TWO DIRTY FOR D.C.

Five Soviet grain irradiators filled with Cesium 137 have been smuggled out of Kazakhstan. A CIA agent finds them on a Venezuelan freighter, but is discovered before he can report their destination. A Russian mastermind has infiltrated factions of the US government, and is plotting to smuggle the irradiators into the country in a way no one expects. His dirty bombs will put countless Americans at risk for radiation poisoning, and slow, painful deaths. Robert Carlton, the US Deputy Attorney General, and Lt. Col. Grady Barlow realize, too late, that their actions have helped the Russian and his wealthy investors. Time is running out. They must risk everything to stop the Russian from detonating his bombs.

J RUSS BRILEY

TWO DIRTY FOR D.C.

PUBLISHING

Liz Russel Productions L.L.C. ™

Two Dirty For D.C.
Copyright © 2017 by J Russ Briley

Liz Russel Productions L.L.C. and
the LRP logo are Trademarks of
Liz Russel Productions L.L.C.

Written by J Russ Briley

Edited by Liz Russel

First paperback edition 2017

ISBN 978-1-943882-06-9 (Paperback edition)
ISBN 978-1-943882-07-6 (eBook edition)

www.jrussbriley.com

Dedicated to my gorgeous wife
without whom this novel would not have been possible.

TWO DIRTY FOR D.C.

<u>Chapter 1</u>

Moving unheard through the cargo ship was easy. With all the noises around him, he could shout and never be heard. Passing unseen was another matter. Exposed ladders, narrow gangways, hidden corners, and very few paths to choose from made avoiding the crew difficult and dangerous, even at night. The hold was dark, which helped him hide, but so dark that he could barely see. There were a few sparsely spaced dim lights, covered in a film of diesel and dirt. Craig crept slowly down the aft starboard ladder into the hold. The ladder, made of bent rebar crudely welded to the side wall, was rusted and brittle. A rung under his foot creaked loudly, hinting it might break. He hesitated even though he knew the noise was drowned away in the general cacophony of stressed metal and machinery. The thrumming of the engine and frequent groans of steel joints twisting in the rough seas masked other sounds. Craig paused again when he reached the last rung. Peering through the gloom, he stepped off into the maze of corridors made by thousands of crates and the chains that bound them. He could barely see, but he didn't want to turn on his flashlight. Trusting his instincts, he moved forward through the cavernous hold.

The ship had seemed small and fragile crossing the last of the Atlantic. It had pitched and yawed unceasingly. Even here, in what should be calmer waters as they approached the southernmost Caribbean Sea, it rolled from side to side. Heavy wood boxes, teetering over his head in the deep belly of the ship, strained against their chains with each pounding wave.

Weighing in at about eight thousand tons, the ship was a converted tanker from the fifties. Rust, age, and general abuse disguised its purpose. The engine was in prime condition under blotchy, deliberately aged paint. The propeller shaft spun smoothly in its bearings, surrounded by rusted mounts. Dented and chipped, the propeller itself was carefully balanced and tapered. Its brass had been washed in acid to hide its newness.

Craig was on board because this was a smuggling ship. A former Soviet government smuggling ship. Walking slowly through the aisles of wooden containers, Craig reached his marker. He had made three trips below in three nights over six days, when the laziest crewman had the night watch, and when the fewest sailors were about. Pulling his old chewing gum from the chain, he tossed it between the floor slats into the lower bilge. This was the spot where he'd left off the last time. Reaching into his back pocket, he took out his thin flashlight and a new stick of gum. He didn't switch on the flashlight; instead, he pulled on the end cap. It had a push-pull safety cap, requiring a twisting action. Drawing out smoothly, the casing telescoped almost a foot as he turned the cap. The flashlight contained a normal looking halogen bulb, but inside there was also a small LED hidden to the side. It now blinked faintly and went dark.

Craig had activated his very sensitive Geiger counter, the only hi-tech tool he had in his cover as a Venezuelan merchant sailor. He put the gum in his mouth, tossing the wrapper through the slats below his feet. The gum tasted sweet and minty in his dry mouth, turning it suddenly wet with saliva.

Making his way forward down the starboard side, he thought he saw a glimmer from the flashlight's LED. Swinging to his left, he saw the flicker appear again. As he stepped between two huge crates the ship lurched from a big rolling wave. The boxes above him shifted against their chains. Craig ducked instinctively, but the chains held and he moved on. The LED began to beat a slow, regular rhythm, as the Geiger counter picked up radioactive traces. Craig's breathing quickened as he approached five boxes of similar size and construction. The wand in his hand beat a faster rhythm of red flashes from the LED. They rushed to a frantic pulse each time he waved it near one of the boxes. Closing the Geiger counter back into its flashlight form, he switched on its white light.

The five crates were made of stained and battered wood. They measured roughly three-by-three by four feet. They lay on their long sides, stacked on top of a single pallet. The Russian and

Spanish markings indicated that the boxes contained machine parts. Seemingly older markings read something about plastic parts, but these had been scratched out as if the boxes had been reused.

Pulling a crowbar from his belt, Craig stepped up on the edge of an adjoining stack and jammed the iron blade under the edge of the top box lid. Prying against the lid, he felt the chain which held the crates steady in the rocking ship strain against his efforts. He gained only the barest glimpse of the inside packing material before his belt was grabbed and he was pulled off balance. Bouncing hard off the corner of a box, his head split as he was thrown to the oily floor. His flashlight careened between the boxes and dropped through the slats into the bilge.

"So," a man spoke from the darkness in deep, grating Russian. "You are looking for something." He held the beam of his large metal baton-shaped flashlight in Craig's eyes.

Craig's training kept him from responding quickly. The small delay gave him time to think—to stay safe; disguised. The simultaneous shocks of pain, being discovered, and hot blood oozing down his head pulled at his ability to maintain his cover. Craig couldn't make out the man's face in the dark, but the voice was easy enough to recognize. It was the Second Mate, Vlad. Craig had not seen him do anything on board except walk around, listening and watching. Craig avoided him and the two large men that stayed near him. All the crew avoided them.

"I don't understand," Craig responded in halting Russian, keeping up the impression that his knowledge of the language was limited. "Let me explain, Sir," Craig tried answering in Spanish, while he attempted to regain his feet.

The crowbar, freed from the box and now held by one of the bodyguards, crashed down on his shoulder, slamming him back to the ground. The loud crack of his breaking collarbone echoed in Craig's head. Searing pain shot up his neck and into his skull.

"Silence!" The Russian came closer, shining the flashlight into Craig's face again. "I know you speak Russian. You try my patience, Arnulfo."

Craig had worked in the Venezuelan merchant marine for three years as Arnulfo. His American accent hid nicely behind the guise of a Castilian-speaking Venezuelan, sounding like the Spanish spoken around the Canary Islands. The Venezuelans on the ship thought he was avoiding arrest somewhere. They didn't care where he was from. It was easy to buy their silence and deepen his cover. The Russians thought the crew all sounded alike, with their lightning fast clipped forms of Spanish. Until now Craig had thought his cover was solid, and that his identity remained hidden.

"I don't understand." Craig's voice cracked as the Russian words came out slowly. The broken bone digging into the meat of his neck continued to bring fresh pain with any movement.

Vlad pressed the bell head of his heavy flashlight under Craig's chin. The Russian asked slowly in Spanish. "Who sent you?"

Free now to respond in Spanish Craig said, "I was just checking the cargo tie downs."

The flashlight fell away as a hand crashed against Craig's cheek, snapping his head to one side. Craig cried out, his face contorted in agony as the muscles in his chest and shoulder cramped around the snapped collar bone. The ragged and sharp splinters at the end of the bone threatened to pierce through his skin from underneath.

"I think you found what you have been looking for." The Russian stood up. "Bring him!" His hand waved aft as he stepped away. The two men grabbed Craig by his arms and lifted him.

"Ahhg!" Craig felt his broken collar bone pushing through the skin as the men dragged his body face up and backwards through the boxed corridors to the engine control room. His heels slammed into the elevated water-tight door sill. Craig didn't notice. The pain in his head from bone jutting through his skin was overwhelming.

Pushing the heavy door mostly closed, Vlad switched on the bright white overhead lights. Craig was dropped to the floor, his head bouncing hard against a gray, rusted-looking controls cabinet. Hidden inside, the new modern electronic control circuitry quietly managed the engine and wheelhouse equipment. Craig's neck bent forward against the box, his chin to his chest, choking the air in his windpipe.

"Now, why are you here?" Vlad pressed his flashlight against Craig's broken collar bone. The pain shot through him, increasing as Vlad pushed harder, making the raw, splintered end of bone jut further out of his chest. A slow stream of blood ran from the torn skin and spread around the collar of Craig's dirty t-shirt.

"Gahhh." Craig responded with a guttural sound of pain.

Vlad lifted the flashlight away. The drop in pain felt like pleasure. A relieved sigh poured from Craig's lips.

"Who do you work for?" There was a long pause, then agony exploded through Craig's head as he felt the heavy flashlight slam fiercely into his jaw, cracking it in half. He felt his teeth shift as his jaw deformed into an angular shape. Blood coursed from his mouth.

"Who sent you?" Vlad asked in Russian again. He'd lost his temper and his patience.

Craig struggled to translate Russian through his pain-mangled mind, but it wasn't working. The throbbing and numbness alternately swept in between spikes of agony. He was slipping rapidly into unconsciousness.

"I know you understand me! I'll not ask again!" The Russian punched Craig's face on the remaining good side and switched back to Spanish. "Who sent you?"

Craig lifted his head and glared through the bright lights at the cloudy vision of the Russian. A hint of a smile came to the still intact corner of his mouth, but the pain from his badly broken jaw twisted it, creating a grotesquely disfigured expression.

He managed to croak out, "Ffffk uoo."

The Russian nodded at one of the men who then reached over and squeezed Craig's jaw.

"Auuuuuurg." Craig's pain was unbelievable. He passed out briefly, but the man held his head up to face him and slapped him back to consciousness.

Changing to English the Russian asked one last time, his voice thick with his Russian accent and anger mixed together, "I won't give you another chance. I know you understand me, American. Who sent you? CIA?"

Craig spat blood at his face.

Standing up the Russian wiped his cheek. He spoke Spanish to the men holding Craig. "He will tell us nothing. Kill him, and throw him overboard."

Craig felt the impact of the crowbar on his head and blacked out. He was unconscious, but breathing, as they heaved his limp body into a cargo net beneath the small hatch. The hoist lifted him easily out of the bay into the open air and ocean spray. A wave hit the bow hard enough to send a blast of sea water over the deck, splashing Craig in the face. The water seemed cold after the heat from below decks, despite its almost eighty-degree temperature. The salt water stung angrily in his wounds, waking him just enough to open his eyes in thin slits. One of the ruffians noticed.

"Hey, he's waking up!" he shouted over the wind.

"Who cares?" The other answered with a grimace of bad teeth. "Dump him over. I'm getting soaked out here." They both fell silent as they saw Vlad emerge from the hold, glaring at them.

They lowered the net and released all the loops but one from the hook. Raising the net again they spilled Craig out on the deck.

"Get his shoulder." With one man on each side, they hefted Craig up against the rail, his chest striking the hard steel. The exposed bone sticking out of his shoulder should have forced a scream, but there was nothing left in him to cry out.

He could see the ocean whitecaps below, illuminated more by the moon than the dim ship lights. He could hear the wind and the grunts of the two men as they each grabbed a leg and lifted. His chest slid against the rail as they forcefully heaved him overboard. His face scraped down the rusted gunwale as he fell.

Vlad turned, marching off to search Craig's berth. He would find nothing. The only hard evidence of Craig's mission lay in the oily water sloshing in the bilge. The GPS locator transmitter in the flashlight lay useless beneath the heavy steel of the ship.

One man watched as Craig's body dropped down the ship's side into the water. The other walked away toward the crew quarters and the dryness inside. The white splash of water was all that could be seen under the moon as Craig's body hit the ocean. There was no sound of the splash over the engine noise and wind.

The warm water wasn't enough of a shock to wake Craig fully. He couldn't seem to move. He knew he was sinking and instinctively held his breath. It was a futile action. He knew that the deep, black water would soon consume him.

Sinking slowly; his arms and legs wouldn't function, but his mind held on defiantly. His descent was not fast enough to pull him down past the churning propeller. The last thing he felt was the pull of the blades sucking him in, the heavy brass hacking his body into ragged chunks. The gore of blood and meat spread like a slick behind the ship in the darkness. Small and large fish quickly converged on the unexpected midnight buffet. The few chunks that made it to the sea bottom were picked over by crabs. Craig no longer existed.

<u>Chapter 2</u>

Robert Carlton, the newly minted Deputy Attorney General of the United States, stood in his home office with Lt. Col. Grady Barlow. Just outside the congratulatory party continued, but in the closed room he and Grady were discussing their next move.

"Seriously, that was Secretary of State Vance on the phone just now?" Grady asked. "What's going on?"

Robert smiled as he filled Grady in. "First, he congratulated me on the promotion."

"Did I say congratulations?" Grady offered his glass as a toast and Robert clicked it against his own.

"Thanks. He and my boss, Jack, decided to have me take over something for them. Duties of the new job."

"No rest for the wicked." Grady grinned as he sat down in one of the armed leather guest chairs.

"True." Robert seated himself in the matching chair.

"So, is this connected to this trip to the Caribbean that you mentioned? You're serious about us going down there?"

"Yes, on both counts. Apparently, the State Department and Department of Justice are involved in the President's Commission on Terrorist Attack Preparedness, and there's an issue that needs to be addressed by someone from the Commission. Probably just a formality, but they want a 'presence.'"

"Never heard of that Commission," Grady commented, pouring them both more champagne.

"The Commission is new, and with a name like that I doubt that it will go public. It includes the Secretary of State, Justice, Homeland Security, and the Secretary of Defense. It also includes the Directors of the CIA, FEMA, the FBI, and the Chairman of the Nuclear Regulatory Commission."

"Whew! That's a loaded list." Grady took a sip from his glass. "So, Jack Crain wants you to carry the heavy bags, or is this more on the level of look important, say nothing, and report back?"

"Well, it would be normal for Jack to pass off anything that didn't specifically require his presence as Attorney General to me. He is my boss, and I'm his Deputy. He's asked me to take his place on the commission—for now, anyway. He's tied up with some bigger issues." Robert let the sound of that sink into his own head. Only hours into this job and he was going to sit in for Jack Crain on a Presidential Commission. This responsibility took him from feeling like Jack's errand boy to someone who carried clout.

"That's a pretty big bump up the ladder." Grady voiced what Robert was thinking. "No pressure involved, right? Well, I'll be glad to do what I can, as long as it doesn't turn into an investigation like this last one. I'm not sure I'm ready for any more explosive situations."

"No promises." Robert laughed. "I'll try not to get your next house destroyed." He realized that they were already joking about Grady's recent brush with death.

"Seriously, Grady," he continued, "I have to admit that I'm not sure what we're signing up for with this Commission." After the OPOV plot, Robert figured that he shouldn't assume that anything was routine. "That said, a trip to the Caribbean can't be all bad. This kind of thing is usually just a matter of meeting a few people, and making sure nothing they talk about is going to raise red flags. We'll probably get a great meal or two out of it, and maybe a little sunshine." He stood and stretched. "We should go back out to the party. I'm sure Tracie is wondering where we are."

"I'm willing. Speaking of great meals, I could probably force myself to eat some more of the food out there." Grady grinned, standing up. "They've put on quite a spread. Your wife and her friends know how to throw a party, Robert."

. . .

After an hour of socializing Robert and Grady escaped back to the study. The event had wound down, and only a few of Tracie's friends and fellow hostesses remained. The stragglers had moved into the kitchen with Tracie, helping her organize the remains of the buffet.

Both men were tired, but neither was ready to admit that they needed sleep. Each was hiding occasional yawns. They had endured strenuous, sometimes horrifying events in the past weeks, struggling to uncover a conspiracy. The investigation had taken its toll. Robert's ideas about his President and the government had been shaken to the core during that time, and he'd learned to use some hardball tactics—even with his father. Grady was still recovering from physical trauma. The battering his body had taken wouldn't fully heal for a month.

They could hear the remaining women laughing in the kitchen. Robert knew that while the Kennedy Center hostesses liked working with Tracie, his promotion made her more important in their circle. His new role came with greater prestige—not only for himself, but also for her. Her dance card would be filling rapidly with a fresh level of Washington DC elite functions.

"Did you get a chance to think about any of this?" Robert asked.

"About what?" Grady had exchanged his champagne glass for a tall glass of cold water. He leaned back in his chair and lifted an eyebrow at Robert.

"The party," Robert answered with a tinge of sarcasm, waving his glass toward the living room. "Come on, Grady; what do you think I'm talking about?"

"Nice party." Grady took another sip of water, trying to rehydrate. When the glass pressed too hard against his lip it hurt a bit. The split had not completely healed. It reminded him of the bruises that were still sore on his body and face. "For a second there I thought you were going to ask me about something serious." He touched his lip checking for blood.

"Grady, I feel like I've been nothing but serious for a month." Robert delayed for a second or two, swirling the water he'd added to his own glass.

"Here it comes." Grady grinned, which hurt the lip again. He winced. "Are we back to Secretary Vance's call?"

"Not yet. Grady, how do you feel about the job I'm recruiting you for?" Robert wanted to know whether Grady was fully on board with the new team idea he'd pitched earlier. He needed his help.

"I'm in, but I don't really know what I've signed up for, yet," Grady responded frankly. "One minute we're talking about a new team with members from the Pentagon, the DOJ, and NSA, and as though he's reading your mind, Secretary Vance calls with an assignment that you want to attach me to—and we're headed to the Caribbean. What are we really doing? Is this part of your team idea, or are we both attached to that terrorism commission now?"

"I guess I don't have enough information to answer that question." Robert sighed. "I just know that we need a team set up for any future problems we encounter that require interdepartmental cooperation. If we learned anything from the OPOV situation, we learned that." He paused. "Well, I'll know more tomorrow after the meeting with Vance's staff. I'll keep you posted after I drop you off at the Pentagon in the morning."

"Rental car place." Grady corrected. "I need to get a car." Grady smiled again. "You got my last one blown up, remember?"

. . .

With the last of the partiers gone by a respectable eleven p.m. Robert, Grady, and Tracie cleared up the last of the liquor, and bagged a few things that had to be thrown out. Tracie finally won the argument to call it a night by saying that Alicia, the housekeeper, would get the rest of the cleaning done in the morning.

Tracie set Grady up in the guest room, putting fresh towels in the adjoining bathroom, and showing him where she kept extra toiletries. It was, after all, she reminded Robert, his fault that Grady didn't have a home to go to. Robert took the criticism in stride, glad that Tracie didn't mind having a last-minute guest. Exhaustion hit all three of them. Robert's two sons had retired to their rooms hours earlier to play games, but now the whole household fell soundly asleep.

Chapter 3

The conference room table in the Zurich office building seated twelve comfortably in tall leather arm chairs. Clean lines of glass, steel, and hardwoods were the only decor, save for one large modernesque painting of white splashed with color.

In front of each chair was a Victorinox Swiss Army leather portfolio, and a Caran d'Ache writing journal with matching pen case. The case contained an Alchemix graphite pen. The portfolio held an electronic tablet synched to the presentation that would be shown on the large wall-mounted screen. The Swiss luxury items set the importance of the meeting as well as the value.

The seats were filled promptly. Each arrival was carefully choreographed to avoid awkward encounters that might occur in hallways or elevators. The attendees were doing business as a group, but they were not friends. Except for two of the individuals, each was an investor as well as a representative. Of the exceptions, one, a woman from America, and a man from Germany were substituting for investors who held political positions and could not attend in person. The others forgave the politicians this slight as part of the burden of being too recognizable.

No movie, sports, or music stars had been recommended to the club. They were unreliable with their fast money. Here today, and gone tomorrow.

The presenter arrived as the clock on each tablet hit the top of the hour. She spoke English rather than the local German.

"Welcome. We are pleased to have you here today. We have placed the particulars of the transaction in the electronic tablets before you. There are two icons on the screen. The blue one contains the presentation written in your native language, and the red is for the financial details. If you would please touch the blue one now, you can follow along with the brief presentation."

When the main screen illuminated with the first slide, the tablets corresponded with their translations. They automatically updated each time the presenter switched slides.

"Your individual contributions of twenty-million Swiss Francs will be deposited in separate accounts. Each of your tablets holds the account numbers for you, and for each of your clients. The deadline for deposits is tomorrow, end of business. That is eighteen-hundred hours, Zurich time. All confirmed deposits will then receive the time schedule and updates via this device on secure link. The card inside the folio has the current password for your tablet, which should be changed prior to leaving. You may use this device to make your deposits if you wish. It is secure."

The austere presentation echoed the crisp feeling surroundings.

"One-quarter of the deposit will go to expenses; the other three-quarters will be used to make trades on the stocks listed in the prospectus appendix A. The participants agree to not purchase any financial instruments related to these stocks themselves. Exchange costs, but no brokerage fees, will be assessed to the transactions. Trades will be limited to no more than the agreed franc or dollar amounts of those stocks listed in appendix B, prior to the event date. This is to protect your investments from market disruption and dilution. Failure to stay at or below the agreed-upon quantities will result in removal from the club, and forfeiture of the moneys in the account. You will each receive activity announcements via the tablet at the same time, and as soon as available. After the event, you may make trades outside the stocks listed in appendix A."

The presentation went on to highlight the expected returns, relevant disclaimers, and anonymity clauses contained in the prospectus. In every way, it appeared as any other financial agreement, except for the steep initial fee. Around the table, thirty clients represented a total investment of six-hundred-million, plus non-refundable expenses of one-hundred and fifty million. Even these numbers were insignificant compared to the external transactions they would be making independently. Each stood to make profits nearing a hundred million dollars, depending on their investment size and appetite for risk. Even an investment this predictable contained random perils and was subject to the vagaries of the stock market. It was no club for the weak at heart.

"Are there any questions?" The presenter queried.

A gentleman with a heavy Western US accent spoke. He was the only new member of the club. "Now, I understand that we can buy and sell as much of any stock not on the list that we like?"

"That is correct." The presenter was patient.

"So, ya'll are gonna sell the stated stocks using 'puts' on the appropriate exchanges before the event, and then buy balancing 'puts' after the drop-off?" He didn't wait for an answer. "What if I want to buy on the dip, and how do I know you will get the best prices?"

"Don't worry about the process." The pinstripe-suited man seated next to him told him. "Your principals have done this before." The man's condescension was palpable.

"I'm the principal, Buster, and I like to know what is going on with my money. And I want to know what ya'll call 'minimal collateral damage' refers to, as well as 'limited defense infrastructure impairment'." The Westerner was undeterred by the man's contemptuous attitude.

The presenter quickly responded. "Your questions are valid and deserve a complete explanation. I will be happy to innumerate the exact manner of transactions, and approximate timings for you at the end of the presentation. As for your other two questions: our by-laws strictly prohibit the intentional long-term damage to critical defense infrastructure. It is our intent to avoid creating a global military imbalance, or long-term economic downturn. Collateral damage, including human casualties, cannot be avoided, but our team will use methodologies designed to minimize the potential, avoiding risk to club members and critical personnel. The projected locations are listed in your prospectus. Changes will be noted on your device prior to the event."

She looked up to address the total audience. "Our presentation is complete. You will find details and a copy of the material on your tablet. If you wish to remain for the detailed review of our financial process, you will be most welcome. For those who are ready to depart, please take your gifts with our thanks for participating in the club." Her smile was clinical and unemotional.

Everyone but the Westerner rose to leave. The presenter waited patiently as they filed out. New members occasionally joined the club and often had further questions. Each new member was recommended by a full member, and well vetted, but not fully informed until they were committed. That commitment often occurred in a meeting like this one, when money was transferred. It was always a substantial amount of money. If the participant wanted to know more, that was understandable.

The representatives silently left, most meeting bodyguards. All were met by drivers. Each handled their money transfers in whatever way they felt most secure. In previous meetings, the transfers had been required immediately while in the room, but the days of trusting someone else's electronics were gone, and most investors had developed individually preferred methods. Their transfers would be conducted on selectively cyphered devices that matched on both ends, or in face-to-face transactions while physically present in Zurich. Most of the participants went directly to their banks to make the arrangements by hand. After the money was taken care of, some also went to "cover" meetings to complete their trips.

· · ·

After an hour's drive northwest to Basel, Switzerland, the man in the dark blue pinstripe suit with red tie arrived at Tower One. A distinguished gentleman in his early sixties, he stepped confidently out of the limousine.

"Mr...." A man greeting him began.

With a quickly raised hand, the investor silenced the greeter.

"Of course. My apologies, Sir." The greeter was contrite after his breach of etiquette. He had forgotten that names should not be used in the open. Technology now pervaded privacy at any but the most secure locations. "They are waiting for you upstairs," he told the investor.

The businessman looked up at the half-pyramid shaped tower. The tallest building in Switzerland at one-hundred and seventy-eight meters, it was a mere forty-one floors, but it looked impressive standing alone against the blue sky. Nothing of even half its height was within view as it loomed over the river. Although the newly opened headquarters of this large pharmaceutical company was usually referred to by their company name, the building was marked simply Tower One.

The meeting was to be held on a leased floor with no name on the doors.

Entering the room, the man was welcomed immediately by a half dozen executives like himself; Senior Vice Presidents of huge oil companies, strategically titled below such arbitrary law boundaries as Sarbanes-Oxley and its international counterparts. SOX had taken its toll as far back as two thousand and six, forcing meetings like this one to take root. The result of these meetings was a new conceptual layer of executives; critical influencers held back in the SVP ranks with power well beyond their titles. Bigger titles created criminal liability under SOX, and financial accountability. This new layer of management now ran the quiet backrooms of business.

"Gentlemen, let's get started. Should we discuss the Molasse Basin first?" An ice-breaking chuckle ran through the group. The joking reference to the Swiss oil basin tucked between the Jura Mountains and the Alps was the official reason for the meeting. It would be the first and last thing mentioned. Everything in between would be forgotten.

. . .

An hour and a half west by car from Zurich sat Berne. Berne held the capital and Embassy Row. Inside the guard gate, at the American Embassy front entrance, the American's long legs swung out of the car. Her tasteful dress, coat, and scarf reflected diplomatic stature and a sense of couture fashion. The chauffeur offered his hand, which she gracefully accepted. Her wrist gleamed with a gold charm bracelet as she held it up.

"Ms. Morrison, welcome to Switzerland." The Ambassador's aide greeted her with the deference accorded to the US State Department Under Secretary of Arms Control and International Security Affairs.

"Thank you," Lillian Morrison answered.

"The Ambassador and staff will meet with you in a few moments. Perhaps you would like to freshen up from your trip?" The aide inquired.

"Yes, I would," Lillian answered as they walked into the building towards security.

"After your meeting, you will meet with the head of the Swiss Federal Department of Defence, Civil Protection and Sport (DDPS) at Bundeshaus, if that is acceptable."

"Of course. Thank you." She was shown to an executive waiting room, complete with a lounge and lavatories.

This would be a quick meeting as part of a European tour, and the last leg of her trip before heading immediately back to DC. The trip had been cut short in order for her to join a meeting there, so the usual pleasures of Berne would have to wait for the next visit.

Chapter 4

The morning after the party Robert was feeling a little worse for wear. Tracie was friendly toward him, but didn't get out of bed to see him off. She extended her hand for a kiss goodbye before curling back under the covers. Grady was up, dressed in a new uniform, and ready to go. Robert found him seated at the kitchen table with a cup of espresso in his hand.

"Good morning." Grady cheerfully greeted Robert.

"Morning. I'm glad to see you got the machine to work." Robert's headache was better after a shower, but he cringed at the sound of ice falling inside the refrigerator compartment. He heard the clock chime in the hallway. It dawned on him that Alicia was not coming through the door. "Where is she? Where are the boys?" He said half to himself, half aloud.

"Alicia?" Grady answered. "I met her when she came in at seven. Woke me up with a start. Scared the heck of her when I popped out to see what the commotion was. She was fit to be tied with the boys, but corralled both, and hauled them out the door. I don't know how you slept through it. Must be that parent selective hearing thing," he said, shaking his head. In his opinion, the boys had been loud enough to wake the dead.

"What time is it, then?" Robert asked, realizing he'd forgotten his watch.

"Eight."

"Thank God Vance pushed out the meeting to ten. I got a calendar message update earlier. We'd better get going." Robert spotted his watch on the counter where'd he apparently left it the night before. He grabbed it, heading to the hall closet. Coat, scarf, phone, and the two of them were on their way before the clock hit eight-fifteen. Grady explained which rental agency he wanted to go to, and gave Robert directions. He'd made the arrangements first thing after calling his insurance company.

Robert's mind was on his meeting with Vance's staff, and he almost missed the turn-off. He suddenly heard Grady say, "Hey! Turn here. Here! You're going to miss it!"

Robert hit the brakes on his BMW hard, glancing up to see if he was about to be rear-ended. Making the turn too fast into the shopping area, he realized he was in front of Grady's coffee bean den—the cult of java pleasures. That wasn't the name of the shop, but he thought it should have been. "Coffee?" He acted surprised.

"Don't mind if I do." Grady's already cheerful mood picked up a notch in anticipation. "Espresso for me, I think. You need one, too. I can tell."

"But you had coffee already." Robert was not completely up and running. He'd forgotten that Grady's "usual" was a four-shot "Eye-Opener."

"That machine of yours is okay for an auto, Robert, but the pods just don't cut it for an avid Espresso drinker. Besides, life is too short. I learned that lately, thanks to you." Grady was up and out of the car as soon as Robert put the car into park. "What'll you have? Latte? Mocha?"

"Mocha, nonfat." Robert called out through the closing passenger door. He remembered that he wanted to cut back on caffeine. "Decaf!" he yelled out as he opened his door. He was too late. Grady was already across the parking lot and nearing the coffee den door. By the time Robert got into the espresso bar, Grady sat on one of the window stools, grinning.

"Smell that aroma. I feel better already." Grady's crisp new uniform seemed contradictory in the laid-back atmosphere, but there were several other uniforms coming in, and a few standing in line. Some wore their ABUs, or what Grady's dad would have called "camo fatigues." Grady was wearing his blue service dress uniform. The ribbons on his chest and silver oak leaves on his shoulders were conspicuous. Combined with his tall good looks, dark complexion and bright smile, he looked like a recruiting poster.

Some of the military personnel came in wearing their blues, or the Army and Navy equivalents, with dark, matching sweaters to battle the cold weather. Grady didn't like the sweaters. Even with the rank on each shoulder, he thought they looked sloppy and soft. He avoided them except when he needed to "fit in." In the summer, he would wear the no-sweater blues and skip the jacket—that was his idea of a casual day. He preferred the service dress uniform. He'd learned to be comfortable in his Academy uniforms, and had always liked their sharp appearance.

Wearing a broad smile, the barista brought over Grady's eye opener and Robert's mocha.

"Beth, you're the best." Grady accepted the drinks. "You made my day." His genuine happiness and natural charisma put a bounce in Beth's step as she headed back to make more dark liquid joy.

"You and your coffee." Robert's heart rate had finally calmed from the sudden stop.

"I got us to-go cups so we can keep moving," Grady told Robert. He waved at Beth as they got up to leave. The other girls behind the counter also looked up. "Don't forget to put the tip on there, Jill." The girl at the cash register waved her acknowledgment. He smiled and turned to Robert. "Let's go."

Three blocks later, Robert pulled into the car rental parking area. "I'll call as soon as I have an update from Vance." He told Grady. "We might be headed out soon, so get what you need and let me know if I need to talk to anyone."

"Roger that. Thanks for the lift." Grady was off to the rental office as Robert pulled away.

. . .

Arriving at his office Robert saw that Lorraine was no longer floating on his promotion high. She was her normal, efficient, stable self, but somewhat subdued. She had been with the Department of Justice for decades, but was always passed over for successive appointments. It hadn't taken her long to remember that Robert would probably use Jack's admin, and she'd get his replacement as her new boss. It wasn't that she wasn't appreciated, it was just typical in the system. Promotions from within were rare. The second and third-tier administrative assistants seemed to come with the furniture. Lorraine wasn't politically inclined enough to strategize her career into the higher ranks.

When Edward Bradley, Jack's former boss, had died, Bradley's admin remained at her station. When Jack Crain had become the new Attorney General he'd kept her, and now his former admin was in limbo. Ed's admin was much better connected and could make calls and meetings happen for him more easily, so it had been a logical switch. Lorraine sighed to herself, assuming that Robert would make the change to Jack's former assistant.

"Good morning, Mr. Carlton. Secretary of State Vance's office called with your itinerary. I booked a flight for you this afternoon." Lorraine handed him the documentation.

"That was quick." What Robert wanted to say was "presumptuous." So, this was what dealing with Vance would be like. No wonder Jack had handed it off so fast. Robert looked over the ticket and handed it back after writing Grady's cell number on it. "Contact Colonel Barlow at this number and get him set up on the same itinerary. Then call my wife to let her know, and send her the information in an email. Get the AG's office in Puerto Rico on the phone for me, Lorraine. I need to talk to them this morning. Thanks." Robert walked into his office, noting again his name and new title in the gold letters on the door. It felt good.

Before he'd had time to sit down Lorraine arrived. She set a cup of hot coffee and plain bagel on his desk in their usual spots. She left and closed the door without a word spoken by either of them.

. . .

Grady had a busy morning. He made it to the weekly thirty-minute staff meeting on time. Next, he was supposed to see his commanding officer, Colonel Brand. Since the staff meeting had been Brand's, there was no delay between meetings. They moved to the Colonel's office where Grady now stood at-ease.

"Barlow, I had a call before the staff meeting from Deputy Attorney General Robert Carlton's office. He's requesting your ongoing support of his new team. I'm sure you are aware of this, and obviously, it relates to your recent performance." He looked up briefly from his folder. "I read your report, and that of the Attorney General's. Well done." He didn't pause for a response and looked down again at some papers. "The General has approved the requested assignment. This does not affect your chain of command, and you will continue to report to me."

"Yes, Sir," Grady answered, surprised that the paperwork had already come through and that it had been authorized.

"I assume this meets with your approval." He looked up at Grady again.

"Yes, Sir, it does," Grady responded. He stood stiffly, despite not being formally at attention. "The functions of the role are not yet clearly defined, but I believe I can provide value to the mission."

"Perhaps 'not clearly defined' to you as of this time, but a 'roles and responsibilities' document has been provided to me by Colonel Mayer. I'll forward it to you. This is considered a liaison role, in addition to your support of this office, and our continuing support of intelligence. We see a certain alignment of the two, so we're going to add the responsibility of working with National Security and Homeland Security. Here are the officers you'll need to contact." He handed Grady a folder that had a brown elastic band holding it closed. On the outside was the seal of the United States Intelligence Community, known as IC. "Your former responsibilities for strategic planning and staff support have been moved," the Colonel finished.

"Thank you, Sir." *Short and sweet,* Grady thought. The Colonel was not the type to expound broadly on any topic. Grady recognized that he'd been dismissed.

This was exactly how his boss liked to do things, Grady reflected. Brand brought officers junior to himself up in the ranks and moved them forward. He and the General were aligned in this approach, and had built their careers around these actions. Grady's recent achievements and his expanded duties had just become a resume builder for his boss. The General had his sights set on becoming one of the Joint Chiefs, and Brand would be climbing with him the whole way.

Not surprisingly, the wrap up of his involvement with OPOV had positioned him in a liaison role between the Department of Justice and the Pentagon, along with an attachment directly to Robert's office. What was unexpected was the inclusion of the NSA and DHS. The National Security Agency and Department of Homeland Security were not typically encouraging cross-functional cooperation, other than in press conferences.

Grady's challenge was going to lie in navigating between high-level military personnel and civilians. He knew that these groups would be filled with 'promotion hounds' looking for their next move up, via his reports and PowerPoint presentations. They would spout rhetoric, declaring the obvious, and push for change that everybody agreed with, but no one actually worked on. It didn't matter if they wore a uniform or a suit, they were politicians, and he'd been pushed into their world.

Grady was sure he could handle it. The General was convinced of that, as well. He had become aware that Grady's understanding of a wide range of subjects, from combat to technology, was surprising in its depth. Grady understood how they interrelated, making him right for this job. His ability to get things done, even in a political environment, had been improving every day.

Five minutes later Grady sat in his suddenly disordered office surrounded by boxes of files that were being carried out. Other boxes had arrived. Sitting on the table, Grady's smartphone silently illuminated with a message. "Border management and surveillance meeting in 45 minutes." His calendar had already been updated. It was starting.

The reminder was followed immediately by a text notification of, "Call Mr. Carlton's office for itinerary." It was going to be one of those days.

Chapter 5

Vlad was standing on the foredeck fuming. The search of Arnulfo's room had come up empty. There wasn't the slightest hint of CIA to be found. Even the toothpaste in Arnulfo's bathroom kit was Venezuelan. It was all too clean. The rest of the crew's gear contained a variety of products available in South America or the West Indies, including a few from the U.S. That was typical. This convinced Vlad that Arnulfo had been CIA. The fact that the man was dead did nothing to allay Vlad's concerns. How had Arnulfo become one of the crew? How much had he known about Vlad before the five boxes had come aboard?

Vlad had confirmed that Arnulfo served as a Venezuelan crewman/deckhand for three years. His home port was listed as Pamatacual, and there was an apartment there in his name. No drugs or arrests were connected to his history. Some of the crew had experienced minor skirmishes with the law, but not Arnulfo. Yes, the records were too perfect. He had to have been placed on the ship by the CIA, but why? Why at this time?

Another thought came to Vlad as he watched the ship cut through ocean swells, powering its way toward Guiria, Venezuela. Was there another spy onboard?

The captain and first mate were shocked by Arnulfo's quick demise. Like the crew, they were now scared to the point of paranoia. Side glances and hushed voices permeated the ship from the bridge to the engine room. On deck, no one spoke.

The crew was paid well for their work on this smuggling ship and knew better than to ask questions. They did what was asked of them, ignoring what the boxes contained in the hold. No one minded the long trips and heavy work. They couldn't make this kind of money anywhere else. They were accustomed to special passengers and strange cargo, but the brutal killing of Arnulfo was something new.

Vlad's two bodyguards weren't part of the crew. They did no work, and since they took turns standing next to Vlad whenever he was about, the crew knew he was important. He was obviously no simple second mate. Now the crew had good reason to keep their distance from these three.

Vlad had one plant within the crew. Bastian was a tall islander from Isla Margarita, just off the shores of Venezuela. He was one of six crewmen Vlad hired after coming aboard as second mate. Bastian spoke the local Castilian Spanish. He'd learned English in his years on a fishing boat in Trinidad and Tobago. Bastian was too new to be trusted much by the crew, but he could mingle and overhear things said loosely, or too loudly. Like Vlad, he had joined the crew for the trip to Pointe-Noire, Congo, on the west coast of Africa. Arnulfo had already been part of the ship's crew.

Vlad and his operatives had sailed one round trip to establish themselves, and to witness how things ran aboard the ship. They were now at the end of the second leg of their real voyage. Their cargo lay amongst the oil industry equipment, next to machinery and spare parts. The industrial disguise worked well. Any coastal guard inspectors would find nothing to concern them. There were no drugs on this ship—ever. This was a ship that would not take that risk. Customers like Vlad needed special packages delivered, and paid enough to support the smugglers profitably. The rest of the cargo was camouflage. It provided incidental profit, and cover for the frequent smuggling of arms to Africa. This shipment was coming west for a change.

. . .

This trip had not gone smoothly. Vlad wasn't concerned about Arnulfo's demise. After he'd been seen on his dark walks through the hold, Vlad knew he'd become a problem. Disposal had become necessary. Now Vlad needed to know if there was another spy on board. Along with his bodyguards and the first mate they turned over every crewman's bunk, locker, sea chest, and duffle. The galley had been searched, along with every nook and cranny throughout the ship. They found nothing. Even the captain's cabin had been searched. He'd allowed it readily to protect his reputation and his life.

Vlad was still not satisfied. It was not yet time for his plans to be revealed. He had to know if there was another spy.

Vlad went below to the officers' mess. He had spoken discreetly with Bastian, who relayed that there was unrest in the crew. They were talking about Arnulfo's murder. They knew that Arnulfo had overstepped in some way—how, was not their concern, but some took issue with the killing. They didn't like a stranger making that decision.

Vlad knew their rebellious thoughts would have to be stopped.

The officers had been with the ship for many years. Vlad saw no reason to distrust them. They had everything to lose if their clients became unhappy. They had created this successful smuggling operation and had no interest in it being compromised. He focused his attention on the crew. He asked for half of them to be brought in.

One by one the men were questioned. The six Vlad had hired were mingled together with the original crew. It was the newer men he suspected most. After harshly questioning all the men, he made his selection for the second round of interrogation.

The two bodyguards brought the four men chosen to the hallway, leaving them standing there. One bodyguard remained in the hall, guarding. The other accompanied each crewman taken to Vlad for questioning. One by one they were pulled into the room. Those left in the hall heard pain-filled screams coming from inside.

The last of the four crewmen, Renzo, now sat with legs and arms strapped to a hard metal chair. Sweat poured down his face as Vlad paced in front of him. The straps bit into his wrists. There had been no bindings in the previous sessions. Fear filled the man's eyes as he stared at Vlad.

At first, there was no question; Vlad only paced. Vlad's size alone was intimidating. Renzo watched the tall broad body, thick with muscle, move. Without warning, Vlad turned and slapped Renzo hard across the face. Renzo felt Vlad's large hand hit him and thought his eye would pop out from the blow. Feeling the strength in the blow was terrifying.

"You are the one!" Vlad accused. "SEBIN!" he spat, referring to the Bolivariano Intelligence Service of Venezuela. His hand hit the same cheek again, snapping Renzo's head around. "If it is not the secret police, then you will tell me who you work for." It was unlikely that the illiterate crewman was part of the Venezuelan secret police, but Vlad wanted to make sure that Renzo's dimwitted expression wasn't simply a good disguise.

The crewman hadn't answered, seemingly dazed by the blows and questions. Vlad casually picked up his black steel flashlight. The knurled grip fit Vlad's large hand. He hefted it before the face of his victim. "Medellin!" he snarled at Renzo.

The mention of the Colombian drug cartel caused Renzo's eyes to widen, but still he did not speak. Vlad immediately jabbed the narrow base of the flashlight into the man's gut.

"Uuuuff!" The air mixed with spit, bursting from Renzo's mouth as his body crumpled forward against his bindings. Still there was no response.

"Cartel de los Soles!" Vlad tried. Again, he slammed the heavy flashlight into the man's gut, this time higher, almost hitting the ribs.

"Uurkh!" Everything went black for a moment, then Renzo's eyesight returned, starting in the center. Bright sparks spread across his vision, like fireflies in a motorcycle's fast moving headlight. "It's not me!" he cried. Tears poured down his face.

This one was too easy to break. "Get him out of my sight." Vlad waved him away.

The bodyguard took Renzo out into the hall, standing his weak, bent over body against the wall, across from the others. Vlad had made sure the sounds from the mess were loud enough to hear in the hall. Fear showed in the faces of the three crewmen as they waited their turn. "You. You are next," the bodyguard said. He grabbed the nearest man and dragged him into the room.

. . .

Word spread through the ship as the beaten men were heard sobbing, pleading for mercy, or yelling. The cook and his assistant had heard it all and spread the news to passing crew members. Vlad had intended that to happen. He wanted there to be no question about his willingness to inflict pain on any who might oppose him. He meant to skin any exposed traitor alive, and he wanted all aboard, officers and crew alike, to know it.

The last man to be questioned was standing in the gray steel corridor. The three men in front of him had been beaten, each one more severely in succession. The last could barely stand. Blood coursed down his cheek where the flashlight had struck. Vlad had stopped using his hand.

"You. You are next." The bodyguards told him.

"No! I didn't do it. No!" The sailor pulled against the hands of both bodyguards as they dragged him screaming into the room. "Nooooo....!" The slammed door cut off his last cry, temporarily. The latch hadn't been secured. The door eased back open, letting the sound of interrogation carry into the hall.

Pushed down into the chair the man continued to weep. The weeping irritated Vlad, who stood in front of him smacking the bloody flashlight into his equally bloody red palm. "Shut up!" Vlad snarled. He was becoming bored with these weak men. He was losing the excitement that had originally invigorated him; tiring of the game. It was time to wrap up this exercise. "The more you weep and whine, the worse this will be for you."

Sniffling, the sailor tried to override his panic. He choked back the sobs, waiting for Vlad's questions.

"You are Tiljo. Yes?" Placing the bloody light's bell under the chin of the man, Vlad pressed his head up, so that he could look directly into the man's eyes. "I know that two of the crew lied to me. You tell me which two, or it is you I will punish."

The man did not believe that any of the crew had lied to Vlad, but he broke immediately. His eyes gave it away to Vlad, who had seen it before in the camps. Tiljo would tell Vlad anything to escape. The last vestiges of humanity clung by a thread inside him. "I...I," he began, then stopped—saying nothing.

The black metal impacted Tiljo's nose, breaking it instantly. Blood rushed out down his chin, neck and chest. "You feel that?" Vlad smiled. "Feel this then." Vlad's eyes flashed with intensity, his mouth stretched in a grimacing smile. With his huge finger and thumb, one on either side of the broken nose, he snapped it back straight.

The pain shot through Tiljo's head and he prayed he would pass out. His head fell back and his muscles went limp, but he was still conscious. The bodyguard held him up in the chair.

"Which two men are the liars?" Vlad's face was so close they could feel each other without touching.

"Renzo." Tiljo said in anguish.

"And?" Vlad sounded menacing, holding the flashlight close.

"Julito." Tiljo collapsed forward.

"Bring them. And the cook," Vlad barked to the bodyguard who quickly untied the broken man and dragged him up from the chair.

The beaten men were marched down the hall by the bodyguards, following Vlad as he headed aft. As they passed the galley, one of the bodyguards dragged the cook from the kitchen, pushing him into the line.

Emerging from below decks, they stood on the fantail. The five crewmen were pressed face first against the rail, looking out at the white prop wash and open ocean.

"Traitors!" Vlad yelled at their backs above the noise. "I won't tolerate it! Do you understand?" There was no response, but Vlad wasn't expecting any. Pulling a pistol from his belt he fired two shots. One slammed into the back of Renzo's head, and the next into Julito's. Their bodies crumpled at the waist and then toppled off the ship into the water below.

The remaining three were spun around to face him. "If you, or anyone, speaks about this, or anything else EVER, you will join them. There will be no questions next time. Just this." He waved the gun at them, glaring sadistically, then marched away.

Vlad's teeth showed through his stretched lips as he walked forward to the bridge. He would tell the captain that the spies had been found and executed. He was now sure that there had been no other agents on the ship, but discontent about Arnulfo might have fueled talk. Only fear could assure complete silence. The men must never speak about this trip.

The cruel expression on his face was one of pleasure. The blood on his hand was sticky. He flexed it to feel the life it once fed. His fingers rubbed against each other until the blood dried and flaked off in granules, falling to the floor as he walked. He shrugged and felt the blood engorged muscles flex in his shoulders, stiff from the exertion of striking the men. His ears rang with their cries.

It felt good. It felt very good.

<u>Chapter 6</u>

Robert's stop at his office was brief. After a quick run through messages and files he needed for the meeting with Vance's staff, he was in a cab heading for the Harry S. Truman building, home of the State Department.

Robert was met in the lobby by Mary Whiston. Even at twenty-eight years old Mary looked like a college student. Her straight, dark brown hair came within an inch of her shoulders, flipping under slightly at the ends. The side-parted bangs hid her right eyebrow, but the left was straight and dark above closely set eyes. She was a full head shorter than Robert, with a roundish figure and rounder face. The youthful smile that came with the shorter stature emphasized the collegiate impression.

"Mr. Carlton, I'm Mary Whiston from OIA—the Office of International Affairs." She offered her hand to Robert, shaking his solidly. "We met at a holiday party. I don't know if you remember me, but I'm the IA Specialist responsible for Florida and the Caribbean. I work for the Criminal Division Deputy Assistant Attorney General, in charge of the OIA."

"Of course, I remember you," Robert lied. He wanted to clear up her role. "Are you assisting on this trip to Puerto Rico? Or do you have another agenda?"

"I'll be assisting you, Sir. I got a call from the State Department coordinator. He said that they assumed you would want me along for the ride, since I was involved in the last meeting. I assisted Mr. Crain on the Puerto Rico issue, as well. It's your decision, of course." Robert was now her boss, three levels up. She looked anxiously at him as they stood in the busy lobby.

The huge glass wall was causing the voices and footsteps hitting the hard stone floor to echo all around them. Above flew all the flags of countries maintaining diplomatic relations with the United States. There were more than one-hundred and fifty of them. Visitors nearby were expressing their amazement at the combination of glass, stone, and the dizzying array of color. Baffled dignitaries searching for their own flags could be heard measuring the perceived value of relative positioning to other flags in the room.

Robert felt disoriented by all these things as he mentally questioned Mary's role.

The OIA, as part of the Criminal Division of the Department of Justice, reported to the Attorney General's office, and directly to him, the Deputy AG. When he had been the Associate AG, the OIA was on the large section of the organizational chart not associated with his duties. It was a huge group. Robert would probably never meet everyone in it, and choosing someone to work with would take more file review time than he had available. He'd prefer not to have someone who might potentially report back to Jack directly, but it could be advantageous to work with someone who knew what Jack had said. He decided to take the easy path and stick with Mary.

"I'm glad you're here, Mary," he told her firmly. "Tell me about the last meeting, and why this trip to Puerto Rico has become necessary."

Mary debriefed him on previous events, filling in some detail on her own background. Robert discovered that she was a political science graduate of Northwestern University. Her communication skills were good, Robert thought, listening to her briefing. He understood why Jack had chosen her.

The meeting in Puerto Rico was going to be a standard meet and greet with the Governors of Puerto Rico and the US Virgin Islands. It would be followed by a working session with Puerto Rico's Attorney General and his immediate staff. There were some general legal issues on the agenda, but nothing special was involved. The original meeting had been postponed due to the death of Attorney General Edward Bradley. It had been placed back on the calendar before Jack Crain had officially replaced Bradley. Jack's schedule was full, so Robert had been called.

Robert understood that while the meeting sounded important, it was going to be pretty standard. It was a hand-me-down assignment. These tended to be time-consuming, filled with paperwork, and generally weren't of much importance or political value. Once in a while, there was a hot potato involved that somebody up the ladder didn't want to handle, but that didn't seem to be the case with this meeting. Robert wouldn't have elected to take Jack's place on this, but he didn't have much choice.

Mary ushered Robert through security where they were met by a waiting administrative assistant. They were escorted down the hall and up the stairs into a well-appointed conference room. At the far side, seated among her staff in the center of the large elliptical table was State Department Under Secretary of Arms Control and International Security Affairs Lillian Morrison. She was better known as "Mako" Morrison.

"I'm in serious trouble," Robert thought. He knew Lillian Morrison by reputation. Her previous business colleagues had dubbed her a "shark," eventually nicknaming her "Mako," after the large predator. The designation had stuck. She was known for sporting her metaphorical dorsal fin, and for taking a big bite out of anyone who got in her way. Robert wondered what about this Puerto Rico trip required a briefing with her.

Robert heard Mary's sharp intake of breath after seeing "Mako" Morrison. Mary looked like she was going to pass out. He noticed her take out her phone and start rubbing it nervously.

Robert didn't notice Mary staring at Morrison's gold charm bracelet. It had a small teapot with inlaid blue sapphires that was nearly identical to Mary's phone cover graphic.

"Mr. Carlton. Thank you for being so punctual. Let me introduce my staff." Ms. Morrison pulled his attention back to the room. Pointing to her right, she began calling out names and titles. No one moved to shake hands until the introductions came around to those nearest Robert. These few reached forward to shake his hand. Robert and Mary introduced themselves to the group, then moved to the table, opposite Lillian Morrison. Robert noted that Mary had pulled out her computer pad and was taking notes. He hoped they were good. The introductions had gone by too quickly for him to remember everyone in the room.

"Ms. Whiston, it's unnecessary for you to take notes. We're recording the minutes." Lillian's hand gestured toward the corner where a stenographer was taking down everything on a court recorder. "You don't need to try to capture everything, just the immediate actions, and assignments."

Mary flushed, looking embarrassed, but also relieved.

"Please, sit down," Lillian continued. "Would you like a beverage? Water, coffee, soda?"

Robert pulled out the one empty chair immediately across from Ms. Morrison and answered for both himself and Mary, who looked too nervous to hold a drink steadily. "No, we're fine. Thank you for taking the time to brief us today. I'm looking forward to understanding how Justice can assist in this Puerto Rico meeting." Robert seated himself, and Morrison's staff followed suit. He didn't notice that Mary took a seat in one of the subordinate chairs set around the wall of the room. He counted eleven people at the table. This wasn't feeling like the relatively casual briefing he'd had in mind. This trip was starting to feel less like diplomacy, and more like a hot potato.

Lillian Morrison's reputation was well known. She was the State Department's "bad cop" to Vance's "good cop." When there was a warlord, international arms dealer, or rogue state prime minister who needed to be hog-tied, Lillian was the one Vance sent. Her habits of being blunt, fact-based, and aggressive were legendary. Her discussions took place behind closed doors and details weren't released, but the results were noticed.

"I'll get right to the point, Mr. Carlton." Lillian began. "We need a comprehensive multinational plan to head off any attempt to infiltrate the United States with nuclear, biological, or chemical weapons from nearby nations. This effort is underway with Mexico and Canada. We know that the advancements made in delivery methods are ahead of our capabilities to detect possible varied attacks, so we must become more agile and adaptive. Our allies are farther behind in this than we are. We need to not only partner with them for continuity and intel, but also to help them improve. Am I clear so far?"

"Yes, quite clear." Robert fell back to the safe, short answers of court. Nuclear, biological, and chemical weapons were out of his league. He wondered where this was going. Robert began to wish he'd snagged Grady for this meeting.

"Good." Ms. Morrison opened a folder sitting in front of her. A similar folder sat in front of each chair—precisely in front of each chair, as if a ruler had been used to center the object, placing it one inch from the edge of the table. "If you will look at your brief, the staff will hit the highlights of our current position."

Robert opened his folder. One-by-one, each person around the table described the broader context of each concise paragraph. There was exactly one paragraph for each staff member. The sections had been distilled down as though they were Cliff Notes on the aspects of a pending international disaster preparedness plan.

Robert might expect something like this facing the Joint Chiefs in a military strategic planning session, or in the White House Situation Room, but he hadn't been prepared for it here. The intensity of the meeting was growing, and his illusion of the State Department having endless cocktail parties and shaking hands was diminishing. Place cards and petit fours weren't part of this agenda.

"Your role, Mr. Carlton, is to set the stage for these talks." Morrison paused to gauge Robert's reaction.

Robert was unsure what she was expecting him to say. His father would often make statements like this, expecting a response when no question had been asked—usually to gain insights into how to manipulate his listener. Robert fell back to his legal strategy training; when in doubt, ask a question.

"Where do you need to begin, and how far do you hope to get during this meeting in Puerto Rico?" He felt good about that response. It put the responsibility back on Morrison to more precisely define the objective.

She pushed away slightly from the table, closing her folder. "Let's put the cards on the table," she said abruptly. "We want this to be a low-key conversation. Each entity involved needs to determine their role and commitment before we do. Some will want to step forward and approach us. Others will want the reverse, depending on their local political needs.

We need to give them that opportunity. So, before we move militarily or diplomatically, we need someone indirectly involved to open the dialogue. As the Department of Justice, you can approach this as an issue of controlling criminal acts, and through questions of extradition. Find out how much each entity is willing to contribute to the process, and what they are capable of doing. From there we, or the military, can get involved to help rather than to dictate. Starting in Puerto Rico, or the US Virgin Islands keeps this casual and neighborly. The British Virgin Islands will be joining the meeting as a pre-disposed ally in the discussion. I've already spoken with them. I believe we will have all NATO related islands on board very quickly, but we cannot speak to their level of resource commitment."

"I understand." Robert actually did understand. His role was to get the process started, but make it look like it wasn't being driven under pressure by the United States. "And how far do you hope this first meeting will take us?" He asked.

"I'd like PR, USVI, or BVI to take on the role of bringing at least half of the top ten island nations together for a meeting within the next thirty days."

Robert was surprised. He'd expected a more general expression of commitment to be the goal. "We can't advise our Governors that they need to make this happen?"

"No more than we can tell the Governor of Texas or New York what to do. I don't want to play that card, anyway." She put her hands on the arms of her chair as if she might stand up. "There will be further discussions of course, but can I count on you to make this happen? It is imperative that we get started immediately."

"Yes, of course," Robert replied, feeling a little stunned. He didn't have a choice in the matter—that decision had been made for him when he'd been assigned to this project.

Morrison stood up, followed immediately by her staff. "Thank you, Everyone. Mr. Carlton, could you stay for just another minute?" The room emptied out. Mary left with them, after a quick glance at Robert, leaving him standing across the table from Morrison. When the doors closed, Morrison came around to his side.

"I appreciate you doing this." She pulled out the chair next to Robert indicating with her hand he should sit down with her. "You need to know that there is time pressure involved. I can't share the details with you at this point, but I need you to establish if you can, an immediate agreement that allows us to supply intervention support in the case of any attempted incursion. We need that agreement. Some of these little countries might see intervention as a military action on our part if they don't agree in advance."

Robert remained quiet. He didn't like going into a situation without the background information that was prompting her sense of urgency.

"Imagine if a crate of Syrian nerve gas arrived at a small island on a container ship or charter plane," Morrison told him, identifying his silence as reluctance. "The manpower we would need for handling and disposal could look like an invasion. We need to protect the inhabitants, and they would need to willingly allow us to do whatever was necessary. Most importantly, the situation would have to be handled there, without delay. We'd also need to stop anything coming long before it reached us."

"It's a tall order," Robert said slowly.

"I'll make it a little easier for you," Morrison told him, smiling. "You can't make any commitments. Your job is to bring back requests. For you this a unilateral discussion. Get them talking amongst themselves. Help them decide they want to work with us because it's important to them. That's it."

Robert didn't think that made it easier in any regard, but clearly "Mako" considered the conversation complete. She stood, shook hands with him, and left without another word.

Mary was waiting for Robert outside the room. As they headed back out through security and into the lobby he asked her what DOJ OIA could do to assist with this project.

"My duties are in relation to the Department of Justice Criminal Division—specifically the multilateral work, as well as international treaties. Any documents you need analyzed or created, we can handle. Our team can work out the details, validate the legalities, and create the write-up. I have been told to facilitate any function you deem necessary, and bring it back to the team."

"Then pack your bags," Robert told her. "You're going with me."

Chapter 7

By the afternoon, Robert was back on his "to do" list. With Lorraine orchestrating, he met individually with department heads who now worked for him. Each brought their current objectives and assignments, and most had a list of recent achievements they wanted to show off. The sheer volume of work done at the DOJ was staggering. Robert had been generally aware of the majority of Justice's functions, but he knew he'd never keep track of the numerous activities in progress.

Fortunately for him, Robert thought, Jack Crain wanted to keep his own fingers in every pie. He loved the pace and power of the Deputy position that Robert now filled. Edward Bradly had been a "hands off" Attorney General, happy to have Jack handle the day-to-day. Jack planned to be a different kind of AG; he was going to continue to run the show. The organizational structure was a straight line from the President to Jack, and then to Robert, so Jack had plenty of leeway for commanding the workload. The Department of Justice pyramid fanned out just below Robert, allowing him powers of delegation, but Robert's job was to do whatever Jack requested.

Robert had thought he was fine with that—more than fine; he'd have been completely underwater if Jack handed off everything. As the afternoon progressed, he began to realize that there was a problem with Jack's micro-management. Each department head was aware that Jack was still the operational head. Robert might be overseeing the entire DOJ, but he wasn't really the boss. Robert recognized that he might be perceived as Jack's errand boy—plus, his direct reports could be going over his head to Jack all the time.

Why couldn't control effortlessly have fallen into his lap along with the title? Was he missing some stand he should have taken with Jack? He thought about how his father always "controlled the room." It was his particular talent. Even when someone higher up the ladder was present, his father held sway. Why wasn't Robert able to do that? Why couldn't he countermand the impression he wasn't in charge?

Robert Carlton senior always told Robert there were three kinds of people in the world: those who "can do," those who say, "I want," and those who "will have." "Great doers," he said, "become managers who get the job done. The 'I want' people fill the lower executive ranks and push 'doers' around. It's the 'I will have' mentality of the top executives that gets them what they want." Robert couldn't quite get his arms around how they made that happen. President Baxter and his father were both "I will have" people who never let anything get in their way. No opposition, sentiment, or reality could deflect their demands.

Robert wondered when that mindset would take over his actions. Intellectually, he knew it wasn't something he would ever be "given." He was going to have to take it. He needed to make things happen, but right now he didn't have the first clue about how to do it. When would that "I'm the boss" sense of power kick in?

Robert had been in charge of thirteen departments before he'd received this promotion. Now he managed double that amount, but with a lesser sense of control. He thought about how some people seemed to be power brokers from birth. Lillian Morrison certainly ruled her roost. Robert had been frustrated with himself after leaving her meeting. Somehow Mako Morrison made him feel subordinate, as if he now worked for her. That feeling lingered in his mind now.

"The Counsel for the Office of Professional Responsibility to see you." Lorraine was standing in the doorway. Robert snapped out of his reverie at her announcement. Lorraine was determined to keep him on task and on schedule. He'd have to figure out his power-broker strategy later.

"Thanks, Lorraine." He told her. "Send Ellen in."

Ellen had just seated herself when Lorraine knocked and opened the door again.

"Mr. Carlton. Pardon me; Jason Carlisle, Whitehouse Chief of Staff, is asking if you can come over to the White House right away."

"Tell him I can be there in forty-five minutes," Robert answered.

"Yes, Sir." Lorraine ducked back out.

"I'm sorry, Ellen, but we'll have to reschedule." Robert apologized.

"I understand completely," Ellen told him as she stood up. She knew, as anyone in Washington DC did, that a call from the West Wing took priority.

Robert had Lorraine reschedule his afternoon, then set out on foot from the DOJ, scanning for cabs. Ride-sharing apps were currently considered a security risk, so he couldn't check their availability. He'd considered driving, but parking could be a nightmare. On a nice day, the little over a mile distance from 950 Pennsylvania Avenue to 1600 Pennsylvania Ave could be covered in about half an hour, but that would be cutting it close to his appointment time. Cabs and buses weren't on the restricted list this week, and the bus had a direct line. He'd taken the path toward its stop, in case a cab wasn't handy. He got lucky, catching a taxi almost immediately.

Once inside security at the West Wing, Robert was taken quickly to Jason Carlisle's office. As he neared the door, he could hear Senator Gregg's deep booming voice back in the main reception area. He wondered whether Gregg was arriving, or leaving.

"Mr. Carlton, Mr. Carlisle asked if you would wait in his office," Carlisle's secretary interrupted his thoughts.

Gregg's voice was fading, sounding as though he was exiting the building. Robert turned toward the secretary and followed her, seating himself in one of the two visitor chairs. He hadn't been there more than a second or two when Chief of Staff Carlisle walked in the room.

"Mr. Deputy," Carlisle began, "thank you for coming over so promptly." Jason moved with speed and confidence as he shook Robert's hand. "I wanted to thank you personally for your efforts on the President's bill. It is sure to pass the Senate now. I had no idea you had such a strong connection across the aisle." He moved to the other side of his desk with three long strides and seated himself. "You could have knocked me over with a feather when I heard you pulled in eleven votes for us."

"Glad I could help," Robert responded, wondering what vote Carlisle was talking about. He was framing a question that might get him that answer when the door to Carlisle's office suddenly opened. In walked President Baxter.

"Mr. President." Robert nearly jumped from his chair.

"Jason, Robert," the President acknowledged as Carlisle stood. "I hope you don't mind me dropping in."

"Not at all, Sir," Jason answered with a smile.

"Robert," the President continued without skipping a beat, "you really impressed me with this. When Senator Gregg told me you convinced him to support my bill, I was stunned. We've been talking with him—how many times now, Jason?"

"At least six times, Sir," Carlisle responded, shaking his head.

"Felt like a dozen," Baxter said. "Well, when he asked for five minutes and brought his support, I was stunned. He named your arguments as the motivating factor for his assistance. Well done, Robert; well done." The President moved to leave the room. "Jason, make sure this gets moved up the docket before these votes have a chance to get away."

Halfway out the door, the President stopped. "Jason, get with the strategists. Gregg hinted he would be retiring at the end of this term, and I want to take our best shot at winning his seat. Again, Robert, good job on this."

"Thank you, Mr. President." Both Robert and Carlisle said as he left.

"I knew he would want to tell you face-to-face." Jason was enjoying this affirmative moment in the day.

"I heard Gregg leaving. Was he here long?" Robert asked.

"No, just about ten minutes. I got a heads-up from his office that he was coming over. You must have been very convincing to turn him to supporting our bill—and to get him to bring ten votes with him." Carlisle eyed Robert speculatively, pausing for a moment. "Whatever you said, Robert, we appreciate it. We needed the win."

He moved toward the door, signaling the conclusion. "Keep up the good work, and let me know if you have another of these miracles up your sleeve. I'm always happy to help give an extra nudge." It was a gentle reminder that freelance achievements might tally up personal points, but there was value in shared wins.

Robert was soon standing in the lobby, somewhat in shock. He had gained valuable ground with Carlisle and the President, through Senator Gregg. He didn't know how, but he would figure it out.

. . .

Grady was also busy with his "to do" list. His was much more basic. He needed clothing, shelter, and food. He'd been checking out apartment complexes inside Crystal City. A blend of offices, residences, shopping, and easy transportation to the Pentagon put the high rises in demand. Most had underground corridors that provided sheltered access to everything. Hot, sticky DC summers and frigid winters made that a desirable feature.

Grady's insurance company was making him rebuild his house. They required an almost identical design—a "replacement," not an improvement. That meant he didn't have to spend much time with an architect or builder, but the place was going to take a year to finish. He figured that would give him time to decide whether he was moving back in, or selling. The home he'd shared with his wife had been a refuge for him, but since it was gone, it might be time for a change. A rental just south of the Pentagon would be incredibly convenient, and an apartment lifestyle might give him more time to get out and about.

Grady was finding that convenience came with a big price tag. What was available had discouragingly high rental or lease rates. Even going way out to Columbia Pike was expensive. He didn't want to contemplate a commute down ninety-five towards Fredericksburg—that traffic was crazy in the morning.

Remembering the Pentagon housing board, Grady called in to check on what might be available from re-assigned personnel. Here he caught a break. One of his past flight students who had been flying C-17s had been deployed overseas on a two-year assignment. The pilot was in deep on a small condo his parents had helped him buy in Crystal City, and he'd lost his renter after a year. The condo came with everything—it was furnished right down to the dishes. Grady would only need to buy personal care items, food, and a pillow he liked.

Even better was the fact that Grady had casually kept in touch with the guy through social media. A quick email opened the conversation. Hearing that Grady's house had burned, the pilot dropped the price on the rental, matching the rat trap, smelly-carpet, two-bedroom apartment Grady had just viewed. The condo only had one bedroom and one bath, but it was in a great location. Grady agreed and was told that the facility manager would have a key ready for him in the morning. The place had already been cleaned, so he could move right in.

Grady called Robert. "I have a condo! It's available immediately, and has just about everything I need in it."

"That's great! How did you manage that so fast?" Robert tried to not sound too excited. That was easier to do, now that he was back at the office handling routine paperwork. He genuinely didn't mind having Grady as a house guest for a short time, but he knew too long a stay would wear on Tracie.

"A former flight student needed to rent his place, pronto." Grady was feeling cheerful. "I can't move in until tomorrow. If it's all right, can I impose on you for one more night? If that's not going to work, just let me know and I'll get a hotel," Grady added cautiously. He knew that Tracie and Robert had experienced some discord recently. She'd arrived back home from her mother's at the same time Grady had become Robert's guest.

"It's not an imposition," Robert told him sincerely. "Not at all. I'll tell Tracie. She'll be fine with it; really. Can you be back by six for dinner?"

"Let me take the two of you out." Grady offered.

"Thanks, but with the boys, I'm sure Tracie will already have plans made at the house. Dinner at six. Okay?" Robert figured that was the safest course of action since he didn't know what Tracie might have on the schedule.

"Okay. Thanks, Robert." Grady answered. "I really appreciate it."

"No problem. I'll call her now." Robert got Alicia on the phone when he rang the house. Tracie had already re-filled her calendar and wasn't expected home until late. Alicia had no problem adding one for dinner, so they were set. Robert hung up and prepared to face the next one-on-one interview.

. . .

Robert and Grady sat down to "Lasagna ala Alicia," a strange combination of pepper spices with chicken, white Mexican cheese, and wide noodles, topped with sour cream. It was a favorite of the boys. They wolfed it down amidst loud laughter and punching each other. Robert's efforts at keeping them quiet failed. Alicia had much better luck with threats of fewer video games, and more time devoted to homework. Dessert was French vanilla ice cream with cinnamon-chocolate sauce, after which Alicia hustled the boys off to their rooms to take baths and do homework.

Grady found himself relaxing after the boys left. He wasn't used to rambunctious kids, let alone kids who didn't straighten up when their father told them to behave.

"You don't have any idea what it's like until you have your own," Robert told him. "I used to think it was Tracie's fault, or that the problem was that I was never around. So, I tried to spend more time with them. I joined in with their activities and tried to take an interest in their games, but even young kids don't want their parents around now. Video games, cell phone apps, and the Internet—that's all they're interested in. Believe me, other people's kids around here are worse. I want to blame the electronics world, but I know that we let them get too involved in it. We can't take it away, and frankly, I don't know what we'd do with them if we did. It all sounds like an excuse, I know." Robert finished, knowing that what he was saying was exactly that, an excuse. Trying to "retrain" the boys would take more time and energy than either he or Tracie had available.

"From what I've seen..." Grady paused for a minute to think through what he was about to say. He'd been hard-pressed to keep from taking over the disciplinary duties at dinner, and was sure he wouldn't let any kids he ever had behave like Robert's, but child behavior conversations were right up there with bringing up politics or religion. Some things were better off not being discussed with friends. "No...you're right, Robert." He laughed and shook his head. "Until you have your own, you just don't know what it's like."

There was a long, quiet pause. Robert needed to fill Grady in on what happened at the White House, but he didn't really want to. Robert got up so that he could reach the bottle of Chilean Malbec wine he'd opened for dinner, and refilled both their glasses.

"I had a meeting at the West Wing today, with Carlisle and the President," he began.

"You're becoming a regular over there. Impressive." Grady was honest in his praise.

"I earned some big points, and it took me a while to figure out why." Robert knew the punchline would disappoint Grady, so he was easing into it. "It seems a Senator from the opposition jumped sides in support of legislation the President was trying to get passed. Evidently, the Senator dragged votes with him because I convinced him to do so. A total of eleven votes came with him. Now the bill will pass."

"That's a big deal! Congratulations!" Grady raised his glass.

"Yes, it is a big deal, but I had nothing to do with it. The Senator I supposedly convinced was Gregg," Robert told him.

Grady lowered his glass back down slowly. "He hasn't resigned?" Neither of them had checked to see if Gregg had resigned as he said he would. There just hadn't been time.

"No, he hasn't." Robert continued grimly. "I didn't know what Carlisle was talking about, or what the President was congratulating me for having done. It took me a few minutes to put two and two together, Grady, but it's clear that Gregg used this situation to extend the deadline we gave him. Gregg has announced his retirement at the end of the term."

"Not immediately." Grady was gritting his teeth as he spoke the words.

"No," Robert said again. "Obviously, any attempt by us to force him to resign immediately, as we originally told him to do, would put the President's bill in jeopardy. He found a way to box us in." Robert admitted.

"Leverage." The disgust on Grady's face needed no translation.

"I guess we should feel okay about it, though, Grady," Robert rationalized. "Gregg is still leaving, just not as soon as agreed. He is doing some good on the way out. Sure, it's not altruism. He could have done the same thing and left, but he would never do that. The only reason he did this was to strike a silent bargain." Robert knew his reasoning sounded weak to Grady, but what choice did they have? They had to accept the situation, or they'd undermine the President's agenda.

"His word is worthless. You can't trust him." Grady had good cause not to trust Gregg.

"No, you're right about that, but it's less than six more months." Robert persisted.

"It's a deliberate move. He's the kind of politician that will always find a way to get what he wants." Grady ranted. "He tried to get rid of me—permanently, Robert! It's a little hard to swallow the idea that he can find a way around paying for that." He took a breath and sat back in his chair. "The guy is good at this game. I suppose there's nothing you can do about it?"

"Not a thing. If we exposed him we'd create one hell of a scandal, and still might not get him out the door faster. He knew exactly which strings to pull. If it's any comfort, I guarantee that those votes he swung cost him dearly." Robert told Grady.

"Then enjoy the brownie points, but watch him. Maybe that's how these things work. Hell, I wouldn't know." Grady smiled and picked up his glass again.

"You're right there—that's exactly how these things work." Robert tipped his glass in a responding salute.

They decided to call it an early evening, retreating to their rooms to unwind and read. Grady didn't have a replacement computer or an electronic reader, yet. His had both become part of the melted mass in the fire, so he'd bought a paperback book. He'd chosen a thriller. Hopefully, it would be almost as exciting as his life had recently been.

. . .

After their morning routines, Robert and Grady split paths to get a few things done before each headed to the airport. Grady picked up the key to his rental first, then managed to fit in buying some much-needed clothing. He also bought a plain black officer's travel backpack from the MCSS uniform store in the Pentagon. He and Robert met at Reagan National airport for the twelve-fifty-nine flight to San Juan.

"You didn't tell me that DOJ work was going to be hot standby alert duty." Grady joked once they arrived on the inside of security. "I'm thinking I'll need to keep a bug-out bag ready. I hope I have the right gear for a trip like this."

"Whatever all that means, I'm sure you'll be fine." Robert wasn't sure he had the proper clothes, either, but that felt secondary to the lack of information preparation. This was all still too new to him. "I take it your commanding officer approved?" He asked, trying to make conversation.

"I had a quick, but positive meeting with him yesterday. You certainly greased some skids." Grady laughed. "He asked if I approved of the assignment, but by then I'm not sure I had a choice. They had already started processing paperwork."

"Lorraine is efficient." Robert smiled. Lorraine certainly had taken his new job in stride and was being her typically effective self. He would have to remember to thank her for her consistent work.

"I would say so." Grady grinned. "I think the General is anxious to have a spot at the Intelligence Community table, by the way."

"You're probably right." Robert agreed. Who wouldn't want to be part of the United States Intelligence Community? It had been steadily gaining power since Reagan established it in 'eighty-one. "You still work for him directly, right?"

"For Colonel Brand; yes. Most of my old office and my planning duties have been handed off to a newly promoted Lt. Col. and a 2nd Lieutenant. I picked up the interface duty to the NSA and DHS, in addition to working with you. Now I have the total IC responsibility for my group." Grady and Robert walked toward their gate, which was conveniently close.

"It took two officers to replace two-thirds of you?" Robert joked.

"Story of my life," Grady nodded, grinning.

Mary Whiston was sitting at the gate, waiting for them. She stood up as they approached. The contrast of her pale complexion next to Grady's dark skin drew Robert's attention. That, combined with her short, wider stature alongside Grady's fit form towering over her struck Robert as comical. He shook off his momentary inner chuckle and made quick introductions.

Grady checked his watch to see how much time they had before the flight left. "Coffee, anyone?" He asked. Robert and Mary declined. Grady quickly headed off in the direction of a coffee kiosk.

Robert settled into a chair next to Mary's. He and she briefly reviewed their meeting strategy. He'd decided to treat it as a management checkup for general disaster preparedness, as in the case of natural disasters, as well as for preventing or dealing with illegal importation or smuggling of anything, including terrorist weapons, into the US. The inherent issue was the permeability of the Caribbean, and their lack of expertise and crisis management capabilities. In addition, all the islands, large and small, had a plethora of harbors and airports. Most of them held international status, and few of them had solid customs controls, much less security. They also had little or no equipment or training in the detection of any weapons.

Robert kept the conversation with Mary general, and some of his thoughts to himself. Mary hadn't been included in his one-on-one discussion with Morrison, so he'd decided to keep her involvement on more of an administrative assistant level. Was it reasonable to ask these islands to do more to check for possible terrorist weaponry? It should be. Whatever form the terroristic threat took shouldn't be hard to spot—if they'd begin by checking boxes and luggage more thoroughly, and did more inspections on large shipping vessels while in port. He made a note to discuss this with Grady later.

Robert began mentally calculating how to begin building an agreement around security and the incursion of massively destructive weapons. The combination of foreign affairs and military defense made for an interesting challenge. Robert carried with him the nod from Secretary of State Vance's office as the first line of foreign affairs, so between him and Grady, they were reasonably well positioned to open the dialogue. Neither of them had any special training, or even much experience in international affairs, but then, neither was there to solidify an agreement. Lillian Morrison had made that quite clear.

"Water?" Grady was standing in front of him with a capped paper cup of espresso, and three large bottles of water. He handed a bottle each to Robert and Mary. "You can't fly without hydrating."

"Thank you." Mary smiled. She looked genuinely pleased that Grady had included her.

"Thanks. You didn't have to get these," Robert told him.

"No problem," Grady told him. Robert turned to Mary and asked her a procedural question about the meeting. Grady sat down and popped open his book. He almost gave a sigh of relief, reveling in the knowledge that their seats were not all together. He knew he would be asleep before the wheels were up on the plane.

. . .

They landed in San Juan at seven-thirty. Taxis were everywhere and well managed, airport style. Palm trees illuminated with "up lights" and swaying slightly in the warm breeze instantly provided a tropical, calming effect. The last remaining glow from the sun was fading, but the air remained a comfortable seventy-three degrees.

Their taxi was actually a van. In typical island fashion, it used open windows for air flow instead of air conditioning. Mary was finding the breeze from the two front windows troublesome for her hair, but she didn't complain.

When they drove past the Santurce district and took the bridge to San Juan Antiguo, or "old San Juan," the view opened up to the spectacular lights of the city reflecting on the water. Their hotel was the "Caribe," which sat on a point of the islet facing the San Gerónimo de Boquerón fort ruins. The stone battlements were lit just enough in the growing darkness to inspire thoughts of pirates and cannons.

Pulling off the main road, the taxi rumbled toward the modern hotel structure. Multiple buildings of white concrete architecture rose ten to twenty stories each. The Caribe's mid-twentieth century styling included a huge pool area, with a large curved glass wall dining area. The grounds looked perfectly manicured. Robert thought each palm tree had been measured out exactly to fit the landscaper's plan.

"I could get used to this," Grady commented, instantly one with the island. Even in uniform he seemed quite at home.

Puerto Rico was new to all three of them. Each had been through the airport on the way to other destinations, but none had ventured outside the building. Robert and Tracie always talked about coming, but between the cost, their schedules, and the boys, they hadn't visited the island. Grady was anxious to explore. He'd wanted to spend more time in the Caribbean and Grenadines, but hadn't done much traveling outside work since Keisha had died.

San Juan seemed somehow more familiar to the three than they'd expected. Being so much a part of the U.S. made it an easy travel experience. Everything flowed smoothly, with none of the uncomfortable barriers or colloquialisms of some of the smaller islands.

Grady's uniform and Robert's winter-weight suit felt hot in the moist, warm air. They made a beeline for their rooms after checking in, shedding the coats and ties. Meeting Mary back at the restaurant a few minutes later, they opted to dine inside where air conditioning brought down the humidity and the temperature. They weren't alone, although the patio restaurant was packed as was the outdoor bar. From inside they could see the palm trees and light tropical dress of the diners through the tall, curved windows. The scene looked appropriately vacation-like.

When the food arrived, it was excellent. There was a distinctive flair with the spices even on the very American menu. They each ordered a light meal and kept the drinks to one a piece.

Mary seemed a bit awkward with her ornate umbrella'd rum punch in hand. The drink, combined with her youthful round face, made her look years younger. She appeared to be still in college, Robert thought, reflecting that his own college years were long gone. He noticed that her phone, left upside down on the table, sported a pattern of little blue teapots and daisies.

It didn't take much time for the long day and heavy air to take its toll. The three were yawning by the end of their meal, so they ended the evening early. There was nothing to figure out tonight. The schedule, agenda, and transportation were pre arranged. Instructions had been waiting at the desk in an envelope for Robert when they'd arrived at the hotel.

"Maybe working with Vance won't be too bad," Robert thought to himself. Like Grady, he felt like he could get used to this.

Chapter 8

Their day started at seven-thirty. An aide met Robert, Grady, and Mary at breakfast and drove them to the State Department of Puerto Rico, located in the Palacio de la Real Intendencia. It was a classic white colonial building, located just west of the Plaza de Armas. Mary was the first to spot that famous square as they drove by its well-known round fountain.

"There it is!" She exclaimed excitedly. "We studied the square in architecture class. The fountain statues depict the four seasons. My favorite is 'Winter.'"

It was hard to miss. The large statue of a bearded man completely covered in a heavy blanket from top to bottom stood out distinctively in the warm sunshine, while summer's half-naked Venus-styled woman stood across the fountain.

"Classical with an original spin," Robert commented as they passed the square. "Winter looks almost modern in style compared to the other figures."

"It's all over a hundred and fifty years old." Mary's rapt gaze drank in the historic buildings. Grady seemed more interested in memorizing the streets and watching people.

Upon arriving they were escorted rapidly from office to office, meeting key personnel in the State Department. It turned out the trip was important for three reasons, the first being that Jack had never visited Puerto Rico. Robert discovered that there were a number of legal responsibilities the State Department had been hoping to discuss in person.

The second reason surrounded drug trafficking and refugees; both were on the rise. Mary, Robert, and Grady were besieged with requests for an understanding of how to get more help with both problems, and who could be their liaisons in these areas.

The second half of the day was dedicated to the third problem: the issue of allowing the U.S. to intervene in cases of disaster—

natural, and otherwise—and working with the islands in a joint effort to expose more smuggling of terrorist weapons, keeping them from reaching the U.S. mainland. Most of the afternoon resulted in a closed-door session, attended by the Governor of the US Virgin Islands, with three high ranking staff members, the Governor of Puerto Rico, and the Governor of the British Virgin Islands, attended by his entourage. The US Ambassador to the British Virgin Islands made an appearance partway through the afternoon, apparently invited to do so by the BVI Governor when they'd met for breakfast that morning.

Robert had studied the cheat sheet provided by Vance's staff on the plane and was well-prepared for the formalities of the meetings. Calling the BVI Governor "Your Excellency" seemed awkward, but he found that it was expected. The governors and ambassador suggested dropping some of the other unnecessarily formal aspects of protocol since their time together was short—a suggestion Robert readily agreed to follow.

Mary dutifully took notes and passed a few to Robert regarding background points. Grady spent most of his time trying to stay attentive through all the diplomatic maneuvering and formalities. Robert was worried about being pinned down on points he had no authority to negotiate. While the two US Governors were amiable and smiled frequently without saying much, the British Governor Edward Collins was amiable to the point of being casually friendly. Robert kept waiting for the verbal knife thrust he was sure must be coming.

"Mr. Carlton, as I see it, you need our little islands to protect you from invasion by mad men in small boats, and tiny planes descending upon you like locusts over vast amounts of sea and air." Governor Collins finally summarized, not without humor in his voice. "However preposterous this may sound, it is clearly in our best interests to help, but as you know, we are already doing our utmost to stem the tide of drugs racing to market in the States. While we are eager to help, it is difficult to see how you can expect us to protect you on all fronts, and from all these threats simultaneously with the minimal support we have from the U.S. today. Surely we can do no better than your country in detecting terrorist threats."

There it was, thought Robert. Grady glanced over at Robert, one eyebrow slightly raised.

Without giving Robert time to respond, the BVI Governor continued, "Mr. Carlton, we are more than aware of your continuous surveillance flights and crisscrossing ships by the Coast Guard, Air Force, and Navy. Yet you still have tons of cocaine and heroin arriving on shore every day. How can you possibly expect us to stop this when your vast resources are unable to do so? What is it that you believe our already overtaxed resources can do?"

Robert took a breath, preparing his answer, but before he could speak the Governor was again commanding the conversation.

"We understand what you want us to do, but here is what you must do," His Excellency continued. "Redouble your efforts on drug intercepts. Triple customs control in Puerto Rico and the USVI, and finally, include your weapons of destruction tests at all of these points. As for our friends throughout the Caribbean, they will need training, equipment, and funding from the States in order to carry out their efforts in support of your security. I am speaking, of course, on behalf of many, but each island nation must raise their individual concerns. In our case, Her Majesty and Parliament have already graciously equipped us to handle any of these threats, and we extend our support to our ally in arms."

The Governor's speech seemed to have concluded. Collins rested back into his chair and pulled a carafe nearer to pour some water into his glass. Robert found himself thinking that he looked like the proverbial cat that had swallowed the canary. Robert was pretty sure he was the canary. He opened his mouth to respond, but was once again cut off by the Governor's verbosity.

"You are not to worry, Robert; your ambassador and I have already engaged several of the regional governments and we think our proposal will suffice at this stage." At a wave of his hand, one of his staff members rose and engaged his laptop to put on a presentation. It outlined a proposed meeting that included the islands that formed a geographic band across the Caribbean Sea, from the Caimans to Antigua, crossing below Cuba, and then south from Antigua to Grenada. The resulting two-sided box encompassed most of the area, with the Dominican Republic and Haiti holding the largest single land masses in the group of islands.

There were several slides of existing efforts and statistics covering the massive drug smuggling trade, and how it had exploded in volume over recent years. There were slides of recommendations for increasing drug and weapons smuggling controls dated from two years earlier, along with recommendations for curbing the demand for drugs in the US. It was a rehash of many such types of presentations, but reiterated here as an exclamation point to the issues in question.

Finally, the slides changed tone to a hopeful alliance against the threats, showing a map of islands and nations with circles around those that had already agreed to meet.

Assuming that this wrap-up was a point at which he could enter the conversation, Robert was beginning to see some light in the presentation. He addressed the BVI Governor. "Your Excellency..."

"Edward," the Governor corrected, smiling in a benevolent fashion.

"Edward," Robert managed, "you are saying you can bring these islands and nations together in conference to discuss how best to address this threat, but that it falls to us to work with Cuba, the Bahamas, and Mexico separately." Robert broadly summarized. "Why the Bahamas, Governor?"

"While the Bahamas have chosen to continue recognizing the Queen as their monarch, they are, as you know, an independent nation, Robert." The Governor answered instructively. "Strategically, it seems best to have the U.S. in control of a definite region, not a mixed area with questions about responsibility."

"I am glad you grasped my other points," Collins continued. "We will be happy to facilitate and host talks with representatives, as designated on the map, to discuss our mutual concerns. We would welcome the United States' active participation in this discussion. It would be best to proceed from the perspective of each island's danger, with regard to drugs, arms, natural or unnatural disasters, and weapons of terror—should such weapons come to them."

The BVI Governor had come to the party ready to be a bigger supporter than Vance had apparently expected, but he was not going to let the U.S. off the hook for supporting the costs and burdens. Plus, he was apparently looking for a new Caribbean counter-narcotics strategy that would emphasize prevention at home, along with rhetoric geared toward a more "flexible" approach overseas.

While this could complicate matters, Robert felt a weight lift. He could tell Vance there would be a meeting. Someone with the authority to negotiate would be able to come back with trades in mind.

"That would be greatly appreciated, Your Excel...Edward." Robert responded gratefully. "Thank you. Is it possible to move forward with your idea quickly?"

"I believe the first meeting will be in three weeks? Am I right, Steve?" The Governor queried.

The Governor of Puerto Rico nodded. "Yes, and you'll be hosting the first session, isn't that correct, Edward?"

"Quite right." The Governor nodded. "Each subsequent meeting will take place on another island nation territory, to encourage participation by all. Now, Mr. Carlton," the Governor turned toward Robert, "are you prepared to foot the bill?"

"Well..." Robert began, stalling while he thought about how to answer the question.

"I mean the U.S., of course, and not you personally," the BVI Governor said, making a joke of his question. They all laughed. "This will prove to be rather more expensive than it seems. The islands have many susceptibilities, which will necessitate a great deal of funding."

Robert had worried that the Governor was referring to all the expenses associated with the meetings, which was a difficult enough decision. He hadn't expected this initial discussion to encompass any commitments larger than that, but he now realized that he was, indeed, being asked for the entire cost of this project. This could easily turn into a massive windfall for the Caribbean economy via U.S. taxpayers, and it was not in his power to make that call.

At least this was the kind of jousting Robert was used to in DC. It was easier to formulate his answer than he'd expected. "Edward, we are more than happy to openly and jointly evaluate the equipment and manpower needed from the United States. I will pass on our discussion notes and requests to our representative in the discussions."

"You won't be that representative, Mr. Carlton? I am devastated." The Governor sounded disappointed, but smiled mischievously. "Of course, we must let the bureaucrats have their moment in our glorious sun, but I think we would all be very happy should you be able to join us."

Following many handshakes and well wishes, the Governors receded to a smaller meeting room to continue other discussions. Their staff members stayed to hash out a short list of details with Robert and Grady. Grady ended up with four pages of Coast Guard, Air Force, and Navy notes to be clarified and documented. Mary had many more that included Customs, DEA, and ATF issues, with notes she'd compiled in a scrawl that Robert hoped was some form of shorthand. Robert's summaries held the main points and requests from the discussion.

The full day of meetings was followed by a PR State Department dinner, sans Governors. This took place at a restaurant perched on a shoreline of rocks that bordered a small section of beach. It was a beautiful location. The breeze from the open patio gently wafted under a blue and white awning, bringing the scents of moist salt air up from the ocean. The colored Christmas lights hanging from some of the palm trees should have seemed out of place, but they somehow fit perfectly with the burning torch scents of citronella and kerosene. The aroma of delicately fried foods wafted in from the kitchen.

Grady and his counterparts seemed to be hitting if off at the far end of the dinner table. Jackets came off and shirt sleeves rolled up early. Robert finally gave in, taking off his tie and rolling it up neatly to put in his coat pocket. Mary sat timidly in the middle of the two groups. She didn't seem to know how to participate in either group's conversation, but was trying hard to not look forgotten.

Robert's conch and fritters were fantastic. He'd deliberately opted for local, but somewhat familiar sounding foods. Grady was more adventurous, taking recommendations from the Naval and Army officers around him. On his sample plate was mofongo stuffed with seafood, fried snapper chillo, and lechon with plantains and caimitos. They all finished with black, rich, Puerto Rican coffee. Grady seemed to be in heaven.

Once back at the hotel, Grady enthusiastically announced, "We have to have mallorcas for breakfast in the morning."

Robert looked queasy. "You know that our flight doesn't give us much time for finding a breakfast spot," he tried. He wasn't sure he wanted to get on a long flight after eating local dishes.

"No, really, Robert, you'll love this." Grady's enthusiasm was overflowing. "It's sweet bread with fillings. The place they gave me directions to has the best café con leche in San Juan. It's on the way to the airport, so we won't waste any time getting there."

"Okay, I'm in." Robert gave up. He'd been thinking about ordering room service—scrambled eggs dry, toast, and bacon. Maybe coffee. He figured that if nothing else, the café con leche would be all right.

. . .

By the time they reached the airport in the morning, Robert was overstuffed and exhausted. He hadn't slept a wink all night. Grady's proclamation that the evening's exceptionally dark-roasted coffee had no caffeine in it conflicted with the evidence of Robert's bloodshot eyes, but he had to admit that he'd enjoyed the mallorca for breakfast. Grady had been right about that. Robert got his scrambled eggs and bacon, after all, stuffed inside the powdered sugar-topped bread. Robert had eyed the concoction suspiciously, but it was delicious.

He'd passed on the offer of more coffee at the airport, opting for a bottle of water, while Grady went from shop to shop in the big airport collecting trinkets to take home. He was also ferreting out very collectible bottles of rum. He lobbied to convince Mary and Robert to carry back a bottle each. Mary finally acquiesced and so, eventually, did Robert.

Grady was full of energy. The mallorca and black coffee had him in top form. Mary had demonstrated a hearty appetite and was now eager to follow Grady's lead with more coffee.

"You don't know what you're missing!" Grady insisted when Robert passed on the coffee.

Robert made a mental note that Grady was going to be hard to keep up with on trips together. When their flight finally left, he was glad to find that their seats were some distance apart.

The first leg to Miami was typical, but there a ground delay put them three hours behind schedule. Finally seated on the next plane, Robert succumbed to his nodding head. He didn't wake up until the wheels hit the ground in DC. Grady, after noticing that Mary was sound asleep when he went back to the lavatory, contentedly followed suit with his book laying in his lap.

When they met again outside the jetway at Reagan International, they all had noticeably bleary-eyed expressions.

"Good trip. Thank you for coming along. My office, nine in the morning?" Robert told them, ending the trip with a schedule reminder.

"Tomorrow." Grady acknowledged tiredly.

Mary nodded, and the travelers parted ways as they left the airport.

. . .

When Robert arrived home around seven-thirty, Tracie was already upstairs in the dressing room with a facemask, glass of wine, toenail polish, and her dressing room television playing a movie. The boys were absorbed by their video games in their rooms.

"How was your trip?" She asked cheerfully.

"Good. Well, worth it." Robert responded. "Sorry again for the short notice."

"That's okay," Tracie said, clearly unconcerned. "I had invitations from several of the hostesses at the party. We had a marvelous time last evening. Don't plan anything from here on out without checking with me, though; we have commitments for every day through Christmas Eve, and we are invited to the New Year's Gala! So, no more trips—and you'll need to get your tux cleaned. I want you to put it on before you do that, so I can see how it fits. I sent you everything on a list, so make sure your secretary gets it all on your calendar. I'm exhausted! It's all just been a whirlwind since I got back." Robert could tell she was excited behind the tired eyes. She was happy as a clam in that green face of mud.

"Well, I'm dead tired, as well," Robert confessed. "I fell asleep on the plane, but I guess it wasn't enough. My neck is so stiff I'm not sure I can relax."

"Take a pill," Tracie recommended.

"I was thinking about a hot shower, and then reading a little. The pill sounds like a good idea." Robert agreed.

"I like it." Tracie gave Robert a hug and headed back to finishing her nails.

"Oh, your parents called," Tracie called to him as he headed into the bathroom.

"What about?" Robert asked.

"Just wondering how your trip went. They would have come over, but your Father was traveling."

"Where this time?" Robert was not actually interested. The question was reflexive.

"Switzerland. He had some kind of big business meeting over there. He seemed to be really happy with the way it turned out. He asked what I've been up to."

"Really? I'm surprised." Robert was surprised. His father didn't usually spend time idly chatting.

"Me, too. He actually seemed interested in talking with me." Tracie seemed flattered.

That was out of character for his father, Robert thought as he got into the shower.

By the time Robert finished Tracie was in bed reading. Within minutes of opening his trip notes, he was fast asleep. Tracie nodded off at almost the same moment. Both had left their lights on, and pages held in their hands.

Chapter 9

Sailing on a broad reach from Martinique to St. Lucia, Mark and Julie enjoyed the steady breeze and light seas of the Caribbean winter. Winter was prime tourist season, with visitors flocking south, running from the cold. It was also the dry season, with easy yachting weather. Mark and Julie set out on their sailing adventure just after the hurricane season, flying to St. Croix the second week of December to finish the purchase of a sailing yacht. They'd spent the holidays on their newly acquired Beneteau 423 in the US Virgin Islands. Celebrating Christmas and New Year's Eve on the beach, they'd traded wind-blown snow for sand, sailing, and eighty-degree days. It was a dream come true. Their Christmas present to each other was the yacht, and the time to leisurely sail it. The weather was perfect as they traveled south from one paradise island to the next.

It was the end of their fourth-week sailing. Both were fully settled in with the boat. They'd previously spent holidays in the Grenadines and West Indies, returning there many times for sailing trips, so they adapted to the Caribbean lifestyle quickly. Planning to sail their new boat to Grenada, they were winding their way through the West Indies.

Mark had gained his protected waters captain's license three years earlier from a yacht club in Grenada. It was something he'd always wanted to do. When his small electronics company had been bought out he and Julie had taken a one-month break to sail, and at the same time earn the license. As soon as his "stay" package that the new owners of the company had required was finished, he and Julie had officially retired and made the decision to buy the boat.

They now felt rich—or at least rich enough for the two of them. Mark at forty-four and Julie at thirty-seven were enjoying their financial freedom. They planned to be "serial entrepreneurs," already concocting their next business idea, but for now, they focused on sailing.

Mark was in good shape, even compared to twenty-something guys, and young looking, despite gray temples just starting to come in. Julie was attractive and fit, her Pilates-toned bikini body tight and active. They still felt like newlyweds. They'd met five years earlier, when Julie had started working for Mark's company, but had been so busy working they hadn't had much time together.

This was their first sail in their own boat. The Beneteau was originally from Tampa Bay, Florida. The owner had sailed it down to the US Virgin Islands and decided to sell it there. It was a $125,000 bargain. Forty-two feet long, with a displacement length of one-hundred and forty-eight, it contained two spacious bedrooms, two heads, and an awesome galley. It was similar to the Beneteau Oceanis 37 they'd rented several times, but fit them better. They loved it. Somewhere they had gotten it in their minds to sail it to Grenada, and then, later, sail back home to the Savannah Yacht Club. That would take place when the winds shifted and were favorable for a long beat north.

For now, they just loved sailing the Caribbean. They could steer where they liked, when they liked. They had stopped at Martinique to shop the fantastic French island for perfume, new bathing suits, and a stock of Beer Lorraine. Yesterday had been St. Lucia to resupply food and fresh water, and visit the master woodcarver's studio. They would spend today running back south, on their way to Bequia for scuba diving and lobster pizza at Mac's. Tomorrow, assuming favorable winds, they were thinking of heading to Mustique, and Basil's bar for its incredible fresh Grouper. That is, of course, if they sailed from Bequia at all. Two straight days of lobster pizza, Bequia nightlife, and seeing what was new in its art studios sounded pretty good right now. If the winds weren't favorable, who cared? The galley was fully stocked, and the day was theirs. It was perfect.

At the helm, Mark steered a course of 190 degrees, the apparent wind coming directly over his left shoulder. The sails were full of soft air. The sun was just over the top of the mast. Soon it would be hidden by the sail—a much-awaited moment after a long morning filled with the sun's bright glare. The breeze was light, so Mark set the Genoa instead of the jib. The larger staysail, or "jenny," as most called it, extended past the mast and came low to the deck. It made the boat go faster, and was preferred unless the wind was too heavy. The only downside was that some of Mark's view forward was blocked.

It had been perfect sunbathing weather all morning. Once they were on a steady course, Julie took full advantage of it. She was lying out in the sun on the bow where the deck was wide and smooth. It was an area spacious enough for a dinghy to rest, but they towed theirs behind the yacht to keep the sail from rubbing it when tacking.

Usually modest, Julie had surprised Mark by buying a very skimpy bikini she'd found shopping on Martinique. Out here, and alone on the ocean—save for a few distant boats—she had even foregone wearing the top of her suit. She wanted to escape "strap lines." She'd purchased some plunging back gowns and spaghetti-strapped tops for dancing and going out to beachside restaurants. She seemed to be enjoying the breeze as it tickled the delicate skin of her sun-warmed breasts.

Mark was enjoying watching her from his position at the stern. Julie was an essay in braille, ready to be read over and over again by his fingertips. Smart, beautiful, and sexy, she was a real page-turner.

Julie rolled over on her side to face Mark standing the helm. Her shapely leg bent upward, but Mark was enthralled with her tanned breasts and the shimmer of water misting over them in the sun. Julie was admiring Mark, with his windblown hair, broad shoulders, and very cool sunglasses.

"Mark," she said languidly, and just a touch sexily. "It's your turn to cook."

Galley duty had fallen to Mark for lunch.

"I was hoping you had something else in mind," he smiled.

"Maaaybe," She said drawing the word out. "But food first. I'm starving."

"Your wish is my command!" Mark grinned. "Come take the wheel."

Julie got up, stowed her cushioned mat under a bungee and grabbing her towel, headed aft. Mark handed off the wheel and as he moved toward the galley he let his hand brush across Julie's breasts.

"Get my top while you're down there. I can't drive topless." She smiled coyly.

"You sure?" Mark was still grinning. "I think it looks great."

Once below he handed up her top, making her bend way over to get it.

"Thanks." She said, knowing exactly what he was doing. Mark laughed.

Julie held the wheel with her knee while she tied on the bikini top, and Mark got started with the food. They had brought some Jamaican style jerk fish, which he spread extra jerk spice sauce thinly across, then laid over rich, dark bread. It smelled terrific. A few slices of canned mild green Ortega chilies and Monterey Jack cheese completed the tasty-looking sandwiches.

"Honey," he poked his head out of the door facing aft and looking at Julie, "what do you want to drink?"

"Beer Lorraine, of course." She smiled broadly, calling out her request over the rush of the wind and sails.

"You got it." He ducked back below to retrieve the beer.

There was a growing sound from downwind, but the wind in the sails and slapping rigging on the mast hid the increasing thrumming. Neither of them noticed how fast it was coming.

"Mark!" Julie screamed as she threw the wheel over hard sending the boat lurching to the left. The wind grabbed at the sail leaning the boat over even farther. The sudden shift in the listing deck sent Mark across the settee into the bulkhead. The drone of diesel engines was now clear throughout the yacht.

Bursting from behind the blind spot of covering sail a gray metal-hulled boat rushed past the heeling sailboat, throwing spray over it and soaking Julie.

"Mark, get up here!" Julie turned the boat back to its original course as the huge wake of the gunboat crashed into her bow and sent Mark sprawling back across the lower deck and into the galley. There were no cushions to break his fall as he crashed into the counter, scattering all the food and utensils not already on the floor.

"Mark!" Julie yelled again.

"What the hell happened?" Mark managed to catch himself. Reaching hand over hand he used the stair rail to pull himself up and out of the cabin. Staggering to the wheel and grabbing the console, he could see the stern of the gunboat behind Julie as she fought the nearly foundering sailboat.

"He tried to ram us! I couldn't see him. He came from behind the sails."

"He's turning!" Mark pointed at the diesel craft, its stack pouring black smoke as it turned sharply, heeling over radically. It was not much more than fifty feet long, old, and ill maintained.

Neither of them spoke as they watched it come to bear on them. They had read all the warnings of pirates stealing yachts, drug syndicates, and worse. Now those warnings flared in their minds.

"It's got a flag," Mark said. "It must be military, or some kind of coast guard."

"What are they trying to do?" Julie was scared. So was Mark, but he was trying not to show it.

"Don't worry. They're just being idiots. It'll be fine." He tried to reassure her.

The boat came along their port and windward side, blocking the wind enough to stall the sails. A black man in a white uniform called to them in island accented English over a megaphone.

"Drop your sails, and prepare to be boarded!"

Mark waved his agreement and moved forward.

"Hold her steady, honey." He called back to Julie. "Everything will be all right."

They held close hauled—too close for Julie's comfort. The boat's tall cabin killed the wind and calmed the sea making it easier for Mark to drop the sales. In moments, three uniformed men stood on the wallowing sailboat. Two held small machine guns. The third man, the one with the megaphone, had a forty-five at his side and wore rank on his shoulder boards.

"Papers, please." He demanded.

Mark went below and came back with the boat's papers, customs forms, and his captain's license. Handing them to the official, he asked, "Is there something wrong, Officer?"

"Passports, please." The man returned gruffly.

"Passports?" Mark asked, wondering what the hell this was all about.

"Yes, passports. Now." The officer looked up from the papers sternly.

Mark went back below. Even with the bumpers cushioning the impact, the heavier boat jostled the sailboat around in the water making it hard to stand. Julie held onto the boom and wheel as she waited for Mark to come back up. She could see one of the armed sailors openly ogling her, but she couldn't let go of the wheel and boom to cover herself up with her towel. She could only glower at him, which had no effect.

"Here they are." Mark handed over the passports as he came up the ladder to the officer.

Almost snatching them from him, the officer said. "You are leaving St. Lucia territorial waters. Do you have a visa?"

"Visa? We just came from there. I wasn't told..."

The officer held up his hand and continued thumbing through their passports.

"You have no visa...Chief!" The armed man next to him snapped to attention. "Place them under arrest."

"Now, just a minute!" Mark protested. "What flag is that? Who are you?" Robert pointed at the stern of the gray boat.

"No talking!" The Chief admonished Mark, using the barrel of his machine gun to indicate that Mark and Julie must get onto the gunboat.

"This isn't necessary..." Mark began.

"Quiet." The officer frowned at Mark, interrupting him.

"At least let us get some clothes." Mark felt an immediate jab in his back ribs from the other man's barrel.

"Just do as he says," Julie said quietly. "There must be an explanation for all of this."

"No talking!" The Chief reiterated with a frown.

The officer climbed onto his boat first. The effort to switch boats even in the light seas was awkward, even hazardous. Other men from the metal boat had jumped over to secure the sailboat and fit it with a towing line. With frightening speed, Mark and Julie found themselves hauled over the steel deck, down into the boat's hull, and handcuffed to a pipe below decks. Their scant clothing left their bare skin exposed to the harsh metal surfaces covered in oily film and rust.

The diesel motor boat lacked the stability of the sailboat. It tossed in all directions, pitching, rolling and yawing like a cork. Once the boat got up to speed it became more stable, but the motion bruised Julie's and Mark's buttocks and shoulders against hard steel with each roll. Occasionally a larger wave would jolt the boat, pitching its bow upwards and sending their heads thumping against the hull. The ride seemed to drone on forever. Dense diesel fumes pooled in the boat and in their lungs. The lack of fresh air soon sent them both into a dizzy, nauseated stupor. They frequently passed out. Each time they awoke they could feel their bodies becoming increasingly limp and helpless.

Julie and Mark couldn't see that their yacht had been cut free, and was being taken on a different heading by another boat. In a few hours, it would be pulled to another island, and into a small harbor that contained some large, rusted metal buildings and workshops.

Mark and Julie lost track of time as they rocked in and out of consciousness. They didn't notice when the boat moved closer to shore into the smoother waters on the leeward side of the island. Once at the dock, they were ushered off so quickly that they had little time for noticing the missing yacht. Groggy and dehydrated, they didn't notice the lack of insignia on the boat or the men, who were now looking more like fishermen than sailors. All they saw was the waiting panel van, the paint on the windows, and the stains inside the filthy truck.

<u>Chapter 10</u>

Robert was glad to see the New Year's celebrations come and go. The day and night schedule of events since his trip to Puerto Rico had left Tracie elated, and him exhausted. All of December, thanks to Tracie, had been filled to overflowing with parties and social engagements. The boys, after a glut of high-tech gifts at Christmas, were addicted to their new toys and already demanding more game disks, apps, and a never-ending supply of batteries. Alicia had taken a week off. The resulting chaos left the house in shambles. All in all, Robert was happy to go back to work.

Entering his offices from the hallway he found boxes filling the reception area. Lorraine was busy labeling another one to add to the stacks.

"What's going on?" Robert waved his arms around the room ending with his eyes on the door to his office. It was open. Inside more boxes stood in the center of the room. Behind the boxes stood a junior admin, packing files and books.

"Lorraine? Was this on the schedule? Did I miss a memo?" He asked, feeling annoyed.

"Attorney General Crain sent a memo, Sir. He has recommended Mr. Franklin as your successor, and wants you to move into your new offices as soon as possible." Lorraine answered, casting a worried eye at him.

The new offices were next door to the Attorney General's. They had been Jack's. Apparently, he'd decided it was time to let go of them, and install Robert closer at hand.

"That's right." Jack chimed in, unexpectedly striding in from the hallway. "I want you where I can get you at a moment's notice, or less, Robert."

"Jack, how was your holiday?" Robert was quick to turn and shake his boss' hand.

"Great, and yours?" Jack responded.

"Great," Robert answered, completely forgetting the chaos at home. "So, I guess I'm moving today." Robert realized he felt okay with that. It was a disconcerting start on his first day back, but he'd been wondering whether Jack was going to let go of his old offices.

"Here's the thing, Robert." Jack moved the two of them into the connecting meeting room and closed the door. "I like the direction you're headed, and I'm pleased with the way you've taken on special assignments. I've decided to keep you flexible on assignments. I discussed this with the President and he agrees. I know this isn't typical for the Deputy position, but I have several ongoing initiatives that I want to carry through with the staff. That will keep me tied up, but there's always something coming up in the system that needs special attention. It'll work best if I can have you available for those situations."

Robert knew this was executive-speak for, "I am a non-recovering micromanager and I can't let go." It was certainly true for Jack. He was also a little obsessive. He could be demanding, but in a surprisingly congenial manner. Robert had no illusions about running the AG offices; that wouldn't happen with Jack around.

"We'll have to take things as they come," Jack went on. "I hope that works for you."

"Sure, Jack. Whatever you need, I'm ready to step up," Robert responded firmly. It wasn't as if he had a choice, so he might as well look positive and energized by Jack's decision.

"I'm going to do some rearranging of my office support staff. Can you live with Lorraine as your admin?" Jack queried.

"No problem." Robert had not given it much thought. Now that Jack had suggested it, he realized it was probably the best course of action. Lorraine knew him well by this time and was familiar with how he liked to work.

"Good." Jack had clearly expected an affirmative answer. "Now for the tough one: I want to recommend Franklin as your successor. Who would you like heading up Legislative Affairs?"

Robert would have preferred to have more time to think the decision through, but Jack liked quick, decisive pronouncements. The Legislative Affairs department was important to the AG office's cooperative and productive relationship with Congress. Usually, it went to a politically talented individual, who was on his or her way up the ladder. Robert's recent experiences, particularly in dealing with the President and the powerful Senator Gregg, had taught him that political interaction was key to his long-term success—and maybe to his survival. He needed someone he could count on to work hard, but who would be content to be secondary to Robert. Someone not necessarily craving the limelight.

Jerry. Yes, Jerry would be the best choice.

Gerald Turner, head of the Office of Intergovernmental and Public Liaisons, had been a direct report to Robert. His skills at analysis and his performance levels were both efficient and dependable. He wasn't as pliable as Robert sometimes wished, but he was good at his job. If Franklin was replacing Robert, then Jerry now worked for him. Robert would prefer that Jerry stayed on his own team. This would be a good way to keep his abilities available.

"Jerry," Robert stated solidly, pausing to see if Jack required justification of the decision.

"Jerry." Jack mulled over the idea for a few seconds. "I think I see why. At first glance—I like it."

Jack opened the door to the conference room. "I'll get back to you in twenty-four hours on that." He made his way to the outer door, past the boxes. "Once again, congratulations on your initiative. I'm looking forward to your continuing hard work, Robert."

"Thanks. You, too." Robert suddenly realized that he'd been less than adept with that reply, and mentally cringed.

"Ha! Good one." Jack chuckled as he left.

Robert was berating himself for his inept rejoinder. Yes, Jack had taken it as a clever remark, but it could just as easily have fallen completely flat.

He noticed Lorraine standing still, deliberately not staring at him, but clearly hoping he'd pass on whatever had been discussed with Jack.

Robert cleared his throat. "Lorraine." Robert placed his hand on a stack of boxes, and then removed it, feeling awkward. "How soon can you have us moved into the new offices?"

"Us?" Lorraine looked surprised. She had been passed over for two decades, so she'd assumed she'd be working for whomever Robert's replacement turned out to be.

"Yes, 'us.'" Robert reiterated. "You and me. When can you have us situated?"

"Tomorrow afternoon," Lorraine responded automatically, still trying to get used to the idea that she'd be moving, too. "We should have everything moved and in place by then." She still looked a bit stunned.

"Great. I have a meeting in an hour, and since my office is a wreck, I'll go now, and get there early. I have my cell phone if you need me." Robert grabbed his valise and coat. "Congratulations." He mustered a smile and extended his hand.

"Thank you, Sir." Lorraine shook his hand, perhaps for the first time since they'd met.

Robert wasted no time leaving the building. He headed toward the Naval Research Laboratory, calling Grady's cell.

"Lieutenant Colonel Barlow speaking, may I help you?" Grady sounded formal.

"Grady, it's Robert. I got away early, so I was thinking of stopping for a coffee before heading to our meeting. Do you know a place near the NRL?" Robert didn't want to sit in a lobby or a parking lot, but the only places he knew that had coffee in the area were hotels and tiny drive-thru kiosks.

"Sure." Grady immediately sounded more cheerful. "There's a little spot at the corner of 2nd and L, as in Lima. If you're taking the 695, exit on S. Capitol, go south, then left on M, as in Mike, then left on 2nd. I'm done here, so I'll meet you there."

"Great. I'll see you in a few minutes." Robert was glad to have a moment before the meeting to chat. He started to say that, but realized that Grady had hung up.

Grady arrived about fifteen minutes after Robert.

"Sorry I'm late," Grady said as he strolled over to where Robert was sitting. "Parking issues—first getting out of the Pentagon, and then finding a spot here."

"I'm early, and this wasn't planned, so it's not an issue." Robert was sitting with a mug in his hand and his valise on the table where he could see it.

"I know this place isn't fancy, but the coffee was good enough last time for me to remember it. How is it today?" Grady questioned.

"Fine." Robert fiddled with the mug handle, not sounding particularly enthusiastic.

Grady cocked an eyebrow at him. "A glowing review. I'll be right back." When he returned he had a latte in hand. "So, what's up?"

"Nothing. They have my office all boxed up, so I thought I'd get out and be early for a change." Robert told him.

"Boxed?" Grady now had both eyebrows raised.

"Yes, I'm moving to the new office. Jack Crain's old office." Robert explained.

"Right." Grady remembered that Robert had wondered when the move would take place. "Nice office?" Grady sipped his espresso drink.

"Almost identical to the old one. Same furniture. It's adjoining Crain's, so it'll give him quick access to me." Robert said.

"Bummer." Grady smiled. "I didn't get much advance information about this meeting we're headed to today."

"It was originally set up for Lillian Morrison to attend as an orientation to current and developmental airborne weapons detection programs," Robert explained. "She's not going, but we are."

"She probably knew she would be sending someone else." Grady gave his mug a slight frown. "She doesn't like orientations."

"Bad latte?" Robert inquired. He was familiar with Grady's quest for the best espresso drinks.

"No, it's fine. I think the pull was a little slow, or the machine was a little hot." Grady told him. "So Mako's sending us instead of going herself?"

"Ms. Morrison; yes." Robert was now questioning his coffee's flavor. Grady was going to turn him into as much of an aficionado as he was.

"Airborne weapons—meaning in-flight or chemical, and biological aerosol?" Grady ventured.

"Aerosol plus nuclear. I think they have decided to consider radiation airborne." Robert said, recalling the brief.

"Makes sense." Grady mused. "Well, that's good. I could use a refresher."

"You? I thought you could write the book on this." Robert was genuinely surprised.

"Delivery of these airborne weapons maybe, but detection is a whole different game. NRL is always playing with new ideas, so they may have some I haven't seen. It's a good thing that they're working on this stuff. I've always thought that a bomb-sniffing dog approach would be a bad idea looking for nerve gas. Really bad for the dog."

He took another sip. "And canaries are so nineteenth century," he joked. "I have a feeling this is going to be like a chemistry class."

. . .

They'd left Grady's car in the coffee shop parking lot, riding in Robert's. Grady directed Robert toward the sign reading, "Visitor Control Center" at the front gate when they arrived at the NRL. They got their passes there, then were directed to the building where their meeting was scheduled.

Walking into the Naval Research Laboratory, Robert took note that the building seemed old and a little run-down. It was populated by a number of civilians. "Who are all these people?" He asked Grady.

"I've only been here twice myself, but I can tell you that the NRL is more about military funding than about uniformed personnel. The wife of a friend of mine works here, and she's not military. There seem to be a lot of PhDs, along with their graduate students, in every project I've seen come out of this place." Grady elucidated.

Checking in at the appointment desk Robert introduced himself and was told that a manager from the department would be with them momentarily. When she entered the lobby, it was a shock for Grady.

"Faith? I didn't know you would be at this meeting. Don't you work in one of the other buildings?" He asked, surprised to see her there.

"I do," the woman answered, "but this is a special meeting." She turned toward Robert. "You must be Deputy AG Carlton." Faith's outgoing personality was friendly and welcoming.

"Yes, I am," Robert answered. "Please call me Robert." He told her as they shook hands.

"Faith Atherton; pleased to meet you. And of course, Colonel Barlow and I are acquainted." She said, nodding to Grady. "As

Grady noted, I work out of the main administration building, next to the dish. I'm the Office Manager for most of the projects around here." She explained.

Robert couldn't help noticing Faith's blond hair, curvy figure, and bright smile. Her cheerful attitude was impossible to ignore. She laughed at almost every sentence, managing to keep the conversation flowing with Robert as they walked.

"Is this your first time at the NRL, Robert?" She accepted the first name usage easily.

"Yes, it is. I haven't had any occasion to be in on these discussions until now." He answered.

"Then welcome to the NRL, and prepare to become part of the team." Faith laughed.

"Sounds like I'm joining a football squad." Robert kidded.

"It does, doesn't it?" Faith's good humor and effervescent personality bubbled over, but somehow she stayed in command of the conversation. "As I said, I am the group office manager for the ONR, or rather, the Office of Naval Research. I have been asked to coordinate your meeting today. First up is an overview with the Director of WMD, or Maritime Weapons of Mass Destruction Detection, followed by a briefing from the NRL Aerosol Optics program and the MISTI/SuperMISTI group."

"And MISTI stands for…?" Robert asked, wondering if he'd remember all the acronyms.

"Mobile Imaging and Spectroscopic Threat Identification—it was created to detect nuclear weapons. Wow, I'm surprised I remembered that! We just call it MISTI—nobody ever asks that question." Faith laughed again.

They arrived at the conference room. Like the rest of the building it seemed tired. It felt very empty with no one else in the room.

"Faith, can you tell me how old the Naval Research Laboratory is?" Robert asked her, thinking that it didn't look much like a technical research lab.

"It does feel a bit old for high-tech research, I know." She admitted. "These main buildings were constructed back in the forties, but the NRL actually began operations back in 1923. In 1915 Thomas Edison made a public statement that had a lot to do with everything here getting started. You'll see his picture and quotes everywhere here. Don't let the buildings fool you; we do research in every discipline, from Autonomous Vehicles to Zettabyte storage banks."

"Zettabyte?" Grady asked, wondering where Faith had conjured that one up.

"A Zettabyte is a thousand Exabytes—which is a lot." Faith grinned. "I memorized that for the tours. We take turns giving it." She seemed to be waiting for the next question from either Grady or Robert.

"I have a question that's off the subject," Robert asked. "How do you two know each other?" He was curious where Faith fit into Grady's life.

"Mike, Faith's husband, and I both went to the Academy." Grady chimed in. "The three of us are good friends." Grady left out the part about his wife Keisha being one of the group. They'd all gotten married about the same time, and Keisha and Faith had been close right up to Keisha's death.

At that moment one of the two doors opened and the WMD Director walked in with three other people.

With quick introductions, the meeting started. First came an overview of the Office of Naval Research, and the Naval Research Laboratory's role in WMD. Robert reminded himself that this was all about detection of weapons, not creating or destroying them. Eventually, the discussion turned to Airborne Weapons Detection, the primary focus of the meeting.

Dr. Patel from the WMD group led this discussion. "My team has developed a method for single aerosol particle discrimination and classification, using infrared absorption spectroscopy, which we are transitioning to the next generation of chemical detectors." He continued with a description of this method, assisted by his staff.

After an hour, Robert's brain had overloaded, but he got the gist of the material. Currently, there was limited capability in detecting chemical and biological weapons. It was necessary to have a properly trained and equipped team of humans get up close and personal with the dangerous stuff. The next generation of detection coming on-line allowed for testing via robotic sampling, which was slower, but safer—as long as particles weren't spreading on the wind. Dr. Patel's development was exciting because they'd been able to detect some important known substances at much safer distances. The method also made covering more area from a single vantage point possible. Dr. Patel hoped to have a system ready for field tests very soon.

Grady seemed to have a strong grasp of the limitations and implications of this research. He had a working knowledge of the most effective delivery systems, and how they might be used around the world in combat conditions, depending on equipment and terrain.

Then the MISTI team arrived. Clad in a green tweed jacket, Dr. Alan Browne's appearance contrasted sharply with Naval Lieutenant Katherine Davies' crisp service khaki uniform blouse and skirt. Her collar held the insignia of two silver bars, similar to that of an Air Force Captain's. Robert was generally familiar with the Air Force and Army, but Navy rank was a bit of a mystery to him. A Navy Lieutenant equaled an Air Force Captain, he reminded himself. He found himself wondering why the armed forces didn't all use the same rankings.

Robert's attention was brought back to the presentation. He knew he was in over his head with the first MISTI slide illuminating the wall.

Dr. Browne was presenting in a dry, clinical fashion. "The Mobile Imaging & Spectroscopic Threat Identification system, or MISTI, is a stand-off detection, identification, and localization capability for locating radioactive materials, even those deliberately concealed. The primary purpose of MISTI is to detect hidden, specialized nuclear materials. Our project parameters are to image a radioactive source in 3-D to within ten meters, by detecting a 1 millicurie source in 20 seconds at 100 meters."

Robert felt he was going to suffer serious brain damage in trying to absorb this material. He decided his best bet was to gain a very general understanding of MISTI's work. It was unlikely he'd ever have to explain the technical end of it in his negotiations.

At the end of the table, Faith was watching Grady, trying to assess his body language. She wasn't interested in how he absorbed the presentation, but rather in how he was responding to Lt. Davies. Grady was covertly eyeing the Lieutenant. He'd quickly glanced back toward the presentation slide when she casually looked his way.

Lieutenant Davies' professional appearance didn't detract from her pretty face and smile. She'd pulled her dark brown hair back and up, pinned sleekly to fit under the uniform hat she'd wear when outside. Her skin was a shade darker than Grady's own, setting off her white teeth and lush lips. Grady noticed that her figure showed seductive proportions under the khaki uniform, but he couldn't stop looking at her glowing brown eyes.

Faith pulled her attention away from Grady and back to the material. Dr. Browne had reached their pre-arranged break point, so she jumped in when he finished speaking.

"I suggest we break from the formal PowerPoint presentation and turn this discussion over to the Lieutenant, who can show you MISTI up close and get your feet wet." She smiled mysteriously, wondering if they'd catch her pun during the next segment of the orientation.

"I couldn't agree more." Dr. Browne started shutting down his computer.

Grady snapped back to the activity. He had momentarily lost track of what was being said, but everyone was suddenly standing. He was surprised to see Browne shaking hands in preparation for his departure.

"It was good to meet you. You're in good hands with Ms. Atherton and Lt. Davies," he assured Grady and Robert as he left.

Grady lifted an eyebrow at Faith, who grinned at him.

"You're coming along?" he asked her, surprised. He figured Faith had heard this stuff a million times.

"I wouldn't miss it," she said, winking devilishly at him.

Faith and Lt. Davies led Robert and Grady down several hallways, and out the side of the building. Turning toward the river at the end of the complex, Grady realized they were heading to a dock a few hundred yards ahead. A fifty-foot barge at the end of the long dock seemed to be their destination.

Robert was asking Lt. Davies about the origins of MISTI. Faith dropped back to walk beside Grady. "How's the rebuilding of the house coming?" She asked.

"It's coming along. Not fast enough for my taste, but it gives me some time to consider," he told her.

"Still thinking you might move back in?"

"Right now, I feel like I could get used to the condo life. It's pretty sweet to be so close to work. Not much left for me back in the old neighborhood, since everything in the house was vaporized," Grady told her.

Faith squeezed his arm briefly in sympathy. She knew it had been hard for Grady to have everything he'd shared with Keisha destroyed, but she wondered if it wasn't the break he needed to move on with his personal life. He hadn't dated much since Keisha had died. She and Mike thought he'd spent too many nights alone in that house. They'd tried to have him over to their place as much as possible, but they both knew that couldn't fill the hole in his life. When she'd heard about this meeting coming up, she'd asked Mike about fixing Grady up with Katherine, but he'd advised her to keep out of it.

"If there's a spark when they meet they'll make it happen, Honey," he'd told her. "No reason to push either one into a forced situation."

Faith looked up at Grady and wondered. He'd certainly noticed Katherine.

"Better get back to the tour-guide part of my job!" She told Grady, grinning. She quickened her pace to catch up with Robert, and started giving him some historical information on the rest of the complex, pointing back toward the buildings. Somehow she maneuvered Lt. Davies back to walk beside Grady.

If Katherine had noticed Faith's tactic, she didn't react. She'd been thinking about the next part of the orientation. Realizing that Grady was looking at her, she smiled.

"You seem familiar with the NRL, Colonel. Have you been here for other meetings?" Lt. Davies asked.

"Yes. It's my first time seeing MISTI, though, and please, call me Grady, Lieutenant," he commented, smiling back at her.

"Katy." She corrected him genially. "Then let me tell you about MISTI. The sensing equipment is inside the two 'A' containers you see on the barge."

They were now within twenty yards of the barge, with the set up in full view. The ISO containers were the kind of metal crates seen on container ships, trains, or semi-haulers. The 'A' size was twenty feet long. In front of the containers were two tanks.

"Facing us are two cylindrical tanks to provide ballast for keeping the barge level," Katy continued. "The cylindrical tanks are positioned behind the containers, which shelter sensors facing the Potomac."

Everything looked solidly mounted to the barge, with several tension wires holding the tanks and containers to the deck, but the barge itself didn't seem seaworthy. It was only a few feet taller than the water.

"The system uses both Germanium and Sodium Iodide detectors. The Germanium provides spectroscopy and unique isotope identification, while the Sodium Iodide provides two-dimensional gamma ray imaging. By combining the 2-D images with GPS we can derive a 3-D image of the source location. In 2011 trials, MISTI met all the initial design parameter requirements. At that time, it was transitioned to the Department of Energy. This is actually SuperMISTI that you're seeing today. It met its on-water requirements in 2012, both active and passive."

"How far has it been deployed?" Grady's interest in the device grew as they got closer.

"So far only as a few test modules," Katy replied, "but the testing is moving forward rapidly. I'm in charge of conducting the sea trials. Right now, funding is the only thing holding back large-scale deployment."

Robert spoke up, "What is its primary function—as in, what does it do best?"

With that question, Katy stopped. They had reached the end of the pier and were standing on the edge of the dock overlooking SuperMISTI, and the Potomac River. She turned and looked at Robert.

"It is very good at spotting a radiation source, even if it has been intentionally hidden. For example, if it was in a container onboard a ship, in a block of warehouses, or inside business buildings, MISTI could determine the type of nuclear source, and its location—within about ten meters." She replied.

"How close does it have to be?" Grady asked.

Katy quickly responded, "It has been tested fully at four-hundred meters. Theoretically, it should be able to work well up to four miles, line of sight, depending on the strength of the source."

"Line of sight?" Robert questioned.

"Well, if the source was below decks in a ship's hold, for example, or behind a power plant, that interferes to some degree with MISTI's ability to read information," Katy answered. "Gamma rays could still pass through the metal, concrete, or other materials to some extent, since they penetrate well. They can go through most things, but the more absorbing or reflecting the clutter, the less reliable the reading." Katy tried to put the data in more practical terms for Robert. "The idea is to have a system that can spot nuclear WMDs being smuggled. MISTI is flexible. We can deploy the equipment by train, or trailer-truck as well. That's why the arrays were built into the two, twenty-foot containers. We have a unit mounted on a truck being tested now."

"Let's go aboard," Faith invited Grady and Robert. "Katy can show you how the arrays are laid out."

Katy's descriptions became more technical as they looked inside the containers. Each HPGe array was about five-feet tall and four-feet wide, consisting of twenty-four square, boxy-looking sensors. Robert thought it was a scientific geekfest. Grady seemed excited by the display, and Faith had obviously been through this presentation enough to be very familiar with the equipment. Robert felt out of his depth when Katy delved into the more scientific aspects and began checking his watch. Faith noticed and gave Katy a discreet nudge.

"That about wraps it up, Gentlemen," Faith interjected when Katy finished summarizing. "Any questions?"

The conversation migrated to general discussions about the Naval Research Lab. Faith did most of the talking. Katy took over when the discussion turned to the many other projects the NRL had in development. Drone technology, stealth systems, advanced communications, and bullet proof transparent aluminum brought Robert's attention back into the dialogue. Both he and Grady regretted that they had other meetings to attend; the subjects were enticing. They thanked Faith and Katy and headed back to the car.

. . .

"What do you think?" Robert asked as they headed toward the parking lot.

"It got my attention. So, this is what we would deploy, if necessary, in the Caribbean?" Grady asked.

"I assume so, but there's a limited amount of equipment. Getting them moved around looks like a real issue to me." Robert added.

"Agreed." Grady mentally began considering the problem." That thing is fine in a harbor, but it won't handle the open ocean. We'll have to find out what their projected transport options are, and how fast it can be deployed."

. . .

Faith and Katy made their way back to their offices. On the way, Faith grilled Katy.

"Well? How did you like him?"

"Who?" Katy answered absently, still thinking about the equipment.

"Grady, of course!" Faith said, giving her a little push.

"Oh, so that was why you asked to have me in that meeting at the last minute. Don't you think your tactics were a bit obvious?" Katy sounded a little annoyed.

"I didn't tell him anything about you, Katy," Faith reassured her.

"But you knew he was coming." Katy was a bit peeved at Faith. This was another in a long series of set-ups. Faith had hauled out a series of available bachelors since Katy's divorce.

"Honestly, I didn't know he was coming until the last minute. It was supposed to be someone named Morrison. Once I knew it was Grady, I realized that it was a perfect chance to have you meet him without going through another blind date." Faith explained.

"No more blind dates," Katy said firmly.

"I know. I promised." Faith had made that promise more than a month earlier.

"I should have added, 'no more set-ups.'" Katy told her. The dating games had worn thin fast. She'd sworn off men, delving into her work.

"He's a nice guy, Katy. I've known him for years, remember? He's not a player." Faith tried to get Katy to smile. "I was right about him being good-looking, wasn't I?"

"Yes, but pushing for me to be in the meeting was too much. Just drop it." Katy was in no mood to cheerfully accept Faith's meddling.

"Okay." Faith buckled momentarily, but rebounded with, "How about the four of us..."

"Faith!" Katy almost yelled.

"Okay, okay." Faith responded, shaking her head. She'd have to think of some other way.

Chapter 11

Hunching over a desk jammed against a rusted corrugated steel wall, Vlad examined several different sailboat design graphics. Three black haired, dark-complected men walked up, standing together on his left side at a respectful distance. Next to them stood an oddly placed ceiling pole and two filthy vending machines. The massive sliding metal doors which lead to the boat ramp made little sound as four men pushed them together slowly, and locked them with a huge steel hasp.

Turning to look at the three men near him, Vlad's face remained unreadable in the darkness. He reached forward and flipped on the desk lamp, casting oddly shaped shadows against the curved Quonset hut wall. The men obediently waited for him to speak, knowing they should only listen. Vlad's low-toned voice rasped from decades of smoking, making his Russian accent sound harsh.

"I want nothing missed. The boats must be exactly the same as they arrived." He ordered.

The boat that had just been pulled in out of the water stood dripping on the floor.

"I want no fingerprints, no shoe scuffs, no beer bottles, and no cigarette butts. Nothing to tell the boats left the water, or that anyone was on them," he emphasized.

The men had heard this speech twice already, but they obediently listened to it again. The three supervisors understood Vlad's English better than the other men standing by the closed doors, but none of them were anything more than basic laborers. They would remember and follow instructions. They had no leadership skills, no drive, and no ambition. Vlad would not have employed them in any other location, but on this island, they were as good as he would get.

"No mistakes." Vlad's harsh voice reiterated.

He stood slowly, towering over the men, taller and bigger than all of them. His appearance was intimidating, and his permanent scowl made it look to the men as though he frowned at them.

"These are the last two boats. There will be no lazy mistakes. Each of you is responsible for one task. Just one. Do it right." He pointed at each man, naming their jobs as he said, "Mounting, fiberglass, finishing; you will all keep these boats clean inside and out. You will do as these men tell you." He pointed to two men who appeared to be in their fifties, standing apart and to one side of the others. "Get it right. Your assignment here will be over when the last boat is finished. Do it well, and you will be chosen to work on the next job, starting right away. Remember, you will say nothing about your work to anyone; not to friends, and not family. Never...or you will lose the next job."

The workers nodded sheepishly. The threats alone were enough, but the prospect of another job was too much to risk. It was good work; good pay. Not going home for almost two months was a small inconvenience. Plus, the food was free. Their family and friends knew they had jobs on another island and weren't expecting to hear from them for a while.

None of them called this island their home. Only two came from the same island, and one had lied about being from another to get the job. There was no one to visit on this island, and no reason to leave the building.

The men had been working for Vlad for three weeks. Each time a boat came in they got the same instructions. Now only two boats remained.

The Quonset hut was a large forty-by-one-hundred-foot WWII warehouse model. The center of the half-round building reached twenty feet. This provided plenty of room down the middle, even for the tall boats. The hut was spacious enough inside to house living arrangements for the men. Nearby tables were stacked with boxes of food. A make-shift kitchen was filled with familiar smells coming from pots on the stove, and something cooking in the oven.

Island spices permeated the building. The military surplus sleeping cots were set up on the sides of the hut.

The newly acquired yacht stood in line with another, both on dry dock stands. Masts and rigging lay to the sides of each hull. In the adjoining floor space, two more yachts were packed tightly together on stands. Those boats were finished. They would be re-launched during the next week while the moon was dark. Each would slide silently out on separate nights.

The Russian crinkled his nose as the spicy food smell became stronger. The odor was not to his liking; sometimes the smells were offensive to him. He did not eat with the men. He spent little time in the building.

"Get to work," Vlad ordered, turning back to the desk and design plans.

The islanders dispersed to hold ladders and handle hoists. The two older men went to a small kennel and led out two dogs. They spoke quietly to each other in Kazakh. To the dogs, they spoke Spanish.

"Come, we hunt now," they told the dogs. The Venezuelan dogs were government trained. Happy to be released from their kennels, they pranced beside the men as they were led to the boats.

The two men were technicians from a farming district in Kazakhstan. They were trained to transport and work on seed irradiators. Their job was to handle the irradiator radioactive sealed sources sitting in wooden crates near the boats. Working with the dogs was secondary.

With their dogs, they climbed up into each boat as it stood in the dry dock. Like the other men in the hut, they wore off-white leather full-fingered sailing gloves made by a US manufacturer, plain white Hanes T-Shirts, Levi's, and white-soled Rockport boat shoes. Even the dogs wore white cotton booties on their feet while on the boats.

The floor of the Quonset hut had been filthy when the men had arrived. The entire building had been thoroughly cleaned by degreasing, then scrubbing with seawater. No detergent was used. Discolorations remaining in the concrete were well washed and permanent. The workers were careful to avoid contamination to the boats. Vlad had been concerned about the cooking smells in the hut, and hoped that they would dissipate once the boats were back in the water.

Outside the immediate boat work area, the hut was typically trashy and rusty, like most workshops on the island. The windows were painted dark or frosted. The outside looked worse, matching other workshops in the area.

The sailboats rested upright on rolling platforms with their keels two feet or more off the ground. The weight of each boat rested on stand tops made with TPE surfaces, designed to protect delicate finishes like epoxy, gel coats or fine wooden craft. These fiberglass boats wouldn't get as much as a scratch. Each deck stood well above the ground.

Everything had been handled carefully and quickly when the boats were brought in. Locals in the work zone would say nothing. They had been well paid with the promise of more to come. No unnecessary chances had been taken. The boats had arrived in the harbor randomly over the past week. These two boats had been brought in from their unassuming harbor anchorages late in the night. It had been the same for the first three. Late night wanderers through the district and local barflies had been conveniently distracted at critical times, usually with free drinks.

Now the boats were being thoroughly examined for anything a Coast Guard inspection might consider suspicious or illegal. One dog sniffed for drugs, the other for explosives. The men searched every nook, planning to remove anything that might be found.

An hour after they began, the two men were finished. They stood near the Russian's desk. Vlad turned in the wooden swivel chair to look at them.

"Well?" He demanded impatiently.

In very rough English the first man stated, "We found marijuana in the Gozzard 36-foot boat. The other was clean except for this gun." He held up a heavily oiled revolver.

The three island supervisors had been standing in the background, listening. Now they came closer, knowing there would be assignments.

"Flush the marijuana and put back the gun. Clean the smell of the drugs away." Vlad directed the two technicians.

"Da, Vla..." One of the technicians started to respond, immediately shrinking back when he realized that he had inadvertently used Russian and Vlad's name.

Vlad glared at the man. As he stood, his stare slid across to the three supervisors who looked decidedly nervous. "I noticed one of the workers near the boats without his gloves," he growled at them. His stance shifted and his voice lowered dangerously as his fists came to rest on the desk. "Make sure everyone keeps their gloves on."

All the men in the room stiffened.

"If there is another infraction, I will deal with it and you three, personally." His voice rose above the sounds of the work area. No one moved. "Tell them!" He barked, slamming his open hand down on the desk. The smack of his hand echoed off the walls. The workers froze where they stood and watched the three supervisors, not daring to breathe. The supervisors began moving quickly, scattering into the work area. They began yelling and pointing at the workers' hands and gloves.

The technicians remained.

Vlad moved closer to two wooden crates stacked one on top of the other. Two of the original five had been opened and now stood vertically against the wall, empty.

"You have a full week to mount these two and finish the boats. That is plenty of time to do it right." He mandated, reaching out his hand and resting it against the top crate. "You have done well keeping them intact. I have detected no leaks, only ambient readings. For these two boats, I want the same small charges placed on the baffles as before, and the same ductwork construction for the masts. As with the other boats, the secondary larger charges must be placed on the sealed container body, opposite the baffles to blow the boat upwards. I want enough charge to break it apart, on a separate remote detonator. Set the failsafe auto timer for ninety minutes to give the blower time to do its job. Understand?"

"Yes." One of the technicians responded hesitantly.

"What is it?" Vlad waited only a few seconds. "Speak up," he commanded impatiently.

The technician stiffened. "The bulb will seem large, and oddly placed on the Gozzard."

Vlad considered the statement. Pulling out the boat plans he placed the Gozzard design next to the Gulfstar. He pointed to each of the keels. "Both are shoal keels. The Gulfstar leading edge is farther back." He told the man.

"Yes, we placed the bulb in the center, and ducted it at an angle." The technician confirmed.

"Then do this one the same way." Vlad decided. "I agree that the bulb on the Gulfstar seems oddly shaped, but it will look fine in the water. This time, make the bulb longer, so it tapers the length of the keel."

"Yes. Thank you." The technicians answered as they retreated.

Vlad replaced the boat plans and pulled a small folding knife from his pocket. He used the file from the knife to clean a fingernail, while discreetly checking the radiation badge sensor cleverly disguised as a logo on the bright red knife. Twenty mSv. He was still safe, with no more than the exposure that two CT scans would cause. The sensors located around the work area had been deliberately manipulated to be inaccurate. Vlad limited his time in the room as a result. He was conveniently away when the protective boxes were opened, and the sealed sources mounted.

"Before you put the fiberglass on I will inspect them," Vlad spoke loudly enough for the techs to hear from across the room.

Both men turned and nodded. He motioned both back over. In a quieter tone, he said, "He will be here in five days. I want these mounted and the fiberglass done before then. Allah help you if you fall behind schedule."

With that, he turned and left the men to their work.

. . .

By the middle of the second day, the sealed sources had been mounted with the ductwork and charges in place. What remained were the final supports, fiberglass, and paint. It was a tight schedule, but the technicians would make it. The Russian had not been in the hut except to examine the mounting prior to fiberglass work. Pictures were taken at each step for him to review.

The two technicians met with Vlad at a local street bar.

"You have done well." The technicians were relieved. Vlad rarely praised anyone's work.

"Thank you, Sir," they responded, almost in unison.

"The last crate and both dogs have been loaded, along with the supplies for the staging island, onto Amador's boat. I want the three of you to go ahead and get things set up. The second round of money has been sent as promised. Your families are now well cared for. Here is the portion for each of you as spending money." Vlad continued, handing over two envelopes filled with cash. It was true, the money had been sent.

The men gave visible signs of relief at his announcement. Now they knew, even if something went wrong, their families would benefit. Vlad was known in many villages and small towns as a man who paid well. Only on occasion did his employees become martyrs by their death and never return home.

"I want the two of you to help Amador set up the island. He has instructions for you. When you are done, you will continue with the dogs to Guiria where we will meet and make plans for the next project." Vlad dismissed the men.

They thanked him again and left to meet Amador's boat.

. . .

On the boat with Amador, the Kazakhstanis felt at ease. Amador was the man who had brought them, along with the five crates, up from Venezuela for this job. When they got to the small island it was not hard work to unload the supplies the other men would need when they came. The most labor-intensive part was unloading the cases of rum and the last sealed source crate.

The small island had only one building, a vacation house with a large patio with several small tables and chairs. Next to the patio the three men began digging a hole in the sand. The soft digging didn't take long, then Amador read them more of the instructions.

"Attach a large charge to the casing of one sealed source, so the Cesium will be released into the sand, then cover it. If you can, make the sand look undisturbed after the charge is set off, so we don't have to smooth it out." Amador's expression was deadpan, his eyes as lifeless as an iguana.

"It will leave a lethal exposure." The technicians looked genuinely concerned.

"Yes. Now get to work." Amador returned to the boat as the techs donned fresh radiation suits from two duffle bags. Soon they had buried the sealed source and the empty crate was back on the boat. They had placed a shaped charge against the source casing, facing downward. The sand pushed back on top formed a small hill. It didn't take long, but with the suits on it was hot work. Done, they walked back to the boat and got on board.

Amador started up the engine and released the stern line. They were now ready. With the remote switch in his hand, he fired the charge.

There was a strong deep thump that emanated from the island. The sand lifted several inches before falling back in a shallow hump. A dusty cloud slowly settled over the now broken, unsealed radioactive source. On his meter, one of the technicians confirmed a jump in Gamma radiation.

"The meter says it broke open."

"Wide open. Yes?" Amador asked in stilted Spanish, the only language they shared with reasonable fluency.

"Yes, it was a strong pulse. No question."

They released the bow line, motoring quickly away and upwind from the island with its deadly burial mound.

The detectors indicated little more than background radiation now. They removed their sweat soaked suits with visible relief and stored them back in the duffels.

They settled in for the boat ride.

Still sweating from the suits, the men drank eagerly from two bottles of water Amador handed them from the cooler. Then they took a deep draft from the rum bottle Amador broke out from the six they had liberated from the island stash.

"Done." Amador toasted with the rum bottle and handed it back. The plan was that they would head south, traveling at night, and smuggle themselves back into Venezuela.

The rum was kicking in as the heat and waves made them feel woozy. The effect was so strong it was hard to remain standing, or even sit on the rail. The first technician collapsed to a sitting position on the deck, his back to the transom.

Amador had drunk the rum, too, the technician thought hazily.

As the second technician stumbled with the roll of the boat, Amador walked over to take the rum bottle from the half-sitting, half-laying man on the deck. "Don't spill this. It is good rum," he told him.

The second technician collapsed heavily to the deck, barely able to prop himself up on one elbow. The other was now face down, prostrate and unmoving. The rocking of the boat tossed them unwillingly from side to side, causing them to bump the rail wall over and over.

Amador didn't bother to tell them what had happened. There were pills dissolved in the water—pain pills. They would feel nothing as they passed out. He would not need a bullet. That saved time cleaning blood off the deck. Taking two men down alone required skill rather than brute force. Besides, a rocking boat was a poor place to test one's marksmanship. Amador watched patiently as the second man fell over and passed out.

Satisfied they were out cold, he stopped the boat near a line of reef. He calmly heaved them over the side, one at a time. With a fishing gaff, he pushed down the feet of each man until their shallow breathing pulled in water instead of air. Only one gave a convulsive jerk as he sank, leaving a small trail of bubbles. The fish from the reef and sharp coral would make quick work of them.

"So, my friends," Amador spoke to the two dogs in their carry cases. "I have a treat for you and then you will see your new home. They will take good care of you, and you will guard the farm. He tossed a piece of meat to each dog. They wagged their tails happily, but remained silent. Well trained dogs, thought Amador as he smiled. He pushed the throttle forward on the engine, whistling a tune as he tossed the two water bottles over the side.

With easy winds and unusually light seas, Amador decided to make his heading straight for his friend's island home. The friend had a farm there with some pigs, chickens, and vegetables in rows. It made for comfortable living. The occasional odd job kept him in enough money to live and buy what he needed. The dogs would be welcome, providing protection in exchange for their keep.

The farm was a lengthy boat trip away. It would take several hours overnight to get there, but a nice sand bar was on the way. The sand bar had some bushes and plant growth that remained above water year-round, except during storms and the surges that came with them. He would stop there to sleep and give the dogs a run.

<u>Chapter 12</u>

In an off-white sling chair of strong, soft cotton canvas, Maxine sat facing the calm water of Elbow Creek. Just north of the Melbourne airport in Florida, Elbow Creek nestled in an inlet off the Intracoastal Waterway. Elbow Creek fed the Eau Gallie River, which emptied into the ICW, or "river," as locals called it. Just inside the first bend was the Eau Gallie Yacht Basin, with boat works, and repair area. It was one of dozens of possible locations where Maxine might find what she wanted.

Max, as she preferred to be called, was on the deck of an old-school, local seafood shack. Yachtsmen and sport fishermen didn't come here. This was a bar for workers and a few barflies who already sat on their designated stools inside. A short conversation with the bartender had yielded a potential match in a guy named Rayberg.

"Yeah, Berg fixes boats." Gary wasted no time serving Max and answering a few questions.

"Think he can work on a sailboat keel?" Max asked him.

"Sure. I think he can work on pretty much any boat. He'll be in when the sun goes down." Gary told her.

"Just like that? Every day?" She queried.

"Ever since I've been here." Gary had opened the beer in front of her. No on-tap draft for her and no glass. A bottle was just the way she wanted it. She avoided open drinks in places like this. Not that anyone would try to drug her, but she wasn't the kind of girl who gave anyone that chance.

Holding a chilled bottle of Yuengling lager in her hand, she watched the seagulls. The fishermen who came here to have a beer at the end of the day drove working boats big enough to do well at sea, but which were easily tucked away in small inlets at night. Some lived on their boat in cabins barely big enough for a hammock. They used "jon boats" to get around to the scattered stores and bars.

Chapter 13

The AFC championship football game was playing on the TV. Grady had moved it to the condo second-floor deck just for today, but he wasn't paying much attention to the game. In his opinion, the U.S.A.F.A. Falcons were the only team worth watching—and maybe the Vikings. Grady had liked the Vikings since he was a kid, but had no recollection of why. And okay, yes, he'd watched some Redskins games with the guys at a bar. He did work at the Pentagon, after all. Football was not really his game, even though he watched the Super Bowl at parties most years. He only paid attention enough to do well competing with his fantasy football buddies. It also helped to be able to talk articulately with rabid fans he knew. Mike was one of those.

Right now, Grady was focused on the burgers sizzling on the small deck grill. He was waiting for the perfect moment to add the jalapeño jack cheese and bacon. Katy, Mike, and Faith were sitting at the small table on the deck. Mike was glued to the TV. Katy and Faith were talking a blue streak about something. They would be headed inside soon. Grady could tell by the way Faith was clutching her Redskins jacket tightly around her.

The weather in DC had suddenly gotten warm for a few days. Warm that is, for January. They were taking advantage of the sunny day while it lasted. For the girls that would be another five minutes, maximum.

"Another beer?" Mike nodded at Grady with a tip of his Miller Light bottle.

"Nope, thanks. I'm good." Grady acknowledged with a nod back. "But help yourself." He pointed to the cooler with his Sam Adams bottle.

Mike got up and went to the cooler conveniently placed about three feet away.

They had met at the Air Force Academy when Mike was a four-degree "doolie" under Grady. Grady preferred the acronym "SMACK"—Soldier Minus Aptitude, Coordination, and Knowledge. The two-degrees used the word to refer to the sound made by underclassmen when they hit the marble terrazzo, upon being commanded to "trench!" Upperclassmen thought this command was great fun when the doolies were late and rushing to class.

Grady had hit it off with Mike, and kept an eye on him through graduation. Grady's career had rushed along a little faster than Mike's; he was considered young for a Lt. Colonel, while Mike had steadily progressed to the rank of Major, consistent with his age.

In their late thirties now, the two men couldn't appear more different. Mike had a full "dad bod," while Grady was very fit. Grady's dark skin showed almost no sign of age, while Mike's face had visible crow's feet and two horizontal lines creasing his forehead.

Faith, Mike's wife, had been skinny with noticeable breasts and narrow hips when they'd met at an Academy social event. She'd been an Academy High School senior when Mike was a first classman. Faith was a wild child and very popular, with fast hands that Mike loved. Mike was almost as wild. They got married two days after his graduation and moved to Hill AFB, Utah, where Mike got stationed. Faith almost didn't have time to graduate from college at Weber State when Mike was re-stationed in Enid, Oklahoma, before ending up at the Pentagon.

Two kids had given Faith more substance, adding to her chest and hips. She'd acquired small love handles, but Mike had to admit he liked the curves. Neither one had lost their wild natures.

Mike walked over to the smoky grill, popping open the beer and dropping the church key on the grill side stand.

"Hey!" Faith called over with a raised eyebrow and nod toward her empty beer.

"Sorry, Babe...Katy?" Mike reached in the cooler while looking back for an acknowledgment.

"Not yet, thanks," Katy replied without looking at him, moving right back to her conversation with Faith. They were talking about work. Katy was telling Faith about getting MISTI open water certified.

Faith and Katy had met when Faith started working at the NRL. Katy had just turned thirty, was finally over her divorce, and a little more than anxious to get her promotion to lieutenant commander. Career was her focus. Faith had been trying to set Katy up with someone from the day they'd met, despite Katy's determination to avoid entanglements.

She'd thought of setting Grady up with Katy a couple of times before, but until lately Grady hadn't really let go of Keisha. Faith had loved Keisha, too, and had grieved right along with Grady when she'd died. She understood that Grady needed time, but now he needed to move on.

After the meeting at the NRL Faith had thrown a little party, inviting both Grady and Katy along with some other couples. Then she worked on both of them until they'd agreed to a double date with her and Mike. They'd gone to dinner and out dancing, and had a blast. It worked out well enough that Grady finally asked Katy out on their own. They'd been dating since then.

Faith was convinced they were a good match. She also thought that each needed a friend in the worst kind of way.

When Katy ran out of steam talking about MISTI, Faith decided to change the subject.

"How's it going with you and Grady?" Faith inquired.

"I'm here; right?" Katy replied.

"Yes, but what's going on? Are you guys an item now?" Faith was clearly dying to get the details.

"Shhhh." Katy gave Faith a withering look and glanced toward the guys who were only a few feet away.

"They're not listening." Faith had that devious smile again.

Katy frowned back with a hint of, "don't go there" in her eyes. "Change the subject," she told Faith.

"Come on! Haven't you guys...." Faith began, but Katy cut her off.

"I said, 'shush!'" Katy glared at Faith.

"So...used to condo life yet?" Mike asked Grady as he handed the new beer toward Faith, who stared at him blankly until he opened it. "Ha, ha; sorry! Here you go, Gorgeous." He still had that young pup grin Faith liked, so she grinned and let him off the hook.

Grady didn't look up. It was almost time for the cheese. "It's different. Still feels small, but then I don't have much stuff to get in the way."

"I hear ya. What a shock to have it all burn down that way. Still, a fresh start and getting a big payoff isn't all bad." Mike was under the delusion that insurance companies simply paid out the total and that Grady had come out of the deal with a fat check.

Grady sighed. He'd tried to explain it all to the first dozen friends and relatives who'd had this same reaction. He had a replacement policy, so theoretically he could purchase everything that had been lost. Robert Carlton's official intervention cleared the way for the fire to be listed as accidental, without some category of criminal act that would nullify the insurance. That helped, but the reality was that he had to get the house plans originally submitted to the city, show bids for rebuilding, and then actually build. He had to come up with receipts, serial numbers, pictures, or witnesses who would swear that he owned the stuff he was putting in a claim to have replaced. Then he had to re-purchase each thing, and submit receipts for reimbursement. Every single thing, one at a time. Trying to prove he'd owned 90 DVDs, 200 CDs, assorted tools, four pairs of jeans, twenty pairs of underwear, an extra ink cartridge, a computer, a reader, a particular bicycle, or anything else, then having to go buy the stuff again, and finally, process the expense, was a brutal process.

Mike was one of his witnesses to ownership, since all Grady's receipts and pictures had gone up in flames with the house. Mike still didn't understand the procedure, but Grady didn't really blame him for that. If it hadn't happened to him, Grady would never have believed that trying to remember the model of saw, hammer, or television he'd bought could be such a pain. Grady had given up on worrying about replacing a lot of the small stuff. He was concentrating on big stuff like his Jeep, Motorcycle, computer, and furniture. It wouldn't all be done until the house was rebuilt. There were still appliances to be bought, carpets and flooring to choose, but he knew he'd never take the time to try to replace everything he'd had. Some of it was gone forever with no chance of replacement, like mementos of his life with Keisha.

Grady had not told anyone, even Mike and Faith, about the attack, incendiary grenades, guns, and two dead men. It was an official "need to know" situation. As far as his friends were concerned, it was just a freak accident.

"Yeah, well, it wasn't as big a check as I'd like but you can't win every battle. I have a year to go purchase as many replacements as I can, or as many as I'm willing to hassle over." Grady told Mike.

"Damn insurance companies. They're worse than the mob." Mike shook his head.

Grady raised his beer. "To legalized crime." They tapped the bottle necks together.

"Assholes." Mike cheerfully added. "Where are you putting all the stuff you're buying?"

"I add it to my self-storage place whenever I find time to buy something," Grady answered.

"Hope the place doesn't get robbed. Sounds like a big pile of treasure." Mike looked concerned.

"Thanks for that thought," Grady said sarcastically, frowning. "I found one of the storage places that has a lot of cameras, alarm locks—all the stuff that's supposed to make it harder to steal, so hopefully it'll work out."

"What are you two talking about?" Faith chimed in.

"Insurance companies. Bastards all." Mike responded in good humor.

Grady checked the meat and called out. "Burgers are done!"

"Great! I'm starved." Faith jumped up, happy for the chance to get her burger and take it inside where it was warm. Potato salad, bean pasta, and a fruit salad were set up on the kitchen counter. Faith grabbed her plate from Grady and headed inside. Grady just had time to put the other burgers on plates before Katy and Mike headed in through the sliding glass doors.

"This looks delicious. Faith you make the best pasta!" Katy told her, taking a small portion of each heavily mayonnaised dish. Faith cooked fattening food the way her kids liked it, and expected everyone to eat a lot of it. With full plates and beers, they scrambled for spots at the coffee table where they could see the TV outside.

Grady was thankful that there were no screaming kids to handle. One of the great things about Mike and Faith was their willingness to drop off the kids with "Gramps" and "Grand." Both sets of grandparents came from military families and knew the drill. They'd all retired near Arlington and were more than willing to give Mike and Faith time off from parenting.

"Have you done your shopping for the trip?" Faith asked Katy excitedly. She loved shopping and was thrilled to have a good reason to go.

"No. I haven't even had time to think about it." Katy answered. She was still unsure about the whole trip idea.

It was Faith who was driving the plan. She had been concocting a vacation for the two couples to St. John's ever since she'd watched

Katy and Grady dancing together. Faith had locked in the reservations after Grady and Katy's first date.

Katy and Grady now found themselves trapped in a double date vacation trip. They knew it wouldn't be boring with Mike and Faith, but both were feeling a little awkward.

Faith was not only the managing type, she was also a romance junkie. She and Mike loved their kids almost to a fault; they would roll in the grass with the kids, play games, and go crazy having fun as a family. Weekends were events even when nothing was planned. They knew where every kid "freebie" in the area was, and the kids had more toys than time to play with them. But Faith never felt like they got enough time as a couple. For them, trips like this St. John vacation were over-the-top, getaway extravagances. She was going to make the most of it. Grady and Katy were the friends that would be dragged along in Faith's exuberant wake, like skiers behind a fast boat.

"They're bringing out the new bathing suits, now. We have to go shopping." Faith was unstoppable.

"My suit is fine." Katy glanced at the boys who were watching an instant replay on the TV through the sliding glass door.

Not satisfied with this answer, Faith blurted out to Grady, "Grady, don't you think Katy deserves to have a new bathing suit to take with us?"

Startled by the sudden question, Grady and Mike turned and looked at the girls. Fortunately for Grady, who had no idea what to say, Mike jumped in.

"Are you shopping already? Seriously?" He shook his head. "You girls will have to handle all of that. We're watching the game."

"Oh, you're worthless." Faith returned.

She turned back to Katy while the boys took the opportunity to go back out on the deck, and watch the remaining few minutes of the game with sound.

Faith continued verbalizing her plans for the trip, while Katy went along with them grudgingly. The first week of March was coming fast, and Katy still wondered whether going was a good idea.

Now that the boys were back outside, Faith pressed again. "Well? Have you and Grady…"

"No!" Katy cut her off and spat the word out with emphasis. "Stop it, Faith. It's not like that."

"Don't you like each other?" Faith was definitely prying. "Come on! You've gone out with each other for over a month. And after all, we're going to the beach," she said, somehow making it sound like intimacy was part of the beach package.

"Beach plans don't equal sex, Faith." Katy was perturbed by the intrusive question. "Look, you have to let me and Grady handle our relationship at our own pace."

"He's a nice guy. Sexy, handsome—and he clearly is into you. What more do you want?" Faith was persistent. She really didn't understand Katy's resistance to getting involved with Grady.

"One room, two beds. Don't push it." Katy shot back.

"Don't worry. If you guys want to go slow, it's your business." Faith sensed the need to back off.

"Sorry, I really don't intend to pressure you, Katy. We should still go shopping. Come on! It'll be fun." Faith regained her eagerness for trip preparations.

"Let's figure out our schedules at the office. Right now, let's clear this stuff." With that, Katy grabbed two platters and stood up.

. . .

The weekend was in full swing for the Carltons. Robert and Tracie's boys were taking full advantage of their Taekwondo competition. One was on the mat facing his opponent, the other jumped, kicked, and in general flailed around on the sidelines.

"Watch what you're doing!" Robert admonished his youngest. "You'll end up kicking someone."

Taekwondo competition had originally sounded like it would be an organized activity with judges, referees, and rules. Robert had hoped it might instill some discipline in the boys, but soon realized that in the hands and feet of his kids it was random, spastic thrashing. The yelling sounded more like screaming animals than a sports activity. The coach assured both Robert and Tracie that sometime this season the older boys would suddenly have a breakthrough, and become poised and skillful. They would find a Zen-like state of self-awareness and calm strength. Robert held no such hope. To him, this all looked like a monkey fight at the zoo.

"This is ridiculous," he told Tracie. "They have no idea what they're doing." He waved his arms around at the swarm of boys randomly jumping and flopping on the floor.

"They're learning," Tracie responded without looking up from her tablet. "Give them time. It's supposed to be fun. It's their first competition."

Tracie was mostly ignoring the activity and the kids in general. She had her seat, computer tablet, flavored water bottle, and lap blanket. In her view, this was quality parenting time, and Robert was acting as a disturber of the peace. "Try enjoying the nice temperature," she told him.

"We're in a gym," Robert commented dryly.

"Climate controlled," Tracie emphasized.

"Who's winning this competition? Is anyone keeping score?" Robert continued, feeling frustrated. This did not fit his idea of sport.

"Your older son's age group starts keeping score next year." A father next to Robert explained. "Right now it's not important who wins, just that they move up to the next belt." The man shrugged his shoulders. "Go figure. All I know is that it keeps them busy."

"So, this is how parents spend their quality time with their kids on the weekends," Robert grumbled to himself more than anyone else. Saturday had been spent buying clothes for the boys, followed by soccer registration. Sunday morning was mandatory church. "Politicians must keep up appearances," Tracie had told him. Now it was Taekwondo. Next weekend the cycle would repeat.

None of this fit Robert's interests. He liked quiet weekends with more organized and civilized activities. Beach time, mountain hikes, or lake activities were his preference.

These kinds of weekends had become unattainable fantasies lately. He needed a vacation. He berated himself for not taking time off in December after the voting system fiasco. Actually, "fiasco" was a nice, politically correct way to describe the deaths and corruption associated with the mess. He and Grady had spent days sorting out what happened, debriefing the Secret Service, Homeland Security, local police, politicians, and testifying in some public OPOV hearings.

Robert had yet to feel any step up with his promotion. The reserved parking spot and new office were both nice, but even with double the staff, he was still short employees. It felt like he had tripled his previous workload. This should have kept him busy and completely distracted, thinking only of work. His subconscious had other ideas. He still woke up in cold sweats a couple of times a week. He dreamt of exploding cars and burning hands hanging from fire engulfed trunks. He hadn't told Tracie about that; not the dream, or the actual moment when a car had blown up in front of him.

Tracie kept things to herself, too. The fear and anger, the Secret Service agents suddenly guarding her and the kids left scars she wouldn't admit existed. She trusted strangers less, and she trusted Robert less. There was a new, more elaborate security system on the house and trackers on both cars. The boys had a new school with full security, where many of Washington's elite sent their children. Tracie didn't know, ask, or care how it all got paid for. She hid her concerns behind the glamorous political face of promotion and invitations. Tracie focused on mingling with higher status moms every day, and she liked that. Outwardly, as far as she was concerned, everything was back to normal.

That included Robert being more involved in family activities. Tracie had insisted on it, saying it was part of a more normal existence for the boys. Robert wondered about that. Was anything going to fit his definition of "normal" again?

He sighed, watching the mayhem around him. Maybe this was as normal as it got. Monday, he would go back to work and try to act normal there, too.

Chapter 14

One a.m., the last Monday of January. Vlad stood watching from a hundred yards away as the final yacht slid into the water on schedule. The mast would quickly be lifted into place. The guy wires would be reattached with precisely the same number of turnbuckle rotations as they used to remove them. When the sun came up, the boat would be quietly rocking at its mooring buoy. None of his men would be in sight.

Alexi stood next to him.

"Your work is excellent." Alexi had to concentrate to not roll his Rs with his natural Russian accent, and speak flatly like an Englishman. He found American English difficult, so he stuck to the London style.

Vlad took the compliment silently.

"The men will be taken care of?" Alexi asked.

"Yes," Vlad answered. Both men used English. They were too smart, and too well trained to slip and use Russian where they could be overheard, no matter how unlikely that possibility seemed.

"When?" Alexi continued.

"Today," Vlad responded.

"Good." Alexi almost smiled.

Silence followed as both men strained to hear the winch lift the mast. Even at this relatively short distance, the sound of water and the breeze completely obscured the whirring of the well-greased motor.

"I am pleased," he added.

Vlad nodded acceptance of the compliment. "When will you wish to start Step Two?"

"Give them four weeks to arrive, then start. You have a plan for any that fail to go?" Alexi wanted verification.

"I have two buyer paths. With good weather, they will all arrive." Vlad reassured him.

"Good." Alexi turned to leave. "No leak before then."

"None. Not possible."

"Be sure and give me twenty-four hours of notice before you start."

They walked up the ramp to the Quonset hut building and stopped by the side door. Vlad held a smartphone next to the wall. It connected to the Bluetooth radiation logger on the other side. It was mounted in a locked wooden cabinet above the desk area and was the only accurate Geiger counter mounted inside the building. The app on his phone displayed a time-graph of radiation counts. There had been a spike 4 days ago when they mounted the sealed sources to the boats, but the levels were down again and safe. He nodded to Alexi and the two men entered.

"The total?" Alexi asked.

"Five-hundred mSv—millisieverts. Some would be sick by now if it was more."

"Deaths?"

"No. Not from this."

"Good, it is important they know nothing before it is time. Then it must be swift and clear."

"It will be obvious. There will be no question." Vlad had everything carefully arranged.

The only light on inside the building was one dim bulb high in the ceiling. It was enough to allow walking without tripping, but the high curved roof kept it from being noticeable outside in the dark.

Alexi wanted more verification that everything was set as planned. "Make sure one gets to her in Melbourne. If one is sold, that would be easiest. If not, she must arrange the theft of the one that stops closest."

The side door opened and the workers entered along with the three supervisors.

Alexi took up an executive pose behind Vlad who spoke to the last man to enter.

"Close the door and turn on the lights." The workman did as he was told and the bright bluish green lights flickered on. Where the boats had been, a panel truck now stood, alongside two vans. The truck had been brought in as the last boat was taken out. Some of the men had already loaded the cots, bedding and kitchen gear with the food supplies in through its rear doors.

"Pack up the rest of this; load it on the truck, and take it to the launch. I want all the special gear in the four crates. Nail them shut." The special gear included the protective clothing and tools that had been used for dealing with the sealed sources and explosives. While they worked on packing and loading, Vlad talked to the tallest supervisor quietly in the far corner.

"When you load the launch, I want the crates put in the locked hold. After you get everyone to the island you go to deep water and scuttle the launch as I showed you. Flood the locking compartment with the pump before you transfer to the small boat. Set the timer and move away one hundred meters. Wait thirty minutes to make sure nothing floats to the surface. If it does, you will have to sink it separately. Then go back to the island and wait. I will be there in one week to take all of you to the next job. Understood?"

The supervisor nodded. This had all been carefully discussed twice before. He had helped with the installation of the explosives that would sink the launch which resembled a gunboat. He understood very well that the Russian wanted precision, and that his job was to listen and obey.

"Nobody leaves the island until I get there." Vlad reminded him.

The man nodded again.

The loading complete, the men climbed into the truck and vans along with Vlad and Alexi. They pulled out and headed to the dock. It was almost four a.m. by the time the gear was properly stowed in the launch and the men were ready to leave. A small open fishing boat had been clipped to the launch stern using a D-ring and tow-line. All but two dock lines had been released.

Vlad carried two black tote bags to the launch. "This is your pay and there are bonuses for each of you," he told the men. He pulled out a stack of paper bills, thick enough to be valuable in any denomination. "You each get a full share." He put the money back in the tote.

"You will speak to no one, or you will not have the next job. I will meet you in one week." With that, he tossed one tote to the nearest supervisor on the launch and left the dock.

"They will obey?" Alexi asked as Vlad came up to the van.

"Money is everything to them," Vlad answered disparagingly.

"When will they guess?" Alexi knew what would happen, but not how soon.

"If they guess at all, one week, or maybe two. It was low dose here, so there is no sign. There it will be high." Vlad seemed unconcerned.

"As long as it is delayed long enough." Alexi worried.

"It will be." Vlad's tone convinced Alexi.

The two men clasped wrists. Alexi turned to one of the empty vans and drove away without any further comments.

Vlad did not stay to watch from the dock preferring to watch from the other van some distance away. From his vantage point, he could see the boat depart, and when it cleared the first harbor buoy. He looked for anyone who might attempt to leave the launch. None did.

· · ·

In a little more than 10 hours the launch had reached an island south of St. Vincent. Several tiny islands were scattered around this area, but most were too small to attract any yachters to their rocky beaches. On one of these was a rentable vacation home. The skipper was familiar with its location. It wasn't much, being more of a hut than a house, but it had a small dock, a large deck, and seclusion. The launch pulled up to the dock and the men quickly unloaded the supplies they carried, as well as sleeping, cooking, and personal gear. There was already a large stash of food, and most importantly there was rum on the island from Amador's trip a few days earlier. Everything else stayed on the launch. The four boxes, now stuffed with the hooded safety gear and tools used by the Kazakhstani men, along with the protective bunny suits used by the others remained in the locked hold. Just like the rest of the vessel, the hold was all steel. It was located near the engine room.

The men were aware that the sailboats they had worked on were stolen, and that the launch was easy to recognize. It made sense that it must be sunk with the crates so that nothing could be traced. The skipper, Jamarco, and the tall supervisor, Bastian, sailed away with the boats. The two other supervisors stayed behind with the six men, organizing food and opening the rum. With, food, rum, and more work coming it was a vacation party.

In less than two hours of motoring, the two boats were beyond sight of the island, or any other land. Other boats might be within view due to the early hour, so Jamarco and Bastian waited until the sun began to set. Now the late fishermen would be headed to port, and the tourists would be watching west for the sunset—not east of the islands where they were.

Jamarco flipped the switch for the number two bilge pump. This pump had been rigged to push sea water into the locked hold. They both listened as the loud motor and rushing water filled the boat below decks. The hiss of escaping air around the bulkhead was louder than they expected. It soon became a raucous whistle. When water began leaking from the top of the door Jamarco moved on to the next task.

The boat was listing noticeably to one side from the weight of water in the hold, but the time was right. Soon the sun would sink below the horizon, followed quickly by darkness. No ship or boat lights were visible, so Bastian went below to set the timer on the charges while Jamarco pulled the fishing boat up to the fantail. The listing deck brought the rail much lower to the water on one side, so he pulled the boat near to that lower corner.

It was awkward going down the ladder. Below decks Bastian connected the red wire to the battery. Double checking that the timer switch was off, he connected the black ground wire.

Grabbing the D-ring that held the line, Jamarco squeezed it to release the boat, but the ring was frozen shut. It wasn't rust, so he thought it must have gotten locked somehow. He fought it for a few moments, then reached for his knife and started sawing at the rope.

Below, Bastian watched the display light up showing 10 minutes. With a flick, he threw the switch, but the display did not start counting down as expected. It was much faster. It was counting seconds! 8...7...6 seconds. His eyes dilated as he rushed to the ladder but by the time he grabbed the second wrung the blast was ripping through the ship, and tearing the skin from his body in shreds. The metal hull exploded out into the ocean and the sea rushed in.

On deck, Jamarco was thrown overboard. His ears rang as the explosion's fireball burned his hair and clothes before throwing him into the black water. The knife fluttered downward to the ocean bottom.

A second explosion erupted, sending flames into the air and igniting fuel oil on the water's surface. The flames rushed toward him as he tried to swim away, forcing him to dive. Flames raced overhead. He came up gasping for air beyond the pool of fire, which lit up the launch on the ocean. The boat heeled far over to one side, then with many gurgles and hisses it slipped under the small waves.

The timing had been good for the explosion. The orange sky was just bright enough to disguise the blast's flash of light and flame, while the deepening night hid the rising column of smoke.

Treading water, Jamarco realized that the small fishing boat was still tied to the larger metal launch. He tried to swim around the small burning patches left from the fuel, but had no chance of reaching it in time. The weight of the sinking hulk pulled its bow under, and took it to the sandy bottom two-hundred feet below.

Jamarco looked around in disbelief. The patches of flaming fuel flickered and went out one by one. There was no point in yelling; no one would ever hear him. They had motored at ten knots for almost two hours. It would be twenty miles back to the island, fighting the tide and wind all the way. He kicked off his shoes and tried to float on his back. With each small wave that splashed his face, oily water went into his nose and mouth. He had to stop often to cough and tread water. He was feeling his resolve float away with his strength. He couldn't survive this way.

With a deep breath, he inhaled fully and let himself slip under the waves. Bobbing with his back to the surface, he bent at the waist and released his belt so that he could pull off his pants. He was back up for a breath before he needed it. Treading water, he tied a knot in each pant leg at the ankle and then zipped up the pants. By flipping the waistband up out of the water and then straight back in several times, he filled the pants with air until the legs floated and the butt was full. Then he cinched the belt around the pants waist. With his right hand, he pulled the belt under to arm's length, and reached between the inflated legs with his left arm, grabbing the belt. Then he reached through with his right arm. Now the pant legs were under his armpits, and he was floating.

With his head above the smaller waves, he felt almost relaxed. The pants would leak air, but slowly. With the very last glimmer of light on the clouds, he turned to the west and began kicking.

Jamarco had confidence now. He knew the sea. He could overcome this if he stayed calm and headed west. The current would take him north, but there were islands that way. In the morning, fishermen would come out to sea. They would find him.

The pants quickly proved more porous than he expected, needing more air. His awkward position made it difficult to add air, so he compromised. With one arm through the crotch, he could swim sideways, giving him one arm and both legs to paddle. Adding air was easier this way, and he could switch sides when one arm became tired.

It was pitch black now. The stars seemed uncertain—was he headed the right way? Were the waves growing? The distant flames had long since burned out. Even the moon shed no light on the water. It was only a sliver of white in the sky. The buoyancy of his body gave him a tangible sense of up and down, but he had no sense of direction. His right shin was aching.

When he reached down to check his foot, it felt normal, but the pain persisted. He imagined the railing of the boat must have hit him as he was thrown over. He kept kicking, but more and more his mind was wandering.

Why was the D-ring frozen? What had happened to Bastian? Why did he start the timer and not come up? He wondered what time it was, wishing he had a watch or a phone. Both would have proven useless in the water, he knew. Only the tourists and divers spent so much money on waterproof toys. Besides, he was far from any land, much less a cell tower.

His leg ached more now. With a deep breath, he reached down again. His fingers felt the toes, foot, ankle, and up his leg.

"Ahhh!" His head jerked up from the water. His fingers had found the scrape running up his shin. It was deep. Until he'd touched it, most of the scrape had been numb from the salt water. Now the freshly exposed flesh was stinging angrily.

He thought about sharks for the first time. Caribbean shark attacks were rare, but the fish could smell blood in the water for miles. He tried to calm himself with logic. In places like Florida, wave action made the water turbid. A foot could look like a flounder. Bright metallic bathing suits on an Aussie Surfer could look like the flashing scales of a silver fish. Clear, fairly calm Caribbean water made it easy for a shark to identify its food, didn't it? But what about at night? Jamarco tried to stay calm and kicked slowly toward the west.

Had he been bumped, or was it his imagination? He tried to be still and float without moving his arms or legs. He was sinking again. The pants needed more air. He needed to scoop the waistband again.

Another bump. Jamarco scrambled to get on top of the inflated pants and lie still. He waited a long time, holding his breath. His balanced slipped, and he thrashed to stay up and centered on the floating pants. He lay still again, panting. Again, something bumped his leg, and then brushed against his foot. It felt rough and scraped against his wound, sending pain up his leg and panic to his brain.

He fought the urge to kick, but when he felt something again, panic took over. He swam as fast as he could. He swam faster than his hands could hold the pants—faster than he could breathe. By the time he stopped he was out of breath, and spinning in circles in an attempt to see through the dark. Panting, he started swimming again; slowly at first. Now the waves pulled at his foot, or was it the waves?

He spun again, this time sinking too far and coming up coughing with water in his throat. The bump came again, this time with a tug at his foot. His face splashed into a wave. His foot jerked back and forth five times, then pain screamed up his leg. He reached down slowly as he drew his leg upward trying to feel his foot without dunking his head. The water rose into his face. His searching hand only found his ankle. There was nothing below the ankle, just warm water.

Fear took hold of Jamarco. He kicked at the water. His arms thrashed at the surface, trying to swim away. When the bite came again, it was halfway up his thigh. Pain and water mixed. His cry only made bubbles, streaming into the blackness. He went under the surface, down deeper with every vicious shake, succumbing to the ocean with a great inhale of water and blood. His mind mercifully shut down. He passed out before the last beats of his heart echoed faintly in the black Caribbean Sea.

Chapter 15

From the harbor, Vlad drove to the far side of the island. The rocky dirt road was hard on the van, but it had survived these conditions many times. He made his way through one small village, passing only occasional farms after that. He wound his way up a steep hillside, reaching its crest.

Just over the top stood an old concrete building. It had been the school master's house, destroyed in a hurricane, years earlier. Inside were two large rooms and a toilet that no longer worked. Two openings for windows were covered in colorful shower curtains. The door, while functional, clearly had belonged to a different building's smaller opening.

Vlad parked the van next to a small white panel truck and went inside. Three men greeted him. They sat on wooden boxes and a chair in front of a rusted table, eating. Next to one of them was a pistol. In the corner stood an old assault rifle. Vlad sniffed at the lack of discipline and their complete disregard for security.

The three men were charged with guarding, feeding, and supplying water to the hostages. Vlad realized he should have checked on them more often. They had no sense for the responsibility of the situation.

For a big man Vlad moved surprisingly fast as he approached the table. He pulled out his pistol and shot two of the men at close range. The third fell back from the table, his hands raised defensively.

"Boss, no! What did we do? I can fix. I fix!" The man yelled. Vlad holstered his pistol and picked up the one on the table.

"All right. You fix." Vlad snarled at the man. He hoisted the thin man out of his chair easily and pressed the pistol into his hand. "Shoot them."

"You killed them, Boss!" The man stood frozen, confused by Vlad's command.

"Shoot them!" Vlad ordered again. The pistol had no magazine. Vlad had released it. There might be a round in the chamber, but he wasn't intimidated by what the man might do with it. "Shoot."

With Vlad behind him holding his arm, the man shakily raised the pistol and pulled the trigger. A single bang erupted. Vlad knocked the gun out of the man's hand. He fell to the floor and scuttled to the corner where the rifle stood. It was not his intent to use the long gun, he just wanted to get away from Vlad.

"Pick it up!" Vlad ordered pointing to the rifle. With shaking hands, the man touched the rifle just as Vlad's pistol fired again. The man was dead.

Walking over to grab the rifle, Vlad lifted one of the men toward the door and stood him in the corner the best he could, then stepping back, opened fire with the rifle.

He sprayed the body and wall indiscriminately, then tossed the empty rifle back to the far corner with the other dead man. Snapping the clip back into the pistol, he fired three rounds into the other two men, then dropped the weapon.

From his pocket, he pulled a number of papers and threw them across the floor. Each was a ransom note. One for each person who they'd kidnapped from the boats. They were poorly written, marginally addressed, and the envelopes had random stamps on them, with varying sums of postage. It now appeared that these men had been amateurs in the ransomed hostage business, and that an argument between them had turned fatal.

Pulling away, he drove back the way he had come. He wasn't coming back to this island.

• • •

Overlooking a small picturesque bay, and a little farther down the hill from the schoolmaster's ruined house, sat the abandoned concrete schoolhouse. Plants covered most of the outside bare walls, where only tattered bits of light green or yellowed white paint clung in the cracks. Where there once had been a reasonable roof, corrugated aluminum and fiberglass sheets now lay weighed down by cinder blocks, rocks, and tree limbs. The windows were tiny, high, and barred with rusted iron. Before the building had served as a school, it had been a jail.

Its original purpose had returned when the hostages were brought inside.

Mark and Julie sat in one corner of the twelve by twelve concrete and dirt-floored room. They huddled tightly together under a tattered, smelly blanket, protecting themselves as much as they could from chilly nights and mosquitos. Chrystal and Jeff sat in the other corner, leaning against the outside wall where the sun had warmed the concrete. It became surprisingly cool at night on the hillside. The wind, humidity, glassless windows, and their minimal clothing made it hard to sleep. There were bugs; so many bugs. The two couples had given up swatting. Chrystal's skin was raw from rubbing the insects off. Julie itched around her ankles unbearably, but would not scratch. The bites would start bleeding again if she did, and her fingernails were filthy. The mosquitos ignored Mark, but his scalp seemed to be crawling all the time. He tried to rub the feeling away with his arm, avoiding the desire to scratch. Jeff wouldn't talk about it. They were all having a hard time not freaking out.

All four of them had scrapes and cuts decorated with garish streaks of mercurochrome. The reddish-brown liquid stung angrily each time it was brushed on, but Jeff knew its medicinal value from when he was a kid. It had vanished from United States drugstore shelves in 1998, when it was banned from sale across state lines by the FDA. It was better than getting infected, though, Jeff insisted. Their jailers provided the old-fashioned mercury-based antiseptic along with a five-gallon bucket, two army cots, and two filthy blankets. There was rough brown paper on a roll and two meals a day. Mark and Julie had learned from Jeff and Chrystal to save half the morning fruit for midday. They had been held captive a full week before Mark and Julie arrived.

Water came from another bucket of questionable background, but miraculously none of them had gotten sick drinking it. Chrystal complained of stomach pains, but hadn't had any other adverse reactions. There was barely enough water for drinking, so none went to washing. Jeff's and Mark's hands showed considerable damage from trying to raise the roof to escape. Jeff had discovered the dirt floor was years of accumulated dirt and debris over a cracking concrete foundation, but that hadn't stopped all four of them from trying to claw through in several different places. The mix of blood and mercurochrome gave their hands a horrifying appearance. The rocks and blocks holding down the roof were too heavy, but they kept trying to push them up each night when it got quiet, sometimes just out of frustration.

That frustration was rising again as the sun was setting. Today, there had been no breakfast, and if the sun went down without their jailor arriving, there would be no dinner.

"I don't think he's coming," Mark whispered through cracked lips.

"Shhhhh!" Julie hissed. "They'll hear you."

Once, on the second night, a jailor had barked at them to shut up. From the barred window of the locked doorway a small bucket of fish guts had splashed into their cell. The smell was awful. They had used some of the day's water to sluice it over to the drain hole on the outer wall, but the smell continued, and the flies never stopped coming. That was the only punishment they had received since arriving.

"I agree," Jeff spoke. "Not a sound all day. We have to try again."

"No!" Chrystal whimpered. "No more."

"Com'on, Mark." Jeff got up. He was shaky, more so than he realized. Mark was more solid on his feet.

Mark braced himself against the wall and laced his fingers. Jeff, who was lighter, stepped up and gripped the top of the wall in between the corrugated recesses of roof.

"Try pressing up with your knuckles," Mark whispered.

"I am." The fiberglass flexed but there were too many blocks on this section too. Maybe there were concrete screws, as well. It wasn't long before both had fallen again to the floor.

"Stop it!" Chrystal whined. "It's no use."

Mark moved over to the door. "Larry!" He called in a loud whisper making Chrystal scrunch down deeper into the corner, hiding from what might happen.

From the door across the hall he could hear Larry, another captive call back.

"What?"

"Any luck?"

"No!" They heard a sudden crash, as Larry fell through his door into the hallway. The cracking of wood, screeching hinges, and Larry's body hitting the concrete sent them all running for the dark corners.

It seemed a long time before the lock in the door to their cell room made a rusted dull clacking sound. The door swung slowly open. A tall, thick, dirty man with a scraggly salt and pepper gray beard stood in the doorway. It was Larry.

"They're gone." He told them. "I don't see them anywhere in sight."

Mark was up quickly. Jeff followed. The three men began exploring the hall. Larry held keys in his hand. Soon every door was open. Nine people stood huddled together, terrified of what might happen next.

"Jeff, check the main door," Larry advised. "Let's see if we can get out of here." He waved his hand to the rest of the group to get them moving.

Larry and Jeff began to move quietly forward.

"Julie, you all stay here while we check it out," Mark told her, following Jeff.

"No way." Julie was adamant. "We're going with you. I'm not staying in this place a second longer than I have to."

When the men pushed on the outer door, it simply swung open. They looked out at a very small clearing, surrounded by a thick wall of green plants with a purple-blue sky overhead. There were fewer bugs than in the dank concrete rooms, and the smell of spices filled the air instead of rotting fish. The ground was soft and the breeze mild. As one huddled, bedraggled mass, they followed along a path that led to a gravel road. Without a word exchanged among them, they turned to walk downhill.

. . .

In the village below, Jorge sat with his childhood friend Lanny at a small, somewhat rusty roadside table. Each had an island beer and a basket of fried plantain chips. The orange sauce poured over the top of the chips was spicy and hot.

Jorge was the local cop. His beat was the four small blocks that made up the village center. His uniform was little more than a dark blue shirt with a simple emblem. His white t-shirt showing at the open collar needed cleaning, but it was only Tuesday, and Wednesday was when he took out the second uniform. Washday was Saturday.

Not much happened in the village, ever. Its residents worked sporadically between fishing, farming, and odd jobs as the seasons dictated. Over the last couple of weeks an unmarked panel truck had rattled through the village, in and out three times. It had been noticed, but since it was no more distinctive than any other truck on the island, no one had thought much about it. The driver had waved in the usual island manner as he drove past the locals.

The road was little more than a flat, wide path with a few weeds down the middle. It was in keeping with the tattered buildings on each side, leading up the hills to some farms with pigs, spice trees, and the occasional papaya. It was the main path to the other side of the island, so the random vehicle barely raised an eyebrow.

Now Lanny's eyes were wide as he stared up the road. Jorge looked up from his chips to drink from his beer. With the bottle next to his lips, he noticed the shocked, silent stare on Lanny's face.

"Lanny? Lanny, what is it?" Jorge turned to look behind him. The dim light of the store reached part way up the hill through the dusky light. The beer bottle near his lips wavered. His eyebrows lifted and his mouth gaped open.

Trudging slowly down the hill was a clump of nine bedraggled people. Several limped as they huddled together tightly. They wore dirt-stained t-shirts, and bathing suits partly covered by decrepit blankets. A few were missing their shoes. They all crept gingerly down the uneven rocky road.

At the front of the pack, Julie squeezed closer to Mark. "Is it them?" Julie asked timidly, almost whispering.

"I don't think so. We have to chance it." Mark answered.

The group clung closer together and kept walking toward the light.

Chapter 16

The stack of inbox files to his left had grown by three since he'd arrived. Not two inches away, the outbox sat empty. Both the coffee and a bagel Lorraine left on the desk were half gone.

For weeks, Robert had bounced from bureaucratic tedium to political boredom, and back. The administrative nature of his job had erased all the glamor offered by the lofty title of Deputy Attorney General. The trip to Puerto Rico was long forgotten, and his humdrum role as the head of department operations had taken over. Jack wasn't handling the grunt work, and he was leaving a trail of paperwork debris for Robert to clean up.

Robert longed for a relaxing weekend. Dinner and a movie, watching a game with the guys, skiing, or a drive in the country sounded ideal, but unattainable. Even if he had the time, the truth was that there were no buddies to come over to his house and watch the game. There wouldn't have been a fun family vacation at the beach, or in the mountains, and date night dinners for him and Tracie were imaginary—with or without intimate moments.

Admittedly, none of those things had ever been a frequent part of his life. Guys' nights out, football parties, and weekend trips had been occasional college activities. Sure, early in their relationship there had been more intimacy with Tracie, but that all seemed like a thousand years ago. They'd slipped into their demanding work-life schedules, leaving fewer and fewer moments for friends and romance.

None of this deprivation was new. What had been new was the excitement he and Grady shared on the OPOV investigation. The terrifying exhilaration of fiery explosions and billowing smoke was only a memory now. The new job looked impressive from outside, but he missed the stimulation of uncovering a conspiracy. Had that all really happened less than three months before?

Initially, the benefits of his appointment to Deputy Attorney General were gratifying. He'd accepted congratulations from strangers, and warm clasps from powerful friends who, a few days preceding that, had been mere acquaintances. Robert's political stock had skyrocketed. Tracie was drunk with power, and they'd christened the promotion with three very sexy nights. Once the congratulations faded, so had everything else. His work had returned to normal bureaucracy, and his home life was back to the usual chaotic routine.

To Tracie's delight, the higher quality invitations hadn't ended with the holidays. Embassy diplomats, Senators, and Congressman were back from the holidays. The dinners spotlighted influential attendees with equally important titles. Political occasions of all kinds dominated the calendar, frequently including an invitation to the White House. Kennedy Center affairs were being planned for spring, and indoor cultural events were on the calendar for almost every weekend. Now Tracie was more an organizer than a hostess, in charge of determining invitees, and making sure elite guests were appreciated. Robert's promotion had moved them up a full two tables at the big dinners—close enough to say, "hello," to inner-circle elites. Tracie could turn down lesser invitations with gracious disappointment. She loved that. She loved all of it— Robert, not so much.

Robert's tuxedo was getting a workout, smelling of Tracie's perfume instead of mothballs. Sex had tailed off, but was still better than the previous year by a long shot. He knew he should be feeling better about all of this, instead of being frustrated at work and bored with social events which felt like work.

Looking down at the bagel, one hand fiddling with the stack of folders, and the other pushing the coffee mug back and forth, Robert called out through the open door.

"Lorraine!"

"She just stepped out for a break."

"Jeezus!" Robert jumped back in his chair. Jerry was standing in front of his desk. "How long have you been there?"

"Not long; a couple of minutes," Jerry answered. 'You seemed deep in thought."

"You could have said something," Robert told him, annoyed.

"I did. You didn't answer," Jerry said calmly.

"Okay, my heart is almost back to normal." Robert regained his emotional footing and looked at Jerry. "What can I do for you?"

"We have a team meeting at ten. You asked me to stop by and walk with you," Jerry responded, almost grinning.

It was a short walk to the conference room. The Legislative Affairs meeting was the usual stream of updates on Federal Judge confirmations, the status of department litigation initiatives, progress reports on congressional oversight requests, and the schedule of witness appearances. It bored Robert to death, and he was glad that Jerry was handling it all. This was one of those meetings where all he had to do was listen and approve the updates Jerry briefed him on after the meeting. Jerry seemed to be enjoying his new position. As Robert had expected, he was doing the work well.

Back in his office, Robert thought that the inbox looked taller than when he'd left. He hoped that wasn't really the case. The afternoon wasn't shaping up to be any better than the morning.

Lorraine rang his private phone line. He hit the speaker button.

"Mr. Carlton, you have a request for an immediate meeting with the Secretary of State at 1:30. Shall I confirm the meeting?"

"Regarding?" Robert queried. He didn't like to agree to meetings he might not be prepared to handle, even if it was the Secretary of State making the request.

"The Secretary said some people down in the Caribbean have a passport problem, and he wants you to go to St. Thomas to straighten it out," Lorraine explained.

"That would be the Department of State – Bureau of Consular Affairs' responsibility, not mine," Robert told her, wondering why Vance was asking him to handle it.

"Yes, Sir," Lorraine confirmed. "They said you would be working with them."

Robert absently fingered the folder on the top of his in-basket, thinking about her statement. "There must be something more to it than that, Lorraine," he told her, looking up from the folder. "I'm not averse to the idea, but have I got anything from Jack about this?"

"Yes, Sir," Lorraine nodded. "You have an email from AG Crain's office confirming that you are the designated representative. I was copied on it. It's at the State Department. Shall I verify that you'll be attending the meeting?"

"Yes, certainly. Reschedule my two hours on each side, and get them to send up my lunch early," Robert approved.

So, Jack Crain had assigned this to him. That was all Robert needed for authorization, but it seemed suspiciously fast for an official trip. He wondered if this was connected in some way to the Puerto Rico trip.

He pushed Lorraine's extension button. "Is Mary Whiston on the list for this meeting?"

"Yes, Sir, she is. She is actually already in St. Thomas, but invited to the meeting via con-call," Lorraine supplied.

. . .

Robert's turkey and provolone wrap arrived early, as requested, interrupting his work. He'd taken to adding black olives, and spicy mustard instead of mayo on a whole-wheat tortilla wrap, livening up his humdrum, healthy lunch. He'd also begun ordering water, rather than sweetened iced tea. Dropping caffeine and sugar was

Tracie's idea, but it had been Robert's discovery that his pants were tight after the holidays that initiated the change.

Robert was glad to have the break. Lorraine brought in copies of the executive summary he'd prepared, following the Puerto Rico trip. As he packed his computer and tablet into his valise, it struck him that he normally insisted on more information before agreeing to a meeting. These lightning fast summons and trips in between the day-to-day routine were going to take some getting used to.

Lorraine had ordered a taxi for Robert. With traffic and parking, he'd decided that a taxi was by far the most efficient way to get to these meetings. The closest metro on his office's end was the Foggy Bottom Station, and that was a four-block hike. During heavy traffic, the two-mile taxi ride might take fifteen minutes. With the security check, he would be only eight minutes early. Vance tended to run his meetings on Lombardi time, which meant that if the attendees weren't fifteen minutes early, they were late. Robert hoped the traffic was light.

He arrived ten minutes early. He was prepared for and expected a follow-on meeting with Mako Morrison, so he'd had Lorraine make twelve copies of the material highlights and updates from the past few weeks, along with his executive summary.

Like the last time, Robert was met by an admin inside security and escorted, but this time he was led past the conference room and toward the big double doors flanked by flags at the end of the hall. Once inside, Vance's assistant rose to greet him.

"Mr. Carlton, the Secretary of State can see you now." Vance's administrative assistant led him to the door, holding it open for him. She was formally professional in every way, Robert noted. He was pleased to be shown directly into Vance's office without any waiting. Vance wasn't holding his "late" arrival against him.

"Thank you," Robert said as he entered. Vance, standing in front of his desk, was approaching him. On the other side of the room, Robert noticed a door closing as someone exited the opposite doorway. Having both an in and an out door was more common at Vance's level, and probably quite useful, Robert reflected.

"Robert; thank you for being so responsive. I do appreciate that you're able to help us out on such short notice," Vance spoke, shaking Robert's hand briefly.

"Always a pleasure, Mr. Secretary," Robert responded. "What can I do for you?"

"Make it Paul, please, Robert. I think we'll be working together enough to drop the formalities when we're meeting alone," Vance replied.

"Certainly, Paul," Robert replied, slightly surprised.

Robert had met, but not worked with the Secretary of State outside of the occasional Cabinet meetings. Most of the Secretary's issues were international, which generally kept them from running into each other. During Robert's tenure as Associate Attorney General, international problems had been handled politically, not legally. If there had been questions, then the OIA, the DOJ's Office of International Affairs, worked in concert with the State Department. Now of course, as Deputy AG, the OIA worked for him.

"Let me get right to the point, Robert." Vance began. "We have a problem in the Caribbean. Well, maybe not a problem so much as an opportunity," he corrected himself.

"Over the past four weeks, nine American citizens have been held captive on the island of St. Gertach. Now they've been released, and I'd like you to be our representative in St. Thomas when they arrive there."

Robert was a little stunned. Paul Vance was known for his level-headed demeanor and calm presence, which were both apparent at this moment. He could have been speaking about fish poaching, or an exploding offshore oil rig, and his voice would have carried the same intonation.

"What has the OIA advised?" Robert asked, recovering.

"There are no criminal charges to be filed, and no extradition issues," Vance answered. "This would simply be a multilateral discussion."

"And the Ambassador?" Robert was more surprised by the moment. Americans held captive, but no one was being pursued for prosecution?

"The Ambassador is involved, of course, but the local government of St. Gertach is barely more than a village council of elders. The Ambassador is asking for our assistance in keeping this from escalating into a regional issue. Nobody wants to upset tourism." Vance was somehow making this seem like an ordinary occurrence. "I know that involving the Department of Justice may seem backward, but by releasing these people directly to you, and not to us, we're able to prevent this from becoming a State Department issue. It develops as a matter of legal technicalities, property theft, lost passports, and paperwork. The island and its larger neighbors would prefer that this is quietly dispatched. As a result, they are being extremely cooperative."

"I appreciate your confidence, Paul, but the Bureau of Consular Affairs would seem a logical choice to handle this," Robert pointed out. He was still wondering why Vance had chosen him, rather than taking the more obvious route. Suddenly he realized that Vance might take that remark as resistance to his plans, and wondered if he'd made a mistake.

"Oh, don't worry, Robert." Vance seemed unconcerned. "We're better off keeping this to ourselves as much as possible. I'll have my team at your disposal."

Vance rose, smiling. "We've already begun the paperwork; it should be all taken care of by the time you arrive. What I'd like you to do for us is represent the United States and its concern for our citizens. It's best if we can mollify the local officials, and show our rescued citizens that while their experience is being taken seriously, it was an isolated incident that we can help them move on from, and forget. Your involvement and title are low profile from a diplomat's point of view, and high profile from a US citizen's perspective. It's our intent to have you defuse the entire situation."

Robert was uneasy. Vance's assumptions felt too smooth; too expectant.

"I'll have to have my team do some research," Robert countered, "including a review by the legal specialist for the region."

"That's fine, but we need you to be ready to go by 1 p.m. tomorrow," Vance said firmly.

Robert's surprise and hesitation were apparent on his face. Vance showed no reaction, patiently waiting while Robert collected himself.

Robert was thinking fast. He wondered if this was standard operating procedure when working with State. It occurred to him that one of the detained citizens might somehow be connected to a high-profile individual. Perhaps that was why they wanted the issue kept under wraps? Another thought flashed through his head; was he becoming the go-to guy for Caribbean problems?

"We'll do our best, Sir," Robert said, concluding that he was better off going along with what Vance had set up than trying to point out that there were more appropriate channels. He would have liked to know more, but Vance seemed to think everything necessary had been said.

The secondary door opened and the administrative assistant entered.

"Mr. Secretary, they have responded. Could you take a moment to confer with Mr. Makashi?"

"Yes, I'll be right there." Vance turned back to Robert. "Robert, this won't take more than a minute or two, can you wait here?"

"Yes. I'll make a couple of calls," Robert said, wondering what else Vance was going to tell him.

"Great. I'll be right back." Vance left the room.

Robert quickly called Lorraine.

"Mr. Carlton's office, may I help you?" she answered. Robert realized that the phone must not have identified him.

"Lorraine, it's me. Have Gardner pull the latest files for St. Gertach. It's an island in the Caribbean. I want anything we have on whatever's within two hundred miles of it, plus the US Virgin Islands. Have them emailed to me in the morning, and have Gardner available for a call—in case I need him," he ordered.

"Yes, Sir," Lorraine answered automatically.

"Thanks, Lorraine," Robert said, hanging up as Vance returned to the office.

"Sorry for the delay, Robert. I knew it wouldn't be long." He stood next to his desk and did not sit down. "Here's the thing, Robert," he continued. "This is a political mess, since these people were hijacked at sea, and there is some confusion about which country is actually involved. No one wants responsibility, and there are several countries represented in that area. They are all denying involvement, and accusing 'pirates,' but there haven't been any pirates active in that area for years. Nothing like this, anyway. The team has arranged a short briefing for you in the conference room. I would join you, but I have some pressing calls to make." He walked Robert to the door. "If you have any questions, I'm sure they can assist you." He paused before shaking Robert's hand again, and saying, "Thanks for doing this, Robert."

"Thank you, Sir," Robert replied mechanically as he left.

Robert found another assistant of Vance's at the door, ready to lead him into the conference room. Once he was seated, several staff members relayed the State Department's latest information about the kidnap victims. They had already been talking with Mary Whiston, who remained on the conference table speaker phone.

The group of tourists had no serious injuries, but had been treated for minor cuts and abrasions by a doctor, and were now being moved to the US Virgin Islands. They would arrive there tomorrow. Ostensibly, Robert was to be the dignitary in charge when he arrived. He would help iron out any US legal issues. The victims had lost their passports, as well as credit cards, cash, and so forth, but all of that was being handled. His job was to smooth things over, and get them to their destinations without any international incidents being reported.

Robert recognized that his meeting with Vance had been perfunctory. All the decisions had been made before that meeting had been arranged. Vance had decided that Robert was going, no matter what his objections might have been. Robert reflected that it had been considerate of Vance to spend time with him, given that the travel wasn't optional.

Vance's admin handed him an itinerary folder as the meeting wrapped up. Lifting his phone, he compared his calendar with the information in the folder and blocked a week out beginning the next day. He called Lorraine.

"Yes, Sir?" She answered. Apparently, his number had registered on the caller id this time.

"I won't need you to make a plane reservation for me to St. Thomas, Lorraine," he told her, "and according to this folder, I won't need a hotel booking either."

"Yes, Sir—but you're still going on the trip?" She asked.

"Yes. They've already made all the arrangements. I've blocked out next week for the trip." He explained.

"I'll move your appointments," Lorraine responded.

"Thanks. I'll be in first thing to pick up my files, and take care of a few things," Robert finished and hung up.

Clicking Grady's name on the phone brought up his calendar. It was showing that Grady was on vacation.

"Great," Robert muttered sarcastically, remembering that Grady had mentioned going away for a few days. He thought about that for a minute and recalled that Grady had mentioned going to an island. Was it St. John?

He quickly called Lorraine back. "Find Barlow for me. He's on vacation in the Virgin Islands, I believe. Get in touch with him and see if he can coordinate with my schedule somehow in the next two days, and meet me. I'll forward the schedule to you and to him. If he is still in the islands, arrange for him to meet me in St. Thomas. If he is on his way back, see if he can meet me at Andrews for a 2 p.m. flight tomorrow." He paused. "I'll keep my phone handy, Lorraine."

Pulling up his email, he spotted the follow-up notes from Vance's efficient assistant. He deleted all but the attached schedule and forwarded it to Grady and Lorraine.

Chapter 17

Grady sat on the beach soaking up the sun and sipping his rum punch. The trip to St. John was going smoothly. The four of them had talked excitedly as they'd left the airport, taken the ferry, and then taxied to the hotel. Keys in hand, Grady and Katy had suddenly become awkwardly quiet as they faced sharing a room.

Mike and Faith had a room down the hall, four rooms away. The grin on Faith's face as Grady walked past didn't make the situation any more comfortable. Grady let Katy go in first after he unlocked the door.

Katy held her breath, hoping that the two separate beds would be there, as requested. They were. Two queen size beds filled one side of a nicely appointed room. Everywhere were tasteful island prints and white linens. The balcony opened to a vista of palm trees and sand. She quickly went over to open the sliding door. It was easy to hear the waves washing up on the beach. The pool below beckoned, and the palm frond decorated bar was straight out of a postcard.

"Would you prefer the bed by the door so you can hear the waves?" Grady asked her, trying to make the question sound casual.

"Yes! That would be great!" Katy eagerly accepted. That seemed to break the tension. She'd have the waves, a breeze, control of the balcony if she needed to escape in the morning, and there'd be no chance that Grady would bump into her on the way to the bathroom in the middle of the night. She could turn her back in the morning, and he could be up and gone without any uncomfortable interactions.

Grady sighed with silent relief, feeling the first hurdle conquered. There were two suitcase stands, one at the end of each bed, plenty of room to walk around, and two bathrobes. Both of them planned to dress in the bathroom, taking turns, and both their suitcases contained pajamas. The bathrobes would make good extra cover.

"Hungry?" He asked her. They had already discussed meeting Mike and Faith at the restaurant, but asking helped keep the conversation light.

"I'm not sure I'm hungry," Katy mused, "but I should be. In any event, we can unpack later. We should get down there and meet them," she finished decisively.

"Yeah, I'm not sure I'm hungry, either, but if I smell food, that could change." Grady led the way out of the room, and soon they were with Mike and Faith in the open-air restaurant. The conversation never veered from admiring the scenery. They all were impressed with the beauty of the place.

They decided to go with the restaurant's dinner buffet option and were surprised at their appetites. Airport breakfasts and airplane sandwiches left them all hungrier than they'd expected. Mike and Faith were loading their plates with a little of everything, joking about compensating by only eating rum-soaked fruit the next day. Grady was sampling smoked grouper, while Katy reveled in ginger and coconut covered swordfish.

Soon the two couples were exploring the grounds with exotic drinks in their hands. The pool was glowing brightly in the darkening evening, lighting the palm trees with wavy blue shimmers. The beach drew them toward the ocean, though, and the sandals came off. Walking through the sand in bare feet, watching the moonrise was fun. Occasional quick splashes from the thin wavelets rushing up the sand caught them, making the girls laugh as they ran from the water. The drinks made the guy's jokes sound better, but hadn't messed too much with their equilibrium.

Eventually, they all agreed to turn in and meet for breakfast. It was hard to leave the warm sand, but the long day had taken its toll.

Grady and Katy were pleased to find that their room arrangement was going to work out easily. Grady sat on the balcony with his eBook, reading, while Katy got ready for bed. Grady had his turn in the bathroom next. Katy rolled to face the screen door, listening to the waves. She was asleep by the time Grady emerged.

. . .

Grady was up first in the morning, and back on the balcony by the time Katy was awake. After she'd showered and dressed, Faith and Mike sent a message saying they were headed to the covered open-air pavilion for breakfast.

"Morning, Guys!" Katy called to Mike and Faith, as she and Grady stepped into the pavilion.

"Morning," Faith replied, sounding sleepy. Mike raised his hand and nodded.

"Rough night?" Grady asked, wondering what was up.

"No, actually, it was great." Faith answered, grinning groggily. "We decided to go grab a nightcap after you two went up. That became two, which became...well, you know. Without the kids, we get kind of carried away." Faith lost her concentration.

Mike chimed in, "We didn't get much sleep, and I feel like hell."

This drew a round of laughs from the four. Grady and Katy sat down to indulge in the Papaya juice and coffee already on the table, while they figured out what else they wanted to eat.

Their day progressed with lively chatter on the beach under umbrellas, fueled by cool glasses of water and fruit punch. Lunch was poolside with fancy fruit drinks, followed by snorkeling.

They showered and changed for nightlife at a nearby restaurant that had an island band. Mike had been busy making friends with one of the bartenders who'd recommended the place. The food was excellent, and lacking in tacky tourism features that Grady and Katy had been worried they'd find. Faith was a little disappointed that no crazy conga lines formed, but found herself thoroughly enjoying the local music and drinks.

The next morning shaped up to be very much the same. There was a failed attempt by everyone except Faith at windsurfing. She'd excelled at the sport. Why she was good at it mystified the other three.

Faith was constantly chasing Mike with a bottle of sunscreen. By 11 a.m. Mike was red and relegated to the shade of an enormous blue and white umbrella on the beach. Faith was turning decidedly pink. Katy's exposure to the sun had added an almost golden glow to her dark complexion. Grady's dark skin had not changed.

"You two are lucky." Faith rolled over on her beach chaise to face Katy.

"Oh?" Katy said, looking up. She had been reading her book and enjoying the breeze. Grady seemed to be napping. Mike was snoring, but not enough to scare people.

"You always look tanned. I have to go through a pink phase first. Then I get some color, but it won't last a month. Lobster boy over there will just turn red and peel. You get all dark, golden, and look great. Your grandparents were from Brazil, right?" She queried.

"Great-grandparents, on both sides. My grandparents on mom's side moved to L.A. in the forties for business, and stayed." Katy explained.

"Lucky you got their skin. I'm already getting burn lines. See?" She pulled up the edge of her bottoms so high that she had to fix the wedgy when she pulled them back down. Grady noticed the generous flash of white skin out of the corner of his eye. Mike snored a little louder.

"It's a little pink, but you look great. You put on more sunscreen, right?" Katy smiled and turned back to her book.

"Yep. Hey, Grady, are you awake over there?" Faith reached out and prodded him with her foot. "Tell Katy where your gorgeous dark skin comes from," she commanded, trying to continue her match-making operation.

Grady smiled lazily at Faith and Katy. "She never lets up, does she?" He asked Katy. "My great-grandmother was from Morocco, as you well know, Faith. She was tall, beautiful, and very popular in Atlanta. We don't know who my great grandfather was, but when my dad drank a bit too much, he claimed to be half Cherokee."

Both the girls laughed.

The rest of the day was filled with casual talking, swimming, and reading. They all found themselves falling into the relaxing Caribbean lifestyle.

Katy and Faith left the pool early to shower and change for dinner. Grady and Mike came up later, meeting the girls by the bar after dressing. Grady's white cotton drawstring pants and sockless boat shoes were a hit with Faith and Katy. Faith was wearing a low dipping halter dress. Katy was a vision in a bright, tropical silk top and turquoise slacks, with sparkling strappy sandals. Grady slipped a yellow flower into her hair, finishing off her look.

Dinner was casual dining on a covered lanai. The four lingered over drinks until Faith and Mike, not looking a bit tired, decided to turn in early. Grady and Katy took a long walk on the beach before calling it a night.

Grady waited on the balcony while Katy finished in the bathroom and got into her bed. He was thinking about how she'd looked that day in her bikini.

As she fell asleep, Katy was thinking about Grady's smile, the look in his eyes, and how he smelled as he put the flower in her hair.

. . .

The next day started with breakfast in town and shopping, giving Mike's sunburn some welcome relief. Faith found a bathing suit shop and teased Mike with the idea of buying a tiny bathing suit. The hundred and fifty-dollar price tag for "three Band-Aids," as Mike put it, was out of their budget. Mike didn't know whether to be relieved or disappointed. Faith tried it on anyway, letting him peek into the dressing room to see her.

After lunch, they all opted for more snorkeling before heading back to their rooms to change for dinner. Mike and Faith were still talking about bathing suits.

"You should have bought that smaller one." Mike was telling her.

"You wish! This is as small as it gets, Cowboy. Unless you want to run back and spend some of the Christmas Fund." Faith told him.

"I can do that. You want me to?" Mike seemed ready to throw caution to the wind.

"Not unless I lose ten more pounds before you get back." Faith decided.

"You're crazy. You look great. You look so good in it, Babe. You should go for it." Mike was having fun teasing her about it.

That evening was Beach Party Night. Mike and Faith greeted the idea excitedly. Grady and Katy would have rather gone somewhere else. Tourist entertainment wasn't their idea of fun.

As it turned out, the food was some of the best they'd had yet. The limbo contest wasn't all that bad, either, thanks to lots of drinks and fun music.

. . .

Back in the room, Katy ducked into the bathroom quickly and Grady emptied his pockets. Placing his wallet in the room safe, he saw the flashing screen on his phone and dutifully picked it up. There was no point in ignoring it; the app on his calendar would nag every 5 minutes because it was flagged "urgent."

It was an urgent contact from DAG, Robert.

When Katy came out of the bathroom wearing a bathrobe, he was listening to voicemail.

"I have to answer this." He told her.

Chapter 18

Robert sat in his office at home, holding the phone to his ear.

It was late, but he'd been going over notes from Vance's office when Grady called. A large glass of Cabernet, filled just to the widest part of the bowl so the wine could breathe, sat by his hand. The Cabernet was one of Robert's favorites from Beaulieu Vineyards. BV had some special wines that he had preferred since the first time he and Tracie had gone to Napa Valley. These days he couldn't bring himself to pay for the pricey Georges de Latour—he used to be able to afford it, but some luxuries had gone up in price faster than his public servant's salary. Their mid-priced Cabernet was a good compromise.

He'd been talking with Grady for several minutes when, on the other end of the phone, Grady had gone quiet.

"You still there?" Robert finally asked as he toyed with the glass, swirling the wine again.

"I'm here," Grady replied. "I'm still thinking. St. Thomas, tomorrow. You know I'm on vacation, right?"

"Yes—sorry about that, Grady. The trip may only take a few days, but we need to allow for a week. There will be sporadic meetings with dignitaries, and the nine citizens." Robert had rapidly filled Grady in on the details, but he knew he'd surprised him at the end by announcing that Grady needed to be in St. Thomas the next morning.

"Calendar conflicts?" Robert tested.

"No, but I am on vacation, Robert," Grady emphasized again.

"I know, you're on St. John's," Robert told him. "How perfect can that be?"

"Perfect if I stay here," Grady said shortly.

"You were coming back tomorrow anyway, weren't you?" Robert didn't understand what the problem was, or how interrupting a partial day of vacation was a big deal. Hell, he had lost whole weeks of vacation in his career.

"You know I'm not alone," Grady told him. Grady was regretting having called. He should have left the phone in the safe, but he probably would have been tracked down and hauled off the island early whether he had or not. "I mean…" Grady began, trying to get Robert to understand the situation, "Can this wait? We leave to come home tomorrow night."

"Lorraine said there is a regular Saint Thomas Cruz Bay ferry. Grab that in the morning, and we'll have a car pick you up at the dock." Robert was obviously not paying attention.

"I'm familiar with the ferry. The point is, Robert that we are *all* here on vacation." Grady was perfectly willing to go, if necessary. It would not be the first time his vacation plans had been cut short, either, but it wasn't only him being inconvenienced.

Robert came back to earth for a moment. "Who's with you?"

After Grady explained briefly, Robert asked. "Are they military?"

"Mike and Katy are officers. Faith is a GS."

"Katy—that's the one who's your date, right?" Robert didn't wait for Grady's response. "Okay, bring her with you."

"I don't know if she can get leave. She works at the Naval Research Laboratory and…" Grady began.

"She's a Naval officer?" Robert cut in. "Hang on, is that the Katy I met when we were touring MISTI at the NRL?"

"Yes," Grady answered, wondering where Robert was going with this.

"Even better. Bring her. Have her commanding officer call Lorraine, and it will be a work assignment." Robert told him.

"Hold on. I'm still not sure of my role in this, much less hers," Grady found himself thinking that Robert was getting a little ahead of himself with his "orders." "Want to fill me in on why we are necessary a little more?"

Katy, hearing this part of the conversation, headed back into the bathroom.

"Fair enough." Robert had the folder provided by Vance's admin on his desk. He picked it up and opened it while leaning back in his chair.

"You know the basics about the tourists being kidnapped. The first problem is this gunboat that was used. I've spent a little time reviewing the documents Vance provided, and it's clear the vessel wasn't military. From the descriptions—gray, metal, uniforms, and the flag on the back—it appeared to be official. That has me concerned. I'd like your first-hand outlook and opinions as we discuss this in St. Thomas. The officials in the Virgin Islands are also concerned about any paramilitary activities. Having an Air Force and a Naval officer along would show them that we are taking this seriously."

"They have their own military personnel," Grady stated flatly.

"That's true, but I'm going in a federal capacity to show concern for our citizens. That's how diplomacy works. As you know, Ambassadors have military aides—for good reasons."

Grady's father had been an Assistant Air Attaché to an Ambassador, so Grady did know how diplomacy worked. "So, you're an Ambassador now?" He questioned, somewhat sarcastically.

"Well, that's the point. I'm going because the State Department doesn't want this to become an international incident. Nobody in the islands wants that, either, since it could negatively affect their tourist-based economy. You're not an Ambassador's aide, so the whole thing is still discreetly handled, but with a meaningful presence."

Grady was about to respond, but Robert continued, "The second thing is, it struck me that these people, having been high-jacked at sea, might not be ready to settle back on their yachts and sail back. If it was my trip, and Tracie was with me, I doubt that I'd be able to get her back on the boat."

"True enough." Grady did not know Tracie well, yet, but this sounded like a logical statement.

"If you were on a boat by yourself, you'd get right back on and sail where you were going in the first place. Correct?" Robert queried.

Grady thought a minute before saying, "Probably. It would depend on the shape the boat was in, and how convinced I was that it had been an isolated incident—but I'd have to get the boat back somehow."

"My thought is that nine people with five boats could have five completely different reactions," Robert had been thinking about how to handle this. "I think we will need to be flexible. We might need to work with the Coast Guard, and maybe arrange air surveillance for the ones that want to sail home, but are feeling slightly unsafe doing it. There is no doubt that a uniform would be a great help there. What do you think?"

"I don't know if any of us will be able to get the Coast Guard to do that, but I get it. It's a diplomatic trip, and you want uniforms looking official, and speaking reassuringly," Grady confirmed.

Katy came back into the room. She was still wearing the bathrobe, but what had been bare legs under the robe were now legs encased in pajama bottoms. The collar of the matching nightshirt extended up from the bathrobe.

Grady hadn't noticed the bare legs or the change. He smiled at her as she entered the room. She smiled back, and leaned against the television stand, waiting for him to finish the call.

Robert was still talking. "Right. State just doesn't want official diplomats there. We won't be taking responsibility for anything, but we're there to keep everyone calm and moving forward." Robert was still trying to convince himself that Vance's idea of keeping a low profile on the diplomat side was the right strategy. He had to assume they knew what they were doing; he didn't have much of a choice.

"No problems, and no worries. Just a little evaluating and steady support. Okay, I'm in." Grady sighed and began to feel more cheerful. He hoped Katy would like the idea. "I'll let you know how this works out for Katy, and then you can get her orders rolling." He smiled toward Katy, but got back an emotionless look. That got him worried again.

"Great. After you brief her, have her boss contact Lorraine. Lorraine will have everything worked out by then." Robert was assuming Katy wouldn't have any problems with the assignment. He thought for a moment, then said, "You two can fly back with me. You can turn in your return flights."

"Uniform." Grady was starting to think about the details. "I have a bug out bag in my hall closet. I can call my landlord with your name to let you in."

"I'll have a courier get it," Robert told him.

"Okay, someone using your name. Lorraine has my address—I'll text her the landlord's name, and a code word that I'll give him so that he'll let the courier in." Grady said, thinking fast.

"Done. I'll add it to Lorraine's list." Robert said, tapping the note into his message for Lorraine.

"See you tomorrow." Grady clicked off the phone. Katy stood waiting with a questioning look in her eyes.

"What would you think of going to St. Thomas tomorrow, on business?" Grady asked her.

Chapter 19

Robert pulled up to the main gate at Andrews Field. The guard directed him to a secondary building off to the side. While Tracie waited in the car, he received a lecture from a Chief Master Sergeant about sending packages to the gate. A nervous courier sat quietly with Grady's bug out bag on his lap. Robert did his best to graciously accept the instruction, along with several pages of paperwork explaining security do's and don'ts which he had to sign. After he thoroughly inspected the bag, as per instructions, the courier gratefully transferred possession to Robert, who then made his way through the visitor paperwork. Then Tracie had to come in for ID and paperwork.

Finally through the gate, Robert's pulse slowed.

"Maybe Regan and Dulles security gates aren't so bad." Tracie joked nervously. They both knew this was easier, but it was still a bit unnerving. Next time no courier bags, Robert thought.

Tracie held the map they'd been issued and directed where they were supposed to go. Robert watched the speed limits closely. The base required very slow driving. It was a relief when they spotted Arnold Avenue, and, finally, the check-in building.

"There's a rental car place." Tracie was startled.

"That's surprising." Robert was in unfamiliar territory. He felt disoriented. He parked in the designated spot and unloaded their bags. When they got inside the building they were pleased to find the personnel very helpful. Before they knew it, they were in the waiting room.

Another check of paperwork and security scans went quickly. Not until they exited the door to the tarmac did the fun begin to set in. A sleek Gulfstream V sat waiting for them. The pilot was doing final checks, while the first officer performed his walk around.

There was something elegant about walking up to a private jet, Robert thought. Inside they found four people sitting in the back. Two were members of the USVI Governor's staff, and the other two were from the Regional Ambassador's staff. All were hitching a ride following a visit to the State Department. Although they were high-level staff members, they'd been instructed to leave the front entirely to Robert and Tracie. Tracie's smile was big enough to swallow her ears.

The plane was wonderfully appointed. Leather seats sat opposite each other in six pairs. Three stood on each side, facing each other over real tables—not typical airline dinner trays. No sooner were they seated than an Staff Sergeant in a crisp Air Force uniform approached, introducing herself.

"Good afternoon Mr. and Mrs. Carlton. I am Staff Sergeant Waters of the 99th Airlift Squadron, and I will be your flight attendant today. Welcome aboard. Our C-37A is fully equipped, and in a moment, I would like to explain our safety features. First, let me offer you a beverage."

The service on the flight was better than first class. Tracie and Robert had plenty of comparative experience, thanks to their parents buying tickets for them. They had been on Robert's father's company jet twice, but this surpassed those experiences.

There was a custom menu for each of them, and the food provided was prepared fresh. The attendant explained that they typically received Distinguished Visitors' preferences, and would go shopping before the flight. Meals were prepared on board. Robert hadn't expected any of this when Lorraine had asked him what he and Tracie would like to eat and drink.

There was a crew of five. The captain spoke with them before takeoff, and again at cruising altitude. The plane seated twelve, leaving a noticeable gap between the Carltons and those in the back. They even had a separate flight attendant. Tracie couldn't get over how big the jet was inside. She had been excited about having a private plane but expected a small tube, like Robert's father's company jet. This was much more luxurious. Even a tall person could stand up in the aisle.

Tracie checked another box on her mental list of achievements. A diplomatic mission, private jet, and a trip to the Caribbean. She lounged in the comfortable chair. A pineapple-flavored sparkling water filled the champagne flute cradled in her hand.

Tracie's hair was perfectly done, brushing the collar of her white business dress. Her heavy jacket had been hung in the closet, and the cabin temperature was set to her liking. Except for her blonde hair, she looked and felt like Jackie O.

Robert also looked the part he was to play. He had selected a charcoal suit with white shirt, and a silver-gray tie. The clothing set off his hair nicely, giving him a slightly older and very distinguished look. Tracie thought he looked handsome, sitting there reading his files. She pulled her phone out and discreetly grabbed several pictures of him.

"Having fun?" Robert asked without looking up, but with a smile.

"This is wonderful," Tracie admitted.

"Don't get too used to it," Robert warned. "This is a special occasion." Robert didn't want to diminish the moment, but he also felt the need to set realistic expectations.

"I know, but this is wonderful," Tracie said again, lounging even more. The SSgt came to refill her glass and asked if there was anything more she could get. She suggested dessert and coffee, to which Tracie agreed enthusiastically. There was chocolate ganache and freshly ground coffee.

Robert followed suit. "Sounds 'wonderful.'" His grin indicated that Tracie should get the joke, since he'd used the same descriptive word she had. She was too wrapped up in the moment to notice.

"Shannon is fantastic," Tracie gushed. "You know she made the lunch?"

"Shannon?" Robert asked, wondering who Tracie was talking about.

"Sergeant Waters. Haven't you been listening?" Tracie didn't wait for a response. "You have to tell someone, and make sure she gets some acknowledgment."

"I will," Robert assured her, thinking he'd have Lorraine take care of it.

"Does Secretary Vance fly like this all the time?" Tracie asked.

"From what I understand, he usually uses one of the bigger planes," Robert said.

"This is a LearJet, right?" Tracie wondered. She wanted to get the details right when she impressed her friends with them.

"No, it's a Gulfstream V; the military version. They have four of them stationed with the 89th Airlift Wing at Andrews. They are used for high-ranking government and defense department officials, including foreign dignitaries and world leaders." Robert smiled at Tracie's stunned expression.

"How do you know that?" Tracie demanded.

"I read the brochure." Robert lifted the pamphlet from the side of the chair and waved it at her.

Tracie lifted a well-groomed eyebrow at him, giving him a wry look, then said, "I thought she said 99th."

"89th Wing, 99th Squadron." Robert explained, "Wings are made of multiple squadrons."

"And how did you know that? Does the brochure have all of that in it?" Tracie said, lifting her eyebrow higher.

"No, that's something I've picked up from Grady," Robert laughed.

"Are we meeting him at the capital?" She wanted to know.

"Yes, but first I'll get you settled at the hotel," Robert reassured her.

"Good," Tracie said, relieved. "I'll want to freshen up before we see everyone."

Robert checked the agenda on his email, which was loading and sending his messages with normal speed. He had several updates from Lorraine and Mary Whiston, who was coordinating in St. Thomas. Lorraine called about a separate issue at the office. Robert was impressed with how well-equipped the plane was for continuing work on long flights.

Chapter 20

Max crossed Colonial Beach, Virginia off her list. It hadn't panned out. She got in the car and headed to the Washington Sailing Marina. It was a short hour and a half drive if traffic was good. The sixty-mile route would take Max over two tall bridges that crossed the Potomac River.

The first was the Governor Harry Nice Memorial Bridge across to Maryland. It had to be the weirdest old bridge she had ever driven over. Steel girders climbed up at a steep grade so that tall ships could cross underneath. This bridge was known as one of the scariest in America. There were people with phobias about crossing bridges like this one, and for the first time, Max could understand why. She loved it, but then, she loved skydiving. She rolled down the windows to get the full effect as a gusting crosswind knocked her car around. At the top she was easily ten stories off the water. The steep grade down the other side was fun. Max got a kick out of the decent. It reminded her of skiing down a fast slope. She wanted to go across again. She had a timetable to meet, though; it would have to wait for another trip.

Continuing up 301 she crossed the Potomac back to the Virginia side on 495, using The Woodrow Wilson Bridge. This bridge was a more modern style, with a concrete and steel design. It had a navigable height of 70 feet. Yachts like the Beneteau 423, with its mast height of 59' 7", had plenty of clearance, but the bridge gave skippers a tight stomach as they passed below. Knowing that there were 10 feet between the top of the mast and the bottom of the bridge didn't prevent the feeling of imminent collision.

Max had checked out every detail of the route. She knew the height and depth to each inch of the waterway and structures on it. That was important. They couldn't afford mistakes.

She was meeting Luca for dinner at the Indigo Landing Restaurant. She hoped it was as nice as the pictures, and that it served something besides seafood. She was getting a little tired of shoreline cuisine.

Traffic was good. She pulled into the marina parking lot early. The jets taking off from Reagan International due north of the marina were loud, but surprisingly tolerable.

Grabbing her jacket and changing to her walking shoes, she quickly ran a brush through her hair. The unseasonably warm weather had followed her from Florida, making the air humid and sticky. She decided to take it easy at the deck bar, and catch up on some email in the shade—after she walked to the eastern side of Daingerfield Island. She slung the jacket over her shoulder for the walk, feeling the late afternoon breeze begin to cool the air.

The Marina sat in a nook that faced north on the island, but the word "island" was a misnomer. The promontory connected directly to the mainland, not even qualifying for an isthmus, much less an island.

The path was longer than she'd expected and rougher. The road turned to dirt as she passed some junky looking buildings on her way to the wooded shore. This part of the land was shaped like a bulge, providing a greater than 180-degree view, looking east-south-east across the Potomac River. From here it was easy to see a long pier located on the far side, jutting out some 1500 feet into the river. The pier was on the Joint Base of Anacostia-Bolling and the Naval Research Laboratory. At the end of the dock was the fifty-foot barge holding SuperMISTI. With any luck, Max thought, that barge would still be there two months from now.

. . .

Back at the restaurant after her inspection, Max went into the ladies' room. It was well equipped and roomy, equally ready for sailors and bridesmaids. At the sink, Max thoroughly washed away the day's makeup, before going into a stall to change. She had stopped at the car, leaving her jacket and grabbing a small black gym bag and her purse. From the bag, she pulled out a neatly rolled dress and sandals.

When she emerged from the stall the transformation was striking. Replacing her cool linen slacks and turquoise silk top was a dress with wide silver-taupe and thin dark brown vertical stripes. The sheen of the material set off the highlights in her hair. The dress's low, square neck, tightly tailored waist, and mid-thigh hem emphasized her fit body. Max's figure refused to let go of a layer of "protective coating," as she called it, but the softness covered the taut lines beneath, giving her somewhat straight body a pleasing shape. A good bra gave her a little cleavage. Bracelets and low-heeled, sparkling sandals completed the picture. Fifteen minutes at the sink mirror and she felt like a new woman. She found a seat at the bar near the open doors and settled in with a well-chilled pomegranate martini.

Luca arrived early. Max spotted him, but remained on her bar stool and sipped her drink. Luca's dark, styled hair and slight beard tracing his jaw looked distinctly European. His soft, black leather business jacket, white dress shirt, summer weight wool dress slacks, and polished leather loafers spoke clearly of Italy. He smelled of Floid, the classic Italian aftershave. Max loved the scent. She knew that when he got close to her the menthol kick would refresh the air around him just enough to be noticeable. For some reason, the scent always made her sigh.

Luca noticed that Max looked amazing, sitting confidently at the bar, with one shapely leg crossed over the other. Her tanned, smooth skin accentuated her shapely, muscled calves. Her combed hair fell across one eyebrow then down just below her jaw line, exposing the ends of dangling earrings that fell along the line of her neck.

"Maxine, you came." Luca's warm tone rolled across the air, his accent making her name sound decadent. "You look beautiful," he continued. He reached out and grasped the peaks of her strong shoulders, softly kissing both her cheeks. "It's wonderful to see you again," he told her sincerely.

"Luca, you are as handsome as ever," Max responded warmly. She was enjoying being the center of his attention. She found herself as drawn to him as ever. "Please, sit down," she invited, tapping the bar chair next to hers.

Luca removed his jacket and laid it over the back of the chair. His fitted shirt looked even better without the jacket. Even the Italian style of having an extra button undone suited Luca.

Their conversation was light. They discussed travel, cars, and interests as the evening sunset deepened. A chill began to come off the water, sending them into the restaurant.

Max ordered Roasted Chicken a la Chevre, while Luca chose scallops. Their window table gave them a marvelous view while they ate, talked, and laughed with each other. The winds blew the sound of jets toward the building, but a waiter closed the patio doors, muffling the cool breeze and the sound of the engines.

"You can stay a while?" Luca asked as the after-dinner espresso arrived.

"No, just the two days," Max told him regretfully.

"Then you will please me by joining me for lunch tomorrow?" Max asked her.

"I was thinking more of breakfast," Max told him, signaling the waiter for the check.

Luca's flat overlooked Founders Park on the river, next to old town Alexandria. It was just south of the restaurant and didn't take long to reach in Luca's vintage Alfa Romeo. Max playfully struggled with Luca's clothing in the confines of the two-seater all the way. Despite the limited space and stick shift, his shirt was soon unbuttoned and loose, and her hemline had become much higher.

Luca had a reserved parking spot, which was rare in the area. The parking lot was adequately lit, but not generously so. Max was taking advantage of that. When he came around to Max's door, Luca saw that her dress had risen up the remaining short distance to where her legs joined her body. The shiny taupe triangle of her panties showed tantalizingly. She rose from the low car with the help of his hand, swinging her legs out one at a time, exposing more of her hips and high-cut underwear.

"You look fabulous," Luca murmured, pulling her close.

"You look edible," Max said, still holding his hand. She twisted it and turned him around sharply, using the backside of his body to close the car door. With her free hand, she traced down his chest to the front of his hip. Pinned against the car, Luca felt her fingers slip over the front of his thigh, crossing toward the middle, then sliding straight up to where his legs met.

"Ah, you missed me then. I missed you more." Luca laughed, turning deftly in her grip, and spinning them both around. Max's back was now against the car. Their torsos were pressed tightly together, their chests not quite touching. His maneuver had pulled her hands and arms up high, nearly to her shoulder blades, their fingers together.

"I can tell," Max responded, as she wiggled her hips slightly against him. She pulled both their hands upward and back, using their fingers to find the zipper in the back of her dress. Together they pulled it down slowly. His fingers left hers just enough to trace the skin behind the departing zipper, as it went lower, and lower.

"You are exciting me too much." Luca's eyes dilated as his fingers slid across her back, bra, lower back and around the rising curve of her tight rear end. "This zipper is long."

"Yes, it is." Max smiled into his eyes as she reached the bottom and stopped. Her French-cut panties rose high on the sides, barely covering front and back. Now the top inch showed through the open back of her dress.

Luca's hands rested on the skin of her lower back through the open dress. Max's hands came around to his shoulders, moving slowly from the corners to his neck, and then to her own, catching the dress and pulling it off her shoulders.

"Here?" She questioned, giving him a devilish smile.

"Not yet," Luca told her, grinning. He pulled her away from the car. The two walked quickly from the car up the sidewalk to his doorstep. Her dress held on to her shoulders, but the back wafted open freely.

As Luca fumbled with his keys, Max spun him around slamming him into the door. She kissed him hard, with one leg wrapped around his body. Pressing harder with her leg, she released her hands from his body and reached behind for the clasp of her bra.

Luca turned the door lock behind him and they tumbled into the entry. Max's bra was flung halfway up the stairs, while her dress and Luca's shirt slid across the floor tiles. Luca kicked the front door shut with his foot.

Lying naked on the floor and stairs, neither noticed the chill of the tiles on their bare skin. Their panting smiles gave way to intense love making. Max's legs wrapped completely around Luca's back as their passions peaked. Her voice mixed with his in a two-note chord of ecstasy.

Their orgasmic outburst over, Max's head rested against the second step, as Luca leaned on his elbows. Their energy rekindled quickly as they gazed at each other's bodies. Max grabbed Luca's neck, pulling him into a deep open-mouthed kiss.

"You are more than fabulous," Luca smiled, after catching his breath. It was a caressing smile, with his bedroom eyes promising more.

"You keep getting better—like wine," Max said, stroking a line down his shoulder.

"Wine, Si!" Luca carefully and smoothly withdrew from her embrace, drawing a sigh from Max.

"Where are you going?" She demanded.

"Only a moment. Wait for me." He smiled as he got to his knees. He admired her naked form lying on the tile.

"Wait for you?" Max lifted an eyebrow at him.

"Si." He was up and gone, but before Max had moved toward her clothes he was back. Luca produced luxurious white bathrobes with spa slippers in the pockets. He was off again before she had tied the belt. When he reappeared, it was with a glass of ruby red Sangiovese in each hand.

"Grazie," Max told him, smiling.

"Grazie to you, Max," Luca told her, raising his glass. "Salute!" A clink of glasses and the first sip was coursing through her body with warmth and the flavors of pepper, blackberry, and red currents.

They adjourned to Luca's marble trimmed kitchen, where he showed his Garde Manger talents. Producing a tray of prosciutto, cheese, olives, Juliette tomatoes, bread, and sweet creamery butter, Luca placed two chocolate truffles in the center.

Max lifted a delicate slice of prosciutto. Leaning her head back, she placed it into her open mouth, and slowly onto her tongue.

"Mmmm, delicious." Her smile suggestively lifted one corner of her lips as she set aside her glass, and loosened the front of her robe.

Luca's arm swept the tray to the side of the counter, scattering napkins, forks, and décor across the floor. He grasped her waist, lifting her up and placing her on the stone island top. The cold surface chilled her thighs through the robe, promising a contrast of thrills. Max reached into his bathrobe pocket and found the expected condom. This time, instead of letting him handle it himself, she took the package and unwrapped it for him as they fondled each other. Their embrace took on new impatience as their robes opened wide. Max ran her hands across Luca's shoulders, dropping the garment off his strong deltoids and onto the floor.

Luca slid her robe off her body, pushing her back onto the countertop. "Oh, that's nice," Max told him, feeling the chill shock her skin. She ran her hands down his back and sank her fingernails into his muscles.

Grabbing her hips, Luca pulled her closer to the edge. The sounds of their passion filled the room. Rapidly rising and falling waves of electric sensations coursed through their muscles. Her skin tingled all over as her feet flexed and her toes curled. His back arched as his hips pressed against her thighs. Ecstasy flooded over them.

Spent again, Luca's hands slid up along Max's body, caressing every inch. She reached up and pulled his head in for a deep kiss.

Feeling again for their wine glasses, they noticed that not one olive or drop of wine had been spilled.

Chapter 21

The Cruz Bay to Charlotte Amalie ferry left a little after 11:15 a.m., with Grady and Katy on board. They had waved goodbye to Mike and Faith after breakfast as they climbed into a cab.

They both watched from the ferry's deck as St. John receded below the horizon. It was a smooth crossing. They continued their conversation from breakfast, talking about the island, and wishing they'd had more time there.

As St. Thomas grew larger off the bow of the boat, the conversation changed to Katy asking questions about Robert, and what they'd be doing. Grady found himself short on answers. His knowledge about this trip was limited, and he couldn't share much with Katy about his and Robert's recent adventures.

The longer they talked, the more strained the conversation seemed to be getting. Grady couldn't shake the feeling that there was a bigger distance between the two of them than there had been the previous night. He began wondering if he'd done something wrong by inviting Katy along on this jaunt.

Katy was not sending a message as Grady feared. She was putting on her game face. Last night when she'd heard him talking with Robert, she'd calmly gone back into the bathroom and put on the pajamas she had hesitantly left off moments before. When Grady had explained what Robert had asked him to do, and that her role in it was welcome—in fact fortuitous, she'd agreed to participate without hesitation. Working with the Deputy Attorney General was a great opportunity. Any amorous feelings she'd had were washed away by the business talk. It was time to get to work. There was nothing more to it than that.

In the morning Katy had fixed her hair like she did for work, pulled back and tight, so it would look crisp and professional. She didn't have her cap or uniform with her, but the attitude was important. She hated the image women presented when they wore too much loose hair and makeup while in uniform. She kept her makeup simple and understated.

She'd had some concern about her clothing since she only had resort wear with her. She chose her simple white dress and added small silver stud earrings. The sparkling strappy sandals couldn't be helped; she had nothing else with her except beach shoes.

Grady thought she looked great, but kept questioning in his mind whether he had done something wrong. Katy seemed more distant as they got closer to St. Thomas.

Arriving at the ferry terminal it was easy to spot their driver, standing next to an off-white minivan. His white shirt and black pants didn't stand out much against the movement of people, but the large sign with Grady's name that he held up couldn't be missed.

"Mr. Barlow!" The man was calling repeatedly.

"I'm Barlow," Grady acknowledged when he got close to him.

"Yes, Sir. Thank you. I am Peter, your driver. I was hired to take you. If you will please give me your bags, we will be ready to go." Peter loaded up the van with their luggage and opened the door for them to climb inside.

Heading out of the terminal, Peter talked continuously. He described the scenery as they careened about the tiny city streets crammed with pedestrians, bicycles, and small cars darting in every direction. Once they'd cleared the tourist area, he pulled into the left lane and sped up. Honking cars going in the opposite direction flew by within inches on the right. Grady suddenly realized that they were driving on the left.

"I am to give you this," Peter said, interrupting his own monologue, and handing back a printed page with several bullet-pointed sentences. "Mr. Carlton will meet with you where you are staying later this afternoon when they arrive." Grady noticed an ignored stop sign whiz by the van as Peter talked. "They are having lunch on the plane, so lunch is set for you where you are staying." A policeman directing traffic waved left and Peter turned right, without using his turn signal. He continued to recite the list Grady held in his hand. "Your first meeting at the Ron de Lugo Federal Building is at nine-thirty tomorrow." Peter missed hitting a short rock wall by an inch, as two women with plastic grocery bags flashed by the other side, close enough to touch the windows. "I will come tomorrow morning at nine-fifteen to get you." The city businesses had now faded into houses, as the van climbed up one of the lush green hills that encroached on the city from inland.

"Where are we going?" Grady broke in, handing the list to Katy.

"You are staying at Crimson House. It is just here." The driver said looking back at Grady with a smile. He turned back in time to miss hitting a slow scooter inching up the steep hill.

"See it is just here," Peter repeated, pointing out the left window. A few minutes later they pulled up in front of a private home. Peter got out almost as soon as the car stopped moving.

"This isn't a hotel," Katy spoke for the first time since she got in the car, sounding slightly concerned.

"Yes, this is Crimson House," Peter assured her. His smile was as quick as his driving. He was already unloading bags as a very dark, heavy woman came out the door.

"Welcome to St. Thomas," the woman said cheerfully. "I am Dorothy, you must be Mr. Barlow and Ms. Davies. You are very welcome." She held the front door open for them to enter.

The front double doors looked straight through the house to large picture windows and glass doors on the far side. The glass doors opened onto a wide balcony, giving a panoramic view of the city and bay. A giant cruise ship on the far side of the harbor looked like a toy boat. The sun beamed down on the multicolored buildings.

"We have your rooms over here," Dorothy told them, indicating a hallway. "They will be ready for you in the morning," she told the driver. "You can go now, Peter," she said dismissively.

"How much do I owe you?" Grady asked Peter quickly.

"No charge, Sir. Everything is paid." Peter smiled.

Grady reached into his pocket and produced a five-dollar tip.

"Thank you, Sir. I will be here tomorrow at nine-fifteen. If you would like to see the city or go somewhere tonight, here is my card." Peter told Grady. He handed a bent, somewhat dirty white card to Grady, and turned on his heel to leave.

"He's a taxi, according to this card." Grady showed it to Katy as they walked down the hall.

"I thought he worked for the government," Katy said, as Dorothy opened the door to the first room.

"So did I," Grady affirmed.

"This is your room, Miss." Dorothy had picked up Katy's bag and now carried it into the room. Katy followed her in. "I will have lunch ready for you on the deck in thirty minutes if that is all right for you both?"

Katy nodded, and Grady replied, "Yes, thank you," from the hallway.

Dorothy came out of Katy's room and said, "This way, Sir, to your room." She headed down the hall just one door away.

. . .

Robert and Tracie arrived shortly before two. Mary Whiston met the plane and quickly introduced herself to Tracie. She joined them on the ride to Crimson House.

"You and Mr. Carlton are staying at Crimson House, along with Colonel Barlow and Lt. Davies." She told them. "I am staying at the hotel with the yacht owners."

"Yacht owners?" Tracie asked.

"We aren't calling them 'victims.' Yacht owner is a term they have in common and like. No one, to my knowledge, is thinking of taking legal action, but it seemed best to keep everything in a positive vein. I'm sure that will be covered more completely tomorrow in one of the meetings. I don't think anyone knows who the bad guys were, so we're trying to put that into the background," explained Mary.

"Yes, it's early to speculate," Robert stated. He and Mary went over the next day's schedule as they rode.

The jostling speed of the van made it hard to talk. With the sudden turns, stops, and acceleration, Robert found the only comfortable position was sitting straight and looking forward. Tracie was gripping his leg with white knuckles as their driver swung around people, animals and obstacles at raceway speeds.

When the van finally stopped in front of a house, Robert opened the door and got out quickly, helping Tracie out with a steadying hand.

"Welcome to St. Thomas. I am Dorothy, and you must be Mr. and Mrs. Carlton. I am glad to see you here." Dorothy had come out to greet them as soon as she'd heard the van. Her warm smile after the frenetic taxi ride was instantly calming. "Johnny, can you bring the bags?" She asked the driver. "Please, come in," she urged Tracie and Robert, holding the door open.

Mary stepped out of the van behind them and followed Dorothy inside.

Grady and Katy walked in from the deck to meet Robert and Tracie.

"Deputy Attorney General Robert Carlton, I believe you've met Lieutenant Katherine Davies, but Mrs. Carlton, please allow me to introduce you to each other," Grady intoned formally.

Katy extended her hand, as did Robert and Tracie.

"Lieutenant, it's nice to see you again. I hope you'll call me Robert when we're not in meetings." Robert wanted to set a more informal tone.

Tracie chimed in immediately with, "and please call me Tracie."

Katy smiled, and told them, "I'm Katy. I'm happy to save the titles for the meetings."

"And this is Mary Whiston," Robert said, noticing Mary standing in the background. "She works in our Office of International Affairs. As a member of my OIA team, she's responsible for the Florida and Caribbean region." Introductions and handshakes moved around the group again, with Grady acknowledging that he remembered Mary.

As soon as names had been exchanged, Grady chimed in, "I'm sure Dorothy is anxious to show you your room. You probably would like a few minutes to get oriented after the flight. Katy and I will be on the deck, whenever you're done. Dorothy told us she already has dinner planned for the four of us."

"That sounds delightful," Tracie answered before Robert could speak. "I'd love a little time to freshen up."

Mary spoke next. "We have our first meeting at nine-thirty tomorrow morning, with local officials. They have a man coming to pick you up at nine-fifteen."

"Thank you, Mary. Everything looks well organized. We will see you tomorrow." Robert shook her hand. He noticed that Grady looked puzzled, and added, "Mary is staying at the hotel with the yacht owners."

"Oh, then we'll see you tomorrow." Grady grinned at Mary who smiled broadly back.

"Yes, Sir." She said. She turned and headed toward the van. Johnny opened the door for her and then hopped in. The van sped away.

"May I show you your room, now?" Dorothy inquired. Dorothy had one of Tracie's bags in hand. Robert grabbed her second and his own.

"That one is yours," he nodded to Grady, who picked up his bug out bag right away.

"Thanks. See you in a minute." Grady offered.

"Yes, I'll be right back." Robert trailed after Dorothy and Tracie.

. . .

At first, the conversation between Robert, Grady, and Katy was stiff and formal. Tracie came out onto the deck about fifteen minutes later, looking fresh and relaxed. She joined in their discussion about the yacht owners. The conversation gradually lightened up, as the beautiful view and reflections of the setting sun over the bay began to relax the group.

Dorothy's drinks added to the mood. As it turned out, Dorothy was an excellent bartender. Her specialty was a local version of rum punch with lots of spices. By the time dinner was being set up on the deck, the four of them were laughingly discussing their taxi rides.

"Well, however crazy your driver was, wait until you get in Peter's van!" Grady told Tracie. "He's coming to get us—you'll want to close your eyes the whole way," Grady warned her, chuckling.

"I'd almost rather walk," Katy added, smiling.

"If he is worse than Johnny, I think I would rather walk, too! Any chance we can talk him into slowing down, or is that against island rules?" Tracie asked, laughing. They all joined in when Robert made a comment about asking Dorothy for Bloody Marys in the morning, to dull their nerves.

Katy was quickly shedding her 'all business' military stiffness, much to Grady's relief. Tracie dropped her role as queen bee,

Robert noticed gratefully, as he eased into enjoying Grady's gregarious nature. Grady had them all laughing when he told the story about his and Katy's limbo experience.

Before dinner, Katy had excused herself to change into vacation attire. Her conservative white dress was hanging dry. Dorothy had miraculously taken care of that somehow when Katy had asked about cleaning it, worried about what she'd wear the next day. She and Tracie had already decided that they would go shopping at the first opportunity.

Grady's bug out bag had a set of blues, with two shirts and ABU fatigues. It also held hats, boots, shoes, belts, and decorations. He was set.

Katy shared her concerns about not having her uniform, but the group decided that her title would alleviate any confusion. Tracie felt that the fact Katy had been on vacation might help connect her to the yacht owners more significantly. She told Katy that they might relate better to someone authoritative, but who could understand their position from the tourist point of view.

When their dinner plates arrived, they were thrilled. The food looked fantastic and smelled wonderful. There was grilled grouper, local root vegetables, lots of fruits, and a sauce that everyone liked but no one could describe. The island breeze was cooler now, keeping the bugs to a minimum. The frogs came out, singing so loudly that they sent the group into a new wave of laughter. Despite the seductive tropical air, the tired group decided to call it an early evening.

In the room, Tracie continued to be talkative. She rattled on about the scenery, food, what she was planning to do while they were on the island, and her planned shopping.

Robert listened to less than half of what she said. He was thinking about the upcoming meetings. The lack of definition of the work needed had him distracted.

"So, will we have time to shop?" Tracie asked for the second time.

"What?" Robert snapped back to what she was saying. "Yes, I'm sure you will. I don't know the complete schedule, yet, but I'm sure there will be some down time for you." Robert figured that was a safe bet.

"Do you have any idea what I'm supposed to do?" Tracie wanted to fill in the blanks. She intended to enjoy as much of this trip as possible.

"I could use your help in the meetings," Robert told her.

"Really?" Tracie was surprised, and pleased. Robert usually didn't involve her in his job.

"Yes. This is new ground for me. I want you, Grady, and Katy to join me in the meetings to observe, and to help these people see that their experience is being taken seriously. Keep track of what you're seeing and hearing, and give me some feedback when we're not with officials or the yacht owners. You might very well spot some issues that I won't, since I'll be considering the US responsibilities, rather than the individuals' reactions. You can discover where we can best help, and add value." Robert waited to see if that idea floated well with Tracie.

"Of course," Tracie answered, "I'm happy to do that, but isn't the discussion mainly going to be surrounding legal issues?"

"Some of it will be legal discussions," Robert agreed, "but a lot of this is about diplomatically smoothing a path. Think of what you hear as baseline information. We need to find out where we stand, and what everyone is thinking. We don't want mixed messages coming from secondhand information."

"When we meet the players individually we will know what pieces are missing, and we'll work on filling them in." He continued, "I know this sounds very generalized, but nobody seems to have a lot of information about this situation. I think Secretary Vance is right. We need this to be about helping the yacht owners get home safely, or wherever they want to go, and not focus on the victim aspect. It's like when the boys fell down when they were little; if we made a big deal out of it, they cried. If we laughed and helped them up, they usually went back to playing."

"Robert," Tracie said, looking skeptical, "I think this is more serious than a skinned knee."

"You're right," he responded. "and I don't mean to minimize the yacht owners' experience, but we want to find out what may be still bothering them about it, and deal with that, rather than escalate the situation. You're a good listener, and you understand diplomacy. You deal with the problem of interpreting dignitaries' interests all the time. If you can help us find out what these people have actual concerns about, we can move on without creating a further international incident."

"Hmmm." Tracie was still skeptical. "I'm going to take a shower," she said suddenly. Off she went.

Robert knew that by morning Tracie would overcome her concerns by immersing herself in the importance of her role. It would have to be defined her way, but she'd come through with flying colors.

. . .

On the other side of the house, Grady and Katy were already in their beds. Grady lay staring at the ceiling in the dark. His room had a small rock patio with flowering bushes of Hibiscus, and a large Flamboyant tree hanging over the top. He'd sat out on the patio for a few minutes, enjoying the night air, but eventually had decided to get some sleep. He thought about Katy and wondered if she was glad she'd agreed to come.

Katy had opened the window to hear the breeze ruffle the leaves, but was only getting more frog peeps, grunts, and chirps. Her room opened onto a private balcony with a partial view, two chairs, and a small table. She could see the east side of Charlotte Amalie and some of the harbor, but not quite as far as the cruise ship docks—which was a nice omission. The lights reflecting off the water were magical as she lay looking at them.

Katy sighed. She didn't know whether to be glad or sorry that their vacation had been cut short. She questioned whether Grady was glad she was on this trip as she turned out her light.

Chapter 22

Morning came early for Max and Luca. Luca's hand slid softly down Max's back to awaken her. A glistening sunrise was pouring through the skylight in the bedroom, reminding them of tasks to be accomplished.

Luca insisted that Max have the bathroom to herself. She found every toiletry she needed in the oversized, sparkling clean space. After emerging from the warm shower, she discovered an espresso and croissant sitting on a black lacquer tray. Next to the tray sat her bright blue bag, which Luca had retrieved from the car.

Max smiled. This was a man to her liking.

Max pulled on the bathrobe, brushed her hair back, and headed to the small balcony to sit and enjoy her breakfast. Luca grinned as he passed her, heading in to take his shower.

With her feet up on the low balcony wall, the warm robe over her legs, and a strong espresso shot in her hand, Max could almost imagine that she was on vacation. She needed to move on with her day, so she hopped up, and returned to the bedroom. Luca was coming out of the bathroom, fresh, clean, and smelling fantastic. He wore black drawstring silk pajama bottoms. His lightly furred chest was bare and his smile broad.

"Buon giorno," he told her, grinning.

"Buon giorno," Max answered back. "You make excellent espresso," she told him.

"I am delighted to make anything for one so beautiful as you, Maxine," Luca said, walking toward her meaningfully.

"Luca, you are far too enticing, and far too handsome," Max sighed, coming closer to him. She let her robe fall open, the tie dropping to the sides as her body was exposed.

Luca was enjoying gazing at her naked form as he drew near her. His hands glided into the robe, traveling slowly down to the rise below the small of her back. Firmly squeezing her strong glutes, he let his fingers splay downward over the smooth skin.

Max placed her hands on his chest, squeezing. Her nails dug in just a little as she looked into his eyes. At this distance, his two-inch advantage in height felt taller. She rose up on her toes as his hands slid gradually around her legs.

Their bodies merged together. Max pushed her arms up to wrap around his shoulders, touching his neck, her breasts pressing into him.

"We seem to be at cross-purposes if we are going to do work today," Max murmured with a devilish grin.

"Yes, we have much work to do, but there is time," Luca reassured her.

"I admit that would be nice, but it will have to be later." Max pulled away, tying her robe.

Luca gave her the right look of disappointment, followed by a grin. "Later, then it must be," he said, reaching for her hand.

Max turned away quickly. "Later," she insisted. "First we have to get to the other harbor. I want to make sure the angle is right." She was all business, now, as she walked toward her clothes and bent to pick up her blouse. Looking over her shoulder she saw Luca gaze longingly at her bare bottom. "Later," she said again, dragging the word out as she walked by him to the bathroom and closed the door.

Luca noticed the bra and panties left on the floor. Max had a way of making a business day fun.

. . .

They sped along the freeway to the Arland D. Williams, Jr. Memorial Bridge to D.C.

"I'd like to see the view from this side," Max pointed, indicating the water view drive that circumnavigated the East Potomac Park

Golf Course. As part of the recreation center and on the same island as the Jefferson Memorial, the course had an unobstructed view of the yacht harbor and the Gangplank Marina.

Luca stopped the car after exiting to put the top down on the Alfa. Max watched as he walked back around the car. His tight jeans and flair-collared black shirt showed off his fitness and his Mediterranean good looks. Luca's heavy eyebrows lifted each time he looked toward Max, his white teeth shining above his strong dimpled chin.

The breeze felt wonderfully relaxing to Max on this unseasonably warm day. The temperature excited her skin. She wore a tight, bright blue crop top with six closely set buttons up the front. She'd left the top two undone. Her midriff was bare down to her hips. A gathered white skirt gave her body more curve. The skirt ended an inch above her knees. Her sandals were lying next to her bare feet in the car.

Luca drove slowly, below the posted twenty-five mph limit, past the bare trees. The Cherry blossoms wouldn't be popping for another three weeks, even with this unusual weather. The barren trees provided a less obstructed look at the yacht docks on the far side. Max took in the view, noting details. When they came to the end of the divided road, Ohio Drive became one-way in their favor.

"Let's go around the golf course." It was cooler out on the island. Max reached forward to turn on the heater. Luca continued the slow cruising speed.

As they rode, Max started pointing out the remaining features of the harbor. "That is the cantina you mentioned, the Titanic memorial, and that's Fort McNair."

"Si. Yes," Luca glanced back at the road. His peripheral vision caught Max pulling her seatbelt to the side, and loosening the third button on her top.

"So, that would be the Officer's Club, right there on the water?" Max was enjoying the tourist role.

"Si, and that is the National Defense University behind it. The last building is the War College." Another button opened on Max's top, offering a deeper glimpse.

"And across that river is Bolling Air Force base?" Another button was undone. The seatbelt pressed her breast from the far side, accentuating her cleavage. They passed a few more trees, and the last button surrendered to her touch. Max pulled the crop top a bit farther under the seat belt, providing a wider gap.

Max was enjoying herself. She could tell that Lucas' excitement was rising as they played their game. By the time they rounded Hains Point, both sides of the blouse were wide apart, barely concealing the tips of her breasts. Occasional gusts of wind that came across the car would lift the material away on her left side. Pulling the seatbelt off her shoulder and down her arm, Max gave the breeze an opportunity to play with the cloth on both sides. It wafted over her nipples, bringing them to exaggerated excitement. Luca drove even slower.

On this side of the island, there was little to look at over the water, excepting Ronald Reagan Washington National Airport, so the golf course became the view of choice. Luca had ample opportunity for glancing often at Max.

"Have you played here?" Max asked, her tone sounding distracted as the reversal of direction changed the breeze in the car. It lifted her top completely off her chest. She calmly placed it back to barely cover her nipples. The shoulder strap rubbed against her, so she tucked it under her elbow.

"Yes, it is a marvelous course to play." Luca had to force himself to look forward enough to stay on the road.

With a gentle pull, Max raised the hem of her dress. "At night?"

"No, they lock the gates when it is dark," Luca informed her.

She pulled the hem up farther, exposing most of her thighs. The sun flashing through the trees felt alternatingly warm and cold.

Luca pointed out that they were approaching the end of the one-way road section. "Would you like to go around again for a second look?"

"No, that was enough for now." Max pulled her dress down and began buttoning her top. "I need to see the marina."

Luca looked disappointed, squirming slightly in his tight jeans.

"Later." She said with a wink.

Luca pulled over and put the top back up on the car. The trip around to the Gangplank Marina was quick, but the view from the car didn't tell Max much.

"You've made arrangements?" Max asked Luca.

"Si. I have received tentative approval for one transient dockage, but we will not know the slip until one week before. The second dockage has not been confirmed, but I believe they will consent to a second week. The length is no problem. Also, the Woodrow Wilson bridge remodel is done, and needs no advance notice or radio call for boats less than sixty-five feet tall."

"Excellent work." Max was pleased. "I want to take a look at the agency's dock. How close can you get us?"

"You may step on it if you wish."

"You can get us on the base?" Max asked, lifting her eyebrows.

"Yes. I am a student with a project at the center. You can be my guest." Luca answered, smiling at her startled look.

"Seriously? You're a student?" Luca had been assigned all elements of their assignment on the D.C. and Maryland side, but this show of initiative surprised even Max.

"Graduate student. I enrolled in a Master's class. American schools are easy to enroll. They think only of money. Our job should be finished before I need to pass a difficult examination."

Luca has skills, Max thought. In more ways than one, she added to herself.

At the base guard shack, they had to enter the check-in building. Each of them had the standard necessary driver's license. Luca's student card got them approval at the desk, enabling them to sign in. Security was not tight. Visitors were common at the Naval Research Center. Security was controlled by section. Entry depended on "need," and the work being done. Max and Luca were authorized for unescorted entry to presentation and demonstration rooms, as was common in most publicly funded Washington D.C. buildings, and allowed to walk around the main courtyard buildings.

Luca explained that his professor could take them into the lab if she wished, but his project there was unrelated. Inside were some very secure areas he could not enter, and the rest of the base had many sections one could not drive to. Little of that mattered. Max just wanted to get a closer look at the surroundings, and the barge.

The building where Luca had classes was not far from "The Dish" mounted atop the main landmark building. It was a short walk, following the path around the dish building. A gate prevented going far out on the pier, but Max could step on part of the dock.

"So, that is SuperMISTI." Neither made further comment. They both knew how important it could be.

<u>Chapter 23</u>

Robert got up early, showered, and dressed. He wore his shirt and tie, but with the warm island air, he decided to leave the jacket off as long as possible. Leaving the room, he kept quiet to avoid waking Tracie. She would be up after ten minutes or so, denying he had awakened her, but she'd be in a better mood if she had the room to herself.

"Morning, Mr. Deputy Attorney General." Grady's cheerful countenance looked up from a cup of coffee. He held the local paper and had a wedge of equally local looking bread on his plate. "Dorothy makes a great cup of coffee."

"Good morning, Sir." Dorothy chimed in from the kitchen. The open concept layout of the house made her preparations visible. "Would you like coffee?"

"Yes, please." Robert should have been used to Grady's early rising, but he'd been surprised to see him.

As Robert pulled out a chair across from Grady, Dorothy put coffee and bread in front of him.

"Would you like milk for your coffee?" Dorothy asked.

"Yes, and sugar," Robert added. Dorothy set them before him almost instantly. He selected two brown, raw looking lumps, and dropped them into his cup, and poured a little milk on top of them. "You're up early," he commented to Grady. "Did you get a good sleep?"

"I had trouble at first," Grady admitted. "Darn frogs made a racket. You?"

"Crashed as soon as my head hit the pillow," Robert responded.

"Morning," Katy announced sunnily, coming from the hall. She was quickly situated with coffee and more of the local bread. "Thank you, Dorothy," she said, gratefully taking the coffee cup in hand.

"Tracie won't be out for a while. If you want to get caught up, we can chat." Robert hadn't yet drifted into the "island time" pace. He felt they should have a pre-meeting, but after ten minutes they'd covered everything they knew. The conversation reverted to coffee, points of interest, the view, and frogs.

"Good morning!" Tracie emerged from the bedroom. This had to be a record for her, Robert thought. She must have jumped out of bed the second he'd left the room. She looked great, but Robert could tell that she'd decided to take a lighter approach to her makeup and hair.

At the greeting from Tracie, Dorothy swung into action. As soon as she delivered Tracie's bread and coffee, Dorothy began cooking omelets, cutting fresh fruit, and toasting bread to pair with nutmeg jelly.

"This is wonderful." Tracie proclaimed, holding her chunk of local bread up. "What is it?"

"Sweet coconut dumb bread." Dorothy smiled. "I get it at Daylight Bakery."

"Wonderful. Robert, we have to take some of this home with us." Tracie was in rare form, happily partaking of each of Dorothy's offerings.

They took their time over the filling breakfast, drinking more coffee, and enjoying the breeze from the open windows and doors. Robert had not felt this relaxed in a long time.

Dorothy quickly went to answer a knock at the door.

"Nine-o-Five," Robert announced to the group. The morning was progressing quickly.

Dorothy closed the door and came to the table. "Mr. Carlton, Peter, your driver has arrived. He apologizes for being early. There is no rush. May I get anyone more coffee?" Her relaxed and pleasant demeanor made the morning feel like a vacation in itself.

"Yes, please." Grady was the only one to grab more coffee as the others quickly got up to collect items from their rooms for the day.

The van was reasonably clean, rust free, and spacious. Grady opened the sliding door, but got in first to take the awkward back seat, followed by Katy. Robert helped Tracie into the forward row and Peter closed the door.

Peter again talked through the entire ride, pointing out buildings and vistas that they whizzed past in a blur. His unpredictable swerving to avoid potholes, or the occasional local leading a donkey, jostled their previously settled breakfast. The quick turns, honking horns, left-sided driving, and near misses kept his passengers quiet. Peter barreled through the narrow streets without taking a breath between comments. Everyone held their shoulder straps tightly in one hand, and whatever else could provide some stability with the other.

Arriving at the Ron de Lugo Federal Building, the van stopped in a shuddering halt, leaving them all with a burning desire to exit as quickly as possible.

Mary Whiston stood next to Mia Rodriguez from the governor's office, smiling. They waited on the stone steps, anxious to greet the group.

Robert had put on his jacket before the ride and now felt hot and sticky. Katy looked impossibly cool wearing her white dress, washed and dried, thanks to Dorothy. Grady seemed a little warm in his Air Force blues, but Tracie was completely composed in a sky-blue dress, ornamented with pearls, white and blue heeled sandals, and an elegant sunshade hat.

"Good morning Mr. Carlton, Mrs. Carlton, Colonel Barlow, and Lieutenant Davies." Mia greeted them each in turn. "Welcome. I am Mia Rodriquez, Assistant to the Governor." She handed each an itinerary. The first morning meeting was still listed at nine-thirty. The rest of the schedule had completely changed.

"The first meeting is all together," Mia explained. "Lunch is also together at the Governor's mansion. Afterward, Ms. Whiston and I will rejoin you, Mr. Carlton, at the Capitol for a meeting with our Attorney General. Officers Barlow and Davies will meet with the Port Authority Director, and the Coast Guard Commander."

Tracie squeezed Robert's hand, making him turn toward her, but before she could ask about her role, Mia spoke again.

"Mrs. Carlton, the Governor's wife has asked if you could join her while the others are in their meetings. Would that be all right?"

"Yes, of course," Tracie answered, pleased. Her grip eased on Robert's hand.

. . .

The morning was a whirlwind of fast talking. Everything in the meeting was a recap of completed tasks. All of the passports, papers, and boat registry issues had been handled. As it was explained, the boat owners had no complications from local or federal issues and were free to go as soon as they pleased. Their individual driver's licenses, insurance cards, and charge cards were in various states of pending replacement, which was a minor hold-up. As for their financial needs, the bureau of tourism had offered each boat owner a two-thousand dollar, zero interest loan to cover expenses. All but one of the owners had an eastern Caribbean bank account, so the loans were easy to establish.

The Hotel Owners' Association was taking care of all the hotel fees and meals for the yacht owners. A regional airline had provided the transportation to St. Thomas. There was no doubt that the tourism association was doing their best to provide a positive outcome to the difficulties the owners had faced.

Robert and his entourage felt that this was a promising start for their "good will" trip. They loaded up in the van, holding their collective breaths for the trip to the Governor's Mansion. Peter pulled in front of a truck without signaling and hit the gas. The truck didn't even honk. All of this seemed to be normal driving for the area—every driver was behaving similarly.

Peter rapidly explained that the Governor did not live at the mansion, but instead lived at Estate Catherineberg on Denmark Hill, St. John island. Between Peter's driving and fast-paced talking, Robert missed most of the story, but it had something to do with the building, fungus, and contaminated water at the mansion.

"Our Governor is a great man. You will have a marvelous lunch. And here we are," Peter finished. The brakes vibrated a little as they came to an abrupt stop next to Government House. It had been a very short drive.

"Thank you, Peter." Robert managed to say as they exited onto the hot sidewalk. The sun was beating down on the road and three-story building in front of them. Ten massive front steps rose above their heads like a wide pyramid. Down the center the stairs were carpeted in burgundy on both sides of a white rail. Robert had to crane his neck to look up at the front of the large square building.

The first two floors had full-length covered balconies, railed in white wrought iron. The entire building was white, with many evenly spaced windows, each having a cornice and shutters. The structure was impressive. Its bright red guard post to the side made the building look royal. The architecture spoke of the building's Dutch colonial plantation history, while also reminding Robert of a New Orleans hotel.

"Welcome to Government House." The man coming down the tall steps wore a white shirt, black pants, and dull black shoes. "May I escort you to your luncheon?" The man offered.

Murmuring their assent, they followed him. He began walking and talking, giving them the details of the building.

"Government House was built in 1867. It is neoclassical in design and constructed of brick and wood. You will notice that the many pieces inside, including the staircases, are made of local mahogany. Less than a block west are the famous 99 Steps, which if you have time, should not be missed." He carried on, imparting more details to the foursome.

They passed through the main lobby, which was open to the public. The man ushered them into an adjoining room that contained a large round table set up for lunch.

"Welcome, my friends!" The Governor and his wife entered from an opposite doorway. The Governor's lively manner and bright smile projected warmth and a politician's congeniality. After introductions had been made he told them, "Lunch is ready, so please, let us begin eating. We can discuss any questions you might have during our meal."

Lunch went well, with the Governor only lightly touching on the nine citizens and their ordeal. He made no direct requests, but it was clear that he wanted the incident to disappear unnoticed by the world, in an effort to protect tourism. Instead, he focused on how willing he was to help in any way that Robert might find necessary. He spoke about how cooperative the various countries and islands had been, and emphasized their common goal to clear up any problems swiftly.

Once the Governor had established this position, the conversation shifted to commerce, tourism, history, and culture. The Governor gave them some facts and figures on tourism, then delved into the history of the islands, and how the culture had developed. He finished with a few entertaining tales of historical figures' visits, and of 17th century pirates.

At the conclusion of their lunch, the Governor departed for another meeting. Robert, Grady, and Katy re-boarded the van for the trip to the capitol. Tracie was swept away by the Governor's wife, who seemed to immediately form a connection to her. Robert was not particularly comfortable with Tracie being separated from the group, but he was assured that they would be reunited at the dinner planned for the evening.

Reaching the Capitol Building, also known as the Legislature Building, they were given a quick tour, then split for their various meetings. Robert, with Mary in tow, prepared for his meeting with the Attorney General, while Grady and Katy went to meet the Port Authority and Coast Guard commander.

"Do we have any legal issues to contend with?" Robert asked Mary, as they headed to their meeting room.

"One boat had a handgun onboard," Mary told him. "They had traveled through two territories that disallow this, but no charges have been made. One boat had a life ring retention line that was connected incorrectly but corrected by the inspector, and one boat had paperwork issues that can be corrected by the owner within ninety days." These were listed on Mary's file notes. "The authorities are treating these as minor, and have waived any charges or penalties."

"Why are the yacht owners still here?" Robert wanted to know. "I know that some are waiting for credit card replacements, but those can usually be overnight mailed. Are we having trouble getting their passports reissued? I thought that was taken care of."

Mary consulted her notes. "Looks like they're waiting for a couple of issues with their boats to be worked out. I'm not completely sure what the problems may be. This paperwork indicates this should all be taken care of in another day or two."

Mary had melded well with the local team. She and Mia, except for her pale complexion versus Mia's brown skin, could have been sisters. They looked alike, dressed similarly, and had bonded instantly. Mary wore sensible shoes with a one-inch heel, and a plain dark blue skirt and jacket with a simple white-collared shirt. She ornamented the look with a thin silver necklace, a silver watch, and a Loyola Law School ring. Mia looked almost the same, substituting a round-necked white blouse for Mary's shirt, and gold accessories. Both their round figures were minimized by the suits.

"I'd like to see the owners on their way before we leave." Robert frowned. "If we're going to keep this thing low-key it would be best to get them back on their boats and headed out. Let me know if there's anything we need to do to speed that along. Is there anything I should be aware of before we meet with the Attorney General?"

"Don't talk politics or elections," Mary warned. "I've gathered that neither is stable here. Their office is a mess right now, and the AG is new to the position."

"Really? What's the problem?" Robert glanced toward Mia, who was standing within earshot.

"It's all over the Internet," Mary said. "So, it's hard to tell what is true and what is just blogging, but Mia mentioned that there's been a lot of discord. Seems best to avoid anything remotely connected with the problems, at this time."

"Okay." Robert thought for a moment. "Then we'll let him lead the conversation, and see where it takes us."

They walked down the hall the remaining few yards and passed through the open reception room doors.

"Mr. Deputy Attorney General. It is an honor." The Attorney General of the US Virgin Islands was standing in the entry, welcoming Robert. "Come, let's talk." He opened his office door, adjoining the reception room, and in they went.

Robert sat across the desk from the Attorney General, while Mary and Mia were relegated to a small couch at the side of the room. Robert listened to the rundown of possible legal entanglements the AG's staff had been concerned would arise, but the cooperation of the islands had allowed these to be quickly handled. The potential problems vanished, leaving no legal issues. The AG was as determined as the Governor to keep the incident low in profile. No jurisdiction was pressing for hearings, fines, or impeding the yacht owners' ability to leave whenever it was convenient. Robert didn't have to say much. The Attorney General had his statements clear in his mind. This meeting was simply to assure the U.S. that there was no need for action. Mary stayed silent, as did Mia.

Dispensing with the tourist case, the AG turned to issues that concerned the islands. Robert listened and took notes, but the list was typical of any state. Essentially, the AG wanted the feds to stay away from local issues.

Robert seldom visited states, leaving this type of trip to his boss. Politics were Jack's domain, and this was certainly required political side-stepping. He parried the AG's requests with statements of, "We'll certainly take that into consideration and look this all over."

The meeting was over in less than forty minutes. Robert left to go find Grady and Katy, with Mary and Mia in tow. He discovered Grady ending a meeting with a uniformed Coast Guard officer. Katy joined them in the main lobby when she finished her meeting. Led by Mia, they stopped for a quick peek into the Legislature room, then exited by the side facing the harbor.

The spectacular view of the harbor from the double stairway entrance reminded them that they were on a tropical island. Finding that none of them had action items, they took a moment to absorb the view of the water, the green hills beyond the anchored sailboats, and the shore battery cannon.

The cannon had been a necessity back in 1828 when the building had been built for the Danish police, but now it was decorative history. Somehow it gave the harbor a distinctive pirate feeling, as though the skull and crossbones should be flying on a nearby brigantine.

"The United States bought the Virgin Islands from Denmark in 1917 for twenty-five million, in gold coin," Mia told them, after describing the color green that had originally adorned the white and yellow building.

"Fits right in with the pirate doubloons theme, doesn't it? What do you think? Was it a good buy?" Grady asked Robert, over the noise of squawking seagulls.

"Did you pick up on why we wanted to buy it?" Robert found himself mildly curious.

Katy chimed in at that point, "It had to do with securing the Caribbean. The Lusitania was sunk in 1915 and there were concerns Germany might annex Denmark. This whole area of the Dutch West Indies could have become a sub base."

"It was all done under a treaty. President Woodrow Wilson orchestrated it," Mia added.

"Did you know he was born in Staunton, Virginia? I visited there one fall to see the leaves. Great little town," Grady was enjoying the history lesson.

"What's next on our agenda?" Robert asked, thinking that it was time to move on. They all pulled out their pages.

"That was it for me until dinner." Grady folded the paper and put it back in his small notebook.

"My schedule is the same as Grady's," Katy added. "I'm free for the next several hours."

"I am on your schedule," Mary told Robert, meaning she was at his disposal.

"Mine says dinner at six." Robert put his paper back in the valise "That gives us three hours."

"I could use more to wear." Katy had done well through the day without a uniform, but with only one reasonably suitable outfit, her situation was going to get awkward.

"Actually, I could, too. I think the uniform is overkill from here out, but my resort wear might be a little too casual." Grady's uniform had helped set the stage for the first meeting, but seemed a bit pushy once introductions had been made and the initial ground covered.

"Right. Where do they need to go?" Robert turned to Mary.

"I only know the tourist shops," She said, turning toward Mia.

"Mia, is there a mall around here?" Robert asked.

"We have many malls, and plenty of shops," Mia told them, smiling.

"I also need something nice for tonight's dinner," Katy added.

"Mia," Robert suddenly had a thought, "can you tell me where my wife is?"

"She and the Governor's wife are already shopping," Mia said and began walking in the direction of Peter's van, parked nearby. "We'll avoid the places where the cruise ships go. Those shops have t-shirts, jewelry, swimsuits, and liquor. Those sorts of things. Very good prices, but I know a few places where you can find nice clothes that are more suitable. Some of the hotels have nice shops that we could go to, but they tend to be expensive."

"Let's try the places you know, Mia," Katy stated, worrying about her budget.

"Let's get going, then." Mia took charge and herded them toward the van. Robert realized that he was going along for the ride.

Shopping was a confusing experience. Peter offered his usual barrage of information and advice, but Mia took charge. They visited some island style malls but had their best luck at some boutiques that were located along the principal streets of Dronningens Gade, Royal Dane Mall, and Palm Passage. Soon enough they were well equipped for the evening and the next day.

With bags in hand, Robert, Grady and Katy headed back to Crimson House to change.

Chapter 24

On the tiny island eight men sat in shade, where they could find it. The small house was not much more than a hut. It was crammed with eight cots, and the supplies that couldn't survive sun or rain. Insects harassed the men day and night. The worst were the no-see-ums; tiny biting midges that attacked incessantly. Their supplies had not included bug spray, an unfortunate oversight. Islanders rarely used the spray, but the men waiting for the boat to come and take them to their next job wished they had some.

The boat was late.

The euphoria of the first night had dissipated by sundown of the second day. By the evening of the third day arguments broke out, fueled by fear, and too much rum. The two men given the task of scuttling the launch hadn't returned. They should have been back by the first morning. Motor trouble could explain the delay, but now they knew something had happened. If those men had run away they would all be in trouble when the Russian arrived and found out. Even if those men had drowned, how would the men on the island prove that to the Russian? What if they'd been caught? How long would it be before the police arrived at the island? The men argued about their fate and the consequences.

Uncertainty clouded the long, boring hours. Each day had dawned with higher tensions and irritability. The food tasted bad. Water ran low. The rum was no longer satisfying.

Today they waited again. Now eight nights and nine days had passed since they were dropped off. The boat to take them to the next job should have arrived after seven. Only one ship had been sighted, and it had been far away at night, its lights shining along the edge of the horizon.

The waiting was hard. The uncertainty was worse, but there was more. Blisters. They all had blisters and they were becoming unbearable. Every one of them had blisters on their feet. They appeared on half the men the third day. Some had popped by the fourth, leaving tender under-skin that oozed clear liquid, or cracked and bled. Most of them could barely walk now. Their ankles were swollen, and the skin on their legs showed red blotchy sores. Hands had become increasingly puffy, sore and painful to bend. Even simple tasks, like making food, were so painful that only three could still manage it. Four men were dizzy and light-headed, unable to stand. Two had what seemed to be severe sunburn on their faces and blisters on their lips. Both those men had trouble seeing clearly, and their eyelids brought pain with every blink.

The men didn't know that they had radiation poisoning. They were all showing symptoms of radiation dermatitis.

Beneath the sand by the deck, the broken sealed source was exposing them to powdered Cesium-137. The explosive charge had distributed most of the radioactive powder into the sand. The Cesium powder stuck to the small particles. The remaining portion of Cesium in the container was slowly working its way upward and out.

Each time the men walked through the sand to the deck, they kicked up the fine dust. The more they walked through it, the more they came in direct contact with the Cesium. It burned more each time.

At first it attacked their bare feet directly, sticking to the soles, and riding on the tops of their toes. These blistered first. The beta rays from the Cesium traveled only a short distance, but easily penetrated their skin and soft tissue. The gamma rays traveled much farther. Those penetrated through their entire bodies, even making their way through bone. The men who were the worst off were those who slept on the deck at night, avoiding the heat trapped in the hut. They'd moved their mattresses outside, placing their faces closer to the ground and the radioactive source. They inhaled more of the dust in the air, and they were near the source for more hours of the day.

The dose for every man was climbing. After the fourth day of pacing through the sand, they'd all had direct contact with the cesium powder. One man started throwing up on the seventh day.

The men didn't understand what was happening to them. They thought it was the fault of the sun, bugs, or food. Tempers ran high. They cursed the dwindling supply of water and fretted about the boat that did not come back. They hoped the Russian would soon appear on the horizon and take them to the next job. They ignored the two men lying on their cots, not eating, not sweating, and not drinking their ration of a small cup of water twice a day.

Now they were out of rum.

. . .

Vlad sat in a comfortable hotel on the southern edge of Key West, Florida. The distinctive Victorian building with its red roof, cream paint, and pale Florida-green trim had a nice pool, great views, and was within easy access to bars and restaurants.

He was glad to be away from the southern islands for a while. Their laissez-faire approach to work and life irritated him. The Americans here were only marginally better, but the volume of tourists kept the pace a bit faster.

Key West's small Boca Chica Key airport had been easy to use to get into the U.S. They were used to foreign tourists.

Not that he would have had any trouble elsewhere. His cover job was as regional sales manager of a multi-national textile and accessories company. The company was real and had existed for more than ten years. His true clients were only too happy to launder some of their money through the dozens of small manufacturers he represented. The sales were real, with real products, but the work was all on-line, requiring none of his time. He got paid commissions, they got quality products which they used or sold, and everyone got clean money. The legitimate multi-million-dollar business was run by dozens of people, so Vlad could make his special deliveries without encumbrances.

The moment Vlad arrived he'd contacted a Florida boat broker. The process was simple. He provided a list of features he was looking for in a boat, and the broker would find him some to consider.

It was common for clients to have models they already knew they liked. Vlad had his list. He told the broker that he had read an article talking about the best sailing yachts. The Gulfstar 39, Hunter 356 and Beneteau 423 had caught his eye.

Quality used boats were available from ninety to a hundred and fifty thousand dollars, depending on equipment and condition. Listings from all over the Caribbean, the US, and Europe existed on-line. "Carl," as Vlad called himself, simply did not have time to look for a boat. He traveled a lot, so he wanted the broker to search, provide pictures, and when the right yacht appeared, arrange for a professional inspection, plus delivery.

The broker was happy to provide these services. Communications would be via email and through Vlad's pre-paid Key West cell phone. The transaction would be completed with a wire transfer when the broker found the right boat.

Grabbing his valise, Vlad headed for the bar to meet with a local Key West yacht broker. The conversation was identical to the one he'd had with the Miami broker. His ID was different. Now he was named Rostislav, who used Ross as his American styled nickname. Ross was a man who made no effort to hide his Russian accent. He visited the Keys a lot on vacation and wanted to sail there in the spring and fall.

By the time Vlad had finished his drink, he had a folder of boat pages he could consider. The broker had the list of boats to find. Now he was covered even if two of the boats went up for sale—he could buy both without raising suspicion. Vlad could relax a little.

Walking down the warm sidewalk, he ignored the placards promising the best food or drink in town. Fake palm trees and another sweet tropical drink with fried conch were of no interest to him. He was going for good scotch and good fish. Vodka, his first choice, would be inferior regardless of brand. The best vodka never got exported from Russia, particularly to the US. He'd had enough of rum last month, and bourbon made no sense to his palate. Fish in Key West was acceptable. They knew how to catch and cook fresh fish.

The restaurant he chose was far from the tourists and their Hemmingway haunts, Jimmy Buffett cheeseburgers, and sunset animal acts. The tourists with their cell phone cameras and loud behavior were a risk, and annoying. He also needed a break from the humidity and heat rising off the concrete.

This place was what he wanted. Eight tables, four outside and four inside, formed the converted house's restaurant. It was hard to tell whether it had been converted last year, or back in the forties. Paint on wood in the Keys never lasted long, and the décor suffered from some ancient Caribbean time lag. Heat, humidity, and the smell of rotting plants seemed to be everywhere on this island, but the food smelled terrific here. There was a distinctive lack of deep frying oil at this place. Instead, he sensed paprika, basil, dill, and possibly nutmeg on the air. The owner assured him that the Dalmore 12 scotch would not disappoint, with its toasty, coffee-rich thick flavor. That, and a baked black grouper with mango chutney, made his evening.

He leaned back with another scotch and thick after-dinner cigar. There were advantages to an outdoor table and warm night air. Now and then he dipped the mouth end of the cigar in the scotch for flavor. He typed two texts into his phone. Each read, "Are you set? V." The answers came back a few minutes apart.

"Okay, L."

"Yes. M."

He sent a text to Alexi. "Ready for step 3. V."

. . .

Max and Luca sat on the balcony. The caramel mocha gelato they were eating followed smoothly behind their decadent meal of double chocolate stout beer, and takeout Philly cheesesteak sandwiches from Al's Steakhouse. In classic style, these were covered in cheese whiz, with mushrooms and peppers, but no onions, piled high on a huge Italian roll. The greasy wrappers skittered in the light breeze, threatening to slip off the balcony through the spindly iron railing. Max crushed them under her chair leg.

"That was perfect." She leaned back, savoring the last licks of smooth gelato.

"Si, it is strange but so good. You must show me Philly one day and we will get some cheese whiz," Luca told her.

"It squirts from a can," Max laughed.

"Can?" Luca was clearly perplexed.

"Some things are best kept a secret," Max answered, as her phone buzzed in her pocket. Moments later Luca's buzzed, too.

"It's him," Max said. "You answer first, then I will a little later."

Luca typed and sent, "Okay, L."

Max waited then sent, "Yes. M."

They sat in silence, finishing their beer.

"I guess it is all set, then," Max said after about five minutes. "Want to celebrate?" She began unbuttoning her blouse.

Chapter 25

The dinner with the island dignitaries and yacht owners was going very well. Tracie and the Governor's wife had hit it off, and even though the Governor had planned a very brief attendance, the couple stayed most of the evening.

If there was any uneasiness, it came from seeing the hands and faces of the yacht owners. Their skin was blotchy and showed red spots from bug bites. Their hands were covered with cuts and bandages. Robert could only imagine what the rest of their bodies might look like. Most had lost weight. It was an hour before Robert realized only one of them was drinking alcohol. They were under a doctor's orders to moderate. They ate carefully, avoiding some of the foods displayed.

"So, what do you think?" Robert asked Grady after pulling him aside. "What kind of feedback are you getting from the yacht owners?"

"Tons," Grady replied. "These sailor types are pretty stubborn. Outspoken, too. They're trying to get back their balance."

"I'm shocked at the positive attitudes, given their appearance. I expected—I don't know—better and worse, if you know what I mean." Robert told Grady. He wasn't sure how he'd thought they'd react, but he'd been surprised at their resilience.

"It is pretty amazing for non-military types," Grady agreed. "When Mark and Jeff were describing their captivity, it sounded bad. They must have had just enough food and water, or they'd be in worse shape. The injuries are all from bugs, scrapes, and self-inflicted from trying to escape. The unsanitary conditions should have made them sicker. I would have thought they'd all be suffering some serious infections."

"I guess we'll learn more, but clearly people are stronger than we think sometimes," Robert said, shaking his head. "I think we are in for some tough conversations tomorrow when they decide to hit us with the hard questions."

"Maybe, but those questions might not be what you might think." Grady took a sip of his rum runner. "One couple—those two," he gestured slightly with his drinking hand, "are selling their boat. They want a bigger one that sleeps three couples and plan to rent from now on instead of owning. They were leaning that way before this happened. That couple to their left is sailing their boat back to the US, side by side with the couple behind them. Their yachts arrived today, via the Coast Guard. The single guy is continuing his trip as planned. He's planning to fly to Saint Gertach, where his boat is still anchored, and keep sailing from there. The last couple might just stay around here, and finish their vacation in US territory."

"That's it?" Robert was astounded. "No lawsuits? Cameras, press, sweeping accusations?"

"Nope. I told you, they're stubborn and indomitable. As one told me, they feel pretty unsinkable. I think they understand the issues relatively well. International waters, no officials involved, and no pirates found. They realize there's no way to resolve this thing immediately, and all of them figure it's a one-off situation. They were wondering how often this happens and why there weren't warnings, but the officials here seem to have convinced them that it's a pretty rare event. I think these people are glad to have escaped with so little damage. They want assurances that it isn't going to happen to anyone else. So, the catch is that if it does they're likely to make their story public."

"I assume the officials have reassured them about that." Robert said, "if that's all we have to worry about, I'm amazed."

"Oh, one little thing," Grady added.

"Here it comes," Robert muttered. He knew this was all too good to be true. Grady had been saving the big punch. He knew it was going to be a tough one, whatever it was.

"The ones who are sailing back want a Coast Guard escort." Grady took a long sip of his rum runner, watching Robert's face.

. . .

When the sun poured through Robert's window in the morning, he groaned loudly. Tracie rolled over and pulled the sheet over her head. By the time Robert had climbed out of the shower and left the room in search of coffee, the household was up. Grady and Katy were enjoying the cool morning on the covered deck.

Breakfast started with the usual admiration of the view, food, and weather. Eventually the subject came back to the yacht owners.

"Indomitable group," Grady chimed in.

"We still have some issues to work out," Robert admitted. "I'm sure they are anxious to have this all behind them, both the local officials and the boat owners, but this seems rather lacking in preparation. It feels as though we're acting hastily." Robert would have liked to get some written agreements all around so that everyone's expectations were clear. Without something in writing, it seemed careless to simply allow everyone to walk away from the situation.

"Katy and I talked about the Coast Guard request last night," Grady interjected. "We don't see any way that that's going to happen, but I know for sure nothing could be done this quickly."

Katy nodded. "The best we could offer them is a clear set of instructions on what routes to Florida will give them consistent coverage by planes or ships that will be within range, and instructions on how best to contact them, or to get help."

"That's what I expected would be the case. I'm sure the Coast Guard has their hands full with drug smugglers, refugees, and overall security issues," Robert responded, sighing and rubbing his eyes.

"That's about the size of it." Katy continued, "Realistically, it's impractical to cover two slow sailboats over a long stretch of water. Planes and helicopters can respond in anywhere between 15 minutes and a few hours, depending on how close they are. That area is well covered with surface ships, and it's very unlikely that these people would have two such incidents, or that they'd actually require Coast Guard assistance if they stay in the typical tourist zones."

"So, it's definite that only two sets of owners are sailing home?" Robert wanted to verify exactly who would be where.

Tracie jumped in with that answer. "Jim and Caroline are selling their boat, and flying back to Miami tomorrow. Jeff, Chrystal, Mark, and Julie are sailing back to Savannah together. Larry is continuing his vacation on his yacht. That leaves Len and Kathy. They seemed undecided last night. I offered Jim and Caroline a ride on our plane, but I assumed we couldn't stop off in Miami, and they are happy with their flight schedule as is."

"Good. I don't know that we can offer that anyway, Tracie." Robert admonished, scowling as much as he dared at her.

"I'm sure we could have worked it out," Tracie said airily, ignoring his glance.

No one was talking. Grady and Katy were sensing the friction between Robert and Tracie. Awkwardly, no one made eye contact.

"May I assume that dinner has been arranged, and that the pilot knows when you expect us to be heading home?" Robert asked Tracie sarcastically.

Tracie parried that comment by saying, "Don't be mad, Robert. Things aren't wrapping up as you expected, but everything's going quite well."

This instantly made Robert irrationally angrier. "I think everyone had made up their minds about this situation before we arrived. I'm not sure why it was necessary for us even to come.

Certainly they could have just sent you, Tracie, since you seem to have this all under control."

Grady cocked an eyebrow at Robert, and waited, giving Katy a wink.

Tracie lifted her eyebrows at Robert, pausing a moment before saying, "You're right, you know; I'm sure the yacht owners did have their minds made up about leaving as soon as possible before we left home, but no one was willing to sign off on the arrangements until you sanctioned everything."

Robert reflected that Tracie was the diplomat in the family. She was happy, the yacht owners were fine, everything was working out well. Here he was blowing a fuse because the situation seemed haphazard without some kind of legal agreement—which he was unlikely to get.

He knew they were waiting for him to give his approval to the arrangements, perfunctory as that approval might be. He was, after all, the ranking member of the delegation. Tracie had laid out the plan, but was giving him the opportunity to be a leader by accepting.

"If everyone agrees that this is the way to proceed, then I guess it's all fine. Let's find out what those two undecided yacht owners are doing, though, and make sure everything's tied up securely," Robert acquiesced.

The day went well. Plans were cleared up with the boat owners and island officials. Robert finally got to be useful as his approval became necessary more than once. The result was a pleasant dinner, and a conclusion that everything would run smoothly from this point forward.

Robert, Tracie, Katy and Grady agreed that none of them was interested in going to a bar after dinner. Back at Crimson House they slowly drank mixed pitchers of beverages, left for them by Dorothy, as they sat on the deck.

Tracie was the first to profess being tired, yawning and heading off to bed. Robert was right behind her, leaving Grady and Katy sitting on the deck's swing chair together.

"Did this trip turn out like you expected?" Grady was looking for something to talk about.

"I didn't know what to expect." Katy was completely relaxed on the swing, and found herself wishing Grady would put his arm around her. "The trip to St. John was great, and this has actually been a wonderful extension of it. Work has never been so enjoyable," she laughed.

"And probably never will be again—but we can dream!" Grady chuckled. "I'd like to get back to St. John sooner, rather than later. That really was great," he agreed. "And I can't believe Mike got so sunburned. He must be peeling like crazy."

"He was in pain that last day. Rum and aloe gel kept him alive, but he still seemed to be in the partying spirit. I think Mike and Faith got a little crazy." She laughed at the memory.

"This is nice—quiet," Grady said. "Even with the tree frogs."

Katy leaned over lightly against him, saying, "It's just us now."

Grady wrapped his arms around her, and Katy relaxed into him. They stayed quiet for a few minutes until a ship's horn sounded in the harbor. Somehow that cue got them both up and leaning over the rail to look out at the view. The lights from the shore glimmered over the water in sparks. The details of the buildings and hills were completely missing in the dark.

Katy turned toward Grady and looked up at him, feeling the warm breeze. Grady looked at her, a smile in his eyes. She reached her arms up around his shoulders, and their lips locked together in a very long kiss.

Grady's arms held her close around the waist. Her fingers delved into his hair and their kiss extended. It became a French kiss, as their embrace deepened. Grady's hands shifted, one higher, one lower. Katy's hands slid down the outside of his arms, feeling the muscles of his V-shaped back.

Katy broke the kiss, leaning her head back, but not releasing him. "Are you thinking what I'm thinking?" She asked seriously.

"I hope so because I can't think of anything else." Grady was being careful to let her set the pace.

Katy let go and took his hand in hers. "Come on." Grady followed.

When they got to the hallway, Grady risked breaking the spell, thinking it was better now than later.

"There is something I should get," he told her.

"Let's just go to your room," Katy said, tugging his arm. Urgency was taking over, now that the decision had been made. "Shhh." Katy pulled him through the door to his room.

She pressed her lips against his, her hands on his chest as he quietly pushed the door closed behind his back. Her fingers flew with excitement, undoing his buttons as he fumbled to find hers. Neither of them was new to this, but both were out of practice. Grady found himself trapped in his own shirt, as he tried to pull it off before the buttons were undone.

"Hmmm. I think I like this." Katy looked at his predicament with amusement. Rubbing her hands through the fur on his chest, she commented, "Nice chest, Mister." She could feel the muscles beneath his smooth skin.

"My turn." He pulled his shirt forward and exposed the hindering buttons. His hands were free to deal with her blouse. It was soon off, and on the side chair. His shirt followed, then his pants.

"Bikini briefs. I like it," Katy grinned.

Grady pulled her closer to him. He took his time, releasing her bra hooks slowly, looking into her eyes as she gazed up at him. His hands spread across her back, his fingers taking the straps off her. With one hand, he tossed the bra onto the chair. With the other he pulled her to him Their kiss came on strong and urgent, hands rapidly exploring skin, curves, textures, and underwear, which soon lay on the floor.

She switched her hands to his shoulders and pushed. They tumbled onto the bed, Katy landing on top of him.

Chapter 26

Just after sunrise, the ocean began putting on a turbulent show past the southern breakwater of Key West. Normally this area was associated with calm waters and hot, humid, dead-calm days. Incoming storms had a nasty way of changing everything. This tropical storm had come across the Grenadines, circling around the Gulf of Mexico across Cancun, and skirting past Texas and Louisiana, making landfall in Mississippi. The gray skies hadn't yet brought rain to Key West, but it was coming. The chop beat against the western shore harder and harder.

Vlad had been awakened by the wind and the sudden slap of his bedroom window's curtain. He could hear the restless waves pounding the breakwater, and the wind rattling the palm fronds. He lifted his electronic tablet and cell phone from the nightstand. He had no messages, but he did have new email.

As the email opened, Vlad fought back his frustration that the tablet had gone into Do-Not-Disturb mode. He expected twenty-four-seven responses from his team.

The email was brief and specific. "Hunter-north, Beneteau-north, Gulfstar-sell, Gozzard-south, Morgan-Montseratt."

"Chyort voz'mi!" He swore under his breath in Russian. "Damn it!" He typed a response. "All known Gozzard information. Dates, destinations, passengers." He slammed the tablet down and grabbed his cell phone.

The boat owners were about to move—finally. Two headed north, one selling, one headed south, and the last was sailing to a small island.

Vlad knew that a plan like this had unpredictable outcomes. That was to be expected. Having delivery mules unaware of their roles was risky. He was ready to adapt. He tapped in a text to Max.

"Be ready to travel tomorrow."

He typed in another email. "Northbound destinations?" And hit send. The Morgan did not matter, it had no payload onboard. Its hull had turned out to be unsuitable. The Gulfstar would need to be acquired. If he did not hear from the agent by tomorrow, he would prompt him.

He turned his attention to the most important thing. What to do about the Gozzard? The tablet illuminated. He had a new email.

"Gozzard arrival in approximately two days St. Lucia. Owner Larry Bledsoe."

Vlad replied. "Send all Gozzard information and photos." He tossed the tablet back on the table."

His email chimed with a new arrival. "Hunter/Beneteau to Savannah GA."

He got out of bed to start some tea. It would taste awful coming from the small coffee maker, but it would be better than nothing while he dressed. It was like the rest of life. Convenience without style.

Like the tea, texts, and emails, efficiency lacked panache. He missed the old days of cyphered messages. What seemed like a hassle then had become nostalgic. Now everything was handled in software, with different filters for incoming and outgoing transmissions. It was all invisible and had no flair.

Admittedly being untraceable was easier now. A cell phone fit in the pocket, a tablet in the hand. The wireless radio he once used was bulky and heavy. Yes, it was better than the old days of a suitcase and Morse code. The team simply bought new devices for each project. New numbers, new email addresses, new internet names. All that was needed was a new charge card, and that, too, was easily supplied. When this project ended, he would have a new tablet and phone. Each operative would also be sent new equipment and would destroy the old ones. Moving fast and making things simple kept snoops like the NSA off balance. He had to admit that reading an email in English was easier than translating code with a book and pencil.

He turned on the shower and steeled himself for a morning of sweet breakfast pastry, weak coffee, and tourists who wanted to chat. As his foot stepped into the tub, the email chime sounded again. He backed out leaving the water running. The email listed everything his operative knew about the Gozzard and its owner Larry Bledsoe. Vlad scanned the information, forwarded it to Max and Luca, then grabbed his cell phone. "Cancel," he texted Max. Then he texted Luca. "Travel St. Lucia tomorrow."

. . .

Sitting on the balcony, Max had finished her chocolate croissant and was sipping her second espresso. Max had awakened in time to see the last touches of pink in the sunrise. Luca came out of the bathroom and walked across the bedroom. He approached, wearing drawstring black pajama pants and an open silk robe. Watching the sunrise in winter was actually sleeping in for both of them. A normal day would start in the dark. This felt decadent. The unusually warm weather made them feel as though they were holiday travelers.

"You slept well?" Luca asked Max.

"Yes, I did." With her heels resting on the lower rail, and her toes up in the air, Max's legs looked lusciously long. The thick, spa-like bathrobe had fallen open, barely covering her.

"You have a message," Luca said, handing her the cell phone.

The message read, "Be ready to travel tomorrow."

"I guess I have a change of plans," Max commented.

"You are staying?" Luca looked pleased.

"No, still leaving, but somewhere different," she answered.

Then the phone buzzed again. "Cancel."

"Now that's canceled. He can't make up his mind." They both laughed.

A minute later Luca's phone chimed from the other room.

"Do you think it's from him?" He asked as he headed inside to retrieve the unit. He came walking back into the bedroom from the kitchen. "It says that I travel to St. Lucia tomorrow. So, I guess it is me, instead."

Both of their phones chimed with incoming email. Luca looked up to see Max standing in the open balcony door. The bright light behind her silhouetted her naked body as she posed with one arm up against the door. Her bathrobe lay draped across the back of the chair.

"Do you have time to say goodbye?"

Chapter 27

Martin and George had been motoring for some time. Their boat was made for fishing, not for speed, but they had no fishing charter today. They were going to set up a house for vacationers. There were several houses, huts, and shacks scattered throughout the area on small islands that could not be reached except by boat. Usually, visitors would go out by water taxi with their supplies for the week. In this case, the place had been rented for three weeks. The renter had his own boat and had taken his own supplies. The schedule said he should be gone by now. Martin had been hired to clean the place up and do maintenance before the next arrivals. Terecia, Martin's girlfriend, was along for the ride, and was sitting on the transom enjoying the fine weather and calm seas.

The boat's forward and open style cabin offered some shelter, but most of the back was uncovered. A large stack of boxes sat secured just under and behind the cabin, to keep the weight as near the center as possible. This left lots of room astern. Terecia was taking advantage of the space to sun herself. She had the advantages of youth combined with a slim figure, but her long torso made her legs appear a bit short. With little endowment on top, she looked younger than she actually was. This pleased Martin, who liked young girls. At twice her age, he was looking to regain his youth.

George was content to drive the boat. At sixteen, he was the youngest of the three and thrilled to be captaining in open water. His usual duties consisted of baiting hooks and cleaning fish.

As they approached the tiny island, it appeared trashed. Boxes and containers littered the sand. The dock held a tattered banner made of what looked like t-shirts and the house looked black, not its normal brown. The closer they came, the more torn up everything looked. The house had definitely been on fire. The t-shirt banner said something and George was the first to realize it was a large E-L-P, the first letter H hidden by a drooped shred of cloth. Two men were coming out of the house. Their clothes were shredded. Their faces, arms, and legs glistened with red and white blotches of blood and puss-filled blisters.

Terecia screamed as they neared the dock. The two men were a mere twelve feet away limping as fast as they could on raw bloody feet. Their hands were held out, pleading for help. George hit the throttle to pull away as fast as he could. Terecia ran from the boat's stern to clutch Martin. The rear cleat of the boat was almost within reach of the man who stretched toward it from the end of the dock. The man's rasping call for help could not be heard over the engine. His mouth stretched wide as his sad, pained eyes pleaded.

. . .

George, Terecia, and Martin sat on the boat, holding their position off the dock. It had been ten minutes. The two desperately ill men stood precariously at the dock edge trying to signal the boat to come back, but they could barely lift their arms and often stumbled just trying to stand. George held the boat steady against the wind and current as Martin looked at the island twenty yards away. He leaned heavily against the rail.

"We have to help them." Terecia pleaded. Her fear was not gone, but her instincts said they had to do something.

"What can we do?" Martin replied without looking at her.

"We have to help." Terecia's eyes were wet with tears beginning to fall.

"It is disease. We can't go back." Martin was strong, but not well educated. Even if he had been, the appearance of the two men was beyond his experience. They looked like something out of a horror movie.

"Look, they are moving away." George was right. Both men were backing away. They did not turn and held their hands down to their sides with open palms. Behind them two more men could be seen, both could barely stand. They held onto the building and did not come forward.

"Please, do something," Terecia pleaded.

"Go in slowly, George." Martin waved his hand behind his back indicating they should move forward and George added to the throttle. They circled to come up easy on the dock from the downwind side watching the two men who now stood on shore just off the dock. They didn't move fearing they might scare away the boat. They knew how they looked.

Martin tied up the bow of the boat while Terecia and George watched. No threatening movement was made. It was easy to see why. The four men were so feeble, decrepit, and injured that for all appearances they were walking dead men. Nothing could have prepared the three for what they saw. Real men, their skin falling off in sheets, with blisters covering their skin, and sticking to their clothes. Their clothes were wet in blotches and clearly torn away from broken, oozing sores. The two nearest the house had eyes that were swollen shut. The two at the dock could see only a little better. Their corneas were almost an opaque milky white.

"Can you hear me?" Martin called out.

"Yes." Came the weak reply. The voice was a harsh whisper barely audible from the beach just twenty feet away. Martin more read the man's lips than heard him.

"Are you sick?" The question was foolish. "I mean, what can we do? I don't know if it is safe."

"Help us, please." The pathetic cry for help was little more than a plea. "We don't know what is wrong with us. They left us here. Help us, please."

Martin moved back to the center of the boat rail and spoke with George and Terecia. "What can we do? They must have cholera, or plague, or something. I don't know what can be done."

"You have to do something." Terecia was crying, and could not stop looking at the men. "They're dying."

"Can we use the radio, and call someone?" George suggested.

Martin thought for a moment. His mind made up, he turned to the men at the end of the dock.

"Do you have food?" He called to them.

"No food, no water," came the reply.

"Wait there!" Martin called back. "We will call for help. We will put water and food here for you, then pull away from the dock to wait for help. Do you understand?"

"Yes," the man answered. "Thank you." They stayed on the land and watched as George handed box after box of supplies to Martin, who placed them on the dock.

"Don't stack them," Terecia said. "They are weak and may not be able to move them."

Martin took the advice one step further. He set the boxes down the dock in a single row and opened them. He even opened several water bottles and food packages. It was nervous work going nearer the sickened men. The stronger of the two looked as if his face was peeling off, but worse, his left leg had little brown skin left. The bloody flesh looked like bare meat with sand stuck to it. Flies swarmed across the surface at will, with no opposition from the man. He either had given up or could not feel them. The weaker man had crumbled to the sand, leaning heavily on his hand. He no longer had the strength to stand, or even look up. Both had stains of fluids down the fronts of their clothes and backs of their pants. Martin thought it was fortunate that the breeze was blowing away from the boat. The men looked as though they would smell like rotting meat.

George called the local authorities by radio while Martin opened boxes. The bewildered response from the other end of the radio frustrated George. He was not sure any action was being taken.

Martin untied the boat and called back. "We will wait there," pointing out in the water. "We will get help!" He pushed the bow away with his foot, and George engaged the throttle. Soon they were at anchor thirty yards out. Martin got on the radio and called the Coast Guard.

"Coast Guard, this is FV Jump Up." Martin gave identification, coordinates, and all the boating information requested, but when it came to describing the scene, it was hard for him.

"It looks like a disease. They are dying, and need help." He went on to describe the open sores and filthy condition of the victims. Reassured that help was on its way, they sat on the boat to wait. They watched the one man capable of still walking shuffle down to the case of water, drinking a half a bottle himself before taking some to the others. Within an hour, two of the men were shuttling some food to the house and doing what they could for the others.

With binoculars, Martin came to realize there were at least four men at the house. Two were on cots. Their hands barely lifted to receive the water, and no food was offered to them. Six, he counted. He didn't know if there were more inside. He could also see the roof of the house had been burned completely away. Perhaps they were all injured in the fire and not diseased at all. Maybe what he saw were burns, but how could someone survive such burns? It wasn't possible. He stayed where he was at anchor.

It was three hours before a speedboat appeared on the horizon. The men on-shore showed no reaction. Terecia had not spoken for the last hour. Her face had lost all expression. She would not look up from the deck. She had thrown up twice, which made Martin worry.

The radio crackled to life. "Fishing vessel 'Jump Up' this is the Coast Guard, do you read?"

"We read you." Martin was quick on the mic.

"Do you see us approaching?"

"Yes, we see you."

"Stand by." The vessel looked like a large zodiac inflatable boat with an enclosed cabin and hard hull. The cabin was disproportionally large for the boat. When they pulled up alongside the men on board quickly collected information from Martin, George, and Terecia.

With binoculars and a megaphone they contacted the island, but could not hear the men's answers. It was too far. That didn't matter. The instructions were clear. The coast guard boat would approach the dock and offload a medic, his equipment and a radio. The instructions were to leave the dock and wait for the medic to radio. What they saw through the binoculars was enough to warrant extreme caution.

When the boat returned alongside the Jump Up, they explained that it was a quarantine situation. Martin, George, and Terecia would have to stay where they were until the medical staff arrived on the larger boat in four hours. They were to move their fishing boat farther away, set their anchor for night, and set a watch. This would give the coast guard boats more room to maneuver while keeping their own boat safer, should they have to stay overnight. They would not be allowed to leave until the doctor made a determination.

After finishing his communication with the base on the radio, the medic confirmed that the others had to stay. No one else was to approach the island. He didn't know what they were facing, but one man was dead and had been for days. One man was convulsing, perhaps from the water he had drunk, and the other four were in bad shape. He had removed the food in case gastrointestinal problems were an issue and instructed the men to take only small sips of water, spaced well apart. He'd put three men on saline drips and had given one medication to stabilize his heart. It was minimal care. Without knowing more, he might do more harm than good.

It had been a long radio call. The small Coast Guard vessel concluded the bigger boat already on its way would need more supplies. A speed boat like theirs would be loaded and would follow the bigger boat to the island.

Chapter 28

Morning dawned perfectly on St. Thomas. A few white clouds floated across the blue sky, pushed by a gentle breeze.

Grady and Katy sat close together on the covered porch, enjoying the view and the sumptuous breakfast of French toast stuffed with heavy cream and nutmeg jam. There was rich black coffee, sweet coconut dumb bread, and fresh fruit slices.

Robert emerged as they were finishing their last bites of fresh mango. Dorothy was quickly at his side with his coffee prepared as he liked it.

"Good Morning," she said. "I hope you slept well."

"Morning. Yes, I did." Robert felt good, despite the previous evening's excesses.

"Morning!" Grady and Katy greeted Robert in unison. Grady added, "Sorry, we couldn't wait. The food smelled fantastic."

"Don't worry. I couldn't have waited either. Did you two sleep well?" Robert asked.

"Sure did." Grady was clearly bright-eyed.

"Yes, thank you," Katy responded, smiling. "This has been a wonderful trip. I wish all my work assignments were so enjoyable. Thank you for inviting me along."

"It was a pleasure," Robert replied. "You'll be a welcome addition whenever we need a Naval presence."

Robert conferred with Dorothy for a moment, and then took a cup of coffee and a piece of the dumb bread to Tracie, who was still getting dressed. Then he returned to his coffee with Grady and Katy.

By the time Tracie came out she was ready to face the day with her usual appearance of perfection. She wore a new outfit Robert had not seen. Katy also had on a new outfit.

"Hello, Everyone! Don't you all look nice this morning," Tracie greeted them sunnily.

Robert drank some more coffee while Tracie chatted with Dorothy, Grady, and Katy. He wondered what she had planned for them that morning.

. . .

Tracie had told them that the plane was available in the afternoon, so she'd planned that the group would go shopping and to lunch before they departed. She'd hoped they'd be able to lunch on the beach at Water Island, but with the plane departing at 3:30, lunch near downtown would be a better choice. Peter would be arriving to take them shopping and would guard their luggage until they boarded the plane.

Robert was glad that Tracie had handled this part of the trip. He was ready to sit back and let her manage the day.

After they'd packed and said they're goodbyes to Dorothy, the group headed out in Peter's van. Tracie had arranged for him to stop at stores where they could buy some island delicacies, like nutmeg jam and syrup, as well as the Dumb Bread, and some rum to take home.

They stopped at Amalia Café for lunch, reveling in its seafood with a Spanish flair menu, and its open-air dining. It was convenient to downtown shopping, and a short ride from the airport, so they were able to take their time over the restaurant's Caribbean version of paella.

When the waitress came by with another pitcher of sangria, she asked, "Have you just arrived, or are you staying longer?"

"We're headed back today," Grady replied. "We were just talking about places we want to try the next time we are here. Have you been to Dinghy's bar?"

"Of course," she answered, laughing. "I think I have been to every place on the island. Dinghy's is on a nice beach. The bay is calm and good for swimming. You can sit at a table in the sand, and watch the water. If you stay for the sunset, I think there is only one late ferry. Make sure you make reservations for it when you go."

"Great tip. I would not have thought of that." Grady responded, smiling.

Robert wondered if Mary Whiston had seen the yacht owners off, and whether she was headed back today. He assumed that she was handling all the last-minute details. Robert realized that his cell phone had not rung once. That seemed odd, but he reflected that Lorraine must be handling his schedule. He'd probably have a pile of messages on his desk when he got back.

"I must not have the vacation gene. I'm already thinking about work," Katy broke into the conversation. "Is anyone else wondering what's on their desk?"

"Not me," Robert lied. "I'm just wondering what's for dessert."

"Don't let him fool you," Tracie jumped in. "He's the worst at going on vacation. I can tell from the look on his face that work was exactly what was going through his head," she added, getting a laugh from everyone, including Robert.

Katy shook her head. "When I go on vacation it takes at least two days to stop thinking about work. When I get home, that vacation relaxation is gone. Just like that." She snapped her fingers.

"Robert is the same way. He drives me crazy." Tracie laughed. "It takes him three days to stop talking about work. Then it takes three or four days for him to stop thinking about work. The vacation doesn't even start until the second week, and if there is one phone call or email, the clock starts over."

"Years ago, she started booking trips to places with no cell phone service, and no Internet." Robert told them. "It works, after the shakes stop." He held out his hand, wiggling it furiously. "See?"

They laughed. "I know what you mean. Our last holiday was two days traveling, and three days there. I never unwound." Grady caught himself too late. The uncomfortable pause held for a long breath. He looked up at Katy, ready to apologize, but she spoke before he could.

"And I thought I would be the first to talk about my past life. You lose the bet," She told him, lightening the mood again.

"I'm sorry about interrupting your vacation plans for this trip," Robert apologized. "I know we touched on this earlier, Katy, but let me say how much I appreciate you both coming to help out. I'm sure it would not have gone as smoothly without you." Robert lifted his Sangria glass. "To a successful trip with new friends. Thank you."

After the clink of glasses, Tracie asked, "Do you think your friends, Mike and Faith, were okay with the sudden change?"

"Something tells me Faith took advantage of our early departure." Grady grinned at Katy. "They needed some time on their own," he explained to Tracie.

"I look forward to meeting those two," Tracie laughed. Robert wasn't sure what he could add, so he kept silent.

"Can I make cutting the vacation short up to you?" He suddenly offered, thinking that would mean paying for lunch.

"You're already picking up the check," Tracie stated.

"I think you should get us something really big—like a trip home on a private plane." Katy smiled slyly at Grady.

"Yes, something stylish. Not some bare bones twin prop." Grady added to the merry chiding.

"Hmmm." Robert looked puzzled, placing his chin in his hand. "Let me see what I can do."

. . .

With too many sangrias and an extra round of banana-blueberry bread pudding weighing heavily on their well-filled stomachs, they found themselves at the airport looking up at the shining Gulfstream V. Staff Sergeant Waters stood at the top of the stairs, ready to welcome them aboard.

"Hello, Shannon," Tracie was first up the stairs.

"Mrs. Carlton; Mr. Carlton. Welcome aboard." Shannon graciously stepped back to let them onto the plane. Then she turned and saluted. "You must be Lieutenant Davies and Colonel Barlow. I'm pleased to meet you." Grady and Katy returned the salute, echoing their pleasure at being on board.

They started off with Robert and Tracie on the port side, Grady and Katy on starboard. There was conversation, laughter, and partway through the flight, more good food. They went light on drinks, sipping them slowly.

They hadn't been on the flight an hour before Robert and Grady began talking business, and Tracie started interrogating Katy. The Gulfstream made chatting across the aisle workable, but the noise of the jet caused a rotation of seats. The guys sat left, and the girls took the right for the rest of the flight.

Tracie got nowhere with her interrogative tactics. Katy was good at turning the tables, and getting Tracie to talk. Katy learned more about the Kennedy Center than she ever wanted to know. Tracie searched conversationally for common ground, and found it in an unlikely place when Katy responded, "You follow the stock market?"

Tracie had been talking about the economy and its relationship with the DOW. It turned out Katy had been following and investing in defense stocks.

"I have several friends in a stock club," Tracie said. "We used to be a book club, but wanted something more challenging." Tracie leaned forward. "We started with little stuff. Ruth's sister, Betty, spotted a little stock, but was afraid to try it on her own. We pooled twenty dollars each and bought the stock as a group. That was three years ago, and now we have a portfolio as a group. I have one of my own online. I started handling the family 401K about two years ago. Robert never has time, and I had some individual stocks I picked, along with the normal balanced array of ETFs, mutual funds and so forth."

Katy had been listening intently. "I got into it because my portfolio is so small no money manager would even talk to me. All I got was the 401K bank pitch of cost averaging, automatic rebalancing and invitations to online seminars. I never made more than nine percent a year after fees, and in the bad years, my account dropped by almost half. That's happened twice now. So, I guess you could say I'm frustrated. One year the market went up fifteen percent, and everybody was dancing in the streets. That same year I made eight percent. It's not right." Katy showed a touch of bitterness describing her experience with Wall Street.

"That's us exactly!" Tracie completely related to Katy's pain. "The promise of retirement on a Wall Street plan only seems to be making the Wall Street guys rich. It feels like you're just handing over your money to them because that's what they tell you to do. Robert and I had two huge loss years, like you, and never got the return we were promised by money managers. Meanwhile, *they* all get million-dollar bonuses. I have friends in their fifties and sixties that have little more than what they put in, despite their investment manager's promises—they might have done better with a savings account. I thought that we were stuck with that being the best we could do. Our club was doing okay, then Robert's father called me recently, and said he could help us do better. We have been rocketing ever since, and I started applying his advice to our 401k. Robert's father has a knack for predicting the ups and downs."

"He's a broker?" Katy asked.

"No, he's an oil executive," Tracie explained. "But he gets the best information from his contacts. It has helped us a lot."

"Tell me more about your club." Katy was hooked.

Robert and Grady were talking about weapons smuggling.

"In fact, our borders are more permeable than Swiss cheese," Robert was saying. "If we were only so lucky as to have just a few holes! It's too easy to smuggle this stuff in." Robert had always asserted that the US ability to stop weapons smuggling was as impossible as shutting down drug trafficking.

"Unfortunately, I agree with that assessment." Grady nodded. "When I was a cadet at the Academy, the assumption was that a warhead was useless without a delivery system. A nuke needed a ballistic missile. Now all you need is a boat or pickup truck. It doesn't have to be militarily delivered in any way."

"IED approaches are too fluid and too flexible to predict well," Robert interjected. "On top of that, we don't know where to expect it. Most of the defense falls on police, Homeland Security, and the FBI getting information from the NSA and CIA." Robert was frustrated by the situation.

"I had a professor of defense strategy at the Academy who thought the global militaries had done a good enough job with defense and mutually assured destruction that militarily devised attacks would not be our long-term problem. His idea was that a rogue individual with the ability to deliver military-grade weaponry on his own would become the real threat—and here we are." Grady was shaking his head.

"Did he have any solutions for that?" Robert asked.

"I think he was hoping that one of us would come up with some ideas before we got to this point," Grady sighed.

By the time they landed and parted ways, Robert and Grady had depressed themselves over the subject. They both had started trying to think of out of the box solutions to prevent weapons smuggling, but were coming up empty.

Tracie and Katy had struck up a relationship. They felt energized and empowered to make a personal difference in their finances. Katy was coming to Tracie's next investment club meeting.

<u>Chapter 29</u>

It was Robert's monthly family weekend. He followed Tracie and the boys to Taekwondo, where Andrew earned a green belt. It cost three hundred dollars.

"Every kid so far made it to the next belt. Is that unusual?" Robert asked the dad sitting next to him. Tracie was doing email and responding to Facebook messages on her laptop.

"Yeah. It's like most 'McDojos.' My daughter is a red belt. Cost me thirty-five hundred, so far. To get her black will probably cost another thousand, and it'll take about a year. But, on the upside, she is in great shape and has developed strong self-esteem. She doesn't know that she can't beat up that tall kid with the orange belt."

"I was getting the impression that belts don't equal fighting skill when I saw an eleven-year-old with a black belt," Robert said.

The father shrugged. "It's about doing the forms, and training the mind. My role is to write checks." He turned toward Robert for the first time. "I was pissed at first, then I went to PTA night and heard about parents who can't or won't get their kids off video games and smart phones. They can't get them to study and have mostly given up. They blame the teachers for not being innovative. My kid wants to kick some ass, here and at school, and is willing to put her phone down to practice. It's worth it."

"McDojo," Robert repeated. "Kind of an upgraded Happy Meal." They both laughed.

"What are you two laughing about?" Tracie queried, looking up from her screen.

"The 'McDojo' expression," Robert smiled.

"Don't let Andrew and James' coach hear you!" Tracie warned. "He's very sensitive about that." She scowled. "This Dojang is not a belt factory. They earn their belts here."

"Of course. We were just joking." Robert turned quickly away. The two men smirked a little and watched the testing. James and the seven year olds would be up next. Robert saw James take his test, tripping twice, but getting rewarded with a yellow belt. Another three-hundred dollars.

..

Grady spent Saturday catching up on work at the office. The new guys needed some help getting up to speed before he could completely free himself of that work.

That evening, he and Katy had intended to have dinner together, but her job put her out on the tugboat. It was a converted Natick-class tug, dragging MISTI out for a test. She wouldn't be back until at least Tuesday.

...

Vlad sat in the office of his boat broker.

"We found a Gulfstar 39 SM!" The broker was proud of his find.

How impressive, Vlad thought to himself. You found the opportunity I made available. What American arrogance. Aloud he said simply, "Good," and waited patiently for the sales pitch.

"I have some pictures for you to look over," the broker handed Vlad a packet.

"This is, as you know, a popular model from the golden era of Gulfstar," The broker continued. "The interior was done in teak, which is a seriously nice step up from the Formica common in those days. But it can be a maintenance issue, and it is hard to match the color stain that Gulfstar used. Fortunately, this owner has preserved it nicely, and there are no repairs needed to the wood. The pictures don't do the yacht justice."

"You have not seen the boat personally, though," Vlad verified.

"No, but my agent on the island has, and I trust him." The broker continued to point out the yacht's features. "She's twelve meters, with a draft of one point four five." Since Vlad was obviously not American, the broker referred to the numbers using metric measurements. "She has a ballast of thirty-seven hundred kilos, with a balance to displacement ratio of forty-three percent. That's very impressive. I can see why you like this model."

"What are the condition of the sails and engine?" Vlad didn't care, but it was something a buyer would ask.

"The engine had full servicing in October. They've provided the paperwork on that. The sails are only four years old. The jenny and main are Kevlar. There is no spinnaker, but is does have the pole and rigging. My agent assures me that, on a scale of one to ten, this yacht is in eight-plus condition—even compared to a boat ten years newer."

"Price?" Vlad wanted to get to the point.

"Ninety-eight thousand, with clear registry in Miami, Florida," the broker told him, as though this news should clinch the deal.

"Where is it now?" Vlad wanted to know.

"It's near St. Lucia." He waited to see what Vlad might say about that.

Vlad thumbed through the pictures again. "That seems high. Your man feels it is without flaws? Cracks, rust, leaks?"

"It has small leaks on two of the doghouse windows, which is common, but I can have those fixed for you. There is minor cracking around the mast and the bow cleats. The anchor winch was replaced with a newer model, and the fiberglass work is visible. The dinghy is an inflatable with a 2-horse motor—both just four years old. And you asked about bridge clearance. It has a fifty-three foot, five-inch—that's sixteen point two meters—mast height, which will give you plenty of clearance up the intra-coastal waterway even in foul weather, or sloppy water."

"Ninety-five thousand, and I want to pick it up in Melbourne, Florida. I will cover up to five-thousand in transfer charges." Vlad stated.

The broker flushed with the excitement of closing an easier sale than he had seen in years. "Will you require an inspection before agreement?" He had to ask, but he was crossing his fingers and toes for good luck.

"Your man says it is good?" Vlad tried to sound unsure.

"Yes, very." The broker spoke reassuringly.

"Then I will trust you." Vlad got up. "If it is not, you will come clean it yourself." He stood.

"I will make sure it meets your expectations. I'll call you to let you know whether they accept your offer."

"They will," Vlad said as if it was a foregone conclusion. He was right. The acceptance call came within the hour.

. . .

Luca had gotten off the plane in St. Lucia at seven p.m., local time. The Gozzard 36 was expected to arrive as early as Monday. There was no way of knowing for sure what time. Sailboat plans tended to change with the wind. Still, this gave Luca only two days to reconnoiter and devise a plan. He needed to make some luck.

The assignment had a slightly unusual twist to it. The moment he'd read the email attachment from Vlad, he'd known why Vlad had switched from Max to himself for handling this assignment. The file showed that the yacht owner, Larry Bledsoe, had broken up with his boyfriend about eight months earlier. It looked like an attractive man might have a better chance with Larry than Max would.

Their last report showed Larry leaving St. Thomas Friday for Sao Bento. Presumably, he'd be sailing directly to St. Lucia. Luca wondered how familiar Larry was with St. Lucia. Where would

Larry go for fuel, water, supplies, entertainment? This was what he must figure out.

Vlad's instructions were clear. "The Gozzard must arrive in Virginia Beach the same week the others arrive at their target positions." Luca knew that if Larry was planning to head north, Vlad would have arranged a more definitive meeting place. Something wasn't going right for Vlad to leave Luca with so many meeting place options. He called Vlad for further instructions.

"Yes?" Vlad answered tersely.

"This boat. It is going the wrong way?" Luca was fishing.

"Yes, but we don't know where he intends to head. You must find out. I want it on target. You make sure it gets there." Vlad did not micromanage his operatives. He expected them to be capable enough to handle the jobs they were given.

"And if it is necessary, I should sail the boat?" Luca had sailed, but not on the open ocean. He was a little concerned about this aspect of the situation.

"It is most important that the boat arrives safely. Don't take chances with the boat, or the schedule. The rest is up to you." Vlad thought for a moment. "Remember, if you must force this, then there will be many nights out on the water to manage the business."

"Yes." Luca had a clear picture, now. If Larry would not head north voluntarily to the US, then he would have to force him to do so, or eliminate him. "I may need identification for US customs."

"If it comes to that," Vlad knew the options Luca faced, "I would rather he brought it in, but do what you must. The schedule must be maintained. Call ahead if you need ID. His boat has an LBO decal. This will help. You understand?"

"Yes. I will have it on target, on time." Luca affirmed.

"Good." Vlad hung up.

Luca was not as confident as he sounded, but he built his skills by doing things he had never done before. He would successfully do this, too.

Chapter 30

Larry left St. Thomas in the afternoon, arriving at the airport nearest St. Gertach in time for afternoon cocktails at the hotel. Tomorrow he would take the first ferry over to the island. Larry had no desire to stay there if he didn't have to. Assuming the boat was in the condition the Coast Guard had said, all he would need was a couple of day's food and water, so he could set sail and leave St. Gertach in his wake.

He absentmindedly touched the marks still healing on his face and hands. They had started itching the previous day. The memory of captivity made him self-conscious and a touch paranoid, but he was healing emotionally as fast as the scabs were disappearing.

The thing that bothered him the most was having no one notice that he'd been kidnapped. His friends and family missed not getting a call or email, but he'd never been consistent with his communications. With the sailboat it was easy to go off-grid for a week.

"I should have given someone my itinerary, or checked in when I came near a cell connection." Larry berated himself. He hadn't updated his Facebook and Instagram accounts with anything that would let thieves know his house was empty. He and the others hadn't even filed travel plans with any official organization. He still wasn't sure what good that might have done. As a group, this had come up several times in conversation.

"Yeah, sending an email once in a while, and a picture or two of Caribbean lobsters on a plate isn't much of a hint if someone needed to find you." Larry had been talking about this with Mark at dinner.

"Julie found something that we're going to use. Honey, show that app you just signed up for to Larry," Mark has insisted.

Julie came over with her phone and turned it on. "Here it is." She showed it to Larry. "Mark and I were thinking there needed to be a service of some kind—our million-dollar business idea for the day. We brainstorm ideas like this all the time. Anyway, we were thinking that there should be a secure tracker that passively monitors your GPS, and uploads it along with a selfie when you take one. Something only your chosen friends can access."

"Yep, that was your million-dollar idea for the day," Larry raised his glass and they toasted.

"Then Mark says, 'You know, there has to be an app for that,'" Julie continued.

"Yeah, there has to be." Larry laughed.

"So, I did some surfing, and it turns out that there are several. We picked this one and signed up in a few minutes." Julie walked Larry through a demo of the software and convinced him it was the best option. With a few clicks, the app was downloading.

Now, sitting at the hotel near St. Gertach, he looked at his phone. Who did he want to give access to his every movement? He tapped his contacts and finally dialed his sister in Denver.

The next morning he boarded the ferry. Before lunch he was on his boat with provisions and fuel enough to get to St. Lucia. He would be there by afternoon the next day even if the wind died, and there was a nice little sand island he could anchor at overnight on the way.

· · ·

Luca sat at the beachside bar of his hotel in St. Lucia. He had on beach wear that showed his physique off to advantage. He was being friendly with the bartender who responded amiably. His goal was to find all the spots on the island where a single gay man might go, and in particular where visiting yachtsmen went.

It was an assumption that Larry was gay. Vlad was quick to make assumptions about gay men that had no validity. He was intolerant of everyone who was not like him, and quick to judge those with different sexual preferences. The title of "boyfriend" could easily have been misunderstood or misinterpreted when Vlad read Larry's file.

Luca tread carefully with the bartender on the subject, since same-sex male relations carried legal penalties on the island. Within resorts most were accepting of affectionate behaviors, but this was not always considered acceptable around kids and families.

Luca never understood intolerance of sexuality. The American prudish view of nudity puzzled him. A topless female was a work of art, and to be admired in all its forms. A nude male was equally worth note.

The bartender's comments indicated that someone with a nice yacht would make one of two choices. They would either anchor off a small beach or go to Rodney Bay where it was easy to rent a slip and resupply.

Luca's instincts told him that Larry would spend as little time as possible in St. Gertach. Resupplying would be first and foremost on his list. The email file indicated that Larry had plenty of money, so that settled it. Luca would chance the Bay, and watch from a restaurant or bar. If he spotted the boat coming in, he would have a chance of bumping into Larry on the docks, or could follow him to a bar or restaurant.

He caught the bartender's attention.

"Yes, Sir?" The bartender was very courteous.

"I'd like another one of these." Luca smiled. He knew the drink would be made in front of him, which made conversing natural. "I was thinking you were right about Rodney Bay. Is there a spot I could watch the sailboats come in?"

"Here, I have a map." The bartender told him, unfolding the colorful green and blue artist drawn map. It had all the highlights of the island marked. The bartender pointed out two restaurants, but Luca spotted one right between the two large docks.

"Thank you, this is perfect," he told the man. He drank his beverage quickly and tipped well before getting up to grab a taxi. He headed to the Bosun's Bar & Bistro in the Rodney Bay Village.

. . .

Luca got up early the next morning, even though the odds were slim that Larry had arrived. He knew it was much more likely that Larry would sail in during the late afternoon. After talking with a couple who were fueling their boat, Luca stopped at the harbor master's office. Any boat coming for an overnight would be likely to have checked there in advance for slip availability, the couple had said. They were right. The office was happy to tell him that Larry had a slip reservation for three days and two nights, starting today. They even provided the slip number to Luca. Now he could relax. He was in the right place at the right time.

It was about four when the sailboat appeared at the harbor entrance, motoring in with sails furled. The clipper ship-styled prow stood out distinctively amongst the other yachts. At thirty-nine feet, she was small compared to the monster yachts tied up at various docks, but she had a pirate feel and beautiful woodwork that evoked romance from days gone by.

Luca watched as the boat approached the slip and slid gracefully in. Luca guessed that Larry would be getting off to report into customs. That would take a while, then he would probably go shopping for provisions.

He was right. As he watched, Larry went to the customs building, eventually coming out and walking back to the boat. He then got off the boat again, dragging a collapsible two-wheeled shopping cart down the dock. As soon as Larry turned to head toward the market areas, Luca walked calmly out on the dock to the boat. There were a few people around, but no one was paying attention to him. Luca knew that these people didn't know each other—all these slips were for short-term visitors. He appeared to be just another yacht owner.

As he walked toward the boat, Luca pulled out his Geiger counter sensor and attached it to his phone. Then he opened up the app. The reading showed a variation from five to ten counts per minute and climbed to twenty-five CPM as he reached the side of the boat. This was nothing. An ambient reading of fifty would not raise an eyebrow. Driving his car in DC could result in higher readings just being around so many buildings, people, and the machines that supported them.

His small, inexpensive, plug-in peripheral unit lacked sensitivity, but he didn't need more accurate information. What he was looking for was a noticeable leak, something over one hundred CPM. These readings indicated that the boat was safe, and the device hidden in the keel was undetectable.

With a casual look around, he boarded the yacht and tested the hatch. It was locked. On the instrument panel just forward of the wheel was a dark Plexiglas sun shield that hung close over the instruments. Luca pulled a three by four by one-quarter inch rectangular box from his pocket, peeled off the backing tape and stuck it to the underside of the sun shield. The backing tape was black. Unless he dipped low to look underneath, he couldn't tell it was there.

This position would protect the microphone in the box from wind, and allow it to withstand dampness and salt build-up for a long time. Longer than the few weeks he needed, or that the battery would last.

Unfortunately, the sun shield would also block any low volume speaking from inside the boat. Luca needed another transmitter inside. Looking forward he saw the first glass air-vent hatch was open about three inches. Just enough. He moved forward and kneeling down, placed a second transmitting microphone on the underside of the glass. He would have to hope it wouldn't be noticed. People seldom looked straight up inside a boat, but Larry might notice it if he closed the hatch. Even if he did spot it, Luca thought, it would still be a mystery as to what it was, or how it had ended up there.

Luca put on his earpiece and switched on the receiver. With a couple of taps on each, he confirmed that the transmitters were working. His task completed, he walked back down the dock to wait.

. . .

Larry came walking back about the time Luca got his beer, sitting at the bar overlooking the slips. He placed his wireless earpiece back on and powered up the radio receiver. A switch on top let him connect to either or both transmitter channels.

The sounds of Larry boarding the boat were too loud. He had to adjust the levels, but the signal was surprisingly good. Larry didn't say anything. He didn't make a call or turn on a radio. Not surprising, Luca thought. Sailing alone, Larry would be used to the quiet, or maybe he'd always been a silent guy.

When he heard the wooden hatch slide shut and the lock snap, Luca knew Larry was headed back—probably to have dinner. Luca paid his bill at the bar and positioned himself by a palm tree to wait. He needed an opportunity to meet with Larry, talk, and find a way to convince him to sail north to Florida.

Larry strolled down the dock and turned toward the village area. It was easy for Luca to follow him—until Larry hailed a cab. The cab was a white Suzuki with a sign in the window advertising its fares. Luca rushed to a cab standing nearby, trying to keep an eye on Larry's vehicle.

"I need to catch my friend. I just spotted him getting into a white Suzuki cab. I think he's headed to a restaurant or bar," Luca told his driver. The cabby didn't seem worried. He nodded and raced down the street as if he knew where to go.

When he spotted the Suzuki, Luca pointed it out to the driver. It was easy to follow. A bright Jamaican-style smiley face covered the spare tire on the back. It seemed to be headed out toward the beach. The Suzuki stopped in front of a restaurant. Larry got out and headed into the bar.

It was early. The sun had not yet begun to set, but the place was starting to fill. The palm frond beach bar served BBQ and burgers, but mostly booze. The cooks were firing up several beachside grills in preparation for the overflow from the nearby hotel. The big, friendly-looking bar's curve made it easy for Luca to pick a stool almost opposite Larry, who was being served a cold Piton beer.

Luca ordered a house specialty rum drink, and soon regretted the choice. An oversized ceramic blue and green parrot showed up in front of him, festooned with straws and a colored paper umbrella. It was a ridiculous looking drink.

"Uh, is this what I..." Luca began, staring at the concoction. "Never mind," he said, as the bartender looked confused. Larry had noticed the drink, and the almost helpless look on Luca's face.

"Not what you expected?" Larry commented over the bar, chuckling.

"Not really," Luca admitted. "I was just looking for a good rum drink." Luca nodded toward Larry's beer, saying, "You seem to know your way around here."

"I've been here many times," Larry said comfortably, smiling. "I come to Rodney Bay almost every year."

"Mind sharing some pointers?" Luca asked.

"Sure, you just arrive?" Larry responded.

Luca picked up his glass and slid off the bar stool. "Mind if I join you? I'll take off when your friends arrive."

"It's just me," Larry reassured him, pivoting slightly on his stool to shake hands as Luca walked over. "Sure, I don't mind the company. I'm Larry, by the way."

Luca extended his hand, shaking hands firmly. "I'm Luca."

"Pleased to meet you. What are you planning on doing while you're here?" Larry seemed to be a good guy, and more than willing to help a fellow traveler.

"It's my second day here. So far, I've been doing the normal tourist things and trying to find my way around. I thought I'd hang out for two more nights, then head north. I had hoped to do some diving—or maybe rent a little sailboat and find a beach that's not as crowded as it is around here," Luca responded.

"An almost empty beach like you see in the brochures?" Larry laughed lightly. "They're here, but not as easy to find as you might think."

The conversation wandered easily from subject to subject. They talked about traveling, as well as other shared interests. After three drinks food became a priority, and the two decided to switch to a table.

Luca had ordered the same beer as Larry to "get away from the parrot," and they both decided on burgers for dinner. Luca veered back to the subject of scuba diving. He'd taken a calculated chance, bringing up the subject. He'd seen the red and white flag decal on one of Larry's sailboat's windows.

"So, what would you recommend if I'm thinking about diving? Is St. Lucia the right choice, or should I hit one of the other islands?" He queried.

"They have some of the best diving in the Caribbean right here," Larry told him.

"I assumed all the diving would be good," Luca interjected.

"Most of the islands have some interesting dives, but if you haven't dived the Piton's you've missed out." Larry went on to describe a dive he'd had there. "The Piton's are south of here—by Soufriere. It's incredible. You start on the boat under this amazingly vertical mountain. You swim over a reef shelf that is flat and fifteen feet deep, extending more than a hundred yards from shore. The shallow, clear water is covered with life. There are seahorses, nudibranchs—the works, and it's unbelievably colorful. Then you go to the edge, and it drops off five hundred feet, just like that. It's a nearly vertical wall. We went down eighty feet. The sea whips come out from the wall twenty feet in orange and yellow, jutting out to the light in long spirals. We even had a huge creature pass below us. It had to be fifty or sixty feet long. It was probably a whale, but it was too deep and dark to see for sure. All we could be sure of was the dark gray shadow image of it, but both my dive buddy and I felt it go by as the water moved us up a couple feet, and then back down."

As soon as the subject had shifted to diving, they'd both stopped drinking—as if they'd both felt the urge for compressed air. They both knew that alcohol, dehydration, and diving didn't mix. Larry was NAUI certified, Luca had a PADI card, and the training for both was clear on the subject.

Larry ordered a mango-flavored soft drink, and Luca followed suit. By the time the second round of plantain and sweet potato fries had disappeared, they'd made their plans for the next day. The two of them would meet at the Rodney Bay dock to go scuba diving. Larry made a call to a dive shop he knew and got it set up. The shop was already doing a Piton Wall dive at 11, then lunch on the boat, followed by a Coral Gardens dive off of Gros Piton. It would be an all-day adventure. He and Luca would meet at the dock at eight-thirty to get fitted with gear.

Chapter 31

Luca and Larry had a great time on the dive. Luca was surprised that it was just as beautiful as Larry had said it would be. The ocean had been quiet for almost two weeks, allowing the silt to settle and the water to become clear. The plants, corals, invertebrates, and fish were both plentiful and colorful.

They started shallow from the boat, almost snorkeling over the reef but when it dropped off, they went straight down. This feeling of flying was new for Luca. He had been diving many times before, including doing some night dives, but this was different. There was no bottom to see. The view sank beyond sight into the darkness. The reef wall gave a reference to gaze upon, as the gray depths gradually overtook the deep water.

As they descended the colors gradually disappeared, too. First red faded at about fifteen feet, then orange at twenty-five, yellow at thirty-five, and soon they saw only blue-violet. The change was gradual but inescapable as Luca strained to see the colors. Whenever Larry took a picture with his camera flash the true colors were revealed for a split second in the white light.

No whale passed beneath them, as it had the last time Larry had been diving there, but Luca could have sworn that he heard distant whale song.

Lunch, a nap in the sun on the boat, and another dive left the two exhausted. Dinner was casual at another beach bar. They made it an early evening, and parted company, agreeing to meet again in the morning.

By the time lunch was served the next day, they had decided to sail together through some of the islands. Luca had told Larry that his schedule was completely open, and Larry was enjoying Luca's company enough to invite him onto his boat. After his recent kidnapping experience, Larry was feeling like a little company might be a good change.

Luca checked out of his hotel while Larry charted their course. Eager to please Luca, he had selected some dive and beach spots Luca had not seen. That took them on a northern course to Dominica, and then to the island of Saba, also known as, "The Unspoiled Queen." The oddly named capital town called "The Bottom" was intriguing, along with the history of Saba's road. They thought they might enjoy some time there, but more diving was the goal.

Luca had sailed in the past and was a ready hand to help out on the Gozzard. The boat's beautiful woodwork and elegant lines had an old-world look, but modern fittings made sailing her easy. Larry had installed some conveniences. Self-tailing grinder winches, and a deck organizer that ran lines aft from key points like the reefing system, as well as a relocated halyard winch were a few of these. Larry had combined these with auto-helm and other improvements, making the yacht a comfortable one-man vessel, but it was nice to have Luca's extra hands. It wasn't long before the two were sailing along the island's shoreline, and having a great time. Their first stop would be Martinique, a friendly French island with some of the best shrimp pizza in the Caribbean.

. . .

Vlad was hoping to leave Key West, now that the boat sale was almost done. It would be the next day before the electronic transfers were complete. The Gulfstar was his, under the name Ross Eliovich Veroslav—a predominantly Czech name. Ownership of the boat would not be finalized until the boat arrived in Melbourne, Florida, on the other side of US customs.

His afternoon lagged with little to do. Luca was on-site and on target in St. Lucia. He had signaled Vlad that he was on the right island, followed quickly by a text that he was in the correct harbor. Subsequent texts reaffirmed that everything was going well. After confirmation that Luca was aboard the sailboat and heading north, Vlad relaxed. That meant his teeth stopped grinding.

He still had to wait until after ten the next morning to see that the bank transfers were complete, and that the agreement papers had been signed. The sellers, Jim and Caroline Barstow, were being very agreeable. The money was now held in escrow, pending completion of the transaction in Florida.

Vlad took a walk down the road to the Gulf of Mexico. That took twenty minutes. The sun beat down on his head. Hot, and irritable with the wait, he headed back to his little house restaurant to soak up some more of the Dalmore scotch with bread and fish.

Vlad spent the next morning making his calculations. It would be two to three weeks before the boats started arriving, so the plan was to get all of them in position in four weeks. He sent notices to the team and his client. The response from the client was "acceptable," so Vlad made one last trip to the excellent restaurant, this time for a red snapper sandwich, before leaving Key West. His destination was dinner in Key Largo, followed by Miami the next day. There was no rush now. He could work on the next project while this one simmered.

Chapter 32

Robert and Tracie sat quietly in the car, heading to dinner at his father's house. His mother Evelyn would as always, be the perfect hostess. The servants would prepare and present the meal as she directed, but she'd indicated that this would be a "casual" dinner. Only their regular staff of three would be present.

As he steered up the drive, Robert felt slightly ill at ease. There were no other cars or awaiting valets to contradict his mother's statements, so there would be no dignitaries who must be kowtowed to, but he still wondered what surprise they would face.

Robert had a nagging feeling that there might be a months-old parental reprisal waiting for him. The last time that he and his father had spoken they had argued. Robert had verbally indicted his father over actions that Robert had discovered during the OPOV mess. He had a thin veil of hope that this dinner invitation was simply the normal three-times-per-year family dinner; then again, it might be a set up for a full-scale scolding.

Robert's pulse beat faster. His trepidation grew, waiting for that first greeting.

It struck Robert as odd that Tracie seemed unconcerned. This was not like her. Normally she talked the entire distance, nervously checking her hair and makeup, and worrying about her dress. Tonight, she'd been ready on time and seemed confident. On the ride she hardly spoke, other than to refer to casual items, like the boys' schedule for the week.

"Are you all right?" Robert ventured as they pulled up to the main entrance, its grand marble stairs climbing from the half-circle drive.

"I'm fine, why?" Tracie turned quickly to look in the visor mirror as she pulled it down. "Is my face okay?"

"You just seemed quiet." Robert quickly added, "You look great."

The nineteen-ten Victorian reached almost gothic proportions, rising up in the center of five acres and towering over the landscape. At one time, the property had contained forty acres, but the original owners gave parcels to their children as they married and produced families of their own. Some grandchildren still lived nearby in somewhat smaller mini-mansions. This home remained the grandest in the neighborhood. Robert's father would have it no other way. He had an image to maintain.

Robert stood outside the car, waiting. Tracie managed the final touches to her appearance, then swung her shapely legs out the open door.

"Good?" She asked.

"Beautiful," he responded automatically.

Climbing the steps to the door, Tracie's high heels slowed them down a little. She'd carefully selected them to coordinate with, but not match her clutch purse. The heels were just tall enough to show off her calves, but didn't make her the same height as Robert's father. Robert was taller than his father was by two inches—something his father had grudgingly been forced to accept, but never acknowledged. Tracie knew this was a sensitive issue.

Tracie's dress was cocktail length, and conservative in style. The dark blue color and minimal tasteful jewelry were chosen to please Robert's mother. Evelyn tended to downplay her everyday wear of a 2-carat flawless diamond ring, platinum and diamond necklace, bracelet, and eternity band, but expected them to be noticed and superior to what Tracie might have. It was both Robert's parents' habits to become irritable if inadequate deference was shown to their expensive acquisitions. If no compliment was paid to their luxuries, they would find opportunities to point out their worth, while stressing the unimportance of the costs.

The door opened immediately after Robert tapped the knocker.

"Good evening, Mr. and Mrs. Carlton." The butler had been with his parents for five years, but his greetings were always coldly formal. He led Robert and Tracie across the large entry with its dark wood and faux-painted traditional Victorian black marble.

They passed the grand staircase that dominated the entry. This rose seven feet, then split to create a twelve-foot long gallery. From there it rose another seven feet on each side to reach the floor above. Every inch showed elaborate mahogany woodwork. Gold leaf molding rimmed its picture-framed paneling. The chandelier above never caught Robert's eye, but it left most visitors feeling as though they were star gazing on a moonless night.

The butler led them to the library, left of the entry. The room was large at twenty feet by sixteen, but its heavily draped windows, ten-foot wide ornate fireplace, and wall-to-wall, floor-to-ceiling bookshelves made it feel smaller. Over the fireplace was a six-foot painting of Robert's great-grandfather, wearing a top hat and tails astride a chestnut and black thoroughbred.

The butler closed the door behind him. There would be a predictable ten-minute wait, so Robert poured himself a scotch and made Tracie a gin and tonic. Both liquors were decanted into crystal with the brand tastefully displayed on an engraved silver chain and nameplate. According to the tags, the gin was Hayman's 1850 Reserve, and the scotch a Balvenie Single Barrel 15.

Robert had little affection for this house. His father had purchased the home only two years before Robert had left for his college dorm. There were no traces of his occupancy left anywhere. Amidst the myriad of pictures of his parents with dignitaries was a formal picture of Robert and Tracie's wedding. A picture of Robert with President Baxter sat prominently on the fireplace mantle, next to a model of his father's yacht.

The door swung open and his father entered. Robert reflected that at this casual family dinner, both he and his father were wearing suits. He presumed that his mother would be wearing a cocktail dress, something like Tracie's'.

"Tracie, you look lovely," Robert Carlton Sr. complimented, giving her a kiss on her cheek. Robert thought that his father appeared slightly more friendly than usual. He'd grasped Tracie in a quick hug. Generally, he was a bit less familial with her.

"Robby! Good to see you, Son," his father said, extending his arm to shake Robert's hand. "Your mother will be down shortly. Can I freshen your drinks?"

This affable greeting was surprising. Robert had expected some level of hostility. He hated being called Robby, and his father knew it, but his father's tone was pleasant. "Nice to see you, too, Father. My drink is fine, thank you." Robert returned cautiously.

"Thank you, Robert, but my drink's still full," Tracie pointed out to his father, seeming much more comfortable than she usually appeared with him.

The three conversed casually about the drive, the weather, and Robert's promotion for several minutes. His father appeared to have forgotten about their last hostile encounter, and was busy complimenting Robert on his advancement. Robert felt off balance. What was his father up to?

"Tracie," Robert's mother swept into the room. "How nice it is to see you. Is that a new dress? You look lovely."

This was also more welcoming than usual, Robert thought, speculatively. Usually, his mother would have added something that held just a touch of criticism or jealousy in the tone. Tonight, she seemed quite friendly.

"It's lovely to see you, too, Evelyn," Tracie gushed, embracing her and exchanging kisses on both cheeks. "You know, I thought this was a pretty dress until I saw you walk into the room. You have such sophisticated taste in clothes."

Evelyn thanked Tracie and turned toward her son. "Robby, don't you look handsome," she observed. Robert also got a peck on each cheek.

His father had been busying himself with making his wife a drink. He now handed it to her. It was a gin and tonic like Tracie's, but a little heavier on the gin.

"Come, let's sit and talk in the living room," Evelyn told them, ushering them out of the library and back across the entry to the opposite room.

Robby gave Tracie a look of, "What's going on here?" She didn't seem to notice his expression.

In the living room the decor changed completely. This was his mother's domain. Wedgewood blue paint with white trim covered the picture frame paneling. Each wall panel showcased an ornate white plaster molding in the center. The room contained antique white-painted, brocade-covered Louis XV furniture, heavy silk drapes, velvety patterned carpets, and a white marble fireplace. An antique harpsichord stood as an ornament, dust free and unused in the corner.

Conversation was kept light, matching the tone of the room. They talked almost exclusively about Robert and Tracie's boys, adding brief comments about the latest book or stage production each had experienced.

The dinner bell rang, and the four adjourned to the dining room. This was a compromise of color and balance, with more plaster adorned paneling in white, and more Louis XV furniture, but this time shiningly polished in its original mahogany. After four courses, Robert and his father adjourned to the library, while Tracie and Evelyn went back to the living room.

Robert was not eager to be alone with his father. He wondered what they could possibly find to discuss. He'd run out of light conversation halfway through dinner.

"Well, Robby, how is the new job?" His father queried, surprising Robert out of his own thoughts.

Seeking refuge in a discourse on his new duties, Robert spoke more frankly about his job than was usual in a discussion with his father. "The job carries a lot of responsibility, overseeing so many different people working on a number of projects, but Jack's something of a micro-manager. In a way that's good; I'm not in over my head, but it can be problematic when I want to take something in a different direction."

"The perks are good," he continued, since his father seemed to be listening. "Jack's not enthusiastic about traveling if a trip is relatively routine, and I'm getting in on some higher-level meetings. I seem to be getting plenty of visibility, so I'd have to say that it's going pretty well."

"What about this new Homeland Security thing where you are taking Jack's place at the cabinet-level?" Robert Sr. poured himself another scotch from his private Johnny Walker Blue label bottle. He offered some to Robert, who found himself uncharacteristically accepting.

Robert was torn between amusement and frustration. It should have been no surprise to him that his father knew exactly what he was doing at work. He'd undoubtedly found out from President Baxter himself, since he and Tom were close friends.

"That hasn't really begun, yet," Robert returned. "The preliminary work has been ongoing of course, but the first joint meeting isn't until next week."

"Well, let me give you some pointers," his father began.

Why did his father have to try to control everything, Robert wondered? He took a long sip of the smooth, expensive scotch, and tried to fight down his resentment.

Unexpectedly the doors opened. In came Tracie and his mother. This was unprecedented, Robert thought, concerned that his father might snub Tracie for interrupting their conversation.

"Robert, Evelyn and I were discussing how much you've helped our investment club. I just had to tell you how excited the club is, thanks to you," Tracie enthused, walking across the room to stand near Robert's father.

Both women were holding dainty glasses of sweet sherry, which Tracie hated, and would find some discreet way to pour out. Robert was surprised when his father warmed immediately to Tracie's flattering chatter and invited the ladies to be seated.

Once Tracie finished admiring his father's stock market knowledge, they began discussing puts, covered calls, and second derivative plays. Most of the discussion was over Robert's head. He knew Tracie was delving into the market with her club, but he had not known that his father had been providing insights. As the conversation continued, he discovered that his father had also been handing out advice, training, and tips on timing the market. He noted that the stock talk surrounded several businesses, but not his father's oil company.

In a complete reversal of roles, Robert found himself talking with his mother about the kids, while his father talked almost exclusively to Tracie.

At the end of the evening he was staggered by the warm goodbyes they received.

"Wasn't that nice?" Tracie broke the silence as Robert started the car and pulled away from the house down the drive.

"Yes," Robert answered shortly, still wondering why his parents seemed so abnormally approachable.

"I think that went very well, don't you?" Tracie pushed, pleased with herself, and fishing for a compliment from Robert.

"It did." Robert was recovering slowly. "When did you and Father start talking stocks?" he asked Tracie.

"Oh, we've been talking since just after your promotion party," Tracie answered vaguely. "Your father has been very helpful. Our little group has been doing very well. In fact, we've been making some good profits. I think we just might be onto something. It's very exciting! We all look forward to the weekly get-togethers," she finished.

"Weekly?" Robert repeated, stunned. "What are you doing that needs weekly meetings?

"Robert, hadn't you noticed that we'd stepped it up from our monthly meetings? As I was telling your father, we have a portfolio selected from about half of his recommendations. The portfolio has earned us five percent in two months. We've also been looking at a list of stocks to play over the next three quarters. I have a report here for this month that I was showing your father." She showed Robert a folded paper she had placed in her purse, but it was too dark for him to make out anything on it. Robert recalled seeing the two of them going over a piece of paper during their discussion.

Tracie playing the stock market, even with its complexities, wasn't what amazed Robert. He knew Tracie could handle whatever she chose. The two surprises were her willingness to take a gamble with money, and even more, the willingness of his father to help her. That last one was a complete shocker. Robert Carlton Sr. had never expressed an interest in helping them with anything in the past. He'd only passed judgment—and habitually found fault with even Robert's biggest achievements. Now he was helping a book club become Wall Street savvy.

Robert drove home in stupefied silence as Tracie talked.

Chapter 33

Bryston Caelle, Senior Field Researcher, sat with the key engineering team. They were listening to Homeland Security talk about deployment and the cost of SuperMISTI. The meeting included an NSA representative brandishing his "Not Invented Here" attitude, when asked about deployment. If the NSA hadn't thought of it first, they weren't going to sanction it.

Since 2014 NRL engineers like Bryston had deployed 48 HPGe detectors, proving they could detect, identify, and localize gamma and neutron sources in a maritime environment. Why, he found himself questioning, were the people in this meeting so clueless? How many times would he have to walk them through this?

The cavalcade of "suits" controlling and manipulating without understanding anything about the inner workings of what they were discussing was confounding. Bryston was 26, and working on his Ph.D. after getting his undergraduate degree in Computer Engineering from Harvey Mudd College. He knew he could run intellectual circles around these "Managers" when it came to this project, but he was supposed to wait for his boss to clarify things for these meatheads.

Bryston hated how often he had to explain that Harvey Mudd was a top five engineering school when these managers would question his background and knowledge. He was not the principle designer of the project, but as an engineer on SuperMISTI he knew it inside out. Sitting quietly while waiting for his boss to speak up was driving him crazy. Keeping silent was not Bryston's strength.

"If you don't find these radiation sources quickly, then what's the point of any of this?" Bryston blurted out in the middle of the discussion, losing his patience.

Bryston's boss glared at him.

"Mr. Caelle, I understand clearly the imperative to control the importation of radioactive substances through harbors on ships.

You're preaching to the choir." Jeff Thompson, NSA Director of Harbor Security, rebuked him. "I also understand the need for rapid detection. Now what I don't understand is how this 17,000 pound, 40-foot-long, trailer-truck-sized sensor is a reasonable method of detection. Don't we have a better chance of detecting from the air?"

Bryston tried to resist the temptation to talk down to the Director. "You have to understand proximity. Distance affects intensity. According to the inverse-square-law intensity is inversely proportional to the square of the distance from the source of radiation." Bryston explained, using what he considered to be layman's terms. "Then there is the diminishing particle count: the farther away you are, the fewer the counts per minute. The result is that more time is needed to get a meaningful sample."

Gordon Carlysle, Bryston's boss, and NRL division chief, motioned to Bryston to dial it back a little. "Mr. Thompson, you just explained part of it yourself." Gordon's Scottish accent was hard for some to understand, but he'd learned to use fewer words to get his message across. "It's big, but it works from a distance. We can scan more area from a single point, and get a target location. Bryston, why don't you walk them through it again, using the presentation?"

Plugging his computer into the big screen, Bryston navigated back to the portion on "How it Works," carefully speaking slowly as he stepped through the technology physics. He pointed out what drove the size of the system, but gave it the 3-D modeling capability that no handheld or aircraft mounted instrument could match.

. . .

Hours later strain of the meeting was still affecting Bryston. He paced around the aft section of the tugboat recounting the gist of the exchange. He was confined to a small section of the usually wide open aft deck by towing lines attached to the SuperMISTI barge.

The heavy lines kept him to a six-foot-wide section, making his agitated pacing look frantic.

"They don't understand even the basics," he fumed while recapping the meeting for Katy, "but Gordon got them to keep the funding in place."

Grady and Katy sat on the stern of the Navy tugboat, YTB-837 Monacan, listening to Bryston rant about the morning's meeting. The recap served as an update before they tried another test from the barge.

The crew of eight busied themselves as their Captain, Lieutenant Katherine Davies, listened to the young engineer. She and Grady both wore their service work uniforms. Hers was the new Navy color combination. Grady's Air Force ABU was geared for desert operations in light browns. The unseasonably warm weather relegated their jackets to the bridge.

Katy had heard enough. "Thank you for the update, Bryston," she cut in, signaling that his download had concluded. "Can you go over your objectives today, and let me know if any of our current course plan needs modification?"

"I'm on it, Captain," Bryston told her, heading below to his computer.

It was a privilege for Katy to have her first Captain command aboard this tug. Few officers got a command so young. It was a one-year assignment. The tug was wanted back in Norfolk after the SuperMISTI testing, but Katy was making the most of the career opportunity. The one-hundred foot, three-hundred and fifty-ton tug had two thousand horsepower. It was enough to nudge even an aircraft carrier to its berth. Captaining the tug was no simple task, but she had proven herself ready.

Grady was coming along for the ride. His current work with Robert related to the MISTI project, but he was on board to see Katy in action, and to spend some time with her. Their schedules had been out of synch since the Caribbean trip. They hadn't had time to get together for weeks. The time apart had created an awkward element in their conversations that Grady wanted to get past. He figured that showing his genuine interest in her work was not only respectful, but might help get them back on track.

He and Katy had discussed etiquette while he was on board. She was the Captain while on her ship as commanding officer. Grady outranked her, but he would be an observer only, unless something happened to disable her. Then he would need to rely on the Chief. She figured that the crew would call him Colonel, as they would a marine, so she wanted to get his role straight.

Grady's challenge was to look like he belonged on a ship, without getting in the way. Fortunately for him, the wide tug had plenty of room on the bridge. The barge they were towing was comparatively small and didn't require a full complement of crew.

Katy's objective was to run a test on the equipment while underway, watching for anomalies. The gentle river rocking presented a challenge for the sensitive gear, as each movement changed the direction and horizon angle of the array. How the software handled these variations, in coordination with data from the six-axis G-force sensors and GPS, would be collected and analyzed. Their ultimate radiation source target had been placed on Chopawamsic Island, just offshore of Turner field at Quantico.

The three engineers monitoring the test were unaware that a second target had been placed at the hospital point boat ramp, also on Quantico. Katy's challenge was to navigate around the island in the hope that both targets would end up in line with each other. Could MISTI differentiate the two?

. . .

Cruising at ten knots as they navigated the Potomac River leveled out some of the river chop behind the tug. After about three hours of heading south, the system successfully came in range of and spotted the mystery radioactive source.

"Captain! We spotted a target on hospital point!" Bryston was panting from running up the stairs to the bridge.

"Mister, I told you about not running on my ship!" Katy admonished him sternly.

"Sorry, Captain." Bryston tried to quell his excitement. "We got a reading as big as the one we expected. Did you know there was a second target?"

"Yes, and I'm glad you spotted it." Katy smiled. "You better get back to the monitors. We've still got the main target to log."

"Right!" Bryston rushed off the bridge.

"Don't run!" Katy called after him. "Kids," she said, grinning at Grady who stood far to starboard, in the back of the bridge.

"He's very excitable," Grady replied. He had hoped to have a nice conversation with Katy as they cruised the Potomac. He should have known better. She was continually giving orders to the helmsman and navigator. Feedback from her crew was constant. It would have been the same if she came with him on a flight if he flew a large crew plane, he reflected. Even if he took her for a ride in a two-seat F-16, the business of flying would come first. Still, it was fun watching her command her crew.

Grady could feel the tension on the tug rise as they got closer to the island. Binoculars popped up more often. Caught up in their anticipation, he grabbed a pair to look in the same direction.

From a distance the island looked like they could easily go around it, but now he could see the spur of sand jutting out. The tug might make it around safely, but sandbars moved over time. It was up to Katy to go through, or make a sharp U-turn after steaming between the island and the mainland. There was a round bay-like area, but the sides of the channel would be equally treacherous with sand.

Katy commanded her ship and trailing barge forward. The barge had a life of its own, moving side to side. Even the act of slowing down had to be carefully managed to limit its movement. The channel looked much too small, now that the two-hundred-foot vessel and barge were passing through it. Grady could see people staring from the far side of the flight line and the Marine Corps University, both of which had front row seats for the unusual spectacle. Military police were stationed onshore. They had received advance communications for this action, but they looked tense as they watched.

The helmsman's forehead was dotted with sweat. Katy appeared calm. She stood stiff and upright, with her feet planted shoulder width apart and hands together behind her back. To Grady, she looked every bit like Horacio Hornblower in command of her vessel.

They were passing with multiple changes in helm, measured off in degrees to starboard until Katy called out the command they had all waited for. "Rudder amidships, Mr. Coyle."

"Aye, Captain," he answered.

"Make eight knots," Katy continued. "Steady as she goes."

"Aye, Captain. Making eight knots," he acknowledged.

Grady thought for a moment that Katy might turn to look at him, but until they were all the way out in the river again, and heading back to dock at ten knots, she didn't take her eyes off the river. Only then did she relax.

Katy turned and walked the two steps back to Grady. "Having fun?" She asked teasingly.

"I am," Grady told her, grinning. It was sorely tempting to reach around her waist for a strong hug and kiss, but he knew she wouldn't like that while Captaining. Grady settled for giving her a wink.

Katy took a quick look at the crewmen. They were focused forward. Turning back to Grady, she responded with a smile and her own wink.

"Captain Davies," Bryston was climbing back to the bridge. "Look at this data—it's great!" He covered the map table with printouts and scattergrams of x-y correlations in the readouts. "We pegged both targets. The first within five feet, and I'll bet we got just as close on the second," he told her.

"That's very good." Katy looked over the charts, asking, "What are these dots?"

"I was trying an algorithm that would take any spurious reading and calculate for CPH instead of CPM, and then measure over the duration of the trip past Quantico. Interesting, isn't it?" Bryston was pushing the technology for everything he could get out of it.

Grady was looking at the information over Katy's shoulder. "These four dots that are together—would that be the radiology section of the hospital?" He asked.

"Either that or the dental area," Bryston responded. "I got those signals when we were approaching the island, so they were behind the island target. I only got the one down-river look, so I expect the results are less accurate, but those are very small, very short signals."

"Impressive." Katy was looking at the numbers. "So, if you can pick up that small a signal, how do you stop every hospital and each dentist's office from showing up?" She was concerned that important readings could be covered, or confused by these signals.

"We have to filter them out," Bryston agreed. "Or not use this more precise equation. My preference is for the filter."

"How about in a naval harbor filled with nuclear-powered ships? Would that cause too much noise to see anything small?" She queried.

"That's where the 3-D value really kicks in." Bryston was most excited about this feature. "By moving the instrument, like our towing it behind the tugboat now, I get an intensity level and a vector. Over time, I get crossovers with each new vector and level. So instead of triangulation of three readings, I get a reading every fifteen seconds of ten-thousand plus delineated vectors."

"Size and location." Grady was following this easily.

"Exactly. We can overlay a map too," Bryston added. "Take your example of a Navy yard," he said, nodding at Katy, "we could say which leak corresponded to which ship, and so on."

Grady was thinking about the implications and possibilities when Bryston volunteered another point.

"Of course, all of these measurements are based on a small leak or intentional radiation source," he continued. "If we had a big one, like a nuke or a dirty bomb, the scale would go so high we could lose the small signals—but then we'd have bigger fish to fry anyway, right?"

Grady and Bryston spent some time talking about the results, and going over different scenarios, while Katy returned to the duties of Captaining her boat.

By the time they finished docking the barge and tug, it was dark. When they reached the parking lot, Grady suggested that the two of them go out for a bite to eat.

"Oh, I'm sorry, I'd love to," Katy replied, genuinely sorry, "but I have our girl's night with Tracie."

"Stocks and bonds with the ladies?" Grady teased.

"No bonds, but yes, stocks every Wednesday," she answered seriously.

Grady realized that he shouldn't make light of the subject. "No guys, I suppose?" He asked hopefully.

"Nope. You guys are too emotional with stock," she responded with a mischievous gleam.

"How about Friday night, then? Are you available?" He pursued.

"Friday." Katy consented. "Pick me up at seven." Katy looked around. Seeing nobody nearby, she stretched up on her toes and gave Grady a peck on the lips. "Don't be late."

Chapter 34

Dr. Prath and his two assistants sat in a CDC conference room in Atlanta, Georgia, listening to a small hospital doctor in the Caribbean describe a flesh-eating disease that had him stumped. Six locals had been found stranded on an island. All were suffering extreme dehydration and vomiting. They exhibited massive skin ulcerations, peeling, blindness, and blood loss. All of their symptoms were significantly advanced. Two died in transit to the hospital. Of the remaining four, two had been in extremely bad shape. They had expired soon after arriving. They'd been in much the same condition as the first two with one big difference: they were completely swollen. The swelling stretched their skin until it started splitting in places. Liquid oozed from the cracks, and their pain had been excruciating.

The remaining men were deteriorating quickly. Upon arrival, they had exhibited deep-red skin, and had all the other victims' symptoms, as well as swelling of the wrists, ankles, and face.

Even though they'd been kept in isolation, there was a growing panic in the small medical unit that they had a disease that would kill everyone on the island. Staff were calling in sick. Ferries leaving the island were full going and empty returning as rumors of an Ebola-like virus spread panic. The panic was unfounded. So far none of the hospital employees had any similar symptoms.

The problem was diagnosis. They could not be sure what they were up against and had no experience with anything like it. The doctor was sure he was going to lose the remaining men.

"We couldn't move them until they could be transported in isolation. The emergency team reported that they were emaciated, and appeared to have third-degree burns over much of their bodies. Their corneas were opaque and white, resulting in complete blindness. Their hair had fallen out, and bleeding blisters covered their arms, hands, and legs from the knees down. Elsewhere the skin was falling off in sheets. On their calves, skin had fallen away down to the muscle." The island doctor's voice was beginning to shake. It was clear that he was attempting to hide his emotions. He was struggling with seeing these men deteriorate without having any ability to help them.

"Doctor, remain calm, please." Dr. Prath needed to get the whole story. "Tell us about the two that are still alive."

The doctor steadied himself, and responded, "Both have extreme redness over all the attached skin surfaces. Both are vomiting and must be hydrated intravenously. We have included essential nutrients, but nothing can be administered orally. Even ice appears to inflict extreme pain in their mouths. Hair loss is significant. Hands and feet have severe blisters. There is a lot of blistering and ulceration—I'd say thirty percent overall, with significant discoloration."

"Is the discoloration light or dark?" Dr. Prath inquired.

"Both. In blotches," was the response.

"Okay. Is the skin regenerating?" Prath wanted to know.

"I think so. It was described to us that the two who were alive on the island, but DOA at the hospital, had moist desquamation at first. Necrosis set in rapidly from an apparent collapse of the dermal vascular system. This occurred in the two men that made it here for treatment, but subsequently expired. I am concerned that the remaining patients are headed the same direction. Their sweat glands are failing, as are their kidneys. My fear is that their skin will succumb completely to necrosis—but they will likely die before that happens."

The doctor took a breath and went on, "Our lab has limited testing ability, but we have CT scanning."

"Okay, Dr. let's go through all your notes step by step," Prath replied. The call lasted an hour longer. The details read like a gruesome science fiction horror story. The Caribbean doctor was clearly exhausted, and at a complete loss for how to proceed.

"Dr. Kirton, please stay on the line. We're going to have a brief discussion and then be right back with you." Dr. Prath put the speaker phone on hold. "What do you think?" He asked his assistants.

"I don't think it is a viral or bacterial problem," Leslie said.

"I agree," stated Prath.

"Radiation poisoning?" Ventured Steve, his other assistant.

"It seems too obvious, but we have to follow the symptoms. They don't fit anything else," Prath concluded.

Dr. Prath tapped the phone module. "Dr. Kirton."

"Yes, Doctor," Kirton answered.

"Here is what we think. This is not viral or bacterial. We suspect Cutaneous Radiation Injury, or CRI, as part of Acute Radiation Syndrome. Do you have a Geiger counter?" Prath inquired.

"I believe the medical school does," Kirton answered, sounding hopeful.

"Get it, and measure the patients. If it registers, you will have to clean them, and the hospital. I suggest you implement radiation procedures for you and your staff immediately. There is a lot we need to go over, but if these men have been heavily exposed and radioactive material is on their skin, you need to protect yourself. Get someone to obtain the Geiger counter, then change your clothes and isolate. When you have a reading, call back. I will contact the Nuclear Regulatory Commission (NRC) to get more information, and to determine what equipment will be needed if we are correct in our assessment." Prath instructed.

"Thank you. I greatly appreciate your assistance, Doctor. I will be in touch within the hour." Dr. Kirton hung up.

"What do you think, Steve?" Prath asked the second assistant.

Steve looked at Dr. Prath. "I think if we are right, we need more than the NRC. There shouldn't be anything of nuclear significance, or with that kind of radiation leaking down in that area to speak of, except some medical equipment. If it was a medical equipment leak, personnel using it would have been the first victims."

Prath looked grim. "I think you're right, which means I need to make some calls. Leslie, get a decontamination team ready to travel. If it is radiation, and the contaminant is on the hospital staffs' skin, there will be more cases. Steve, get Aaron in here. We need some follow-up calls to help locate the source."

Chapter 35

Two weeks out sailing since they'd begun heading home, Mark and Julie were on a reach heading northwest from North Caicos Island to the Plana Cays. These two small islands in the Bahamas were surrounded by white sand beaches and idyllic reefs. A wildlife refuge protected endangered great iguanas and the very rare Hutia, a guinea pig-like rodent native to the Bahamas. Mark and Julie were looking forward to the seclusion of the cays, and their fabulous snorkeling. At eight knots, it would be a long day, but the winds were steady at thirteen knots. No tacks were needed on the long run.

Mark and Julie had become comfortable sailing with Jeff and Chrystal alongside in their Hunter 356. The Hunter had a slightly higher PHRF, or racing handicap, but it was easy for Mark to adjust his sails and keep the gap between them fairly constant. It was understood between the two couples that sailing about a quarter mile apart was preferred for easy maneuvering. Their tendency to race each other a little was eliminated by being out of hailing range.

Sailing together was working out well. Each day they would start early, sail all day, and anchor the yachts near each other two hours or so before sunset. Short conversations over the radio were sufficient for anything that came up, and estimated anchorage locations were chosen the day before. They would meet up after anchoring, hitting the beach or snorkeling, then going into town for dinner or taking turns cooking. They'd found themselves to be surprisingly compatible, and a fast friendship had formed. What had been a horrible experience was now feeling like a vacation again for both couples.

When the sun was about an hour from setting, Mark reached the leeward anchorage of West Plana Cay. The small hill on the island provided some shelter from the breeze. He set three anchors, and the GPS alarm in case they broke free in the night. Shortly after he tightened the second anchor line, Jeff and Chrystal arrived. They anchored in the twenty-five-foot water a proper distance away for boat swing. Before long they were all over the side in their dinghies, headed for the beach. With coolers stacked and fins in hand the four walked north on the beach to the promise of better snorkeling.

"Did you see how clear the water is?" Julie had been hanging over the bow looking at the line as it held fast off the bow. "I could see the line all the way to the anchor."

"It is wonderful, and look, not another boat in sight!" Chrystal exclaimed. "We have the beach to ourselves." The girls had on big hats, bikinis, and short, sheer cover-ups.

"How'd she sail?" Jeff was asking Mark.

"Smooth. One tack all day, and consistent winds. I let the autopilot do the steering." Mark and Jeff had similar setups that allowed for easy cruising, as well as hands-on sailing.

"Have you ever had that three-degree wobble on the helm?" Jeff was referring to how his boat on a reach would drift off course, either to port or starboard, by as much as three degrees regularly enough to feel like it was wallowing downwind.

"We did, until one of the guys at the club adjusted the accuracy settings and the way the rudder pulled to weather," Mark answered, nodding. "Now I never notice the small oscillations. He also taught me to use the other modes on the autohelm. Do you use the compass setting?"

The walk was getting warm. Julie pulled off her cover-up, and Chrystal did the same. The cool breeze quickly refreshed her skin with a race of goose bumps along her arms.

"Oh, that feels much better." She adopted a swing of her hips and grinned.

Julie laughed and responded with an exaggerated heel to toe swing of her own. "Think the guys will catch up to us now?"

"I think so," Chrystal giggled. "Have you been looking for wildlife? I'm hoping that we'll see one of the iguanas." They continued talking and watching the plants near the beach for animal life. Occasionally they would glance back to see if the boys were catching back up.

"Sure, I use the compass part. Should I adjust the settings?" Jeff asked Mark.

"Actually, they told me to only use the compass mode when I need to navigate a tricky area, or for quick control while I set sails or something. The way they set me up, I use the wind mode now, especially when going downwind. From there you change from true to apparent wind, depending on conditions," Mark told him.

"What did you use today?" Jeff was eager to find out more. He thought about going back to the boat for his manual.

"Today was perfect for the true setting," Mark disclosed. "That way the boat could surf down the waves, accelerating as the apparent wind moved forward and then back. Did you notice that?"

"No, you seemed to be sailing straight." Jeff was hooked.

"That's the beauty of it, particularly on a day like this," Mark grinned.

"When do you use apparent wind mode?" Jeff wanted to know.

"When you are sailing upwind," Mark explained.

"What are you boys talking about?" Julie and Chrystal had unexpectedly stopped. They stood facing the men as they walked up, engrossed in conversation.

Mark replied smoothly, smiling, "About you girls. We couldn't help but notice the bikinis come out."

"Well, stop staring at our butts, and let's get in the water!" Chrystal made a quick turn toward the water, swinging her hips with great emphasis. She lifted her mask to adjust the strap and clean out sand, asking, "Jeff, can you bring over my fins?"

Jeff pulled the mesh backpack strap off his left shoulder and followed the girls to the water grinning at Mark. "Smooth."

Mark laughed and pulled Julie's fins out of his mesh bag.

Although the fish were colorful and plentiful, they didn't swim long. The coolers down the beach were calling, so after about forty minutes Mark and Julie, who had made some hand signals popped up above the water.

"Ready for a beer?" Mark asked.

"Sure. Chips and black bean dip, too." Julie started swimming south skirting the beach and Mark made his way over to Jeff and Chrystal. He approached in a circle so he would come up facing them. This helped to avoid that surprise from behind that could feel like a fish nibbling. It also kept him from getting slapped by flapping fins.

"Ready for some beer and chips?"

"Sounds wonderful," Chrystal replied. The two started swimming after Julie. Jeff caught up from behind.

By the time they came out of the water near the dinghies and coolers, Julie had already pulled out the beach towels, chips, dip, some veggies, cheese, and crackers. She brought beers down to Mark, Chrystal, and Jeff, as they sat in the shallow water, pulling off fins and masks.

"Wow! That tastes good." Mark said first, but they all agreed. "There's nothing like a cold beer after a mouthful of saltwater."

They hiked back up to the towels and food, talking about the fish they'd seen. Everyone dug into the food, savoring the tastes and the beer.

Julie fixed herself a cheese cracker while lounging on a towel. "I can't believe it all turned out this way, after being locked up on that little island."

There was an awkward pause. "I want to forget about that entirely," Chrystal finally stated. "I suppose we might never have met you both if it hadn't happened, so I'm going to focus on that aspect of the situation, instead of when we were trapped there. I'm just glad we're done with all of it."

The four were silent for a few minutes.

Mark used a carrot to get a huge blob of bean dip into his mouth. "What's for dinner?" he mumbled, swallowing the dip.

They all laughed at him, and begin considering meal options. It had become traditional for the four to talk about the next meal while eating.

<u>Chapter 36</u>

Robert had been dreading lunch. It had been on the books for two weeks, and he knew it would cause trouble to try rescheduling. Senator Daniel Gregg had requested the meeting, and Robert couldn't outright ignore the senior Senator, no matter what the two of them knew lurked in the background. Gregg still wielded plenty of power.

It was the end of February. The strangely warm weather was gone. Robert missed being in the Caribbean. Had only three weeks passed since he and Tracie were in St. Thomas? The tropical islands seemed far, far away at the moment.

This meeting had Robert concerned. Last time Robert and the Senator met, he had leveraged the Senator into agreeing to retire. They had played political hardball, and Robert had won that day. Senator Gregg had agreed to end his career then and there.

But that had changed. Gregg had played his cards well, and put Robert in the awkward position of having to allow him to push out his resignation date.

Robert clung to the hope that Greg would live up to his commitment. The candidate filing deadline for Gregg's state was in three days, and so far Gregg hadn't filed to run for re-election.

Robert pulled up the register on his computer. Gregg was still not listed. There were two junior members of his party listed. "Wet behind the ear wannabes," Robert thought to himself, shaking his head. The other party had an unfamiliar name filed. They were all only looking to make names for themselves by running against Gregg. Gregg had made no public announcement about retiring, but in three days they would know. Those rookies would suddenly have a real chance of winning. Somebody's life was about to change.

It was reasonable for Gregg to not publicly preannounce his intentions. He'd want to avoid lame-duck status, and his party would want to collect contributions from his supporters. It would also keep a strong opponent from entering the race, since unseating someone like Gregg was nearly impossible. A serious challenge against an incumbent with Gregg's kind of power base took too much money and influence.

"Politics—not a place for honorable men," Robert muttered, thinking that should be a quote written in the history books. Folding up his computer and grabbing his coat, Robert headed for the parking garage.

It was cold. This was a result of a sudden rush of frigid air coming down from Canada. Some battle between El Niño and an arctic blob of some sort continued to rage. The weather had warmed right around Christmas, enough to make the cherry trees show buds in January. This strong cold snap would probably damage the buds and trees. Nobody knew how much, but in some years like this, they'd had to replace half or more of DC's cherry trees.

Robert pulled his coat tight as he exited the building. This fast-changing weather was a hard adaptation.

Robert found Gregg in the bar at the Round Robin. Gregg was sitting comfortably with an empty glass.

"Robert, glad you could come. Have a seat." Gregg's voice was strong and deep, but not as loud and intimidating as usual. His smile was ingratiating. Robert couldn't have been more surprised if Gregg had stood up to shake hands. This was not the domineering, narcissistic Senator Gregg he knew.

"Senator, my pleasure." Robert's pat reply was less than genuine. He'd learned to be wary of the man.

"What will you have? I'm buying." Gregg jiggled his glass at the waiter.

"The same," Robert replied, wondering what was prompting the Senator's generosity. Gregg drank expensive scotch, and he generally preferred that others bought it for him.

Gregg signaled the bartender when the waiter didn't notice his gesture. The bartender nodded and snagged the waiter, who came scurrying over to take their orders.

As soon as the waiter was on his way to get their drinks, Gregg turned back and began speaking. "Robert, I'm sure you know I'm temporarily filling in for Charlie on the Senate Subcommittee on Privacy, Technology and the Law," he began.

"How is Senator Davit?" Robert cut in. He had heard that the Senator from Idaho was ill.

"He's doing well. You know, Charlie and I go way back. Anyway, they think his tumor is benign, but they'll know for sure when they remove it in about three months," Gregg imparted.

"Three months?" Robert accepted the glass of scotch from the waiter. It had just a dash of room temperature spring water added to bring out the bouquet of the Scotch, or "the nose," the waiter disclosed. Robert took a sip, then continued, "Why three months? Why aren't they removing it right away?"

"He tells me they have to shrink it before removing the thing. It's too close to other organs, so they've got him talking some pill to get the size down. The pill wears him out, so he's having to take things a little easier," Gregg supplied.

"Oh." Robert took a sip of the drink. "Good scotch, Senator. What is it?"

"Macallan 12. Quite acceptable, don't you think?" The Senator asked.

"It is," Robert confirmed. He did like the scotch for its smooth, classic flavor and aroma, but this was a reasonably priced scotch. Gregg usually ordered off the list that did not display a price. Another surprise.

The Senator took a big sip and set the glass down. "Robert, what I hope you can help me with is a general legal opinion on privacy so that I can come up to speed on all of this. I could also use some information on the technology that is messing things up, if you're familiar with it."

"Well, I agree with you, Senator. It is a mess. Most of the laws were written before people started putting their personal information on the internet, or posting their images and opinions where everyone can see them." Robert responded, wondering what, exactly, the Senator was expecting from him.

"I'm not as concerned about that right now. That stuff on social media is getting wrung out in the courts, so we're going to leave it to them to set the standards. I'm more interested in Drones and IoT. I'm talking about what is coming—and I think it's coming fast," Gregg stated.

"Again, I think you're right, Senator; that is the next wave of concern. Drones are a big issue, and the current laws are inadequate. We're going to see a lot of court cases over drones. As far as the Internet-of-Things goes, that's going to generate a list of issues, most of which we don't even know about yet. The lack of security is clear enough, but the rest is speculation."

The maître d' got their attention. Their table was ready. They both rose to follow him.

"I think people thought the IoT would be pretty straightforward," Robert continued after they were seated, "but I'm not so sure. We do have laws in place regarding the exchange of data and paths of responsibility in handling it. Those laws should be used to evaluate the cases that are generated." Robert believed in the law as existing, needing only enforcement from court rulings, rather than modification.

"That's well and good, Robert, but let's take, for example, a fitness tracker. What if your wristband collects your location and biometric data, then releases it on the internet while you're having an affair? That spike in heart rate and respiration might be admissible. Can you imagine a flashing red dot on a map, and the place it shows is not your office, or your car, and not home, but a motel, or your partner's home?" Gregg almost laughed at the visual.

"That's a good point, but current laws may cover that if the owner of the wristband set it to regularly release the information. If not, then the manufacturer has liability—at least, theoretically." Robert pointed to his selection on the menu for the waiter who had appeared, and read aloud, "The braised chicken pasta, and blue cheese on the salad, please."

"Yes, Sir. And you, Sir?" The waiter requested. Greg looked up only briefly, saying shortly, "Tell Daniel it's me."

"Very good, Sir." The waiter departed as silently as he had arrived.

"Private menu?" Robert asked.

"He knows me. He came over recently from a favorite restaurant of mine to work as Sous Chef here. The kid has talent." Gregg's glass was empty, but he had not yet demanded a refill. "Yes, I see what you're saying, but what if the data is hacked? How do we apply responsibility? Or do we? Anyway, I'm not as concerned about the personal issues. What I'm wondering is, how much of a problem is on the industrial side of the Internet-of-Things?" He probed.

"I think the first issue the courts will be dealing with is, who owns the data? The cloud will be pervasive, and the information is in the hands of some companies that have little experience in controlling or keeping it safe." This was not the conversation that Robert had expected. He felt comfortable with this line of questioning, and in fact, was interested in the topic.

"Well, Robert, does anyone, including these so-called 'experienced' businesses know how to secure data?" Gregg sarcastically asked. "Hah! I had my credit card stolen by a hacker via a major company breach. It happened at a store where my wife buys clothing. What an ungodly mess *that* was to fix," he continued, shaking his head.

"Getting back to drones for a moment, Senator," Robert interjected. "I think that particular area of consumerism is going to create legal trouble in several areas. The existing laws will be sorely tested." Robert refrained from telling Gregg that he thought Congress should have taken a stronger stand on drone registration.

"That's the thing." Gregg adjusted his girth between the chair arms as he picked up his glass and shook it at the waiter. "It's this traceability and liability stuff."

"Yes, that's a concern. If a drone crashes on a freeway and there's a twenty-car pileup, how do you trace the responsible operator?" Robert queried, making his point.

"Or, it doesn't crash, and just scares a driver into swerving into other cars, or a bridge abutment." Gregg countered. "Then there's breach of privacy with the camera or microphone. Any fool can buy a drone. Right now, there is an assumption people will use them responsibly—which is a joke. I give that zero chance of success. How many neighborhood fights will it take to become a forest fire of legal battles?"

"Or worse, a gun fight." Robert's imagination was filled with examples of what could happen, and what might already be occurring. He wondered: if Gregg felt this way, why hadn't he fought for stricter registration rules? "Proof of invasion of privacy will be tough with owners unwilling to accept responsibility," he added, making another point. "You would think that peeking through windows should be simple to prosecute, but how do you prove it with a drone? I never have a camera handy enough to get a shot of something like that. Plus, I'd have to somehow follow a 'peeping drone' to its owner to be able to do anything about it. That could be difficult."

"What about flying over private property? Isn't that trespass?" Gregg inquired.

"I would say that depends on the drone's flying altitude." Robert had looked into this for Tracie, who had developed concerns about a drone flying neighbor. "The FAA defines five-hundred feet above ground level and higher as navigable public domain. There was a case of a hang-glider being found guilty of trespass at eighty-three feet. I think the courts will have to test the premise of 'uninterrupted use and enjoyment of the underlying land to prevent nuisance.' *Cujus est solum ejus usque ad coelum.*"

"I haven't spoken Latin in years, Robert," Gregg interrupted.

"It's from a class I had, called *The Law and History.* It means 'Whose is the soil, his it is up to the sky.' That was the premise before airplanes."

The two men paused. Robert was still eating his salad, but Gregg's plate had been emptied and removed. The waiter looked disturbed over Robert's remaining pieces of salad when he brought the braised chicken served over freshly made pasta, surrounded by locally-sourced steamed vegetables.

"That's okay," Robert told the waiter, "I'm just slow today." Good restaurants didn't like bringing the next course before the first was finished.

The waiter looked relieved and set down the plates. Gregg's feast of several kinds of seafood looked similar to a Pontchartrain dish, piled high with the emphasis on scallops.

Robert continued, "The main problem is that I think it will be hard to enforce compliance with the existing laws."

"What if some college girl is sunbathing topless in her backyard, or showering with the drapes open on a fourth-floor apartment? Is it her tough luck that a drone's camera gets a shot of her?" Gregg asked, descending upon his seafood fantasy.

"No, she is protected somewhat in both cases." The conversation lagged again as both men concentrated on the food. It was an oddly comfortable silence. Robert was not used to this with Gregg, who normally followed every statement with a question. It had been a congenial conversation, which was unexpected given their last encounter. They continued eating until Gregg finished most of his dish.

"Where was I?" Gregg eased back in his chair slightly.

"Sunbathing topless," Robert replied.

"Right. What did you mean by 'somewhat protected'?" Gregg pursued.

"Well, most, if not all states have statutes addressing the issue of binoculars, telescopes, cameras and so forth from being used from adjoining or distant property. There is also precedent and case law addressing private airspace in most states, but some of it is very individual."

The dessert menus arrived with the waiter, who cleared their plates. Both men made rapid selections. Gregg's was a rum sauced bread pudding; Robert selected black-raspberry sorbet.

"So, you're saying that separate states are going to have a whole bunch of conflicting case laws about these problems. Let's try the question of invited and uninvited. How about paparazzi and the mess they have made of privacy? Where do you think we will go from here?"

Robert paused as the waiter arrived with the desserts. He let Gregg settle into his before saying carefully, "I think we should avoid creating new laws strictly for drones. We should enforce the laws we have."

"But what about a peeper that uses a camera drone from half a mile away, or a hundred yards, or behind your own trees?" Gregg insisted. "There's no way to determine who these things belong to, as we've established. Then there's the problem of actual owners and operators saying they weren't doing anything wrong." Gregg paused to savor another bite of the rich desert.

Robert was amazed. Since when did Gregg care so much about citizens' rights? Or was it his own privacy he was concerned about being in jeopardy? "That's a big issue, Senator. Law enforcement is largely unprepared or staffed for investigations into any of these things. There are certainly many possible considerations. We could attach addendums to existing laws that address the placement of remote cameras without permission. The fact that these cameras are not permanent installations should be irrelevant if the results are the same."

Gregg ordered more drinks, indicating that the conversation would continue, asking several additional questions about drone usage. Eventually he agreed with Robert that enforcement was the goal, with ownership and traceability being the challenge. Robert was glad to see that Gregg had recognized traceability as an issue, but wondered if that would make any difference. In the short time Gregg had left in office, he was unlikely to get anything done about it.

"Well, Mr. Deputy Attorney General, I thank you for your time, but I need to get going," Gregg finally announced.

"Thank you, Senator," Robert responded. "I think it was a meaningful discussion. I appreciate the lunch."

"Mind if I recap our discussion with the committee?" Gregg asked casually.

"Not at all. Of course, it comes with the usual disclaimers until we make the investigation of a specific criteria official." Robert told him.

"Of course," Gregg answered. "Nice working with you, Robert. I think our relationship has evolved, don't you? We're going to be useful to each other, in our new understanding."

The two parted ways at the door. Robert stood in the entry buttoning his coat and reflected on the encounter. Strangely, Gregg hadn't seemed to have any hidden agenda. Robert was puzzled. He wondered whether the Senator had already landed a lucrative job with a special interest group? One that worked for a drone manufacturer perhaps?

Robert thought this was unlikely since so many were made by foreign countries, but he wondered again what the Senator really wanted. His last words certainly indicated that he expected to be in contact. Robert paused, thinking about that. Just what had the Senator meant?

Chapter 37

Standing on the dock of the tiny one-house island, Doctor Prath and his two-person CDC team were sweating in their radiation hazmat suits. Next to them stood two equally overheated members of the Nuclear Regulatory Commission. Two NRC members remained on the rented boat.

The self-contained radiation contamination suits included enough canister air supply to create a slight positive pressure, keeping outside air from entering. The expanding air from the tanks was naturally cool, but it warmed quickly, trapped in the suits. Hanging from their shoulders, thermoelectric Peltier solid-state cooling panels mounted in backpacks struggled to keep their body temperatures reasonable.

The five team members were grateful that three lead-lined crates and the decontamination gear could be lifted onto the island by a small onboard crane. The weight of the gear and exertion of offloading equipment from the boat was quickly turning their suits into saunas. The heat and blazing sun were beyond the limits of the cooling equipment.

The boat anchored off-shore and upwind after the off-load. The two-man NRC crew watched intently. They kept their protective suits on, in case of a wind change that could send radioactive dust particles their way.

The team knew that with radiation, the best strategy was to minimize exposure time and maximize distance from the source. They could shield themselves with twelve feet of water, six feet of concrete, or a foot of lead, but on a boat, these options were impractical. Working onshore, shielding was impossible.

On the dock, one team member was busy assembling the decontamination tent. This was where they would do the first level cleaning when they were finished. The second level decontamination pod stood tied down on the stern of the boat, ready to be used.

Before they had embarked for the island, examination of the two living comatose patients had confirmed the ARS diagnosis. The men had been cleaned as much as their bodies could tolerate, mostly through irrigation. Portions of skin stuck to the cleaning pads, so it was necessary to stop scrubbing before doing more harm than good. The hospital and staff were also cleaned, and their clothing bagged.

The patients still registered radiation on the meters. They had inhaled, or ingested radioactive materials. The prognosis was bleak.

The CDC and NRC teams had come to the island to find the source, verify its composition, and discover what, if any, treatment might help. It was the only chance those two men had. If it was still on the island, the contaminate had to be contained, or removed.

Their instruments were now measuring the radiation levels. They could only stay near the island safely for a day, at best. Less if the radiation was too high. It seemed a short amount of time, but they thought it likely that they'd find the source in such a small area—if it was still there.

After a few minutes of scanning with the instruments from the dock, the team had no doubts. A significant portion of radioactive material was on the island. The shrouded directional Geiger counter sensors pointed them in the direction of the house. The question was, how widespread was the material?

They proceeded up the dock with their tools and instruments. On the open-air porch of the house, they could see four cots; the rest were inside. Large patches of thick, bloody skin stuck to the two cots that were closest to the sand. The skin had dried in the sun, turning black with blood. It was covered in flies. Dr. Prath took pictures of the flies. Fruit flies had been known to survive a lethal dose of 640 Gray, LD640 Gy radiation. The dose was less for larger flies. The flies' survivability didn't tell Prath much, but he documented it anyway.

He proceeded into the house with Leslie. He was looking for food and found several open packets. They saw no mice or rats, but by approaching slowly and carefully, Leslie spotted a cockroach just before it skittered away. Cockroaches could only survive LD64Gy—ten times less radiation than would kill the flies, and ten times more than a human could survive. This was important data. This meant the roaches had not received a fatal dose. It gave the team a useful reference point.

Looking down at her digital readout, Leslie adjusted the scale. Fifteen point eight millisieverts, or mSv per hour. Prath looked over at the reading and with some quick math in his head calculated that fourteen days, twenty-four hours per day, came to a two-week exposure of five-thousand mSv for the men that had stayed in the house. The first responders to the island had reported a gruesome scene that corresponded to the flesh on the cots. The victims who spent the most time near the sand seemed to have been the worst off.

"Steve, what do you read?" Prath said into his radio.

Steve Mahaffey, a nuclear physicist and the team leader for the NRC Southeast Region, was on the far side of the island. "I have twelve mSv."

"I have twenty-five," Alex called out. "I'm by the front porch. I think this is the source."

The team converged on the porch. Soon they had narrowed the search to the sandy spot that was hiding the broken sealed source.

"We need to be out of here in four hours total," Dr. Prath advised them. He had declared earlier that he wanted no more than 100 mSv exposure to the team. In the scientific community, this level of exposure was controversial. The suits generally protected them from inhaling radioactive particles, or gasses, and the team had agreed on the 100mSv number.

They set to work. Prath continued walking the island, mapping his readings and taking samples of plants, insects, and food, while the others dug in the sand. He mumbled as he walked. "Sixty-four Gray times one-thousand, divided by twenty-five mSv, divided by twenty-four hours." He punched the numbers into his calculator. "One-hundred and six days."

They had all been listening over the radios.

"One-hundred and six days?" Steve verified.

"Yes, we saw a live, seemingly healthy roach," Prath answered. He'd forgotten that he'd been talking out loud. "If the source is here, it was placed within the last hundred or so days, worst case."

Digging in the soft sand was relatively easy. In less than an hour, they had the dull green metal container uncovered on all sides. It resembled a metal milk canister. The cylinder was about eighteen inches in diameter, with smaller cylinders on both ends, that measured about ten inches in diameter each.

"Soviet irradiator, broken open." Steve could read Russian. "It's a seed irradiator, using Cesium-137. They use these by dropping seeds in the top. The seeds slide down the chute, and when they come out, they can no longer germinate. Reduces spoilage in storage too. That looks bad." He pointed at a crack along the welding seam of the canister.

"If those men sat near this, the two weeks accumulated exposure was over eight-thousand mSv," Steve continued. "That's why the two who stayed on those cots died first. The ones that tended to be farther back, toward the house, got somewhere between four and five-thousand. The two patients left might have a chance."

"Less of a chance if they ingested it, which is very likely," Dr. Prath commented. "Cesium-137 bonds with sand—and this might be the Cesium salt form. With the men walking in the sand, the dust would be dispersed into the air, and then into their lungs. It would tend to contaminate their food, as well. In both cases, it's a short trip to every soft tissue of the body." Dr. Prath now knew that the two survivors weren't likely to be alive much longer.

"The big question is, how much of the source got out of the casing?" Steve stood aside as two of the team cleared the sand away by shoveling it into one of the crates. "The scorch marks and debris indicate that this was broken open with a small C-4 linear-shaped charge designed to crack it open along the seam, but not blast it apart," he commented, holding up a bag of metal fragments he'd collected. "I think most of the Cesium powder source will still be intact. This could have been a much bigger mess. It looks as though it may have been buried before they opened it. While they kicked up the dust from the sand, the sand actually may have kept the powder from spreading further on the wind, or in the water."

"How do you think someone obtained this canister?" Leslie asked.

"These old-style irradiators were proven inefficient, and largely discontinued in the seventies," one of the NRC team members answered. "The problem is that there are thousands remaining around the world. During the breakup of the Soviet Union, a lot of these were sold or lost. We've also had reports of replenished units that have been worrying nuclear agencies for decades."

Steve took several pictures of the irradiator and the area around it. "Okay, let's wrap this up. We need to box the source, along with as much of the surrounding sand as possible, then quarantine the island."

"What's your estimate on quarantine length?" Dr. Prath asked.

"Cs-137 has a half-life of thirty years. The date on this unit is eight years old. That might be an inspection date, but it's just as likely that it could be a replenishment date," Steve responded.

It took some time to drag the heavy boxes of sand and the canister to the dock and first decontamination tent. They were especially careful in handling the broken irradiator.

"What do you think about this, Steve?" Dr. Prath asked as they waited for the boat to approach the dock. "Why would anyone plant this canister here, and strand those men on this island with it?"

Steve thought about the question for a moment. "I don't know," he finally answered. "There are too many questions. Is this a single lost, bought, or stolen irradiator? I don't think so. Why would you do this if you had only one of these? It makes no sense. There are easier ways of getting rid of people, so I'm guessing this is an opening threat of some kind. Someone just sent us a warning."

"You mean that we're likely to see more of these canisters deliberately broken open, and more people affected?" Dr. Prath worried. "What's next, then?"

"I can't radio this ahead. I'll have to ask you to not talk about the container, what we know about it, or its origins. This is now a national security issue—not only for this region but for the US, as well."

While Dr. Prath and Steve conducted the cleanup operation, Leslie walked the perimeter of the island planting nuclear and no trespass warnings in English, French, Spanish and Dutch.

The lead-lined crate containing the source was loaded onto the boat with the crane and placed inside a larger, thicker lead crate. The crate was then closed tightly. The crates of sand were loaded next. In all cases, they were thoroughly washed in the first decontamination tent on the dock, then again in the second decontamination tent. The team went through the on-dock cleaning, then folded up and bagged the cleaning system. Next, everyone went through the second process on the boat, as they motored away from the island.

All of the team members checked out below the acceptable annual dosage levels, according to their radiation tags. Taking the most contaminated sand was the initial effort—and better than the alternative of leaving the dangerous materials on the island. Much more would ultimately have to be removed from the island and stored, probably in a nuclear waste site in Florida or Georgia.

Under Steve's direction and Dr. Prath's agreement, no effort was made to remove the Cesium source puck from the irradiator casing. This would be done in a federal laboratory. They agreed that the Cesium was the dry powdered type. The liquid form would not have spread so readily with the sand.

Once all the gear was safely stowed, Dr. Prath radioed the hospital. He ordered the immediate treatment of the two remaining survivors with Prussian Blue, ferric ferrocyanide. This was the one effective radiation treatment for Cs-137. If they'd ingested or inhaled any Cesium, the Prussian Blue would bond with it, and flush it from their systems. This treatment historically had shown decreases of the relative exposure by as much as seventy percent if administered immediately. There was a chance that the two men could survive with the treatment, but it was a very slim chance with their long exposure.

"What do we do now, Steve?" Dr. Prath sat down on the boat bench across from the NRC team.

"My team takes it from here. We offload and ship the containers. You take care of the patients and tell everyone as little as possible. You'll need to get me a list of everyone who has come in contact with the patients. Hopefully, we can contain speculation a little while longer. After I make my calls, I'll join you at the hospital. I'll need that list then. Oh, and avoid referring to the source as Cesium-137."

"They already know," Prath protested, "based on the Prussian Blue, it's fairly obvious if they look it up."

"Prussian Blue can treat other things, too." Steve countered. "If you have to say something, say it appears to be Thallium."

"Why is Thallium any better?" Leslie wanted to know.

"It's manmade," Steve explained, "but it doesn't come from a nuclear fission reactor or as a nuclear bomb byproduct."

. . .

Later that evening, Robert's phone illuminated with a message.

"West Wing, eight AM. Crain."

Chapter 38

Seven-forty-five AM, Robert stood in the White House West Wing lobby with his special pass around his neck. He'd expected to see his boss Jack Crain in the lobby, but instead, he saw a woman walking up to him.

"Mr. Carlton? I don't know if you recall, but I'm Jennifer, the Chief of Staff's secretary. Please follow me," she requested.

"Certainly, Jennifer," Robert answered, wondering which room he was being led toward.

As he approached the door leading to the White House Chief of Staff's office his spine stiffened. Jennifer knocked twice and without waiting pushed open the door.

"Deputy Attorney General Carlton," she announced, closing the door quickly behind Robert as he entered.

"Robert! Glad you could be here on short notice." White House Chief of Staff Jason Carlisle stood behind his desk. Robert noticed that one of the two chairs sitting in front of Carlisle's desk held State Department Under Secretary of Arms Control and International Security Affairs Lillian Morrison. "You've met Lillian, I believe?" Carlisle asked.

"Yes, of course," Robert responded, shaking hands with Morrison. Before he could do the same with Carlisle, the Chief of Staff was already moving to the other side of his desk.

"Have a seat, Robert," Carlisle told him, indicating that Robert should take the chair next to Lillian.

Robert took his cue and waited for Jason to begin speaking.

"Here's the situation," Carlisle was jumping right into the point of the meeting without any preamble. "The President, Secretary of Defense, Secretary of State, Homeland Security, Joint Chiefs, CIA, and some key staff members were briefed last night by the National Security Advisor. We have identified a Soviet sealed source irradiator that was opened on a private island in the mid-

Caribbean. There have been six civilians exposed to the radiation, with four casualties. The remaining two civilians are in critical condition. The container is believed to be part of a Kazakhstani stockpile from abandoned factories and farms. There could be more where this came from. You'll learn more details from the Security Advisor in a minute. Now, it is my understanding from Secretary of State Vance that the two of you have been doing advance work with authorities in that region that is pertinent to this situation."

Robert and Morrison nodded but refrained from speaking. It was evident that Carlisle was already well-informed about their activities.

"Okay." Jason continued, "I'll be briefing the President in one hour, at which time you'll need to be ready to answer questions in that meeting. Between then and now you both need to meet with the NSA Advisor, Ron Crest. Get him up to speed on what you have done, and what can be done. He'll be giving information to you about what's been happening in this situation, and what they intend to do."

Jason stood, signaling that the meeting was ending. "You will not be presenting in the meeting with the President, but be ready to answer any questions directed to you."

The door opened. Jennifer came in and ushered them down the hall, past the Vice President's office. She took them to the far corner of the building where the National Security Advisor had an office, introducing them to Ron before leaving and closing the door.

Ron had been scanning a folder of communiques, which he set aside. "Under Secretary, Deputy," he acknowledged. Please, sit," he invited, motioning them to his visitor chairs.

Ron Crest had been an unusual choice for National Security Advisor. He had developed a strong research background while in the Army, and had come to the President's attention due to some insightful strategies he'd developed. Ron had some minor combat experience, but most of his career had been spent in think tank type environments. He also had a significant technology background that included electronics. He tended to prefer titles over names, but left most visitors with the feeling that he knew their middle names and those of their kids, along with every detail of their life story. He also spoke very quickly.

"What we know is this," Ron began, "The private island where the Soviet canister was discovered is very small, and has only one house on it." He handed folders with documents, photographs, and a map to Robert and Lillian. "Six men were stranded there by their employer with enough food and water supplies for a little over a week. They were found after two weeks suffering from radiation poisoning, complicated by dehydration. Four are now dead. The remaining two are under treatment. The Acute Radiation Syndrome was brought on by a deliberately buried and broken open Cesium-137 irradiation sealed source. The labeling indicates it is from a stockpile in Kazakhstan, lost in 2014. The International Atomic Energy Agency reported about 140 cases of missing nuclear and radioactive materials in that area during 2013. Unauthorized uses were also discovered, with more in 2014."

"The canister was deliberately broken open?" Lillian Morrison asked.

"Blown open with a linear shaped charge. Only a crack was made in the housing," Crest informed them.

"What do the two survivors say happened?" Robert asked.

"They gave medical personnel on the scene the information about the food and water, and about being stranded early on, but no one thought to ask the right questions at that time. It wasn't immediately clear what was wrong with the men. They didn't have the diagnosis of advanced radiation sickness until yesterday. The ARS had them in so much increasing pain that morphine was no longer effective, and they were placed in induced comas."

"Even if they weren't in a comatose state, it is unlikely they could still communicate," Ron added. "They now have severe swelling everywhere, exhibited in swollen larynxes, necks, mouths—in simple fact, every bit of their bodies is swollen to the point of being non-functional. I'm told that their hands look like fused baseball mitts, and their eyes are completely shut. The radiation poisoning has decimated their skin. They have a very slim chance of making it."

Robert's mind was racing. This sounded like a deliberate, tortuous act. Was it something they were going to see more of? What could they do to prevent this from happening again? His mind snapped back to the conversation with Ron's next words.

"The local authorities are working on the identities of all six victims now. None of them carried ID, and no one on the nearby islands has been reported missing. This is going to move slowly, given the area and the lack of centralized records. The deceased may not even have dental records. That's a problem since two of them are unrecognizable."

"Unrecognizable?" Robert asked.

"Skin sloughing was the description," Ron said shortly, closing his folder. He opened a laptop computer.

"What do you need from us, and what will the President be looking for?" Morrison cut to the chase.

"My information shows that the two of you are involved in recent activities associated with State to organize the region for the detection and control of WMDs. This irradiator is a WMD. Deputy Carlton, you were the key coordinator of the first meeting, on behalf of the State Department. Is this correct?"

Robert nodded. His head was swimming. Suddenly his simple duties in the Caribbean were taking on more serious implications.

Ron looked at his watch and started talking even faster. "We're going to treat this as a national security threat to get nuclear materials into the United States for terrorist or military purposes. We need to lock down the area in case there are more canisters. The President will be asking for an immediate action plan from State, DOJ, Defense, Homeland Security, the FBI, and the CIA, along with preparation plans from FEMA and the Nuclear Regulatory

Commission. The NRC has already been involved on-site with members of the CDC. The NRC representative should be arriving within..." he checked his watch, "within the hour. He will be joining us with the President. Questions? If not, then tell me about the existing..."

The phone rang on Ron's desk. With a quick look at the display, he raised his index finger. "Just one second. I need to grab this."

Robert made a move to rise, but Ron indicated he should stay seated with a move of his hand.

"Crest here. Yes. Six. Got it. Will you be here in time to join the briefing? Good." Ron hung up. "Okay, I was asking you to tell me the existing capabilities of the region."

Robert filled Ron in on what had been covered with the local authorities in St. Thomas, including their plans and commitments. The first local follow-on meeting had been held, but no cohesive plan had been set in action. The good news was that the various governments were in agreement and cooperative. Individuals from each country and island had been identified as the key contacts for a WMD event, and a chain of communications had been established. They had accomplished a lot in a short time, which was a small miracle by itself. Perhaps some of the hubris from British Virgin Islands Governor Edward Collins, OBE, was justified. He, along with the other Governors had certainly delivered.

Lillian Morrison brought them up to date on the preparations the State Department had made in order to have the Caribbean on a similar page with the Mexican and Canadian agreements.

Ron Crest took the information with a degree of intensity bordering on mania. He was, in fact, adding details in his head to the words spoken, aggregating the information together into his notes to create a more complete picture.

With twenty minutes remaining before they met with the President, Steve Mahaffey, the Nuclear Regulation Commission Region II Chief Investigator, sprinted into the meeting. The four rushed down the hall to debrief with Jason Carlisle. The Chief of Staff asked pointed questions of the exhausted, sleep-deprived Steve, who reported what he had seen on the island. The radioactive materials had been safely loaded onto a Coast Guard cutter before he left. The Q&A continued until there was a knock at the door. Jennifer ushered in the Director of the CIA.

Carlisle immediately addressed the Director. "You think this irradiation canister that's been discovered may be one of five lost in transit from Africa to Venezuela?"

"Yes," the CIA Director replied. "Our operatives were tracking a shipment of five irradiator sealed sources that came out of the Middle East. We first learned of them in Syria. The trail led to Libya, Sudan, and then dead-ended in the Congo port of Pointe-Noire. We'd previously followed a string of arms shipments from there to Venezuela, so we had been gradually adding assets on likely transports. One of these assets was in place for two years. The ship he'd most recently been aboard made port in Venezuela, at Guira, five weeks ago. It has now returned to the Congo, but we haven't heard from our operative. We can't be sure, but we now think the five sources may have been on that ship, and that they were off-loaded in Venezuela."

"Is it normal for your operatives to drop out of communication for a month or two?" The Chief of Staff asked.

"Yes, Sir. Discipline on these ships can be harsh, and often there is no communication in a port because shore leave is denied. We are concerned since he has missed two check-in dates, and his GPS transponder was not sensed in either port. If his transponder was lost or damaged, we should have heard from him in Pointe-Noire where we could have supplied a new one. We have to assume the transponder and our operative are now lost. We are trying to confirm this."

There was silence in the room for a moment as the others digested this information. "This irradiator we now have in-hand is the same type of device as the other five?" Carlisle spoke again.

"To the best of our intelligence," the Director responded.

"But we don't know for sure, and you have no idea where the other five might be?" Carlisle pressed.

"No, but the probability that this is one of five is extremely high," the Director seemed almost inhumanly calm stating this. "The other canisters may have been sent in multiple directions. We don't have any leads at this time," he added.

Again, there was silence in the room, as they each absorbed the implications.

When the knock came at the door, it startled Robert.

Jennifer came in. "He's ready."

They all stood, following Jennifer down the hall and into the President's secretary's office.

"The president will see you now," the secretary said. She knocked twice and opened the door to the Oval Office.

President Baxter sat in an armchair next to the Presidential seal in the carpet center. Secretary of State Vance, the Secretary of Defense, and the Director of National Intelligence sat together on one couch, with their backs to the door. There was an empty chair on the other side of the seal. The Attorney General sat alone on the far couch. Several empty chairs were arranged at the end.

"Come in, come in. Take a seat," the President directed. As they filed past, the President singled out Robert.

"Robert, good to see you again. How is your father? I haven't talked to him recently."

"He's fine, Mr. President," Robert answered, thinking that the President probably talked to his father more than he did.

"Good, tell him 'hello' for me," President Baxter said.

The delay had given the others time to move into the various seats. This left Robert with a seat next to Jack, who had skillfully taken two spots, forcing the others down farther. Jack moved towards the President now, opening space on the couch for Robert. Robert could feel the indignation rising from Morrison, who ended up at the far end of the room. Jason Carlisle took the armchair next to the President.

"Jason, I hope you have some good news on this. I have heard nothing but gloom from these doomsday people." The President's demeanor was light, but beneath his calm exterior ran an undercurrent of heightened awareness.

"I think we have something for you," Jason Carlisle told him. He began laying out the information in a concise style that amazed Robert. Carlisle took the complex data and distilled it down into bite-sized chunks that were understandable and actionable. The summary became positive, despite the negative nature of the situation. Robert could see why the President put so much trust in his Chief of Staff. The download lasted barely ten minutes.

"All right. I think I have the picture," the President said when Jason finished. Turning to Secretary Vance, President Baxter began his directives. "Paul, I want you and Lillian to get your State Department team squarely behind Robert with everything he needs to have another meeting with the Governors, and whatever focal point personnel they've named in their region. Robert, good job getting Edward Collins involved from the start. That Brit really knows how to make things happen. Paul, I like your original strategy of Justice in front, instead of State. Robert, you continue to be the face on this. You're the quarterback. Paul, you hang back and cover Robert. I don't want this to become an international incident."

President Baxter turned back to Robert. "Contact our two Governors and Collins directly. Tell them what is going on, and share the intelligence report that there may be four more canisters, but ask them to not give that information to anyone else at this time. You shouldn't have a problem—they don't want that to become news any more than we do. Your main job is to devise some kind of public position for all of us to use as this unfolds. It needs to be something palatable for the general public, that they could perceive to be a security or training exercise, for example."

Robert was shocked to hear his name and assignment. He'd assumed his job had been to get things started. He hadn't expected to have any on-going official capacity. Vance or Morrison should have been taking over this operation. He could hear Morrison's tense jaw clicking from across the coffee table and knew that she was furious about becoming his lackey.

The President turned his attention to the Secretary of Defense and the Director of National Intelligence. "Bill, I want you and Ron to brief the Joint Chiefs. Warren, pull together the CIA, NSA, and IC on this. Do you have someone who can keep Robert informed, real time?"

"Yes, Sir. Lt. Col. Grady Barlow from the Pentagon is our joint liaison for the Intelligence Community," The NI Director answered.

"Barlow. He's on the team you created for inter-departmental investigation, isn't he Robert?" The President recalled.

"Yes, Sir," Robert answered, grateful that it would be Grady, and not someone he didn't know. "He accompanied me on the previous trip to see the regions' governors, so he is already familiar with that part of the situation. He met with their military liaisons while we were there."

"You're on top of this. I like that, Robert," the President commended him. "I expect you to get this ball all the way to the end zone, Quarterback." The President stood up. "Connect the dots, People. I have a bad feeling about this, and I don't want to see it explode on the news."

"Thank you, Mr. President." They all intoned, almost in unison, as they stood to leave.

"Robert, hang on a second," the President told him, halting his departure.

Robert's blood froze. Jack glanced back as he exited, a cautionary message in his eyes. Robert saw Morrison glare from the corner of her eye as the door closed behind her. This was going to make her hard to work with, he knew. He was going to have to watch out for that shark fin of hers.

Robert waited until the door closed, and he was alone in the oval office with the President and Chief of Staff.

"All right." President Baxter walked to the far side of his desk. "This conversation goes no further than the three of us, for now. I don't want any chance of a panic, but we must absolutely cover every island, landing strip, or rowboat that could bring one of those things here, to the US mainland. If you find them there, keep them there. The island Governors aren't going to want to make this happen, but I want you to find a way. Even more important than the US being vulnerable is us looking vulnerable, so you've got to stop these things getting into the Country. Contact Steve if you need anything. I'll make sure his organization helps you out."

Jason Carlisle nodded, adding, "I'll need reports from you on what you're arranging, Robert."

"Mr. President, Mr. Carlisle, I appreciate your confidence, but..." Robert began. This job was monumental. He couldn't possibly find a way to search everywhere and keep it low key.

"Robert," President Baxter interrupted, holding up his hand, "I know your concerns. Understand that this has to be the way it's done. We need fast action and no complications. We especially don't want any of it in the news. You've already begun the coordination, so it looks better to keep you directing the operation. We can't put the State Department on it for the same reasons we didn't want to send them in the first place."

"And if it goes wrong?" Robert didn't say that out loud, but he was thinking it. He didn't have to ask the President the question because the answer was simple. Robert would be the fall guy.

"Thank you, Mr. President," he said.

Chapter 39

Robert stood in the President's outer office by the secretary's desk. The secretary ignored Robert. People often came out of the Oval looking shell-shocked.

Robert felt drained. The energy of the place seemed to have fed on him—like a vampire sucking him dry.

During the meeting, Robert had felt Morrison's eyes on him. Mako had been sizing him up. President Baxter had double endorsed Robert; it was an opportunity that should have been hers. She had underestimated the situation and had been jammed into the background. He could see her now, down the hall, talking furiously with Vance in hushed tones. Neither glanced his way.

What Robert didn't know was that Morrison had just texted Mary. "Come to meeting one hour early with full update."

Mako was unaware that Robert would have been happy to have this situation fall into her lap. A game was being played, and he'd been thrust deep into it. He didn't know his next move. He felt like a pawn, not a quarterback.

Robert was still frantically considering what to do when he felt a strong grip on his arm. Jack Crain pulled him into the Cabinet room. The huge oval conference table with its many high-backed leather chairs stood empty. The President's secretary closed the door behind them.

"Jack, I..." Robert began, thinking that Jack was looking for information on the last couple of minutes with the President.

"Wait." Jack admonished.

Moments later the door opened. Vance and Morrison stormed in.

"I'm not going to say this is a bad idea," Vance began, looking uncharacteristically fierce and flushed.

"Paul," Jack interrupted, trying to stop what was coming.

"Hold on, Jack." Vance's expression was quickly cooling, as his diplomatic side rushed in to quell the fire. A look of stern neutrality washed over his face. "Let's not make this a big deal." His jaw clenched as he strained to remain calm.

"I wasn't planning on making it anything other than what it is," Jack replied.

"Fine. Neither are we," Vance continued. "This is simply an assignment from the President, and we will deal with it as directed."

Mako was silent, but Robert could see the fire burning in her eyes. She must have been under orders from Vance to keep quiet, just as Robert knew he should be.

Vance turned to face Crain, but the words he spoke were directed at Robert.

"Okay...this is a cross-functional exercise with foreign, domestic, civilian, and military elements," he said. "By the time you're finished, I see a calm region with a single incident on an uninhabited island, and no headlines. This will be the catalyst that unites the area in favor of a strong coalition, determined to detect and control incoming WMDs. At the same time, this should improve infrastructure in the war against drugs. 'Strong Coalition Stops Threats.' That's our headline." Vance turned and began pacing, talking to the whole room, walls and all. "Jack, can we agree that the first action is to get authority distributed to the appropriate organizations?"

Jack moved farther down the table as Vance covered more ground. "Of course. I think the President was right in his decision to follow your initial approach. Having Robert run this reduces the impact, since it is a continuation of the previous discussion. The last thing we want is an international incident."

Robert listened to Jack pull the President into the conversation, deferring to his "higher authority." He was playing to Vance's "assignment" statement and trying to make Vance look smart for keeping the State Department in low profile.

Robert and Morrison were standing on either side of the entry door. Both were watching their bosses work to position themselves and their departments. Robert knew he was on Mako's turf with this assignment, but hadn't Vance deliberately put him there? Had State really not recognized that an incident like this might occur?

Jack and Vance pushed various parts of the assignment back and forth, vying for power positions. Robert could feel himself being tossed around like a ping pong ball.

Listening to the back and forth dialogue, Robert became conscious of underlying problems. If any of this became a negative headline, the four people in this room would be blamed and politically sacrificed—he was the fall guy, but he might not be the only head to roll. More importantly, he now knew this was not the first time contraband radioactive material had gotten this close to the US. Other situations had not been made public. As much as they grappled for power, Crain and Vance were trying to position blame on the other in advance. Robert realized that neither wanted to be anywhere near this problem, but both wanted to control the blame from a safe distance.

If this went badly, Robert realized, Jack wouldn't be his advocate. Robert would be crucified by both Vance and his own boss. Mako wanted the glory if any was to be had, but otherwise, she'd make sure everyone knew how Robert had screwed up.

The door to the Cabinet room swung open. The Chief of Staff and National Security Advisor walked into the room.

"Jason," Vance spoke immediately, taking the lead, "I think we have this under control."

"That's good to hear," Carlisle responded.

Robert raised his hand to get the attention of the group. "I think it should be mentioned that there is a hospital treating patients with radiation sickness. They didn't originally know what they were dealing with, and before they called the CDC they probably talked to other people about it."

Carlisle turned toward Ron Crest. "Ron, did we miss something here?"

"We're working on that," Ron answered. "The hospital wasn't given any specifics on the source, just a treatment plan. As far as the source goes, Mahaffey assures me that they made sure only NRC and CDC personnel saw what it is. It will soon be stateside for examination by the NRC."

"So, we'll need a reasonable explanation for the injuries. Robert, work with Ron and the NRC to get a better than plausible solution for the doctors, staff, etc." Carlisle was forging ahead. "From now on, all messaging comes through my office. No leaks, and absolutely no press. We need a complete list of anyone outside these offices working on the project we'll refer to as 'Sandy Island.' The President expects a report every morning at nine. Run your updates through Ron." He nodded his dismissal of the group and left the room.

Everyone filed out. Robert felt a little air filter back slowly into his lungs. The spotlight was lifted for the time being. Robert walked toward the lobby to exit and found Steve Mahaffey waiting in a chair. He stood as Robert approached.

"Congratulations, Mr. Quarterback," Steve spoke, keeping his voice conversational.

"I'm not sure it's a win," Robert replied. "Not yet, anyway. What did the others say about all of this?"

"I watched them all leave, but nobody stopped to talk. At least not to me. I've been on a few of these. There's always a quarterback, and everyone's always waiting to see who gets the ball. Here, this will help," he stated, handing Robert a thick manila envelope, securely closed with a string loop.

"What's in here?" Robert asked, accepting the envelope.

"Facts about radiation sources. It should speed up your research, and honestly, it will make my life easier if you know this stuff." He grinned.

"I appreciate it, Steve," Robert responded dubiously. It was unusual to get help without asking; it made him wonder about Steve's agenda.

Steve picked up on Robert's wavelength. "If history repeats itself, the technical side will have only a few options and a lot of restrictions we can't get around—no matter how much someone wants to. If you can handle the political mess and get agreement on the things we will do, my team can handle the technical side for you. The catch is that we need a clear roadway through the politics with no potholes."

"Otherwise it gets messy," Robert surmised.

"Sometimes it gets so fouled up, it can't be fixed," Steve warned. "This is the first of this type of incident for this administration, but not the first in history. All the players are new except half of my team and Dr. Prath of the CDC. We can handle this, technically. I think your problem will be Ms. Morrison—but I just overstepped my bounds. Read all of that, then give me a call." Steve reached out to shake hands.

Robert clasped the folder in his left hand, and Steve's hand with his right. "Why Morrison?"

"State always has two faces, and three agendas."

Robert's face expressed concern, but he held back a response. "One more question," he said.

"Shoot," Steve answered.

"How many of your resources do I have?" Robert questioned, looking Steve in the eye.

"One-hundred percent, unless something bigger happens," Steve replied solidly. "That's the only asterisk. I'm not hedging. We have our own budget, so you don't have to worry about that. When we are done, you will have a clear and well-defined handoff you can present to the powers that be."

"Thanks, Steve." Robert held up the envelope. "You will be hearing from me very soon."

"Oh, I'm sure of that." Steve smiled, heading toward the door.

. . .

Robert's trip back to his office was quick. Lorraine sat quietly typing at her desk when Robert came through the door. What she was typing, he didn't know. She was always busy. His inbox was always full, but she managed to keep his outbox clean. He remembered that he'd have to thank her more often for keeping things running so well.

"Good morning, Mr. Carlton," Lorraine greeted him.

"Good morning." He didn't have to ask about messages. The stack was already extended toward him in her right hand. It was much smaller than usual. Lorraine had managed to convince most of his callers to message, text or email their questions, many of which she could assign to others when she saw the subjects. It had lightened his load considerably.

"Coffee?" she asked.

"Yes, please." Robert moved past her toward his door. "Get Grady Barlow on the phone for me. Set up a conference call with the Governors of Puerto Rico, the US Virgin Islands, and Edward Collins—the Governor of the British Virgin Islands. You'll find his information in my contacts list. I need them on the phone for thirty minutes, preferably together, as soon as possible. If not by noon tomorrow, then separately. If separately, put Collins on the schedule first."

"Yes, Sir," she responded.

"For that conference call include Barlow and Steve Mahaffey. This is the contact information for Mahaffey. He's with the NRC." He handed Lorraine Steve's business card, which had been in the envelope he'd supplied to Robert. "Add him to my contacts on my phone." He stepped toward his office door, then paused.

"Get Mary Whiston on the phone after Barlow," he told her.

"Yes, Sir."

Robert went in, closing the door behind him, then opened it again. "One more thing, Lorraine. Get Jerry to come over here." He closed the door again.

Robert pulled out his chair and dragged the inbox toward him while his computer booted. The folder sitting on top was the weekly update. It contained a section from each of Robert's departments. He was way behind on reading this stuff.

A glance at the computer showed it was ready. He clicked it to open his email.

Setting the weekly update aside, he opened the second folder. Department cases and reviews. A quick glance at email showed over two-hundred downloading. Robert wished he could turn it off and take a nap.

There was a rap on the door before Lorraine entered.

"Mr. Carlton, you have been invited to a meeting with Lillian Morrison at the State Department today. The meeting invitation and agenda are on your calendar."

Robert stared at her. Morrison was trying to beat him to the punch.

"Mr. Mahaffey and Ms. Whiston are on the invitation list," Lorraine supplied.

"Get them on the phone for me," Robert ordered. "Try to tie in Barlow. Thanks."

Lorraine ducked back out. Robert stared at the closed door.

Blindsided, outrun by Morrison, he thought. He pulled up the calendar invitation. The agenda covered everything that had come out of the meeting with the President. Action items had already been assigned to Morrison's direct reports.

Robert wanted to slam his laptop shut—slam it hard enough to crack the screen. Sometimes he wished he had some unimportant thing handy that he could break out of sheer frustration.

She must have dictated the call to action over the phone before she even got to her car. Robert was sure this wasn't the first bite he'd feel from her. He could pull a power play and say he was too busy for the meeting, but the fact was that he was going to need her help on this.

The top of the meeting invitation read, "Meeting with Deputy Attorney General Robert Carlton Sandy Island Quarterback, 1:30." He would have to figure out how he could work with this. Mako had better speed than he did and a trained team. Offense or defense, they would pummel Robert's staff. She had a room full of bookworms and researchers. Robert decided that he needed a Jiujitsu approach, with its principle of using an attacker's energy against them, rather than directly opposing it. He needed to use Morrison to his advantage, instead of being used by her, but how?

Robert concentrated on his inbox. Forced by overload, he became a delegation machine. By the time Jerry arrived in his office, Robert was ready to hand off a stack much bigger than Robert's remaining inbox pile. Most of the files had labels for other staff members, but Jerry would have to go over the assignments and follow up.

On the weekly report, Robert's note to Lorraine was, "Set up weekly staff meetings. Find the best time, place, and techniques to make this well attended, and productive. Meetings can be attended remotely." Whatever she decided would be a better starting point than where he was now.

The stack of inbox folders shrank as his outbox grew.

Robert's phone line rang. It was Lorraine. "Sir, I have Barlow, Whiston, and Mahaffey scheduled for a conference call in ten minutes."

"Excellent. Dial me in when it starts."

The ten minutes evaporated quickly. Robert's phone rang, Lorraine connected him and the "joining" sound peeped three times as Grady, Steve, and Mary each came on to the call.

"Thank you for being available on such short notice," Robert opened. "Let's start with introductions." After Grady, Steve, and Mary had given brief descriptions of their jobs, Robert moved to the issue at hand.

He brought Grady and Mary up to speed on the situation on Sandy Island and stressed the need for keeping the situation under wraps. Now it was time to assign duties.

"Mary, I need you to coordinate with Ms. Morrison's office on the meetings and travel. Make sure to include Colonel Barlow on everything going forward, and make sure Morrison's team knows he's integral. I'm clearing my calendar, so there is no need for the back and forth approvals. Work with Lorraine to keep the department expenses straight. We need to treat this as a twenty-four-seven activity. I will be having a conference call with the three Governors prior to meeting face-to-face. This will occur whenever and wherever works best for them, but it will be a.s.a.p. Grady, do you have any conflicts that can't be put on hold?"

"None. I'll take care of transferring my current workload," Grady responded.

"Steve?" Robert asked.

"I'm all yours," Steve affirmed.

Robert didn't ask Mary. He assumed she was available. Robert gave the group a few more details, fielding their questions, and asking Mary to get started with Morrison's staff, then dismissed her from the call. He waited to hear the sound of the conference call system disconnecting from her.

"Okay, Guys. Hang on a second." Robert hit star-two and the computer voice reported, "There are two callers." Satisfied, Robert spoke to Grady and Steve.

"This part is just for you two, and confidential. I need you to determine how many resources you each can assemble—both NRC and Military. This includes personnel, safety, and detection gear to conduct immediate sweeps of as many islands as possible. I need to know how many teams you can field. There may be four more irradiators in the area, and we're tasked to find them or be sure they are not there. The cover story is that we're training special teams in each area. I don't yet know how many countries will be involved, or how many teams they will give us to train. It will help to know how much time it would take to train each team, in each location, including full equipment and what we can provide for loaner equipment. Each location should be able to continue to train while your people move on."

"When you say, 'as many islands as possible,' how many are we actually talking about?" Grady asked.

"I mean every island, every boat, and every plane," Robert disclosed. "How many is relative to time. How many can be done in what amount of time? Can the trained teams carry part of the load? Can we supply some decoy targets to make sure they're doing what we've asked? I think it will have to be an east to west line of islands to form a border, then we'll draw that line south to squeegee the whole area," Robert finished, looking at a map online as he talked.

Grady whistled. "That's a tall order, Robert. We can't pull from the military that easily if this is an undercover operation. If it was a 'Broken Arrow,' that would be different, but then, they would already be activated and we would be trying to catch up." Grady was familiar with military nuclear protocols in a cursory way. He was positive he could not simply pull critically trained personnel for a "training exercise."

Robert realized they'd need to have some private, follow-on conversation, after they'd considered this more and heard what Morrison's team had to say. "Can you two meet with me after the meeting with Morrison?"

Grady's smile could be heard through the phone. "I think we've already given up our nights and weekends, don't you Steve?"

"I'm pretty sure that's what I heard. Does that mean we're engaged?" Steve joked.

"Okay, Guys. Let's stay on track," Robert said, watching the time tick away on his watch. "Steve, where are you staying?"

"Capital Hilton," Steve said.

"Ouch. Wrong direction for me," Robert wasn't keen on backtracking through DC to pick him up.

"Don't worry, I have a car," Steve told him. "I'm pretty good at getting around."

"Do you know the Key Bridge Marriott?"

"I think I can find it," Steve said confidently.

"Grady, do you know a place near there we could go eat?" Robert asked.

"Burgers or views?" Grady wanted to know.

Robert thought his belts were getting tight. "Any place with good, low-calorie food? I could use a little help, post holidays."

"Sure, I'll come up with something," Grady said. "I'd be happier with something a little lighter, too."

They agreed to meet on the other side of the river at five, in the Key Bridge Marriott bar. That would force them out of the Morrison meeting by four-fifteen, and keep them just ahead of the five o'clock rush leaving DC.

Robert arrived at the State Department fifteen minutes early. The closest parking he found near the Truman building was two blocks away. This put his car seven blocks closer to the Roosevelt Bridge, and out of DC Constitution Avenue traffic until the last possible moment.

The Harry S. Truman building lobby was noisy with people pushing through security after lunch. Grady and Steve were already in the lobby. The three made their way to the conference room. Robert didn't have an escort waiting for him this time. The honeymoon was clearly over. The terrazzo floors, marble accents and carved busts of historical figures went ignored as they pressed forward.

Mary joined them outside the conference room. She was quiet and nervously rubbing her phone cover.

Inside the room, Morrison's staff was putting up color-coordinated post-it notes across two large rolling whiteboards.

Robert pulled out the chair directly across from the head chair, centered on the table's far side. He sat, and opened his laptop. It connected to the secure Wi-Fi automatically. Moments later a name tent was placed in front of him and in front of all the other chairs. Next to him on the right was Steve Mahaffey. To his left, Lt. Col. Barlow. Mary had gotten the word out. The others were Morrison staff, and her tent was directly across from his. Mary sat in a chair against the wall behind Robert, with a clear line of sight over his shoulder to Morrison's chair.

At that point, Morrison and her entourage entered the room from a side door. Robert realized too late that he'd given her the powerful grand entrance moment by already being in the room.

"Please, everyone, be seated," Lillian commanded the room. "Here is our situation." She spent the next fifteen minutes recapping what everyone in the room knew. There were no minutes being taken. The pristine agenda was missing, too, but her organized army in lock-step remained. Robert listened to the details that this group would be taking care of, many of which were tiny diplomatic issues that he would have never thought to address. By the time they were done, Robert wondered if his job was simply to show up at the Governor's meeting and shake hands.

"Now we come to story containment on Sandy island." Morrison looked at her senior aide, Lester. "What do we have?"

Surprised, Robert thought back. "Did I tell her the name 'Sandy Island?'" If he hadn't, who had?

"As you know, we are dealing with a Cs-137 contamination. Cesium-137 is manmade, and can only be created through fission, which means it comes from nuclear explosions or nuclear reactors. Our idea is to change the story to one of smuggling radioactive materials that are available in nature, such as Uranium or Thorium. Uranium mine tailings are available in the form of sand, or we could obtain a Radon daughter. Polonium is available, and we can get Thorium-233. We believe these can be substituted for the Cesium on the island and change the story from a weapons smuggling event to illegal mining."

Prior to this, Robert had been content to roll along with the work Morrison's team had done. It was laborious work he didn't have the manpower or time to create—but this idea seemed all wrong. Robert had read Steve's information packet and had also done some research of his own.

"Excuse me," he interjected.

"Yes, Mr. Carlton? You have something you wish to add?" Morrison was courteous, but somehow her expression achieved arrogance.

"I do." Robert opened a file on his laptop from his briefing with Grady and Katy at the Naval Research Laboratory. He looked over at Steve. "Mr. Mahaffey and I have not discussed this, so please correct me if I'm wrong, Steve, but I don't think that idea will work.

Morrison shot a withering look at Mary, who winced.

He continued. "It's too easy to prove the radiation did not come from those materials."

"The sealed source was Cesium-137, which is a byproduct of fission from a nuclear plant or atomic bomb, as Lester said," Robert repeated, standing up. He preferred standing and pacing a little when sorting out this type of problem. "That scares people," he continued. "Fine; I get that, but the patients are being treated with Prussian Blue, which bonds to the Cesium so it can be flushed from the body. Prussian Blue only treats Cesium and Thallium; therefore, the other radioactive sources you mentioned won't be supportable by even a casual investigation. Am I right so far, Steve?"

"Your information is correct," Steve replied.

"Thallium-201 is used in medical cardio-stress testing. It's not that uncommon, and it would support the prescribed treatment. While you could say that it came from stolen medical supplies—which is a fairly common occurrence in some areas—an expert investigation could tell the difference. If we control the site reasonably well, we might delay or even prevent full awareness of the true source for a while. Is that accurate, Steve?"

"I think that's an acceptable explanation," Steve confirmed cautiously, wondering where Robert was going with this.

"Was the medical team told the nature of the radiation, or just to medicate with Prussian Blue?" Morrison asked.

Steve started digging through his computer notes as he answered. "Dr. Prath from the CDC prescribed the treatment, but did not specify the source. I instructed him to avoid mentioning Cesium. I told him that if he was forced to say something, to indicate that it seemed to be Thallium. I'll have to check with him to make sure he didn't disclose anything else to anyone."

"If all that is true then the question is, can we clean up the island enough to plant Thallium-201? Can we make it the less offensive source?" Morrison questioned. Again, she glared at Mary, then caught herself and redirected the disapproving scowl at Lester.

"Where did you get that information about Thallium-201?" Lester interjected.

"Research. Col. Barlow and I reviewed information from Steve and the NRC and did some checking. I'm sure you can find corroboration." Robert was on a roll, and feeling that a courtroom atmosphere had evolved. "In answer to your question Under Secretary, I must advise against a cover-up of the Cesium contamination."

"Mr. Carlton, my staff has..." Morrison began, but Robert cut her off.

"Bear with me here, Ms. Morrison." Robert continued, "The Cesium-137, in this case, is a salt. It bonds easily with sand. It was buried in the sand on that island. Sand dust will be everywhere, even up in the trees, and Cesium can be detected by scanning for 0.667 MeV on a..." He leaned over to check his information from MISTI, "sodium iodide detector. Correct Steve?"

"That's true," Steve agreed.

"Colonel, is that the data we reviewed?" Robert asked.

"Yes, that is correct," Grady recalled the briefing. He could also see the MISTI data on Robert's computer screen.

"If you put Thallium on the island, it would have a half-life of three years," Robert resumed. "The Cesium half-life is thirty years. Can you explain a thirty-year quarantine for a three-year Thallium contamination?"

Robert pulled his chair away from the table and leaned on the table's edge with both hands. "We are going to be helping these islands detect and contain radioactive, chemical, and biological agents in order to protect ourselves and them from attack. Do you really think they won't learn what I have learned in just a few days?"

The room was silent. Morrison glowered at Robert frostily. She shared the dirty look with Mary, who tried to avoid eye contact by looking down at the floor.

"It's too easy to shoot holes in the cover up you suggest," Robert continued, ignoring her. "We need to go in with an inclusive strategy. We'll tell the Governors the truth about the Cesium-137. We will make the story about theft instead of terrorism, by keeping the Kazakhstani origin of the container information secret. We'll say it was old, stolen medical equipment, or an agricultural irradiator from someplace in Africa or South America. I'm sure Steve can dig up a convincing specimen for display. Maybe we could use it as a training tool right back on the island, Steve?"

"I like that." Steve really did like the idea. There would have to be training, and the island had to be cordoned off anyway. "That's something that sounds workable and productive." He looked pleased.

Morrison glared at the aide who had researched the radioactive information, then back at Robert. "Would you mind sharing your information on the Cesium with Lester?" She asked, challengingly.

"Not at all," Robert told her.

Morrison's look made Lester shrink in his chair. "Lester, work with Steve to build this strategy." She ordered. "Write it up, along with a timeline for implementation. Thank you, Mr. Carlton, for your insight." She looked around the room. "Does anyone have anything further?"

The room was too quiet. Robert was still standing, which left him feeling awkward. He also felt compelled to say something.

He straightened up and placed his hand on the back of his chair, trying to look casual. "You have all done a fantastic job pulling this together in a short amount of time. I look forward to working with you on this. Thank you." Robert told them self-assuredly.

Morrison pushed back from the table and stood. "Compile your notes. Put them with the schedule, and distribute copies to the people in this meeting only. Meeting adjourned." She headed for the far door which precluded any face-to-face interaction with

Robert. This suited him just fine. He and his team walked together down the hall to the lobby.

"Mary, have they shared any meeting arrangements with the Governors and Morrison's team, yet?" He asked.

"No, Sir," she answered.

"It's early. I'm sure they'll get to it," Robert said. "Keep on top of that, and keep me in the loop as you learn things. Let Lorraine know if you need anything."

"Thanks, Everyone," he stated. "I'm sure we will be talking tomorrow morning. For now, get some sleep. I think we could experience some long hours over the next couple of weeks." He exchanged casual, yet knowing glances with Grady and Steve. Having a hidden mission was awkward for Robert. He didn't find the art of deception to be his best talent.

Chapter 40

Robert, Grady, and Steve sat at a high-top table in the Heavy Seas Ale House. Robert and Steve had parked at the Marriot and ridden over in Grady's bold yellow Toyota FJ.

"Planning to drive up the Appalachian Trail?" Robert kidded Grady. The vehicle looked ready to take on a mountain, with its legitimate 4-wheel drive, bike rack on top, winch on the front, trailer hitch, and extra fuel jerry can mounted to the outside spare.

"I was thinking more of driving down the beach on the Outer Banks this summer," Grady laughed.

"Nice. Needs a snorkel—so you can drive in the surf," Steve chimed in. "I went up there three years ago. Had a great time."

"Up there? It's south of here," Robert cocked a quizzical eye at Steve.

"I live in Atlanta." Steve reminded him. "That's where our southeast headquarters are."

"Of course. I'd forgotten," Robert wasn't sure he'd have known that. "You fit in so well around here that it's easy to think you live in the area."

They ordered beers and food, then Grady asked the question. "Okay, Robert; what is it that you can't tell Mary, but that we need to know, and how many people on Morrison's team know about it?"

Robert was glad the restaurant was not busy, but he was still careful to talk quietly. "Steve is aware of this, Grady. There is information that five of these canisters were being moved across Africa, and possibly onto a ship. Our people lost track of them in the Congolese port of Pointe-Noire. They think they may have ended up in Venezuela. The one found on our island with the exposed men matches the description of the group that was being tracked." Robert took a sip of his beer while that sank in with Grady.

"They're not sure about Venezuela, but they have reason to think that this one is from that batch." Grady restated without inflection. "Is it possible that this canister is not part of that five?"

"Possible, but there's some evidence that seems to link it," Steve confirmed. "There are a surprising number of these unaccounted for in the world. Most never make it out of the country that used them, but missing is missing. The big concern is who has them. The fact they are out there is old news."

"Just how many of this type are unaccounted for?" Grady hated this kind of thing. It was an outcome of sloppy leadership.

"Thousands." Steve didn't even look up when he said it.

"So, the boss wants us to turn over every rock and plant leaf to make sure they aren't going to show up here without an invitation," Grady affirmed.

"Your boss?" Steve asked, wondering if Grady's command structure was involved.

"His boss—your boss; the big boss in charge of all of us," Grady clarified, referring to the President.

"And while we're looking under every beach chair and behind every bar, no one can know what we're doing?" Steve asked Robert.

"Exactly," Robert affirmed. "Oh, and to answer your previous question, Grady, the Under Secretary's staff is only aware of the Sandy Island canister and its contents, and the plan to substitute its origin and purpose. Beyond that, they have not, to my knowledge, been included."

"This is going to be hard." Grady looked concerned and thoughtful. "I get now why the material had to change to something from a different origin, like a medical source. Has that kind of switch been performed successfully in the past?"

Steve replied. "Yes."

"But you can't talk about it," Grady added.

"Something like that," Steve smiled.

"The next time I see a 'no trespassing' skull and crossbones sign, I'm taking it a lot more seriously." Grady looked back to Robert. "If you hope to do this in less than a year, it will require a lot of manpower. I hope you have some idea of how to pull this off, 'cause I've got nothing."

"I think I do, and I wanted to test out my theory with you two," Robert said.

Both Grady and Steve leaned forward, beers held tightly in their fists.

Robert took a deep breath before beginning, "This is generalized, but what if we get the Governors and the rest of the territories to agree to an all-out training program, with rapid deployment of instructors and equipment across all the islands? Under the guise of training, our people can check all the most likely places, and the trainees can keep working on the rest as part of their certification. We start at the top and work our way down, pushing the risk further away as we move. Plus, that starts us off with our most cooperative allies. If we don't find anything then there's no panic, just preparation, which we need anyway." He waited for their reactions.

"I like it," Steve spoke first. "We can do equipment sweeps with directional instruments to cover lots of terrain fast. Then, to make the training show more results, we can spot survey places like dentists' offices and hospitals. All we need are a few test targets to give them practical experience, and we could cover a lot on an island. There are a lot of islands, though, so I agree with Grady about the time frame. I don't see any way to do this quickly. It could take a year, or a hell of a lot of people if you want to speed up the process."

"That's where you two come in." Robert leaned back. "Steve, you run Region II of the NRC, ten states from Mississippi to Virginia, Kentucky to Florida, plus Puerto Rico and the Virgin Islands. I did a little research and saw that you have the greatest concentration of manpower and equipment in the country. Grady, the Air Force Global Strike Command should have emergency crews scattered around, but I assume Barksdale AFB in Louisiana would have people attached to the 2nd Bomb Wing there, right?"

"You think I can run over to the AFGSC and ask to borrow a nuclear recovery team like someone would borrow a cup of sugar, Robert?" Grady looked appalled. "You know they are the direct descendants of the cold war Strategic Air Command, don't you? SAC didn't play nicely with others back in the day, and I doubt they're more interested in inter-departmental cooperation now. AFGSC is also *very* mission focused, and this isn't their mission. I don't relish the idea of all those Generals saying, 'WTF, and who do you think you are?'"

"No, that wouldn't work," Robert agreed, "but I can request their cooperation, and they may have to provide it. What I need from both of you is the absolute maximum list of resources for assisting with this work, and where they could come from. Then I'll take the concept and the list upstairs and get the approvals."

"You think the 'big boss' will buy into it?" Steve asked, using Grady's euphemism.

"Unless somebody's got a better idea," Robert intoned.

Grady and Steve stared at each other for a while, thinking.

"It could work." Steve looked like he believed it.

"I'll run it up to the Eighth Air Force command," Grady finally capitulated. "We'll still need the big man's approval. I don't know any Generals who will say, 'yes,' without it. They will want to know a lot more about this, and there will be lots of staff involvement. I don't think we can keep what we are really doing a secret, Robert; not from these guys," Grady shook his head.

Robert knew that Grady was probably right, but they had to try. He didn't have any options.

Chapter 41

Mary Whiston was back at her apartment. She opened her bag and removed the teapot decorated cell phone. She carried two phones. One she had purchased for personal use, but the teapot phone was special. It contained preloaded contacts, texts, music, and game apps to disguise the phone's singular purpose: the one number that mattered on the phone. The one named "Teapot."

She saw a text on the phone. "Send copy of files used in meeting!"

Morrison had notified Vlad. Mary could feel the sweat forming on her upper lip. Mary was one of Vlad's teapots. Morrison's charm bracelet indicated that she was, too, but higher up the food chain.

Vlad recruited Mary when she had been newly hired to the DOJ and was deeply in debt. She was perfect as one of his many "teapot girls." Her father had been laid off, and her mother was ill. There were mounting medical bills that her middle-class family couldn't afford. Vlad had fixed that problem. All the medical bills, and Mary's student loans had disappeared. He didn't explain how he'd done that, but there was the promise of more good things to come if she helped Vlad with information.

Vlad had never pushed her beyond the zone of what was easy for her to rationalize. He wouldn't until the stakes were high enough to risk losing his asset. Vlad played the long game. Mary could be useful for many years.

Her first contact with Vlad was frightening. Sitting on her counter next to the bills had been a ceramic teapot she didn't recognize. She'd opened it and found two pieces of paper, folded together neatly. The first was a promise to help her with her mother's medical bills and her student loans. The note made it clear that some minor information would be requested in exchange.

The bluntness of the request, combined with the invasion of her privacy, scared Mary. Someone had been in her apartment and knew private things about her and her family. She grabbed the telephone to call the police, but before she dialed she read the rest. "Do as I say, and your life will be good. Do not, and your life will be very short. Before calling the police, read page two." Mary put down the phone.

She read the second page. It was a copy of a newspaper article on how Livinenko, a former KGB agent, had been murdered in London. He'd been poisoned with radioactive Polonium placed in a teapot.

At the bottom of the page was written, "You cannot taste it or smell it. It dissolves easily in water, and you will not know until it is too late. You will be asked little in exchange for ending your family's financial pain. Place the teapot outside your door if you agree."

At the very bottom of the note was an internet URL. Mary grabbed her computer and pulled up the page. It was a video of Livinenko. It showed him in a hospital bed with no hair and sunken sick eyes. The voice-over in the video enumerated the gruesome details of his painfully slow death.

Mary placed the teapot outside her door. In the morning she found an envelope leaning against the door frame. Inside was the cell phone with its teapot-design case.

. . .

Now Mary sat with the phone. She didn't have the file yet, but she knew that a response was expected.

She texted, "Will get file to you tomorrow."

The reply came quickly. "Quickly" It was then followed by "Report on how many men responding and the schedule."

Mary set the phone down. She needed an excuse to access that file.

. . .

Vlad was sure Morrison had given him the most important parts of Robert's research findings, but he wanted to verify it for himself. He expected Mary to come through. Looking at his watch, he dialed a number and listened to it ring twice, then hung up. Waiting a full minute, he called again. It was picked up on the third ring.

"Yes?" The voice questioned.

"It has started." Vlad was ready to start the clock. "They are responding."

"So, they found it?" Vlad's investor asked.

"Yes." Vlad reiterated.

"You are sure they will respond as planned?"

"Yes. They are predictable. Their resources will drain from the US southeast," Vlad said, smiling at the thought.

"You're sure we can start?" The voice on the other end wanted absolute certainty.

"Americans are decisive when they choose a direction. We use this against them because they do not play chess. They play football and their European partners play soccer. They see only one goal, and they drive to that. They know only defense and offense. They dislike defense and see it as weakness. They do not see the wisdom in playing both at the same time. They do not see diversion and sacrifice, like in chess. They do not see threats from the sides until they strike. We use this tendency to draw them out. When they have a direct goal they can see, it exposes their lack of a rear guard, and we catch them by surprise. They panic. It becomes the global story all can see. We hit in many locations at the same time, so they cannot cover it up." Vlad's confidence was high. He had used the strategy before, many times.

"In this way, we use the strengths of the Americans against themselves. Like Stalingrad, we will draw them in. Let them impress us with their power, then we strike from behind, and cut them off," He concluded.

"Let me know when to be ready for the final stage," the voice ordered.

"Of course," Vlad returned. The call ended. The word would go out to the investors in seconds. Stock buys would be placed around the world. It had begun as planned. Now he had to insure the boats would be in place in time.

Vlad opened the texting app on his phone.

To Max: "Is Melbourne ready?"

To Luca: "Move north NOW. Estimate arrival VB?"

Chapter 42

Luca and Larry had arrived at Jost Van Dyke in the British Virgin Islands two days earlier. Larry was content to stay anchored near Great Harbor with its many bars and restaurants, despite Luca's frequent hints at seeing the Turks and Caicos, or even the Bahamas.

The two had been sailing together for seventeen days. While Larry and Luca were congenial and friendly, the relationship was showing some wear.

Luca's good looks had initially struck a chord with Larry. Although he and Luca had become good friends, the dockside friendship didn't progress beyond sharing expenses, beachside activities, experiences, and cooking. They had lots of laughs, but their relationship remained casual. It had every chance of turning into something more, but there was something that didn't quite click in their chemistry.

Larry didn't know why he didn't feel a physical link to Luca. He chalked it up to the idiosyncrasies of human relationships. Luca knew that his hidden agenda was stressing their conversations slightly. Larry had a desire to head south, but Luca was pushing to go north.

Jost Van Dyke was the furthest north of the British Virgin Islands. North of that was the Dominican Republic, and from there it was a very long day and night sail to the Turks and Caicos.

Luca could tell that he would soon wear out his welcome. Larry was starting to ask how much vacation Luca had. It wouldn't be long before Larry would expect him to head to an airport and fly home.

When Larry decided to take a nap out of the heat, Luca took the opportunity to check his secret cell phone, hidden in his duffle bag. It had one message telling him to move north immediately, and provide an estimated arrival.

Luca turned off the phone and placed it back in the dark duffle lining. He had thought through what he would have to do long ago. No additional planning was necessary. The boat was beautifully appointed with lots of wood below deck, making it unsuitable for his purpose. On the exterior, only the railing outside along with some handholds and trim were wood. The rest was fiberglass. The foredeck would have been the best location for what Luca had planned. Unfortunately, he would most likely have to choose the cockpit, as near the edge as possible.

With the duffle stowed, Luca went on deck and coiled all the ropes neatly away by hanging them up off the deck on cleats and rails, using the gasket coil technique Larry taught him. He then coiled the garden hose used to pump salt water on deck by the aft bulkhead. With everything ship-shape, he went below and propped up a pillow against the galley lounge to read his book. Confident in his preparations, it wasn't long before he fell asleep.

Around four-thirty, Larry started rustling around the forward berth. Not all Gozzards had an enclosed cabin, but this layout did, with a full privacy door. Two single berths in the forward cabin could be swung together to form a double bed, but since Luca and Larry's physical relationship had failed to ignite, they'd tried each taking a berth. Eventually, Luca had taken to sleeping on the galley pullout—Larry snored like a bear.

When Larry came out, it woke Luca and they started talking about food. The island offered some of the best beach bars in the Caribbean, so they gave up any thought of cooking that night.

The dinghy ride to shore was easy. The occasional splashes were of no concern and dried quickly on their island wear. They had a great evening, drinking, laughing, and eating lobster on the sand. It was late by island standards when they finally decided to call it a night. As they motored back to the yacht Luca noticed the bar lights turn off. They had closed the place down.

"How about a swim?" Luca asked cheerfully, manning the helm of the dinghy. Larry was feeling the effects of their alcohol intake.

"Sure, why not?" Larry agreed. Both men liked the freedom of skinny dipping, but nudity on the island was illegal. Night swims were their only opportunity for that pleasure.

With the dinghy tied up, they went below and shucked their clothes. Larry was the first on deck, greeting the night sky with a big stretch before diving in the warm water. The water had felt cool and refreshing during the day, but was now warm and inviting. Luca grabbed a long knife from the sink drawer and climbed up on deck.

"Jump in! The water's great!" Larry called.

"Hang on. I'll get the towels." Luca pulled the deck cabin cushions away from the stern stacking them far forward and on one side. Under the top one, he slid the filleting knife and went below to get the towels.

Without a splash, Luca dove into the water. The two swam around for a while, enjoying the feel of the water on their skin. Luca finally climbed the ladder to get out. Larry was not far behind. Luca went quickly toward the cushions. With a deft movement to the side, he arrived at the ship's wheel just as Larry's hands grasped the railing and stepped up the ladder. Larry's eyes were down to make sure of his footing. Once both feet were on deck, he stood up.

Their eyes met just as the long thin knife penetrated Larry's abdomen below the ribs. In one smooth motion, Luca caused the point to pop straight through the skin. He lowered the handle downward until his fist hit Larry's stomach, thrusting straight up at a steep angle until the handle stopped. The long blade tip stabbed deeply into Larry's heart. The shock of steel interrupted his heartbeat, but it was the twist of the knife that released the blood, allowing it to gush into his chest cavity, dropping the pressure and stopping the flow to his brain.

Larry jerked upward at the impact, then when Luca twisted the knife with all his strength, he hunched forward. His hands reached for Luca's arm and tried to pull back, but Luca held him tight to the blade with his other arm firmly around his back.

Luca had to make a decisive kill. Simply stabbing the heart did not guarantee death in a short time, and perhaps not at all if the blade was small. The fillet knife was long, but the tip was less than a half inch wide.

Larry's hands found no leverage against Luca's arms as they stared at each other. Letting go of his arm, Larry raised his hands to Luca's throat, trying to grip and choke Luca. This was good for Luca. He knew that Larry would bleed out and fall unconscious long before his hands kept Luca from getting his next breath. The two glared at each other in death's grip until Larry's eyes and mouth widened to a silent scream. He gasped one last time for air, then his knees buckled and his hands slipped off Luca's neck, grasping at his wet shoulders as he sank to the deck. Luca held the knife in place as Larry fell to the side, his dying eyes staring up at the dark sky.

For several long minutes, Luca knelt next to his victim, watching for any sign of life. No breath or flicker of an eye appeared. It was dark, and he had to be absolutely sure. He waited, and held the knife.

Very little blood seeped out. The knife handle plugged the wound well. The small stream of red looked black in the darkness as it slid down his hand and dripped onto the white fiberglass. Luca stood up, satisfied there would be no sudden revival of his victim. He had been prepared for lots of blood, but there was surprisingly little. Being naked would make clean up easy. There would be no inconvenient bloody clothes to dispose of.

Careful to not spread blood around the deck, he wiped off as much from his hand as he could on Larry's body. Walking only on open fiberglass, he reached the deck hose and squeezed the handle to clean his hands. He had left the pump on. It automatically shut off when the maximum pressure was attained, but now it jumped back to life with a frightening noise on the dark boat. The sound carried over the water. Luca looked around, but there were no boats anchored nearby, and no one seemed to be walking on the beach. Luca began to rinse off the deck and himself, making sure the body did not block the cockpit scupper hole, allowing the pink water to escape to the ocean.

With all the visible blood gone, he left the water running slowly to keep any new seepage from the body diluted and headed into the sea.

Luca headed below, dressing, and getting to work pulling up the anchors. In less than an hour, the Gozzard was motoring around the point of the island and upwind. Once safely beyond any onlooker's gaze, and the waves and reefs, he set the autopilot and hoisted sails.

It was surprisingly easy to accomplish each task, thanks to the single-sailor upgrades on the boat. The hardest part would have been getting the sails up, but with a self-furling jib and a mainsail that only need the cover removed before hoisting with the motorized winch, even that task had been made simple. Once the sails were up, Luca set the sheets at a reasonable position and disconnected the autopilot. He steered west-northwest for the Turks and Caicos, resetting the autopilot to keep on the new course, and busied himself trimming the sails.

The boat had no radar, and the run was just over five-hundred miles. Luca didn't dare go near land in the darkness. Open ocean felt safer with no rocks or reefs. With a dead body to get rid of, out away from land was where he wanted to be. Luca would wait until just before dawn to dump the body overboard, tied up with a spare anchor. There was plenty of time. The run to Big Sand Cay would take fifty non-stop hours. With wind, weather, and luck, he would make it. He went below to make a snack and to open some twelve-year-old rum.

Inside the well-appointed sailboat, Luca felt surprisingly warm and comfortable. He had gotten used to relaxing while Larry skippered. With the autopilot on and the GPS screen showing all the data, it felt much the same.

Larry's body lay on the hard fiberglass bench beyond the ship's wheel. Luca had turned off the hose when the water ceased to flow pink out the drain hole, to save battery power. He'd covered the body with a beach towel, tucking it under so the wind would not blow it away, but within minutes Larry's face and feet were exposed again. Water spray from the waves soaked the towel. The knife still plunged into Larry's chest stuck out from underneath like a tent pole. Luca remained below looking forward, choosing to ignore the gruesome scene.

After two hours, he realized the computer monitor and instruments were on, draining the battery. It was important to save battery power even though the wind generator was working perfectly. The apparent wind had been steady over the aft starboard beam. The true wind was about fourteen knots, so the small, six-blade wind generator was only feeling a gentle five or six-knot breeze. The speed of the boat had to be subtracted from the wind speed, leaving just barely enough wind to create a trickle of power. Luca turned off all electronics and lights except one reading light, the refrigerator, and the autopilot.

The darkness and rum combined with the steady motion of the boat as it road the ocean swells were seductive. Luca fell fast asleep.

At two AM, he was startled awake by the slapping of the mainsail. The wind had shifted. The loud snapping and jerking motions of the boat were more pronounced in the dark, sailing alone. With no lights onboard or on the horizon, Luca felt panic for several moments until his eyes adjusted enough to stand up and look out at the sails.

Scrambling up, he adjusted the main to stop the noise. He remembered Larry explaining the default for the autopilot was compass mode. If the wind shifted the boat would not adjust. Luca had failed to set it on wind mode which would adjust and optimize the downwind speed and direction, making for a more comfortable ride. It was lucky he had learned so much from Larry, but his inexperience still showed as he fumbled with setting his heading again, adjusting the sails, and then setting the autopilot properly.

Larry's body lay silently on the bench, seeming to mock Luca's struggles.

Luca had planned to sink the body farther from the island but decided that the total blackness around him was good enough. He went below and gathered the spare small anchor and rope. Tying it securely around Larry's ankles and neck, he placed the anchor on the bench. The swimming ladder had been pulled up, but still stuck out the back, and the safety rail was not closed. Luca disconnected both and lifted the ladder onboard. Now came the task of hefting Larry onto the transom, and heaving him overboard.

This was difficult, and Luca struggled with the heavier man. He managed to get him up enough to slump his body over the right direction but it took a long time and a lot of exertion to get him almost ready to roll over the side. Every motion of the rocking boat threatened to drop him back into the bottom of the cockpit. If Luca let this happen, it would be much harder to get Larry's body off the yacht.

Eventually, he had him ready to go and grabbed the body's legs for the final lift. Larry tumbled off the back of the boat. Luca straightened up as the line snaked over the stern. When it played out, the anchor pulled off the bench and dropped on Luca's ankle. The impact knocked him to the opposite bench, and the anchor rolled heavily onto his foot.

Anger and pain took over Luca's emotions. He picked up the anchor, which, under the pull of Larry's body dragging in the boat's wake, yanked Luca's hand into the rail. The motion split the skin on three fingers across the top of his left hand, between the second and third knuckles.

"Ahhhhh!" The string of Italian expletives that followed dissipated in the wind as Larry's body disappeared into the ocean.

Holding his injured hand, and limping a little, he went below to find the first aid kit. He bandaged his three fingers and checked his bruised ankle and foot. He didn't think anything was broken, but they'd be tender for a while.

Luca came back on deck to reattach the safety rail, stow the stairs, and put the cushions downstairs. Satisfied that the boat would now sail itself, he closed the hatch, poured another drink, turned off all the lights and laid down under a blanket.

With the exertions of dumping the body, the throbbing of his injured hand and foot, the strong rum, and rocking waves, he fell asleep again.

. . .

For seven hours the wind was consistent and the waves small. The conditions were ideal for sailing. Luca was now sixty miles from Jost Van Dyke, and that was the nearest he'd come to land for days.

The sails kept the boat steadier in the waves than a motorboat, but the travel was slower. Luca knew it would be a hard trip. If he was lucky, he would arrive safely, and in time for Vlad's plan to be carried out. The new settings on the autopilot were working well, and a quick check of the GPS track showed a reasonably straight course. Everything seemed to be working out fine, but this far out in unprotected waters he was subjected to the rolling swells of open ocean, and there was often the added chop of smaller waves riding on top.

Luca had adjusted to sailing over the past weeks and had his sea legs, but this was harder on his stomach. The boat wallowed with each rolling surge, making the autopilot work overtime. It kept his gut tense. When he was asleep, it wasn't as much of a problem, but he had to sleep on the low side of the boat or get thrown out of bed.

It was difficult to sleep more than a few hours. His sleep was disturbed by the anxiety that went with auto-pilot sailing. Knowing that there was no one on deck watching for other boats or objects in the water was stressful beyond belief. Only exhaustion could force him into sleep. Once awake he had to stay up on deck and watch the horizon, or he'd feel sick all over again.

The sailboat felt smaller and smaller in the darkness, but eventually the sky began to lighten with the coming dawn. Finally, the sun rose above the horizon and Luca's anxiety faded away.

The act of sailing across the ocean to cut the corner off the Florida and Georgia curved coastlines would save days, but at what price? He didn't think about this being the Bermuda triangle. Myths and legends didn't scare him, but he began to understand the reality of the ocean storms and their power as he scanned the water all around him. The thought of fighting a storm in this sea frightened him.

Luca busied himself with small tasks. First, he cleaned off a few remaining blood traces from the deck. Some spots were Larry's blood, but some were from his own injuries. Then he did a system check of the boat and its rigging. The number of buttons and switches he didn't understand sent him to the books and manuals stowed below deck, to read about the navigation, radio, and other features of the modern electronics built into the glossy wooden cabinets.

There was a book on seamanship which Luca read over and over until the evening light faded. He could have turned on a light, but then he would have lost his view of the horizon. Plus, the rocking of the boat would make reading at night and not getting sick impossible. When the sun was finally gone, it was very dark. The moon was little help, illuminating only thin stretches of water. The higher it got, the less any reflection appeared. The horizon was invisible.

Luca could feel the queasiness returning. He would have to try and sleep all night.

He lay below in the dark, trusting to fate. Even with the hatch open, there was little fresh air, and plenty of dank smells. It was the intangible fear that ate at him the most. He was sailing blind. When he was asleep, another boat could collide with him, spelling disaster. Logically, the odds were lower than a lottery win. How many sailors would attempt this route at night without radar? Not many, he thought. At least tonight he'd remembered to turn on the boat's running lights. He never took off the inflatable life jacket harness, but he wondered whether it could really save his life.

With Vlad's whip driving him to hurry, Luca had to keep moving twenty-four hours a day. By not stopping, he saved the time needed to find a place to anchor or dock. He had no choice but to trust the boat, the weather, and his luck that a storm would not reach out and kill him.

. . .

After three days at sea, Luca was desperate to see land. His food was holding out fine—there was enough for two people to last a week. The batteries had charged fully, thanks to using as little as possible. The windmill kept up with the autopilot, refrigerator, and running lights. The wind had shifted far enough two times to force him to jibe, but Larry had shown him how to do this safely so the boom would not damage the boat, or his head as it swung across the boat. When a weak cold front passed through, it poured rain for three hours. The wind stopped completely for one hour in the middle of the rain. Luca had engaged the engine so that he could keep running north. Luca thanked the boat for the hundredth time for being so well-equipped and easy to operate.

After lunch, Luca's good fortune turned. The wind shifted again with the coming of a much stronger front. For the first time, it came down from the north. This put him on a tack. Not wanting to beat hard upwind, he was forced to choose: head further out to sea, or toward the distant mainland. He chose land.

He found sailing upwind against sizeable waves much more punishing than he'd expected. He had sailed a lot, but always in calmer waters. The ocean experience was a very different situation. The waves grew steadily taller, some twice as high as the deck. The boat pounded headfirst into them. Spray lashed at his face, and frequent sail adjustments were needed to keep the boat from feeling out of control. Convinced he could make the sailing smoother he went back to the books, trusting in the autopilot while he went below. In the manual, he found the autopilot setting for wind. It could be set on "Apparent Wind." That seemed to help.

The front came closer, and the wind picked up. Soon it was too much for the sails. The Gozzard carried a cutter rig, with two jib-like sails in front, and a main attached to the mast. The topsail and staysail up front had challenged Luca every time he had to switch them from starboard to port or back, but the trip had required few jibes and even fewer tacks—so far.

When the wind picked up and the ride got scary, he rolled up the topsail by first engaging the motor, and then heading straight upwind and headfirst into the waves. He set the pilot to hold on that heading, and then pulled the lines that wound the sail up on its stay cable.

The waves crashed over the bow. Without the sail pressure, the boat rocked violently in all directions. Luca almost went overboard, clutching ropes when he should have grabbed more stable handholds. It was hard letting out the sheet "rope" that held the sail on one side, while simultaneously pulling in the roll-up line near the hatchway. Luca thanked God for the single-handed sailing equipment Larry had installed.

As the wind mounted, it was obvious that he still had too much sail. He could roll up the staysail, but the book said to reef the main first. The main was simply too big for the wind and needed to be reduced in surface area. He had read about reefing a main, but had never done it, and it was not clear in the book how to do it on this boat. It didn't have a long row of holes along the sail as seen in the pictures through which he could tie gaskets. Soaked from head to toe, cold, and miserable, Luca tried to figure out what he could do.

He thought about motoring, but the prospects of bobbing around with no stabilizing sails in these waves was too frightening. He was forced to go below, trusting in the autopilot again, while he searched the drawers for more books or manuals.

Below deck he had no wave or sky for reference. The boat's heaving motions knocked him around the cabin. He threw up twice, managing to grab the sink. Holding onto anything he could grab was the only way to stay on his feet as he searched the cabinets. Sheer desperation made him flip through every page of every book. Finally, he found the book that had come with the sails. There was a page on the Jiffy Reefing system, with diagrams for the main. Checking the pictures and with a little effort, he had the sail pulled down to the first reef. He rolled in the staysail a foot, too. Now the boat seemed survivable. As long as the wind did not get worse.

Chapter 43

Wednesday morning Robert sat on the phone with the Governors of Puerto Rico, the US Virgin Islands, and the British Virgin Islands. Grady and Steve were on the call with him.

"That's our situation gentlemen. We need to begin the all-out training mission as soon as possible," Robert, having disclosed the true state of affairs and the solution that had been approved, was wrapping up the conversation.

"You paint a bleak picture, Mr. Carlton. Thank you for the depressing course of action," Governor Edward Collins, OBE of the British Virgin Islands, commented, maintaining his dry British humor. "The problem is that I don't believe your idea will suppress the real story for long," The Governor continued. "The news that all six men from the island have died will get out. Containing the story on the island where the men were treated is unlikely. Additionally, the hospital will have to report the deaths of the final two coma victims to their governments. I can only imagine how horrible it would have been for those men, had they awakened, with the kind of pain they must have endured, but, of course, this leaves us all with fewer answers."

Governor Collins chimed in, "We will require a temporary delay, sufficient to coordinate our official statements. I request that you, and your government not release information into our media so that we can phrase it in our local manner—that is, if I may boldly speak for the three governors on this call. We do not want the truth of this situation to leak before we can control the information flow."

"That would be my recommendation, also," Robert agreed. He was only too happy to offload the responsibilities of handling the press.

"Carlos? Derek? Do you concur?" Governor Collins probed the two US Governors.

"Yes, we should coordinate any public statements. Let's keep the US and British statements separate," The Governor of Puerto Rico advised.

"And let's not make any unnecessary public statements. This is simply a training exercise, so the less we treat it as a special event, the less likely the public is to be concerned," The Governor of the US Virgin Islands added.

"Agreed." Governor Collins had his consensus. "Robert?"

"Your Excellency," Robert responded.

"Edward, please, Robert," the governor corrected. "I'll send a message to the coordinators we have established. The three of us will have a quick meeting, and then send team leader guidelines and any schedule requirements to...hmmm...that's a question. How shall we do this?"

"Let's send it through my office," The US Virgin Islands Governor said. "I'll dedicate Ms. Rodrigues to the coordination. Robert, you remember Mia from your trip?"

"Yes, of course." Robert liked the link since Mary knew Mia. "She coordinated our trip with Mary Whiston, so we'll assign her to be our liaison with Ms. Rodrigues."

"Good. That will make it all quite simple." The governor thought for a moment, then asked, "First responses to her in forty-eight hours, with daily updates?"

"Capital idea, Derek. Going through the US Virgin Islands sounds all right and tight. All agreed, then? We have an accord." Edward sometimes imagined himself a modern buccaneer and interjected pirate jargon into his conversation often.

Concluding the meeting with agreement all around, they exchanged goodbyes and ended the call.

The conversation had been much easier than Robert had expected. He thought about that for a minute before he, Grady, and Steve dialed back in on their conference line.

"That seemed to go surprisingly well," Grady began.

"Yes, it did," Robert agreed. "It almost seemed a little too easy to convince them that we'd found the only acceptable answer."

"I have a feeling the implementation will be much more difficult than getting the agreement was," Steve pronounced.

"I'm quite sure that you're right about that." Robert knew that the massive workload ahead was going to be difficult to implement. "Steve, start lining up your trainers and team members. Let me talk with anyone who needs approvals or confirmation. If someone needs more than that, I'll arrange for them to get the authorization they require. Grady, we need to get the final Air Force approvals. Get me a list of Generals that need orders, and I'll have the appropriate communications arranged."

"I should have twelve trainers, and twenty assistants ready in a week." Steve had his people lined up. He was ready to go forward as soon as the paperwork was signed. "The problem I have is equipment," he continued. "We don't have any we can leave behind."

"The Eighth will have the same issue," Grady chimed in. "The trainees should be using the gear we plan to lend them anyway, not what the military guys use. After talking with a specialist at Barksdale Air Force Base who walked me through what they use if a nuke is lost, I realized that there is no way the Air Force will leave that equipment in the hands of the locals." Grady still lacked confidence the AFGSC would willingly agree to participate. The order would have to come from above. The mission-centric groups within each branch of the armed services jealously guarded themselves against being sucked into unrelated actions.

Robert propped his elbow on the chair arm, resting his chin on his hand. He thought for a moment, trying to sort out the answer to their problem. "So, we need a bunch of specialized equipment that isn't cheap or easy to get. Steve, who can we talk to about this?"

"I'll get our senior buyer in Atlanta to put together a deployment package bill of materials that we use, and add the purchasing information for each of the line items, including vendors and pricing. We could piggyback off our purchasing department if you can transfer funding. That way, nobody has to get contracts, credit, or triple bids done. It could take months, otherwise."

"Okay," Robert answered, wondering if short-cutting the paperwork would be possible in releasing the funding, as well. "Get me the list, a contact, and a price estimate. Let's assume we will need twenty-four of those deployment packages to leave behind. We'll use all the equipment you can spare while we wait for those packages to arrive."

"Twenty-four?" Steve asked, trying to figure out where Robert had come up with that number.

"That's two for each Caribbean government we have to work with," Robert clarified. "Some will only need one, but some will need three. Contact me if either of you has any problems," he added, winding up the call. Grady and Steve hung up, and Robert headed into his staff meeting.

Lorraine had dutifully arranged a weekly meeting for him with his department heads. Only two dialed in for the call. One got her remote PowerPoint presentation to work. Robert wondered if he was losing touch with what the other heads were doing, but decided that Jack was probably micro-managing their activities. Unless they or Jack came knocking on his door, he couldn't change anything they were doing. Hopefully, the next meeting would be better attended.

. . .

It was late when Robert arrived at his house. Tracie heard the door to the garage open and then close. "Rough day at the office?" she called to him.

Robert followed her voice into the entertainment room. She was watching something on TV. He had a nice home system with good seating—once you swept the boys' toys off the chairs. It was the only common room they were allowed to have toys in, and they rarely put them away. Tracie had evidently pushed the toys and the video game controls to one side of the room. Robert liked the surround sound and the comfortable seating, but rarely came into the room. TV was an addiction he needed to avoid.

"Not too bad a day," he answered as he entered the room. She didn't turn the volume down, so he spoke louder. "Lots of meetings. I will probably be headed down to St. John again for a quick meeting soon."

"Okay." Tracie hadn't turned from the screen. "Just don't mess up this weekend," she added.

"This weekend?" Robert drew a blank, wondering what she was talking about.

Tracie spun around in her deep leather chair. "The party at the Savannah Yacht Club?" She intoned meaningfully, looking disdainfully at him. "The airport on Friday? The B&B in old town? The dress I bought?"

"Oh, yeah. The yacht club," Robert said, still racking his brain for some recollection of the event. "Is it *this* weekend? I can't believe it crept up on us so quickly." He still didn't remember anything about it. He found himself thinking that he was going to have to start setting his alarm to give him a week's advance notice about this kind of stuff. Suddenly it hit him. "Mark and Julie's club, right?"

The invitation had been issued and accepted enthusiastically by Tracie the weekend they'd met on St. Thomas. Mark and Julie had thought of skipping the annual yacht club party this year, but decided that, given what they'd been through, getting back to normal events might be a good idea.

"Jeff and Chrystal will be there, too." Tracie wasn't convinced that Robert remembered anything about the weekend.

"Right. We leave for the airport at...?" Robert prodded.

"Two-thirty, and no, I can't meet you at the airport, so you should plan to work from home Friday." She spoke loudly toward the TV, making it clear that Robert was losing points for forgetting the trip.

"I'll leave a message for Lorraine," Robert told her. "Have you had dinner?" he asked.

"Some time ago, before Alicia left for the evening," Tracie snapped. "Yours is in the microwave. Four minutes on high."

"Got it." Robert made a fast exit and went looking for the scotch.

Chapter 44

Twenty minutes from their bed and breakfast hotel in old Savannah, Georgia, Robert opened the rental car door and watched Tracie's legs sweep out. Her new dinner dress with its sophisticated slit showed off one leg as she took his hand and stepped onto the pavement. The Savannah Yacht Club sign in Blue with Gold letters read, "Members Only" at the bottom in white. Tracie nodded slightly toward the sign, clearly enjoying the exclusivity of the situation.

It had been a rough week at the office for Robert. Jack had become embroiled in a couple of issues, leaving Robert in charge of more of the department's activities. Handling the Deputy AG workload, staff assignments, and the Caribbean arrangements put Robert on overload.

When the actions were finally set for the "training exercises," with Grady and Steve busy arranging the search teams, Robert realized he might get to take a breath. He was actually glad for an excuse to get away. A trip to historic Savannah was more welcome than he'd thought it would be.

As members of the club, Mark and Julie were their hosts. The SYC, formed in 1869, was permeated with southern charm. A crisp, white, two-rail fence lined the walkway between trim gardens and hedges. The end posts to the fences were weathered brick with large carriage lights on top, shaded under a canopy of old trees dripping with Spanish moss.

The stately, one-story clubhouse presented a low Parthenon triangular pitch roof entry, decorated with many white Doric columns. A large white sea anchor was positioned out front. The view included a long dock with dozens of yachts tied up, resting on the calm tidal waters of the Wilmington River. On the dock, a two-tiered open tower with a green cupola stood watch. A large pool near the shoreline invited sailors to cool off after a long boat ride.

"Nice club," Robert commented as they walked up to the entry. "I wonder when they built it. I doubt that this is the original structure from 1869."

Tracie was content to absorb the ambiance. "I can't get over how the moss hangs down from the trees. This, and the houses in the old part of Savannah are so elegant and..." she stopped, searching for the right words to describe her feelings.

"So *Gone With the Wind*?" Robert tried.

"Yes, and no," Tracie responded. "This is an historic town, so it's not like being on plantations, but it is a glimpse into the old South. I feel that I ought to have a hoop skirt and a fan," she giggled.

They entered the big, double, multi-paned doors and were greeted almost immediately by Mark and Julie.

"Welcome to the Savannah Yacht Club! We're so glad you could come." Mark was shaking Robert's hand as Julie gave Tracie a peck on the cheek. Within moments another couple approached.

"Let me introduce you to our club Commodore," Mark said. Introductions to a large number of club officers and elite members ensued, as they all seemed to be in the immediate area. Tracie was more accustomed to this type of cocktail party flow than Robert. Robert thought it was extremely unlikely that he would ever see these people again, and found it a bit tedious to be introduced to them all. He knew that this was exactly the kind of event he would need to spend more time appreciating if he ever aspired to elected office.

Tracie was not going to miss this opportunity to endear them to the new and old money Savannah set, some who had generational family connections to the club. The handshakes and cheek smooches lasted over thirty minutes.

"Let me show you around." Mark finally led Robert away from the clutch of people. Julie walked with Tracie arm-in-arm as they strolled through the club.

"How do you like The Gastonian?" Julie asked. She had recommended the B&B. She and Mark had stayed there prior to moving to Savannah.

"It's lovely," Tracie responded. They put us in the General Monk Hunter room," Tracie told her.

"Is that the one on the top floor with the pale green walls and striped chairs?" Julie asked, trying to remember.

"Yes, it's charming. Thank goodness you told me to book it right away when we first talked! The place is full to the brim," Tracie mentioned.

"It does get booked up," Julie nodded. "We stayed in the Sheftall Room. All their rooms are nice, and the location is so convenient. We walked around a lot, and it was so easy to get a pedicab to restaurants. Have you tried one, yet?"

"No, but I did see them around. I think we may need to light the fire tonight in our room. It's surprisingly chilly." Tracie had thought about wearing a wrap for the evening, but hadn't wanted to cover up her dress.

"Sometimes the water brings up a chill as evening comes on, but it rarely gets too cool," Julie responded. They had reached the main lounge, nicely appointed with leather chairs and a few sailing decorations. The appointments were sophisticated and understated. The dining room had been updated fairly recently and was very open, light, and contemporary. The granite tables standing under curving wrought iron chandeliers with high, off-white ceilings gave off a modern vibe. It made a nice counterpoint to the darker sitting room and bar.

"Tomorrow night we're going to take you around town. I assume you like seafood? There's a restaurant the locals like called the Chrystal Beer Parlor. It's just a few blocks from where you are staying. It's not fancy, but the food is great. We might have a wait— it's very popular, and they generally don't take reservations. Does that sound all right?" Julie had been following Robert and Mark, but when she spotted Chrystal she pulled Tracie away. "Speaking of Chrystal's...look who I found?"

"Hello, Tracie," Chrystal came right over, dragging Jeff along. She gave Tracie a hug and a peck on the cheek. "How nice to see you again! I see Mark has Robert in tow." Mark and Robert were headed out to the docks, talking avidly. They hadn't noticed Jeff or Chrystal.

"Hello, again, Tracie." Jeff shook Tracie's hand, but he was looking at Mark's and Robert's backs. "It's great to see you, but how about if I let you girls chat, and I head out with the boys to the boats?" He glanced at Chrystal for approval, who smiled and nodded. Jeff sprinted after them, catching up with Mark and Robert as the boys reached the main dock.

"Mark, Robert," Jeff panted, grabbing their shoulders.

"Jeff!" Mark said, turning. "Robert, you remember Jeff, don't you?"

"I do," Robert returned, shaking Jeff's hand. "I wondered when we'd spot you and Chrystal. Do you belong to the club, or are you guests, as well?" Robert asked.

"Chrystal and I belong to the Port of Washington Yacht Club. Mark and Julie belong here, but there is a comradery among the yacht clubs, and some have exchange privileges. Some you can walk into if you sail in; others require an invitation approved in advance. Generally, most are very hospitable. It's nice to be able to sail around, dock, get fuel and ice, and visit other clubs."

Mark added. "You can get a fitting or repair at most clubs, as well. We often need parts that you won't find at a typical dock or hardware store. Plus, the clubs have showers, restaurants, and bars. It makes sailing a very nice way to travel."

Robert noticed that Mark and Jeff got along like they had known each other for years. Being held hostage together created in just days what might otherwise have taken a long time.

Mark was continuing, "When Julie and I first got into sailing, we crewed on an owner's lake boat during regattas. We started renting small sailing yachts when we'd be on a lake or in a port town, and eventually expanded into other waters. We had no idea how nice the rivers are for sailing until someone recommended some to us. Then we discovered the Intracoastal Waterway running down to Key West, and before we knew it we were sailing in the Grenadines."

"Are you thinking about taking up sailing?" Jeff asked Robert, who was looking interested.

"I think Tracie would love being Jackie Kennedy on a wooden sloop off Nantucket Island," Robert smiled, "but I don't know if she's ready to crew for me."

"Here's my boat." Jeff placed a foot on the Hunter 356 in front of them. "Care to take a look?" he asked.

Mark was looking pointedly at Robert's dress shoes. "Robert, how do you feel about going barefoot on board?" he queried. "Shoes like that tend to leave marks on a boat."

"Sure. I should have thought of the shoes," Robert said, remembering day trips on his father's yacht. He was curious more than interested in Jeff's boat, but he slipped off his shoes and socks, leaving them on the dock. He followed Jeff aboard, with Mark close behind.

Robert was surprised at how beautiful the yacht was inside. It seemed spacious and amazingly functional. How so much efficiency got stuffed in the hull seemed remarkable. After Jeff had explained most of the features, Mark suggested that Robert might like to see his Beneteau 423. Robert agreed and was again impressed by the boat and its design.

Jeff and Mark had begun explaining the differences in their yachts and were deep into sailing talk now. Robert was quickly getting lost in their discussion of waterlines, displacement, knots, Kevlar sails, and graphite spars. Electronic this and that became a blur of language. He dutifully replied, "A graphite rudder? Really? Nice," sounding more interested than he was. That created more pointing and explaining by Jeff and Mark, to which Robert returned, "Autopilot linked directly to the GPS with waypoints? That sounds cool."

"Mark claims that his boat is nearly neutral to weather," Jeff was telling Robert.

"Yeah, at first I wasn't sure I liked it." Mark explained, "I wanted a weather helm strong enough to go into irons on its own in an overboard situation, but now that I'm used to it, I enjoy it. Now she pulls to weather inside the autopilot guidelines, but I like the feel. She only pulls head-to-wind at the top of the hull speed. I suppose if I was racing the drag would be an issue, but it's not a class boat anyway."

"Class boat?" Robert asked.

"I've got a PHRF of 135 with the Spinnaker." Jeff was obviously proud of this number but was unaware that his statement hadn't cleared anything up for Robert.

"Mine's 102 PHRFNE, and a 153 from Pascagoula, Mississippi. That was for a regatta I entered." He shrugged his shoulders. "So go ratings, as they say."

"Okay, I'll admit it." Robert couldn't hold back any longer. "What is a PHRF rating?"

"It's a mess." Jeff laughed.

"A red-hot mess," Mark added, joining Jeff's chuckles. "I have a t-shirt from when I raced Lasers that says 'Friends don't let friends sail IRC." Both Mark and Jeff laughed at that.

"I have one that says, 'What's it rate?' That's on the front and, 'Who gives a shit. It's a J-24' on the back." Jeff laughed at his own joke.

Robert pasted a vague smile on his face, wondering if they intended to explain their quips, or if it was time to change the subject.

Mark stopped laughing and began to explain what they were talking about. "So-called Class boats have one consistent design, and, within guidelines, race head-to-head. Then there are people like us who might race a wide variety of boats against each other, so the PHRF, an acronym for Performance Handicap Racing Fleet number, is an established handicap for each to equalize the yachts."

"The thing is, nobody agrees with the rating of their own boat," Jeff was picking up where Mark had left off. "Right now, I think that my boat is faster than his, 135 versus 153, but if we were racing I wouldn't want the smaller handicap."

"So, it's like the golf handicap system which kills me every time a guy with an 8 takes advantage of me, even though I have a 28?" Robert queried. That got a laugh all round.

"Twenty-eight? Clearly, you don't get much time to play, Robert," Jeff ribbed him, smiling. "Me either," he confessed, "and that comparison to golf? Dead on. That's why I never race for higher stakes than buying the first round."

"I'll remember that—only bet for drinks." Robert moved to get off the Beneteau and back onto the dock.

It baffled Robert that they might race what were obviously luxury yachts, designed for pleasure sailing.

"So how long did it take the two of you to get here from St. Thomas?" Robert asked, retrieving his socks and shoes. He was thinking that it had been five weeks since they met. He wondered if it had taken all that time to get to Savannah.

"Almost the whole five weeks," Mark admitted. "We got here two days ago. We just made it in time for the party."

"It was a long sail. We had great weather most of the way, which helped. We did stop a few times to relax on-shore." Jeff added.

"You just got here? How far is it?" Robert asked.

"It was eighteen hundred miles as the crow flies, but we sailed the islands and up the Eastern Seaboard. That's like a big curve, running right along the southern edge of the Bermuda triangle. With a straight shot, sailing non-stop and getting favorable weather, you can do it in nine or ten days." Mark said.

"Good luck with that." Jeff rolled his eyes. "I wouldn't try that with a full crew, much less just me and Chrystal. Sailing at night and never anchoring is for crazy people. Too dangerous."

"We spent some slow days running up the Intracoastal Waterway, avoiding rough wave days out on the ocean, and coming in for food and rest. You can't stay out forever." Mark smiled. "The girls were real troupers through the whole trip, but we're all worn out from long-leg sailing."

"We're all staying two nights to rest up before we head north to DC." Jeff did look a little tired. Robert hadn't noticed that until now. Mark looked fine.

"You're all going?" Robert was surprised.

"Why not?" Mark said. "We've never done it, and we may never have the chance again. Hey, I understand you and Tracie are staying the weekend to see the city," he said, changing the subject. "Tomorrow we're giving you a tour of the Wilmington River."

"Are you kidding? After all that sailing, you're taking us out? That must be the last thing you want to do." Robert was sure they must be imposing on Mark and Julie. "You must have arranged that before you made that exhausting trip."

"Don't worry, Robert. We're looking forward to it. It's as easy for us to sail as getting in a car is for you."

Mark didn't look concerned, but Robert still wasn't sure this was what he and Julie wanted to do. "My point exactly," he told Mark.

"No, really, it's no problem. We're sincerely excited to get you on the boat," Mark reassured Robert. "Ask Jeff! We love showing off our river to visitors."

"It's true," Jeff affirmed. "Come over to the POWC when you get back to DC, and we'll take you around the Potomac." Jeff brightened up at the idea. "But tomorrow, Chrystal and I are going to sleep all day on a huge bed, and order room service." Jeff spread his arms wide as though he was flopping onto a bed. They all got a chuckle out of that.

As they headed back toward the clubhouse, Mark and Jeff talked about the different boats they passed, pointing out their features to Robert. Robert asked if they sailed all year, but both men said that they were looking forward to lazy days by the pool when the hot, sticky summer arrived.

. . .

In the parking lot, Max sat in her car watching. Her vantage point was good enough to see the three men leave the dock and head toward the yacht club. Grabbing the two GPS radio transponders she got out of the car. She intended to attach the transponders to the boats—if she could find a spot where they might not be noticed.

As the men entered the clubhouse, a silhouetted Max wandered out onto the dock, holding a plastic drink cup. She fit in perfectly with the members and guests enjoying the evening air.

. . .

Julie and Tracie had arranged everything for the next afternoon's cruise that took them down the river, not up toward the city and the Savannah River, as Robert had assumed. The leisurely sail took nearly four hours. They didn't turn back until they had a good look at the Wassaw wildlife refuge. Robert had never seen a marsh or swamp like this before. Except for seeing too many snakes, he enjoyed the trip. By the time they got back it was almost sunset. They quickly bundled up the boat so they could head into town.

Tracie and Robert had the following day all to themselves. They hired a pedicab and toured the historic streets and buildings. It was great to get away from DC. Tracie was right about that.

<u>Chapter 45</u>

It had been almost a week since Max had been in Savannah. The GPS unit fit nicely on the Beneteau, but she hadn't been able to find a discreet spot for placing one on the Hunter. She settled for tracking the Beneteau, betting that both it and the Hunter were headed to DC. Her phone showed the Beneteau had started out Monday, sailing north.

It was now Friday, and Max was back in Melbourne. She sat at the inlet bar overlooking the water, a beer bottle in her hand. She was waiting for Rayberg, or "Berg" as everyone called him. Gary, the bartender, had recognized the attractive woman the minute she walked in the door. Her athletic hard body, short brown hair, and strong legs were easy to remember.

When she ordered a Sam Adam's Boston Lager, he remembered to open it in front of her and wrap a napkin around it. Max appreciated a good-looking man with a good memory.

"I'm looking for Berg. I'll be on the deck," Max motioned with her head that she would be outside.

"He should be here, as always. I'll tell him you're out there," Gary replied, smiling at her.

Max couldn't see the docks from where she sat. She was on the far side of a small bridge. Like any place in Florida, it was hard to see very far with all the flat land and tall trees.

The dock facility was the best place she'd found for completing the plan. The boat could be pulled out of the water, and no one seemed inclined to ask questions. The harbor allowed DIY boaters, or those who wanted to hire their own contractors to do work for them. A long repair house was right by the lift crane, where Berg had done a lot of work. He also had a small, fenced lot nearby and a trailer. He would sometimes move boats to his fenced-in work area when they were bigger projects.

That was what Max wanted. A small place with no security, few houses, and an out of the way location. That, and the occasional north wind which put an Air Force Base and the rocket launch facilities at Cape Canaveral directly downwind. These were just close enough to suit the purpose.

The Gulfstar 39 had arrived a few days earlier, and sat at the transient dock. The two delivery agents hired by the boat broker had sailed it up from the islands to this spot that Max had reserved. It could handle up to a sixty-foot yacht with a seven-foot draft; more than enough for this sailboat. The final ownership had not been transferred until the previous day, but now the boat was officially hers, via Vlad.

Max estimated that the Hunter and Beneteau were five days away from Washington, assuming they didn't decide to linger somewhere along the way.

Luca, on the Gozzard, had sent a text estimating he would be in Virginia Beach on schedule in four days. They had talked on the phone once as he sailed along the coast of Georgia, but he was staying away from shore as much as possible. He wanted to avoid any possible encounters with the Coast Guard. His cell connection refused to hold, but she'd heard enough to know that he was exhausted. Luca had sounded uncharacteristically depressed, despite his positive assurances.

Luca's plan was to sail to a little yacht basin in Southport. His intention was to give the impression that he'd sailed up from Florida, to avoid customs rules which would require check-in within forty-eight hours of docking. He would stay overnight, then use the Intracoastal Waterway from there. He'd find anchorage at night.

On cue with the setting sun, the large big bellied Berg walked out on the deck and over to Max. His ever-present beer rested comfortably in the grip of his right hand, and his dirty "Berg's Boats" logo shirt hung over his shorts.

"You got your boat here, and ready to fix?" Berg asked with no preamble.

"Yes, it's here. Have a seat." Max had a few details to explain.

Berg pulled up a chair that looked like it might be strong enough to hold him, if the vinyl webbing held, and sat down. "What do you need done?"

Max cut right to the chase. "I'd like you to fix the cracks in the keel, scrape, sand, and paint from the waterline down. She got a little scraped up by a sandbar."

"Same color?" Berg confirmed.

"Same color." Max verified. "How soon can you start?"

"Next Friday; maybe Thursday," Berg told her. "I'm a little backed up. I can have the boat lifted and moved tomorrow."

"How much for the job?" Max wanted to know.

"That depends," Berg responded. "How many feet is the boat?"

"Thirty-nine," Max said.

"So, two-thousand to paint," Berg calculated mentally. "Can't tell the rest until we lift it and look. Assuming only light fiberglass crazing repair, the bottom scrape from the sandbar you mentioned, and doing the job right, probably less than thirty-six hundred. But I'll have to see before I can tell you for sure."

"Sounds a little high," Max parried. She wasn't concerned about the price, but she had to sound legitimate.

"I can call you with an estimate after I see the damage, or we can look together tomorrow morning." Berg wasn't backing off his price until he saw the work needed. He'd had too many owners downplay damage over the years, trying to get the price down.

"I can look at it with you," Max agreed. "How much to store it until you can get to it?"

"Fifty a day, but as long as I do the work, and you pay the lift-and-look in advance, it'll be free as part of the job. It saves money if we can agree on the estimate same day as the lift." Berg wanted the advance payment.

"Okay. What's the cost of the lift?" Max was getting a little tired of this process, but she knew that most boat owners would ask for breakdowns of all the costs—especially if they were going to a guy like Berg for repairs.

"The lift fee to the dock owner is ten dollars a foot. I charge two hundred to handle it for you. I'll estimate the job while it's on the lift. If you can be available tomorrow, how about a down payment of six-hundred now?" Berg figured that was fair, and would encourage her not to take the work to someone else.

"Agreed. What time tomorrow?" Max reached into her back pocket for her cell-phone wallet.

"I'll move the boat at seven-thirty, or so," Berg said, wondering if she thought that was too early.

"Good. I'll be there." Max pulled six hundred-dollar bills from her wallet and handed them to Berg, along with a key ring. "Here are the keys. It's the white and blue Gulfstar 39 in slip eight."

"No problem. Phone number?" Berg requested.

Max handed him a card with the number written on the back.

Gary came out on deck with a fresh unopened beer in his hand. "Ready for another?" He asked.

"No, thanks," Max told him. "I have some business in town, but get Berg here another on me." Max stood up to leave.

"You don't have to do that," Berg protested as he struggled to rise, less out of chivalry than a desire to return to the bar.

"It's my pleasure." She turned back to Gary. "I'll come by here for lunch tomorrow. Okay if we settle up then?"

"No problem," Gary replied. "Fish and chips are really good this time of year."

Max smiled but did not reply as she headed straight to the parking lot from the deck walkway.

"Serious lady," Gary said to Berg.

"Nice ass." Berg openly ogled her as she walked away.

"Berg, you have a way with the girls." Gary smiled, "You've got a beer coming."

"Make it the twenty-two ounce," Berg grunted.

. . .

Max sat in her car. "Gulfstar ready tomorrow Melbourne" was the text she sent. Pulling up the phone app, she hit the speed dial for Luca and listened as the phone rang without answer. She left no message, sending a text instead. "Text me. I'm ready in Melbourne." She sent a second text to Vlad. "Melbourne on land."

Chapter 46

Max arrived early and watched as the yacht rolled out of the water on the lifting hoist. It wasn't a crane lift; it was a metal frame with wheels on a steel track, like a train. The boat was held up by straps that Berg had positioned for proper support. As soon as it was chocked and safe, Berg was underneath, scrubbing slime off the keel in the places that might show cracks. He was not surprised to find hairline cracks in several spots. The worst spots were around some new fiberglass work done on the keel's leading edge and around a ballast bulb. There'd been some paint work done to cover the new fiberglass. It almost matched the faded original paint.

"There was some work done here." Berg pointed out the bulge at the bottom of the keel. "They did an okay job, but for some reason, they made the keel bigger." He scratched his poorly shaved jaw. "I've seen where people change from concrete to steel, or from steel to lead, to make a keel smaller, but I've never seen one made bigger. Do you want to keep it this way?"

"My friend bought it used, and it came this way. He never races it, and it sails nice and stable, so I'd say no change. Just patch the cracks and paint." Max hoped that would suffice as an explanation.

"Okay, looks like minor cracks except this one." He traced a line across the keel about two feet, just above the odd bulge. "I'll need to grind this out some to patch it." Then he pulled at a flap of fiberglass that was coming off the leading edge. "This I can fix by cutting it off, and putting on new fiberglass. Same on the other side. I'll make sure it's smooth." Berg lowered himself to the ground with an uncomfortable grunting sound. "Don't see any scrape damage from the sandbar. Must have been really soft. Guess the 'glass damage around the bulb is it. If it turns out that any of the other cracks run deep enough to need more repair, I'll call you, but I'm thinking that we're looking at about thirty-three hundred."

"That sounds about right," Max nodded as she watched Berg struggle to get himself back up and off the ground.

Wiping off some algae slime from his knees with both hands, Berg looked at Max. "I'll roll it over to my yard. It'll take a week for the glass work to cure, and another week for the paint."

"One of us will be by to get it in three weeks, if that works for you."

"No problem, as long as I get paid at the pickup," Berg said.

They shook hands and Max made her way to the sandy parking lot. From the pocket of the car she pulled out a cleansing wipe for the green slime from Berg's hand. Her next job was in DC. As she drove away, she went past the parking lot where the yacht would be kept.

Sending a text of her GPS location and one which read, "Melbourne location. Ready," she waited. In a few moments a message came back.

"Received. Proceed next location."

Max put her car in drive and headed for the hotel. Tomorrow she would catch the flight to Reagan to her next task at the Potomac yacht harbor.

· · ·

Vlad set down his phone. The message from Max was good. They were staying very close to the original schedule. The clients would be happy. He would head to Melbourne in three days, putting himself ahead of the predetermined start date the following Sunday. When the wind was right, they would begin.

He messaged his client. "One week to start release. Watch weather."

The exchange of information was brief. "Remember, twenty-four hours' notice. Not Friday or Saturday."

He sent a message to Mary. "Teapot report." His confidence in her had grown since she had delivered Robert's research information. It took her two days to get, but she had come through. She was now responding faster to his inquiries.

He did not have to wait long before the phone signaled a new message.

"Six search teams working a line from Grand Cayman to Jamaica, Haiti and Dominican Republic. Six more teams in Puerto Rico, US and British Virgin Islands." Mary had done well keeping track of the operation.

"Number civilian vs military." Vlad wanted to know how committed the US resources were.

"8 civ, 4 mil," came the answer.

"Reserves?" he queried.

"Unknown," she replied.

Vlad glared at the display. "Find out how many teams left in southeastern and northeastern US," he demanded.

Tossing the phone on the car seat next to him, he stared out at the beach. It was relaxing to watch the waves and sunbathers, although he had no interest in baking himself. Young men and women walked and skated past on the sidewalk in front of him. The scantily clad girls drew his attention. He examined each one. A particularly attractive brunette went past, doing her best to attract a young stud sitting on the hood of his car.

Vlad watched the two tease each other as he thought about the radiation detection teams. How many teams could be mustered? The estimate was between ten and fifteen potential search teams in the southeast, military and civilian combined. Another dozen might be available in the northeast, but that was a stretch. The Americans really didn't have search teams, they used technicians. They were over-qualified for the task. Lesser personnel could be used in greater volume. That's what they would do in Vlad's home country.

Even so, twelve were committed so far. That was a good number. It must have drained most of their qualified resources. In deploying them the Americans had almost emptied out their nuclear search capability within a thousand miles. This severely reduced their only means of finding his dirty bomb sailboats. He smiled. Two girls in bikinis walked by much faster when they saw his face.

. . .

Luca sailed toward a long dock to get fuel and supplies. He had headed in to land from the sea through a large opening connected to the Intracoastal Waterway. The GPS showed a yacht basin, ornamenting it with a knife and fork. Right now, he could use everything, including water, food, fuel, sleep, and a bath. More than anything he wanted to set food on land. He stayed under sail well inside the barrier islands, which were large and long. The channel was also quite big. It looked smaller on the GPS; the auto zoom feature made it hard to judge the absolute size of anything.

Luca took down the sails. Just in time, he remembered to put bumpers out on the sides of the boat. With the help of a stranger on the dock who took his lines, he tied up safely and stood on the floating wood dock. It felt like solid earth to his ocean tired legs.

It was a great relief that no one approached or challenged him. The name and home port of the boat, "Blustery, Tampa, FL," displayed on the stern was enough to fit in with the other yachts, it seemed. His fear of confronting customs, the Coast Guard, or a harbor official vanished. In his pocket, he had the boat's papers, along with Larry's passport. He had replaced the picture with his own, but the less than professional forgery would not pass close inspection or survive electronic checking.

The dock had a store. There he replenished his stores, water, and fuel, and got the information he needed for overnight docking. The hotel nearby had rooms available. Luca settled in to relax for the first time in weeks.

He sent a text to Max. She responded that she was glad to hear he was safe, and on schedule. It didn't dawn on him to wonder which was more important to her. He knew what was more important to Vlad, and he sent a text to him next. The short, "message received," response was as much as he expected.

After food and a hot shower, Luca collapsed on the bed to sleep. After so much time at sea, his body couldn't adjust. The room seemed to be rocking so much that he had to sit up with his back against three pillows. This helped enough. He fell fast asleep, waking well into the next morning. The prospect of getting on the boat again was miserable. It could wait until after he'd eaten a well-deserved, leisurely breakfast.

. . .

Robert's weekly Monday morning meeting had hummed along steadily. The team had adopted its own rhythm, thanks to Lorraine's agenda requests. Rather than tell them what the meeting would entail, she'd begun asking for their subject matter. She created an interactive agenda that they could all see, even as they each made edits. A competition for more impressive agenda items ensued between coworkers, raising the bar from the previous week. The only restriction she placed was the time allotted to each individual.

The conference call included remote presentation capability. Lorraine had all participants, even those in the room, connect through Wi-Fi. When they took possession of "the electronic ball," to present from their own laptops, the meeting progressed smoothly. The lack of cable juggling and memory stick hand-offs saved time and frustration.

All presentations were required to have speaker notes and to be uploaded to the common folder, which Lorraine oversaw and published for the record. She even had name tents at the table. When Robert arrived, he felt a bit like Mako Morrison, with his team marching in formation. It felt good. He reflected that Lorraine was a valuable asset.

With the meeting adjourned, Robert moved toward his office. He found Jerry close on his heels.

"Robert, we need to talk about the..." Jerry began.

"Mr. Carlton." Lorraine interrupted from the doorway. "I have Colonel Barlow on the line, and you said to..."

"Thank you, Lorraine, put him through right away. I'm sorry, Jerry. Can this wait? I have to take this call." Robert was relieved to watch Jerry nod and turn to leave, pulling the door closed behind him.

"Colonel! What's going on down there?" He said it loudly enough to penetrate the door. Then picked up the handset, taking Grady off the speaker phone.

"Take me off the speaker," Grady advised.

"I already did," Robert reassured him.

"So, what's with the 'Colonel' thing? Someone in the room?" Grady read the situation easily enough.

"Yes, but not anymore. Fill me in." Robert was genuinely interested in the Sandy Island project. He had to be since the President expected him to get results.

"We've made huge progress with the small islands. Steve and his guys have almost completed the Caymans while training two teams. They outfitted one boat and a four-wheeler with a trailer. They offload the four-wheeler at each island which runs around the interior, while the boat goes around the shore. It works really well on islands less than ten miles wide, and with few buildings or roads. We run into problems with towns because every road has to be scanned twice—and there are the islands that are hilly or mountainous, like here in St. Croix."

"Why scanned twice?" Robert asked.

"The gear is more sensitive depending on which direction it faces, so mounted to a trailer the reading changes depending which side of the road you're on. Opposing traffic, parked cars, thick concrete walls—these all affect the reading. We pick up trace readings all over the place. As they say, radiation is easy to detect, hard to measure. When we get a spike, we mark the spot and come back to it. If it spikes again, we stop and investigate by hand. We're still fine-tuning the criteria."

"Evidently there is a lot more radiation around than people think," Robert assessed.

"Exactly. I would tune down the gear, but then we would lose accuracy, so the teams have to get used to what is ambient, and what needs investigation," Grady explained.

"How much is the ambient radiation?" Robert asked.

"We call it 'background radiation.' It's low compared to what we're looking for. We're training them to target and react to one millisievert."

"Okay, I'm following you, I think. So, the big question is, after almost a week's experience with this, how long do you two think it will take to cover the rest of the islands?" Robert needed something to feed the higher-ups.

"Four months—except for the big islands," Grady sounded sure. "The Dominican Republic and Haiti are one example of how hard this will be. It could take three months to cover that island with four teams, and we'd still have incomplete data, due to the mountains."

"So, we have to go with containment via portals," Robert guessed.

"Steve and I talked, and came up with that same conclusion. We think we should scan all the transportation points, harbors, and airports. Any point of departure or arrival would have to be considered suspect. To work with current equipment, each possible source would have to be scanned at close range, and the whole area continuously. If not that, then frequently and unpredictably," Grady summarized.

Robert had been thinking along these lines, but the solution would never yield an "all-clear" result. "It's far from a bulletproof solution." He said, a little discouraged.

"True, and we still need a container ship or cruise ship solution. Those monsters are hard to sweep even at close range," Grady reminded him. "Steve tells me it can be done, but the scanners are huge, and expensive. Plus, each container has to be scanned individually as it's loaded."

"That would seem to bring us back to experimental solutions, like MISTI?" Robert questioned. He felt the whole project was looking like a hopeless exercise.

"The problem with MISTI is that we need a seaworthy version and an airborne version." Grady had been researching the fly over option. "I talked to some people about what we have in flyover capability. We've got a plane that can detect airborne radiation. I've been talking to some guys that know 'The Sniffer' pretty well, and they say it won't help us on this. It works by collecting radioactive particles in the air and analyzing them real-time. That won't catch a source sitting dormant or shielded on the ground. My sources think that a downward-looking scanner onboard, say a C-130, flying slow, might work." Grady had been thinking hard about solutions.

"Wait, what is 'The Sniffer?'" Robert questioned.

"The Sniffer is the WC-135 Constant Phoenix," Grady elucidated. "It collects airborne samples. We use it to detect and identify nuclear explosions, like the one North Korea recently set off. It was used for monitoring the air around the Fukushima nuclear plant in Japan to measure airborne emissions, following the power plant meltdown disaster. It has these special air scoops and filters that can be analyzed real-time. Plus, it's got special shielding for the crew that helps during a 'hot' mission. But it looks to me and Steve like our targets on this would be low to the ground radiation sources," he finished.

"If one of these gets turned into a dirty bomb, we might need air detection," Robert ventured.

"If the explosion is big enough, and sends radiation up high enough we could use the system," Grady agreed. "The WC-135 is a military 707 jetliner. Can you imagine it flying over these islands at a few hundred feet?"

Robert thought that would be a disaster—especially in keeping the operation low-key. "No, that sounds terrible. What about satellite options?" He tried. "We must have something?"

"I talked to Steve about that over a beer before we got started," Grady supplied. "He says the VELA satellites and their modern variants won't help us much on radiation sources this small. He's having part of the Atlanta NRC group pull together a report for you on VELA. Also, I contacted some people at the Department of Defense to get you a brief on MASINT. I don't know much about it, but it stands for Measurement and Signature Intelligence. It covers what the DOD is doing with measurement and characterization of data from nuclear radiation, manmade and environmental. Again, it doesn't help us much here, but you'll need to know about it for your big meetings."

Robert was expecting their operation to be a difficult challenge, but it was sounding nearly impossible. "So less than two weeks into it, and it looks tougher than when we started. What do you think?"

Grady hesitated for a few seconds. "The bottom line? Some guy with a Geiger counter has to go door to door. It's almost that problematic, and the bad guys can move the damn things around while we're doing all of this."

"Are you saying that we're wasting our time?" Robert felt a chill go down his spine at the thought.

"Not completely," Grady reassured him. "If they break one open, like on Sandy Island, we'll find it. The problem is that if it is intact, we'll have to almost step on it before our instrumentation tells us it's there."

They were both silent before Robert finally spoke. "It's still the right thing to do." He stated.

"Steve and I agree," Grady concurred, continuing, "and it's good for improving security of the area. We're creating trained personnel, but at the same time we shouldn't set false expectations that we can create some kind of radiation free zone or an electronic fence line, so to speak."

"I hear what you're saying. I hate to admit, it, but I agree." Robert paused, thinking, while Grady stayed quiet. "Okay. You and Steve keep doing what you're doing. Formulate your top three recommendations for how we address this long-term, and we'll meet here in one week, or less."

"We won't be done down here," Grady warned. "Not by a long shot."

"I know," Robert answered. "You'll have to figure out a way for the trainers and locals to keep the project moving forward. It needs to be in their hands eventually, anyway. We can't keep all those people down there much longer. The trainers will have to train their replacements and come back."

"Right. I'll get Steve on the phone. We'll come up with a strategy based on what we've learned so far," Grady responded. "It *is* a needle in the haystack scenario, Robert."

. . .

Vlad, driving up from Miami on Hwy 1, was approaching Melbourne. His next action would be to activate the Melbourne boat on the first favorable wind day during the next week. It might be as early as Tuesday. This would set the wheels in motion for the rest of the plan.

Vlad was feeling good about how things were unfolding. The sequence called for activating Melbourne, followed by DC, Cove Point, and then Norfolk. Max had the DC and Cove Point boats, Luca the one in Norfolk. It was a simple plan. The execution had taken some complicated coordination, but Vlad had managed.

The first outlay of the client's cash had facilitated acquiring the irradiators. The process took months, but success released the next outflow of cash from the client, and the work of importing began. Now they were ready to deliver.

Funny, that Vlad's capitalist client's goal was to terrify other capitalists. Vlad would have once described capitalists as decadent, misguided westerners, but the truth was that his home country, like all the pieces of the former Soviet Union, was entirely capitalist now. He had learned that money was all important, and with each step, he became richer. At the completion of this job he would be wealthier than any of his comrades from his old regiment could dream of; the ones who were still alive.

The tools of the plan were the boats, now turned into dirty bombs. Each dirty bomb was designed to cut at the core of two American treasures: personal safety, and confidence in the system.

Vlad pulled up by the fence of Berg's Boats. Through the chain link gate, he could see the boat on its stand. Satisfied, he pulled ahead toward the bridge that led east. He smiled as he drove across the long bridge to his hotel on the island by the beach. The sun set as he checked in, and soon he was taking a drink to a beach chair. Vlad liked watching the last glimmer of light fade behind him as darkness enveloped the east, and the sound of waves consumed everything. It helped him relax.

Chapter 47

Berg picked up his usual fried egg and bacon sandwich at the food stand as he walked the two blocks to work. He made his own coffee at the shop. He preferred Chock full O'Nuts. Why pay a buck and a half for coffee he didn't like?

With breakfast in hand, and the sun rising above the fence, Berg walked out of the rusty shed into his boatyard. Three boats stood on rolling stands in the yard. Next to the shed was a 1979, sixteen-foot ski and fish Yarcraft tri-hull that needed the center windshield/door replaced. The hinge was shot, so he was waiting for the replacement part to arrive from a junkyard in St. Pete. The Monday UPS delivery had the wrong part in the box.

Next to the back fence was an '03 Boston Whaler Twenty-two Dauntless. The folding fabric top frame had broken off at the mounts in four places after hitting a low bridge. The fiberglass repair was done but needed to cure another day. The customer had insisted on a resin hardener combination that was more flexible, and which didn't "blush," or leave a waxy layer on the surface. The customer thought it would paint better, and handle the wind pressure from the cover. The hardener had a long, three-day cure time. Berg was also trying to convince the customer that the Evinrude outboard needed the carburetor rebuilt. He hadn't heard back. So, it would be the Gulfstar today. The sailboat on its stand towered over the yard against the east side fence.

Berg took another bite of his sandwich, resulting in a drip of egg yolk falling on his shirt midway down his stomach. He wiped most of it off with the napkin.

The boatyard had been there since the fifties, and the neighbors long since accepted the eyesore, and noise. Berg was generally a good neighbor, never using power tools before eight thirty in the morning. He usually worked by himself, bringing in extra hands as needed, and he always knocked off in time for a peaceful sunset.

Finishing the sandwich, Berg went inside for his cup of coffee and his favorite four-inch electric angle grinder. He tightened down a new silicon carbide disk, putting on his safety goggles, earplugs, and mask. He never used to wear a mask, but age and breathing issues were catching up with him. A mouthful of gelcoat dust was more than he could handle these days.

The mask hung around his neck by the elastic band as he carried the grinder out to the sailboat, dragging the extension cord behind him.

Sipping his coffee, he looked over the keel. Wiping off the rest of the dried ocean slime with a sanding sponge, he inspected the cracks. Most of them were simple crazing cracks. The bottom paint would seal and hide most of them. Some he would fix. There was a new repair that ran vertically the length of the keel's leading edge. Most owners would not have spotted it, but Berg had seen plenty of repairs in his day. It was probably a fix after hitting a reef. The repair was okay, but looked like it added a good two inches to the front of the keel. He would run the sander over it to rough it up a little and then paint. Finishing his coffee, he set the mug down on a nearby steel drum, put on his mask, and positioned himself to grind out the long horizontal crack above the ballast bulge.

It was backbreaking work, leaning over and pressing the grinding wheel sideways into the gelcoat and fiberglass. Berg was used to it and rested his elbow on his thigh to support his weight. The wheel ground into the keel, ejecting a cloud of fine dust and powder into the air around him.

He stopped occasionally to see if the crack was gone or if he had to go deeper. He let the tool do most of the work as he slid it farther along the crack. The first pass cut in enough to reach through the gel coat, and slightly into the fiberglass. On the ends of the cut, the crack disappeared, but in the center, it remained. The second pass dug deeper in the middle, past the fiberglass, and into the ballast. Sparks flew as he hit metal. The sparks were straw colored near the wheel, turning to bright white with forked ends indicating stainless steel. This was odd since stainless steel was unusual for ballast. A lead ballast wouldn't have made sparks. The equally common iron ballast would not generate white sparks, only straw-yellow.

Taking pressure off the grinder, Berg was about to stop. Before the sparks ceased, the shaped charge went off, exploding directly into the irradiator. Hot gasses erupted out the side of the keel where Berg had cut it, weakening the fiberglass structure. The shock waves nearly blew the irradiator off the boat completely. The blast knocked Berg off his feet and flat onto his back. Shards of fiberglass stuck out of his face. The grinder fell onto the ground. The spinning wheel pulled the tool around until it hit the cord, quickly coiling it around the shaft. It tore through the plastic shielding and pulled the two copper wires together, shorting them out. Back in the shed, the circuit breaker popped, killing the tool.

Berg lay on his back barely breathing. Something in his body had taken too much of a hit. He was out cold. His hands began to twitch. His thighs flexed slightly as a convulsion tried to sweep through his muscles, but there wasn't enough strength in him. With each spasm, his breathing became more labored and shallow. His eyes started to flutter and his mouth gaped, slack-jawed, straight up at the sky.

Contractions in his chest brought his shoulders together twice. The third contraction held until his breathing stopped in a phlegm-filled gurgling inhale. As his head rolled over to the left, it stopped against a chunk of fiberglass sticking deep in his cheek. A stream of frothy white saliva oozed out of the corner of his mouth onto the ground.

Under the boat and at the front of the swaying ballast bulb a fan was whirring, blowing fine white dust at the cracked container and its exposed interior. The powdery substance formed a thin, smoke-like cloud that drifted on the breeze, hitting the fence and rising up over it to be caught in the high Florida wind. It drifted over the houses and headed north along the coast.

...

Gary closed up the bar at two. The last couple of hours hadn't been worth the trouble of staying open. Most of his regulars came after work for a couple of drinks. A few lonely types would have their typical burger with fries at the bar and socialize for an hour or so.

The grill closed at nine. From that time on it always got steadily quieter, until only the three usual barflies remained. They'd nurse a beer while watching the TV, or maybe talk a little. They'd hang out there forever if Gary let them. With the door locked and his light windbreaker over his shoulder, he started walking home.

Gary lived in a small rental three blocks away. There was no view and no waterfront. It's only redeeming quality was that it was cheap.

His normal path was a block over, but he went this way to take him past Berg's Boats. Berg had not shown up for his after-work beer. It was the first time he'd missed coming by in six months, so Gary was curious.

Normally the rusted shack and surrounding fenced-in lot were pitch black. Lights weren't much of a deterrent to thieves in the neighborhood and just wasted electricity. Berg relied on iron bars and lock mounts he fabricated from scrap metal for security. He had a single row of razor wire on the back side of the fence. It wasn't that visible but had proved effective. Tonight the office lights were on, which meant Berg must be there. That interested Gary. Berg didn't usually work late. Trying the door, he found it open. He swung it inward.

"Hey, Berg! Whatcha up to this late?" Gary called, stepping into the grimy office. "Hey, Berg! You in here?" He called again. It was strange for Berg to leave the door unlocked at night in this neighborhood. During the day Berg left it open pretty often, but Gary figured he must have forgotten to lock it when he decided to keep working into the night. It seemed quiet in the yard. Gary went in further, figuring he'd find Berg taking a beer break.

The back door was wide open to the yard. There was no light on outside, but there was a switch by the door. With a flick, Gary kicked on the two flood lights mounted above the door, illuminating the middle of the dirt and gravel area. Berg was laying on the ground at the far end, just within range of the lights. Gary ran over to him.

"Berg, you okay?" Berg's face was turned away from the lights, but Gary saw some blood on it. The damage didn't seem too bad, but he wasn't sure Berg was breathing. Gary quickly knelt down. Not finding a sign of life, he pulled his phone out and dialed 911. He put the phone on speaker and tried giving Berg chest compressions while he talked with the emergency operator. He had read on the internet that no breaths were needed. He just had to keep the compressions going. Mouth-to-mouth didn't look promising anyway. He could now see that Berg's lips were badly torn in two places.

The firehouse was almost walking distance away, so the EMTs were there in minutes. They tried a few things to resuscitate Berg, but they could tell it was long since futile. Berg was down to ground temperature. A police car that had heard the EMTs call in a dead body showed up, grabbing a few pictures before the EMTs packed up their gear and left. The cop let Gary go home since it would be hours before the coroner and detective would arrive. The cop stayed with the body, waiting.

. . .

Ten miles away, at seven-thirty in the morning, Sergeant Johnson sat at his desk at Patrick Air Force Base. He was reading a manual on electromagnetic spectroscopy. The Airman working behind him was replacing a meter light on one of the instruments they maintained for Cape Canaveral as per the manual the Sergeant had given him. When he turned on the unit to check the display, the audio speaker sprang to life loudly chattering with a series of random clicks or ticks. Startled, the Airman jumped back a step.

"Bunce! What the hell have you done?" Sergeant Johnson spun in his decrepit metal chair.

"Nothing, Sarge! I just turned it on." The airman responded.

"Did you hit something on the inside? Did you use the insulated screwdriver like I told you?" The Sergeant demanded.

"Yeah, Sergeant. I used it. See?" Bunce said defensively, holding up the screwdriver with its long red plastic shaft.

"Well, you must have screwed it up, somehow! That thing shouldn't be going crazy like that." The Sergeant marched over to the workbench, flipped off the power and grabbed the screwdriver from Bunce's hand. "Let me see that."

Placing his hand and the screwdriver on the table, he leaned over to look at the needles on the old spectrometer. It was used to measure x-ray and gamma ray radiation in the inspection of metal welds. When he switched the power back on, it sat silent.

"Okay..." He said, switching it off and then on again. Nothing.

"See? I didn't break it." The young Airman looked relieved.

The Sergeant looked up disparagingly. "Get down one of the new ones." While he looked around the insides of the open instrument, the Airman scrambled up a short ladder and fetched over a newer digital readout unit, plugging it into the power strip.

A jittery line appeared at the bottom edge of the screen. Each time he adjusted a knob, the line bounced and then settled back at the bottom.

"Nothing." Both devices were silent, then suddenly a series of rapid ticks came over the older unit's speaker and a small group of spikes appeared on the newer digital screen. Then it was silent again.

As the spikes scrolled across the screen, the Sergeant hit the hold button on the instrument, then the memory key. He waited. In a few minutes, the ticks started again, continuing for a longer time before disappearing.

"Get the Captain on the phone," the Sergeant ordered. As the Airman quickly headed for the desk, the Sergeant continued to record the sporadic readings. He decided to get another tool off the shelf. This time it was a more specific wavelength analyzer.

"He's on his way." The Airman stood nearby as the Sergeant set up the new instrument. "What's that for, Sarge?"

"It will give me a more accurate reading of the wavelength on this bad boy." The Sergeant fiddled with the controls and waited.

"How does it work?" Bunce wanted to know.

"It will show the kilo-electronvolts if the signal is long and strong enough. If it has one dominant spectral line of gamma-ray emission, then we'll know what radioisotope we're seeing." They waited. Then the signal spiked again and the device readout flashed and held. They got a partial graph with lots of random looking dots. It was several minutes before another tick occurred, followed by a series that lasted much longer. The graph on the screen recorded each reading. The line wiggled down from 4k on the left to 0k on the right.

In the middle of the line graph, there was a pronounced bump. Sergeant Johnson moved the vertical line marker over to the center of the bump. The display read 662 keV. He moved it to a smaller, but still pronounced bump on the left. It read 30 keV. The Sergeant went over to the document he had been reading and looked for the appendix. Running his finger down two pages of numbers he stopped.

"Cesium-137. Holy shit." He muttered.

"What is it?" Bunce wasn't sure what the Sergeant had said.

"Get the van, and hook these up in the hot bay," the Sergeant barked. Johnson ran to the phone.

"But what is it, Sarge?" He asked, coming back in again.

"It's Cs-137. That's on our red list. I'm getting the Captain down here now! Keep loading the van!"

After getting the Captain, Johnson ran his finger down the critical call list. The first was to HQ command. He punched in the number. The Lieutenant Colonel at command tied in a call to Cape Canaveral Airforce Station. In minutes there were half a dozen people on the call. The Captain came rushing in and the Sergeant switched to the speaker phone.

Sergeant Johnson was rapidly grilled by the Colonel at the Cape on what he had seen on each instrument. "What did you use to read the detailed spectrum?"

"I used a Technics UCS-20 with a NaI(Tl) crystal scintillator," the Sergeant responded promptly.

"Confirming your measurement using Sodium Iodide with Thallium," The Colonel ascertained. "How many detectors do you have, and how quickly can you start plotting readings at Patrick?"

The Captain replied, "This is Captain Clark. We can have two vans outfitted in..." He looked at the Sergeant who held up one finger then five followed by two fingers and a zero. "One will be ready in five minutes and the other in twenty minutes." The sergeant nodded.

"Do you have a grid plan to sweep the base?" The Colonel asked.

"Yes, Sir," the Captain responded, watching the Sergeant nod in agreement.

"Okay, Colonel," the Cape cut in. "We need to have confirmation on two instruments in two locations," he told the HQ command officer at Patrick AFB. "If it is positive, you need to seal off the perimeter of the base and search for the source. This is a potentially airborne radioactive isotope alert. You may be downwind of a nuclear event. Cs-137 is a manmade product of a nuclear explosion or nuclear reactor. I assume there was no bomb, which we would have all heard and felt, so it is the later, and most likely a drifting release. It could be an accident or a dirty bomb. Safety gear will be needed. Don't take a chance of inhalation."

Within hours both bases were alive with personnel and equipment. The team at Patrick Air Force Base had made dozens of readings. The readings were stronger on the southern edge of the base, but were rapidly increasing—even on the north side. The base was closed and personnel were being evacuated. Those remaining wore masks or full hazmat gear. One van was dispatched to make measurements on Tortoise Island, where dense housing areas existed. The 404 Pineda Causeway was closed to incoming traffic, and preparations for emergency evacuations from the island had begun. They weren't sure whether to run traffic north or south. Police cruised neighborhoods, announcing the need to stay indoors with all windows closed, but didn't explain why.

Sitting on his balcony overlooking the beach and surf, Vlad heard the announcement over the fire alarm speakers.

"All guests please remain in your rooms with the doors and windows closed."

The message repeated three times. Guests started flooding the desk phones with questions. Vlad knew what it could mean, and he knew he did not want to be downwind. Quickly he made for the stairwell and out to the parking lot. Americans know nothing of security, he thought. There were police and fire trucks moving in many directions, making similar loudspeaker announcements.

A police cruiser pulled up next to Vlad.

"Sir, you need to go inside. There is a gas leak. You will be safe if you stay indoors."

"Thank you, Officer," Vlad said politely, turning toward the hotel door. As the cruiser drove away, Vlad went back directly to his car.

Soon he was driving south on the A1A, headed for the next bridge to the mainland, away from all the flashing lights. He would approach the boat location from the south side since the wind was still blowing toward the north. Then he would find out if his suspicion was correct.

At the first traffic light, he sent a text to Max and Luca.

Max was working out in her complex's exercise room in DC. She'd warmed up on the treadmill, but had spent the last twenty minutes on the dumbbells. The weight area was always less crowded, and she wanted more upper body strength. When she put down the weights from her final set, she picked up her towel and water bottle. Her phone sitting underneath was illuminated with an incoming text. It was from Vlad.

"Melbourne possibly compromised. Your status V," the message demanded.

Max replied. "Ready M."

"Activate zero eight-hundred two days. Confirm," Vlad texted.

"Activate eight AM 2 days," Max confirmed, sweeping the towel across her face, neck, and upper chest.

. . .

Standing on the dock of a small island south of Haiti, Steve Mahaffey was helping offload some gear from a small boat when his phone rang.

On another island, hundreds of miles east, the pagers of the two military detection team members went off.

In Robert's office, Lorraine chimed through his line, "Colonel Barlow, line one."

Robert picked up the phone. "Hello, Grady."

"What the hell's going on?" Grady sounded out of breath like he was running. "I've got two guys bugging out for Melbourne, Florida, and Steve is heading there any minute to meet them!"

Before Robert could reply, Lorraine opened his door. "You have an urgent call from the White House. They want you in the situation room."

Chapter 48

Robert sat in the Situation Room. His special pass hung around his neck, one of only two of its type in the room. He sat second from the end of a long table, his back toward the door. The end wall was covered in display monitors, and several more were scattered around the room. All but three were dark—the rest were on, but showing black screens.

Across from Robert sat three generals: one Army, one Air Force, and one Navy. To his left sat a Coast Guard General who wore only two stars, unlike the threes and fours across from him. To Robert's right sat a thirty-something civilian wearing a crisp suit. He wore the other temporary tag. Five chairs remained conspicuously empty, including the one at the head of the table.

There was no conversation at the table. Robert's short pile of manila folders sat in front of him. The others thumbed through their thick stacks intently. Robert wished he had brought in more paperwork.

Robert had not been in the "Sit Room" before. It had taken six minutes to get through the additional security, even though he'd had a pass waiting for him. Generals had been walking past in a blur while he'd been getting the electronic "third degree." Now that he was inside waiting with nothing to do, he felt nervous and exposed.

The door swung open. "Ten-hut!" the uniformed Marine guard at the door called out.

The generals were up and out of their chairs quickly. The civilian was close behind them, while Robert struggled with his chair before rising.

"Be seated." President Baxter strode in briskly, followed in short order by the Whitehouse Chief of Staff, Jason Carlisle, Secretary of Defense, Bill Trask, The Secretary of the Department of Homeland Security, Talia Snelling, and National Security Advisor, Ron Crest.

President Baxter spoke. "Obviously, this is not the start of World War III. That much seems clear. It looks like a terrorist act, but is it?"

As chairman of the Joint Chiefs, the Air Force General was the ranking uniformed military person in the room. He answered the President. "We are treating this as the use of a dirty bomb. There is no military activity to indicate any war preparation or any government action globally. NORAD reports no surface or orbital actions that could indicate this was a launched attack. No further actions are evident. All we have are readings indicating a single location, utilizing the deliberate surface delivery of radioactive material. There are sufficient readings to indicate this is not a minor release, and neither is it some type of accident; however, we have not located the source. We should have the origin location shortly."

The Secretary of Defense, Bill Trask, spoke. "We don't believe there is involvement by any government, at this time. There is no claim from a terrorist organization. There is no media coverage of what has actually occurred, as yet. There's no unofficial chatter, other than social media talking about emergency search personnel, a supposed gas leak, and the in-home lock down. I just got off the phone with Secretary Vance—there is nothing from State indicating any international action."

The Secretary of Homeland Security, Talia Snelling, was next. "I have Welch, the Director of Domestic Nuclear Detection, on his way to Melbourne, Florida to direct the local efforts." Snelling stood up to go toward a large screen showing a map of Melbourne. "We have twenty members of DHS headed to the area south of Patrick Air Force Base," she said while pointing to the map location, "to assist military and local law enforcement in the evacuation of civilians. Everyone within this 12-mile area will be evacuated from the off-shore protective island, starting at Patrick and going south to the 518 Eau Gallie Causeway. There is an additional team proceeding to Melbourne to help local officials prepare for the evacuation of a portion of the city where the military detection teams believe the plume path originates."

"The original team from Patrick that sensed the radioactivity has covered the island to the 518 bridge, across to Highway 1, and down three miles. They believe the source is somewhere in this area." She circled the area bordered by the Eau Gallie River, Hwy 1, and Montreal Avenue. "They are coordinating with the Nuclear Regulatory Commission, FEMA, National Guard, Navy, and Coast Guard. Local law enforcement has the area closed off, and the Coast Guard is stopping traffic on the ICW and Gallie River. We also have the civilian emergency technician team from the St. Lucie Nuclear Reactor in Jensen Beach, Florida on their way to the site."

She paused giving the President a chance to speak.

President Baxter was careful to get his questions in the order he wanted. "I don't want to harp on this, but I still don't have an answer to my question. Is this terrorism?"

Ron Crest cleared his throat. "Yes, Sir. It is. At this time we do not know if it is foreign or domestic terrorism."

President Baxter's expression darkened. "Is there a danger of explosion? How many people will be affected by the current plume if the source does not change, based on the current weather conditions? When do we expect to find the source? How can it be contained to stop spreading?"

Ron Crest responded, getting up and moving toward the map. "Sir, if the source is there," he pointed, "the wind stays consistent, and the radiation level does not increase, about seventy-thousand people could be within the plume. Could we have the graphic I provided on a screen?" he asked an aide. It popped up on the large central monitor, and he continued, "The estimate we have shows the plume like this." An orange swath painted over the map was displayed on the monitor. "It will continue to expand at slightly less than the rate of wind until it dissipates over the ocean."

Ron let that sink in for a moment before he spoke again. "The current path takes the cloud almost due north. The forecast shows the wind shifting to the east over the next twelve hours. This would keep it headed out to sea, with minimal population exposure and contamination. The population can be sheltered-in-place, or if necessary, evacuated, using four bridges and three main roads on the island."

"Cloud?" The President asked. "You said 'cloud.' There is a cloud?"

"No, Sir, not a visible cloud. It is an expression to describe the shape. It's unlikely that we will even see something visible at the source. It is similar to dust. There should be a finite amount available to spread. We just don't know how much, yet."

"And sheltering-in-place? How does that protect people?" The President questioned.

Robert decided it was time to get involved in the conversation. "Radioactive contamination settles on and clings to surfaces," he explained. "Evacuating people into the cloud increases the risk of contamination. If you stay indoors and close up the house, the radiation settles on the ground and roof, instead of on you and your clothes. They'll only evacuate if the radiation exposure measurement shows that it's too high to stay."

A wall phone rang, and was answered by the aide. She listened for a moment, then announced, "Sir, they believe they have found the source location. Law enforcement is establishing the shelter-in-place rule on the immediately affected homes, as directed. We have a live feed. I have DHS Agent Lopez on the phone."

"Let's have it," the Secretary of Defense said.

In a moment the feed from a drone appeared on a large wall monitor. The drone hovered over a fenced in lot, looking down from about twenty feet up. The view showed a rusted roof at the bottom of the monitor, and a sailboat on a stand at the top. In the center a body was outlined with yellow tape, surrounded by several numbered orange cones.

Snelling took over the call, using the conference table speaker. "Agent Lopez? This is Secretary Snelling. Can you hear me?"

"Yes, Ma'am," the agent answered.

"What do you have there?" Snelling asked.

"The location had a 911 call this morning, just after 2 AM. A man's body was found dead at the scene. You should be seeing that in the picture. The police investigation was well underway when the radiation detection teams converged on the area, slightly after sunrise. The police were waiting for daylight before considering the removal of the body, in order to determine the cause of death with the aid of more light. I think you will see why in these pictures." A series of police photos of Berg's bloodied face rotated on a smaller monitor to the side. "With our arrival, the police backed away and cordoned off the block. They did not have any knowledge of the radiation danger until the teams arrived. Those in closest contact to the body have been taken to the local hospital for decontamination and observation. That's about nine people so far, including the person who found the body and made the 911 call. Since our early readings have shown potentially high contamination, we have instructed the police to move the barricades back another block in three directions. The area is bounded by water on the fourth side."

Descending slowly to a few feet off the ground, the drone hovered around Berg's body. With a gradual scan, the drone moved around all angles of the area. Only the dead man, a power tool on the ground, and the ballast bulb hanging oddly from the bottom of the sailboat keel seemed out of place. The pilot deftly flew the drone closer to the boat. On the screen, they could clearly see outwardly blasted fiberglass, and burn marks from the shaped charge explosion. The video was becoming increasingly snowy.

"What's wrong with the picture, Agent Lopez?" Snelling inquired.

"It's likely to be interference caused by the radiation," Ron Crest answered before Lopez could respond.

"Is the Fido ready?" The civilian in the suit asked.

The Agent on the phone quickly replied, "Yes, they're ready."

"Advise the team to proceed," the man ordered.

Within moments the Agent spoke again. "It should be coming through the gate anytime now."

"Let's see it," Snelling ordered.

The drone turned to show the ground robot. After a few seconds, the aide got an additional live feed from the remote robot onto another screen. Now they could see the drone from the Fido, and the Fido from the drone's camera view, as the robot came through the gate. The robot screen showed a wide shot of the boat lot, with the sailboat, body, and hovering drone in the middle. The screen also had two picture-in-picture views. In the bottom left corner was what looked like a handheld meter display that read "No Threat Detected." This was the actual Fido device for which the robot was named. In the right corner was a gauge reading .0625 mSv/hr.

Once the Fido was inside the fence, the hazmat-clad technician who opened the gate pulled back. They watched as the robot moved forward on its dual tracks. The screen showed the dead man on the ground and the drone hovering over him. The number on the right climbed as the robot turned toward the boat keel. It read 6.40 mSv/hr.

"What is the number on the right telling us?" President Baxter asked.

The civilian in the suit replied, "It is the radiation level in millisieverts, Sir. It will rise higher as the robot gets closer to the source. We can assess the health risk of contamination from that number, calculated against the distance."

The robot stopped to look closely at the man on the ground. The camera panned over and down. The feed was getting snowy, but the camera was more stable than the drone and gave a higher resolution picture.

Sharp fragments of fiberglass were stuck in Berg's face, right eye, neck, and upper body, penetrating deeply. The fragments had been stopped by the bones of his cheeks and forehead. Bruising, probably from flying debris that didn't penetrate the skin, and burn marks from the blast were evident, but the bruising was light in color. Berg had died too quickly for the bruises to become heavily infused with blood. Dried blood appeared around each cut, with small streaks stretching down below them, ultimately gathering in a small pool below his head. His eyes were mostly closed, and his expression of severe pain at death had slackened as death released the muscles. It was clear that he had convulsed before dying.

The robot handler moved the camera up to view the boat. At about four feet the gauge read 25 mSv/hr.

"That's about 4 feet," Lopez told the room.

Robert turned to the President. "Mr. President, that is the same number at about the same distance measured by the team on Sandy Island. I think that thing hanging from the bottom of the boat is about the same size as the Kazakhstan irradiator found buried in the sand on the island."

"It's evident that the irradiator was deliberately disguised as part of the boat in order to smuggle it into the country," Secretary of Defense Bill Trask pointed out. "Is that radiation detector directional?"

The civilian in the crisp suit next to Robert cleared his throat. "Yes, Sir. We'll have to spin the robot around." He issued some directions to the operator and Agent Lopez.

"Mr. President," The DHS Secretary interjected while this was occurring, "this is a standard ROV that we have added an explosives trace detector to, known as a Fido. The Fido, on the left of the screen, is an explosives sniffing detector, which uses amplifying fluorescence polymer technology. It is called 'Fido' after the bomb sniffing dogs. State of the art. There is also a radiation detector mounted to the ROV, and it is about as directional as we can get it to be in this size and weight."

The drone showed a bird's eye view of the action. The robot had begun to slowly rotate where it stood, using its tank-like tracks. One drive track was going forward while the other was going backward at the same speed. The number on the right of the screen dropped down until the Fido was facing directly away from the sailboat, then rose again as it completed the circle back around.

The civilian spoke, "That, Sir, indicates that the source is in front of the unit. It may be the sailboat or something directly behind it. We will have to triangulate at another position to be sure."

Robert found himself frustrated with the simplistic explanations surrounding the jargon-laden descriptions, but the President seemed comfortable with the communications.

The drone backed away to look at the body again. It then pulled high into the air and began surveying the surrounding area. On the perimeter, hazmat teams could be seen in their protective gear. Well beyond that, there were police vehicles blocking all the roads.

The robot moved up to the sailboat keel, pressing the Fido unit right up against the fiberglass where it had broken apart.

The civilian described the action. "The gauge has to be up close to have any chance of sniffing for explosives. More accurate readings can be made in an enclosed space, or with a wipe test, but that is not possible here. The open air makes explosive gasses much harder to detect."

Despite the difficult conditions, the Fido screen turned red and "Nitro Detected," followed by "Military Detected" appeared.

"Okay we have either an explosive residue or a remaining unexploded charge," the civilian told them, assessing the readout. "It is likely that it's C4, but a bomb expert needs to get in there to inspect it, and possibly diffuse what might be left."

. . .

Vlad had been in the area for an hour. He parked near the south side of the barricades, still upwind of the boat. The area where the boat stood was surrounded by police and fire vehicles on three sides, and water on the fourth. Helicopters stayed well away. Vlad recognized that they were upwind, but thought that no one else probably noticed that. The public story was still that there was a gas leak. They had evacuated everyone within the barricades. He could not find a utility truck anywhere. His boat was definitely inside the barricades, based on the GPS location. He got as close as he was allowed. He stayed upwind, trying to maintain a reasonable line of sight, hoping the radio transmitter would reach the area. He pressed the remote control button.

He did not hear a blast, pop, or any corresponding sound that might be explosives detonating. He tried again in three locations without any sign of success. The GPS map showed he was never closer than three blocks away, which was probably beyond the range of the remote. He had originally argued that using a low-tech remote was a bad idea, but there had been the counter argument that cell phone triggers could be easily blocked—would be blocked, as part of standard security procedures in a case like this.

There were news trucks outside the police barricades, and at least three drones flying around. If the radiation had been released, wouldn't they evacuate further away? Vlad wasn't sure, but he was convinced they had found the irradiator location. That meant the timetable had begun without him. He needed to know what they had discovered. It was good that he had given Max and Luca the signal to activate. He headed for a nearby enterprising food truck that had located to the scene. He might hear what was going on from the crews working inside the barricade when they came out for coffee.

While waiting, he surfed the 'net on his phone. He found two short videos of the boatyard, both showing the ramshackle metal building behind a body on the ground. The sailboat was not the subject of the videos. He only got a glimpse of the stand, and maybe a piece of the keel. He couldn't make out the boat's condition. Had his remote activated it? He couldn't tell. He found another video. This time it was from a news helicopter. The body was visible, and so was the boat. Vlad focused there. The keel ballast bulb seemed to be hanging at an odd angle. The irradiator directed charge must have gone off. The rest of the boat looked unaffected.

He switched to the news channel associated with that helicopter. There was a live feed. It showed a black police truck with a man in a heavy suit having a huge helmet placed on his head. Vlad recognized it as a bomb suit.

The video switched to an interview. The news reporter was interviewing a gas company representative in overalls and hardhat. Vlad watched intently on his cell phone and saw what he needed to see.

Walking away in the background, over the gas utility rep's shoulder, was a man in a dark blue windbreaker with a logo. It was impossible to read, but Vlad recognized the shape and letters. It was the Nuclear Regulatory Commission logo. They knew what the boat held. He had to move now.

He sent a text. "Melbourne confirmed compromised. Go Go Go."

An old, 1950s brick hardware store stood across the street. The roads on both sides of the block had barricades, but minimal police presence. The cops were distracted with locals asking questions. Vlad walked directly across the street to the door. It was recessed back from the two side display windows. With his lock pick in hand, he calmly and quickly opened it and stepped inside.

The alarm rhythmically beeped, waiting for the disarm code. Vlad ignored it and moved quickly to the back of the building. He opened the back door and slipped into the alley, where he found ample cover. The alley had been evacuated, so there was no risk of being spotted. Over his shoulder, the hardware store alarm went off.

"Good." Vlad thought, "that will keep them busy, and away from the side streets."

Going through various fence gates and side yards he hastily made his way closer to the boat. He kept trying the remote as he moved. Finally, he heard the boom.

A cloud of smoke and dust rose up above the house tops and small buildings. Vlad stopped. He didn't have time to watch. Now he needed to get out of the area.

. . .

In the situation room, the man in the suit was talking. "Mr. President, I've calculated that the radiation is acceptable at close range for an hour's exposure time, but less would be better. If the NRC team on-site agrees, I recommend the rescue team go in to retrieve the body immediately after the bomb expert makes sure the explosive is safe. Then a second team should go in to secure the radioactive source."

As he spoke they could see the bomb suit clad expert entering the gate of the boatyard. He was just inside when the boat erupted in a cloud of fiberglass and dust.

Without surrounding water, and with the bulb broken partially by the first explosion, the blast furiously launched the irradiator into the keel at an angle. The boat seemed to jump sideways off the stand, its hull cracking in half. The larger explosive charge had been mounted below the irradiator bulb. It shattered the hull and threw as much of the irradiator and debris into the air as possible. The drone lost its picture almost immediately.

The live feed from another DHS drone showed the action. Everyone in the room, including the President, froze.

The Sit Room aide played the explosion back in slow-motion. The heavy bulb of steel and fiberglass shot out of the rapidly expanding cloud of gray dust. Flaming pieces of wood scattered outward, as the bulb hit the keel at an angle, knocking the boat over and off its stand. It crashed to the ground. The bulb shot over the metal roof of Berg's office, past the drone. The blast wave hit the man in the heavy suit, heaving him backward into the chain link gate.

Those in the Sit. Room watched silently as the dust settled over the camera lens that was mounted to the Fido ground robot, now lying on its side. A distant remote camera feed appeared on a third monitor, showing the entrance to Berg's from down the road. Nothing moved except the gray cloud as it swiftly spread out and up.

The bomb suited man lay still for a long moment, then they could see him push down with one arm to roll over. No one could go to his rescue. The danger of radiation was now much higher. With excruciatingly slow movements, he pressed down with his hands and rose up to his knees. Eventually, he stood and began walking out with carefully measured steps.

The President stood up, causing everyone to rise. "General, we now definitely have a dirty bomb. Get control of this situation, People. This is a mess. Find out what just happened, the ramifications and options. I want a full briefing in ten minutes," he ordered. "Ron? What's the next move?"

"Sir," Ron replied, "there is clearly a risk of radiation poisoning..."

"Cut the crap, Ron. Mobilize everyone. I want every agency on this yesterday! You got me? We're having a press conference A.S.A.P. Get your shit together, and have a message ready. We have to calm the public and control the story. Bill, Talia, you've got whatever resources you need. This better get under control fast, or I'm going to want to know why."

"Yes, Sir." They responded. The President stormed toward the door, then stopped, turning toward Robert.

"Robert, what do you think about this?"

Robert had to take in a breath before answering. "It's too coincidental, Sir. I think this is one of the missing irradiators from the shipment of five that the CIA was tracking. If that's true, then it will be Cesium-137 in salt powder form, and, now that it has been spread by the explosion, it will float on the wind like dust. It has a half-life of thirty years, so it won't just go away. It does dissolve in water. If someone swallows or inhales it, they can be treated with Prussian Blue, which will dramatically reduce its medical half-life, and greatly reduce the cancer risks. The sooner everyone gets out of there and is tested, the lower the total radiation exposure."

"Okay, so you work with Ron," the President told him. Then speaking to everyone he commanded, "Take control of this situation. Use the National Guard, the Coast Guard—whatever. I want action, not excuses. Anyone have any comments?" He asked.

The Chairman of the Joint Chiefs added his perspective. "Sir, Mr. Carlton believes this is one of the five missing units, and I agree. We have to assume that the remaining three missing irradiators are threats. We need to close down the waterways, put bases on alert, and heighten the level on all Special Event Assessment Ratings."

"Get S.E.A.R into action, then." The President continued, "Hospitals, football games, and concerts—any large venue that could be compromised." President Baxter looked sternly at the group, saying "I wanted this to be kept quiet. I wanted these things found without headlines, and without people running scared in the streets." He pushed the door open. "Do what you need to do. Get me the written plan—a comprehensive plan, with steps that every agency takes part in, but let's control this centrally. Ron, Bill, and Talia, get together with the Press Secretary and get some sound bites coordinated.

"Talia, you have field operations," the President specified. "Bill, coordinate the military response. Ron, you take point here. Start with the action plan I asked for from State—Robert should have it. Add full military support to that plan. Make no mistake people, we are under attack."

Chapter 49

Chaos best described the scene Steve Mahaffey witnessed as he pulled through the police barricade and stepped up into the DHS communications van. The regional Homeland Security Director and two operators were waiting for him. On the left wall ran a row of communications and video monitors. On the right hung an electronic map that held multi-colored dots, a transparent "plume" graphic, and a row of selectable apps for weather forecasts, wind direction, temperature, and traffic congestion.

There was more, but Steve focused on the live feed showing four protectively clothed technicians lifting the fiberglass encased irradiator into a lead lined crate on wheels. It had been thrown a hundred feet into the front yard of the house next door to Berg's Boats. The bomb expert had checked it over before going to the decontamination tent. He was suffering from shock. Steve figured he would have moderate radiation exposure. The suit and safety gear had kept him from greater harm.

Berg's lifeless body had been shoved over to the shed wall by the second blast wave. It lay there in a heap. No one was sure how to proceed with the body. Any contact created contamination. Decontaminating Berg's body would erase any evidence. If they left him untouched, he was a radiation hazard. They decided to wait on a disposition of the body.

The explosives technician, stripped of his cumbersome bomb suit, got on the phone and confirmed it would take some study to determine how and why the bombs were placed as they were. The remaining fiberglass was covered in highly radioactive dust and would take extensive decontamination before any investigation could occur. It was a mess.

Although covered in fiberglass, the close-up images of the irradiator bulb revealed enough to convince Steve that it was the same model irradiator found on Sandy Island. The doctors looking over the video felt Berg's cause of death was most likely a heart attack, brought on by the first explosion. They were confident radiation was not the cause. The burns were postmortem. The police investigator made a preliminary determination from observing Berg's relative position to the first blast, the tool he'd used, and the cut he'd created in the keel, agreeing that triggering the blast had caused Berg's heart attack.

The findings were still speculation in the middle of the chaos, but the bomb squad's report read: "The grinding stone cut into the trigger wire made of copper. When the grinding stone impacted the wire and removed the shielding, it caused a mechanical connection between the two wires, along with a static charge from the grinding action." It would take some analysis of the badly damaged components to know more. The cause of the second blast was unknown, but a remote or timed detonation seemed likely.

Steve watched as the sealed crate was rolled away. The retrieval team was now exposed to their limit. A new team would come on to start the decontamination process. The contamination boundary had been moved back to the freeway. Geiger counter equipped personnel scanned the periphery. Radiation badges had been issued to everyone on duty. Those taken off duty lined up outside the decontamination tents and hospitals.

The cleanup was going to take a lot of people, and a mountain of work from Steve's southeastern crews. He and the Regional Homeland Security Director started working out job assignments, and how each government organization would support the effort.

"When we're done, is the waste going to be state or federal?" Steve asked.

"What? What are you talking about? Don't your people have someplace they put this stuff?" The Regional DHS Director asked.

"No," Steve answered, "and contaminated debris is going to start piling up. We need a plan where to put it now, and where it will ultimately be stored. I have temporary containment containers on the way to use for transport. We will need more, and they need to be the kind used for storage wherever we are sending the stuff."

"This is a state matter since it happened in Florida," the Director decided.

"Okay, I'll play Devil's advocate on this," Steve told him. "The waste isn't composed of spent rods from a Florida reactor, so you're going to get some pushback from the state. We're going to have a trainload of dirt, roofing materials, fencing, brick, and assorted other pieces of debris by the time we're done. You're going to need to make sure that it will be accepted and that there's room for it all wherever it is going." Steve had fought the issue of radioactive entombment for years, since it always created a hazardous situation. The US had no place to dump, and no plan.

"How about Georgia, or the Savannah River Site? Those are the main controlled landfill sites in the southeast, right?" The Director asked.

One of the control panel operators turned around. "Why not just dump it in Lakeland?"

The comment elicited a reluctant smile from all four men. The Lakeland, Florida incident of nineteen-seventy-nine had left a huge national question about the phosphate mine located halfway between Orlando and Tampa. A ten-square-mile area was contaminated by Radium-226 from the phosphate mining process. From the Radium came Radon, with its byproducts. The cancer hazards of leukemia, lymphoma, and bone cancer were coming from the Radium, while Radon was known to cause lung cancer. The mine had sparked a lot of agency discussions and could have been the largest superfund site ever for the EPA, but resolution was still nowhere to be found.

"Sure, Lakeland. You know that the agencies stopped measuring the radiation there back in January of 2014. In the meantime, everybody's been building houses closer and closer. Apparently, nobody cares," the other tech spoke up. "Even after the September Mulberry sinkhole in 2016, no one knows what to do."

"Meanwhile about a hundred-thousand people are drinking the water and living too close to that mess. Too close, even according to EPA standards," Steve agreed. "So, here we are," he told the Director, "nobody wants to deal with the waste they already have, and there's no plan for disposing of this new problem."

"Too bad we don't have Yucca Mountain, Nevada, but apparently that's still not happening," the Director mused. "How about WIPP in New Mexico?" He suggested.

"No, that's limited to Defense generated Transuranic waste," Steve replied. "We simply don't have a good dump for radioactive materials anywhere. We need a national waste management site for the permanent entombment of high-level radioactive waste. Problem is, nobody wants it in their backyard." His frustration was real, and fact based. It was a decades-old problem.

"So, we're back to Georgia," the Director concluded. "Their Governor is not going to like this."

"Better try to convince Florida it is their problem to store it, first," Steve recommended. "Start with the Senators. You might get lucky with one of them." Steve knew how the political hot potato would get tossed around. He'd done this before.

. . .

Vlad drove west, away from the area, until he found a restaurant bar. He settled in to transmit his key communications. First, he notified his client, who immediately spread the word to all the subscribers. Vlad would wait at least 36 hours giving all clients time to take action on their business plays, mostly stocks. Markets opened and closed as the earth turned, so he had to be patient. Once the confirmations arrived, it would be time to drive the global news cycle. With a few keystrokes, he would notify his team of teapots in fourteen countries. Then he would update his twenty blogs, which each fed twenty Facebook, Twitter, Instagram, LinkedIn, and finally MyMFB accounts—the Facebook of the Muslim faith. The twenty blogs shared links to both of the drone videos already posted on YouTube. All the Twitter feeds carried the hashtag #floridaevacuation. He would start a new one, #floridadirtybomb.

Of the twenty blogs, five had ISIS in the title. Ten blamed Terrorists, and five were on servers located in the Middle East. All declared America under attack. The purpose was simple: to create panic and point fingers.

Vlad smiled to himself as he re-read the first round of propaganda. Over the days of waiting, he had crafted message after message. It was important that search engines and news agencies think all the messages were originals and not copies. Microsoft's multiple languages with spelling and grammar programs helped him sound more American, British, or Arabic, as required. He accepted all its suggestions, knowing that some would be wrong. They were close enough for the amazingly inept blogosphere. All of the posts were already loaded in his blogging platforms, waiting for him to hit the publish buttons. A few hours after the first release, he would send out the next round which contained more detail and speculation about new attacks on the Eastern Seaboard. Round three carried conspiracy theories, and American emergency agency accusations, followed by lists of targets on the West Coast. The only traceability would be to his current IP address at the coffee shop, a series of free email accounts, and five fake charge cards. By the time the government eavesdroppers shut down the accounts, it would be much too late.

Affirmative responses began to roll in. They might be ready sooner than he anticipated. Good.

He sent a message to all his teapots. "Check hourly for update to come soon."

He would provide them with all the information he broadcast. All they had to do was notify their superiors that they had seen the news. All Vlad had to do now was wait and watch. Not long from now, The United States of America would be on global alert, and there would be panic in the streets. Checking that the wind forecast was stable, Vlad smiled and went to a nearby hotel to check in. He had a well-deserved two-hour nap coming.

. . .

Grady had arrived in DC and now sat in Robert's office. It had been a long day. His head slumped to one side as he noisily slept in a chair. His loud breathing could be heard through the door. He had taken a small boat, a ferry, and a small plane, all to get to a larger airport. Then he'd had six hours of flying with more airports in between to get here.

Robert had been experiencing an equally trying day. The work with Ron Crest at the White House West Wing had gone on for hours, following the Situation Room briefing. They had worked without a break on the actions needed to coordinate all the different agencies that were involved.

The sheer volume of people involved in the coordination was mind boggling. They far outnumbered the police and National Guard blocking roads and protecting houses from looters, technicians decontaminating and hauling in and out radioactive material and equipment. Everyone ran the risk of radiation exposure. The droves of press and the estimated million people either running toward or away from the terrorism spectacle had become another problem.

Robert trudged down the hall toward his office. His head was down, and his tired feet nearly shuffled as he walked.

When he came through the outer door, Lorraine picked up on his condition right away. "Would you like some coffee and a bagel, Mr. Carlton?" She asked solicitously.

"Yes, that would be great," Robert sighed, proceeding into his office. He didn't notice the sleeping Lt. Colonel until he had reached his chair and turned back toward the desk.

Surprised, he asked in an even tone. "Colonel Barlow, are you quite comfortable?"

"You could use an easy chair in here, Mr. Carlton," Grady responded without opening an eye. He sat up and stretched with a look of pain when his stiff muscular neck straightened. "Oh, that hurts. So, is it a *real* dirty bomb—another Sandy Island?"

"It's real," Robert confirmed.

"Okay. At least that's settled." Grady answered.

You seem rather casual about that," Robert chided.

"Is it time to panic?" Grady's combat calmness came naturally.

"No." Robert opened his laptop. "You've stayed informed about current events, then." Robert hit Lorraine's button. "Lorraine?"

"Yes, Sir," she responded.

"Could you get Colonel Barlow some refreshment?"

"I have a two-shot, non-fat latte, and a protein shake on their way," she answered efficiently.

Robert looked back at Grady and raised an eyebrow.

"I pre-ordered." Grady grinned.

"Okay, then let's get back to the situation. Tell me what you think about it?" Robert requested.

"I have a direct connection to the support teams of Homeland Security," Grady began. "I suppose that has me up to date with Secretary Snelling and Ron Crest. I'm the Intelligence Community Liaison for my part of the Pentagon, but that doesn't mean I'm fully informed. For example, my information doesn't include what you saw and discussed in the Sit room, or what has transpired this afternoon. I'm hours behind you, although I have seen the footage on the Internet. Does that count?" he asked blandly.

Robert shook his head wearily. "We have some catching up to do."

Lorraine knocked, opening the door and bringing in Robert's coffee and bagel, and Grady's espresso drink and shake. They began exchanging information while they ate, filling each other in on details.

"What's the bottom line?" Robert finally asked.

"You know most of it," Grady answered. "We have two dirty bombs, and the CIA thinks there are five. I think Mahaffey would agree with that, and that securing the Caribbean as a protective barrier to the US is like plugging holes in Swiss cheese. There are a thousand easy ways in and out. There are an infinite number of more difficult options, like using small private docks and open shorelines. You just saw one in action, since this boat was in a small harbor area. The fact is that we'll never get it all locked down. We'd stand a much better chance detecting incoming vessels at our own inlets, harbors, and airports, rather than trying to cover those islands, but it would still be a monumental task." Grady looked certain of his statement.

"So, it was a waste of time," Robert summarized, feeling even more tired than before.

"No," Grady said positively. "It was a good exercise because of the training. It's good to raise awareness with a strategy and equipment. It's good to try anything and everything possible to stop threats before they reach us. It was important for these islands and good for us. Like everything else, you do what you can to make it better, because nothing is foolproof. How about on your end? You guys come up with anything better?"

"There's no silver bullet, Grady. I think we all expected that. Have they found the owner of the sailboat that exploded, yet? I haven't heard anything here." Robert asked.

"Steve's working on it. They know a woman was the contact for the work to be done by Berg's Boats. They don't have a name for her, and nobody's got any pictures, either. No documents or receipts have been found. Even the rented boat slip was paid for in cash, up front."

"No security cameras anywhere?" Robert asked hopefully.

"None. At least none that got a shot of her. The FBI has the assignment to find her. As for the dead guy, the harbor lift fee was paid in cash by him, Rayberg of Berg's Boats, so it is presumed that she paid him in cash. I expect we will have more on the boat before the end of the day. The FBI guys are all over this," Grady told him.

Robert sipped his harsh coffee. "Thanks. I want to be prepared in case the President throws any more questions my way. At this point, it appears that you and I don't have to work on this anymore. It is now the property of Talia Snelling at Homeland Security, and National Security Advisor Ron Crest. They get to carry the ball from now on."

"We're off the hook for the Caribbean search team effort then, too? Can we hand that and the diplomatic stuff off to Vance and Morrison?" Grady questioned.

"Looks that way to me. Let's proceed under that assumption and get it ready to transfer until we hear otherwise," Robert replied tiredly.

"Sounds like a winner to me. I don't mean anything negative with this question, but what changed? Weren't you designated the quarterback by the President?" Grady asked cautiously.

"Talia Snelling and Homeland Security happened. Once they get involved, everybody else has to get out of the way." Robert didn't like the broad, sweeping powers of DHS. The creation of the department and 9/11 had forever changed the power base. "They have taken jurisdiction, and everyone else, like the FBI, are to continue doing their jobs, as long as DHS is informed and ultimately approves. You and I get a pass because they've taken over our workload," Robert explained.

"Centralization has its value, but micromanagement at arm's length—I don't know. It makes it too easy to play the Monday morning quarterback role." Grady didn't like how DHS worked. "I guess we'd better work out the details for the handoff. Then we can officially be done." Grady was irritated and relieved at the same time. He didn't like letting go of a job half done.

"How about tomorrow? I'm beat." Robert confessed.

"Actually, I am completely shot, so that works for me. Meet back here at nine?" Grady asked.

"Sounds good. Lorraine!" Robert called out. Lorraine pushed the door open and looked at him. "Nothing on the calendar tomorrow, right?"

"You asked that it be cleared," she said.

"Good, block it out. Colonel Barlow and I will be having a planning session."

Chapter 50

Max stood at the shore railing of the dock overlooking the Hunter 356 at the Gangplank Marina in DC. At just after eleven p.m. the area was dark. The last restaurant was about to close, leaving enough people walking to their boats or around the area to make maneuvering around security on the docks easy.

Max had arrived in time to see Jeff, Chrystal, Mark and Julie all returning from dinner onshore together. She'd heard enough of the conversation to discover that Jeff and Chrystal were going to lock up their boat, and go back to their home on shore. Mark and Julie planned to tidy up their yacht, in preparation for leaving the next day.

Max waited until Jeff and Crystal headed down the dock, watching as they got into their car. She pulled a small white box from her pocket. It had a button and two sets of rotary thumb switches. She turned the first to thirty-three point-zero, and the second to thirty-four point-zero. The timer was now set for thirty-three hours on the first bomb. The second would go off an hour later. When Jeff and Chrystal pulled away from the parking lot, Max walked casually down the gangplank, heading toward the Hunter.

Wearing a coat over a warm shirt and jeans, she fit in with the dinner crowd. Her light beige gloves were barely noticeable, even under the dock lights. The yacht rested less than fifty yards down the floating walkway. It took no time to reach it.

Standing on the dock extension between the yacht and the next boat, Max checked around her, then peered through a cabin window. Two of the instrument lights were lit. Good. Either the battery or the dock power was activated. She peeled off a protective cover on some two-sided tape and stuck the box on the boat deck, against the white gunwale. It was camouflaged there, with its white housing against the white fiberglass. She pressed the button. An LED inside the plastic housing glowed briefly, then went out.

Now she headed back to shore and turned down the wharf, heading toward the Beneteau.

As she walked, she patted a roll of duct tape in her coat pocket, making sure it was there. Her jeans back pocket had a number of plastic loops sticking out. Over her right-hand was a beach towel, hiding her gun. She'd pulled it out of her waistband, in case she needed to be ready for action.

Max walked nearly the length of the Gangplank Marina, less than five-hundred yards, including the extension out over the water. It was quiet out at the end. Only one other yacht was active, and it was eight boats away.

There were a lot of houseboats in the marina, which Max eyed carefully. She was trying to spot anyone on deck, up on their roof drinking, or star gazing. The place seemed devoid of outside activity. The Beneteau floated at the far end of the dock where it was dark. There was only one small light. Max could just make out the name "E-Vent" near the bow. It was painted or stenciled in a high-tech font.

As she quietly approached, she watched for movement in the windows. It was likely that Mark and Julie were on board. She figured they must be in the bow stateroom or the bathroom. The curtains were closed on both.

If she could manage to get aboard undetected this would be much easier. Max passed the windows as quickly as she could without making noise and made her way to the stern. The vertical portion of the hatch that led below was open, but the top cover was pulled shut. She would have to slide it forward to get in.

Max knew that getting on the boat would make it rock, and sliding the hatch would probably make noise. If they spotted her too soon they might shout out, or put up a fight.

Listening, she heard nothing. She made her move. From the dock, she stepped very slowly onto the boat to make the added weight shift the boat to that side gradually. She tried to look casual doing it, in case there were any onlookers. The hatch had a wood frame, with a shaded gray Plexiglas insert. With a careful look inside, she saw no one. She pushed as gently as possible to slide the hatch forward. It slid quietly. With the vertical door plank out already, she was now able to step in but only got to the first step before Mark came out of the bedroom door.

"Hello, can I help you? Are you looking for someone?" Mark was surprised to see this woman, but didn't immediately perceive any threat.

Max pulled the towel off her hand, exposing the pistol. "Shut up and get on your knees."

The bedroom door slammed shut behind Mark. Without hesitating, Max leaped forward and side kicked Mark high in the chest, followed by a knee kick to the gut. Then she hit him on the side of his head with the heel of the pistol. Mark had no time to react. He crumpled to the floor. Max stepped on him to reach the bedroom door, forcibly turning the handle, then immediately bashing the door in with her shoulder.

On the other side, Julie was trying to dial her phone with one hand and brace the door with the other. Max' first hit surprised her, knocking her back half a foot. Max had expected resistance and was already lined up to push off of Mark's body with the strength of both her legs. The powerful second thrust drove Julie onto the bed and sent the phone flying. Max was on her as she fell, pushing her face first into the bed and pulling her arm around her back with a twist. She pressed the barrel of the pistol to her cheek.

"Don't move," Max ordered, tightening her twisting grip. Julie groaned. Max then tucked the pistol back in her waistband. Keeping Julie immobilized, she reached forward, grabbing the phone off the mattress pad to make sure it was not connected or dialing. It wasn't. Tossing it back on the bed, she realized that Mark was starting to move. She pulled a zip tie handcuff from her pocket and yanked it harshly over Julie's hand. With a tug, she tightened it.

"Ow!" Julie cried out.

"Shut up!" Max pulled her to the side to get to the other wrist. Pulling her free hand backward, she zip-tied it to the first, then shoved Julie onto the floor in a tight, confined ball.

Max launched herself onto Mark, pulling and twisting his arm around until he was face first on the wood floor. She pulled another zip-tie out and fastened it around his hand as he let out a yelp of pain.

"Be quiet, or I will knock you out again," Max threatened. With a yank of his pained shoulder, Max pulled his arm up while stepping on his thigh.

"Arrhhh!" Mark was in severe pain now.

Max ignored him and grabbed the other wrist to twist it up and into the open side of the handcuffs. With another tug, he was strapped around the silver mast that came down all the way to the floor.

Julie had been trying to get up, but Max was able to subdue her easily by grabbing a handful of her hair. She dragged her to the bench near the mast, and duct-taped Julie's cuffed hands behind her, and around the mast above Mark's arms. It was a little bit sloppy, but effective.

"Okay." She stepped back and pulled the gun back out for show. "You both need to be quiet. I will not hesitate to hit you over the head with this. Putting the gun back in her waistband, she pulled out the duct tape again and covered both their mouths. Looking at Mark, she said. "Pull your legs up to your chest, feet together." When he obeyed, she put her shin down on his feet with her full weight, taping his ankles together, and wrapping them all the way up his calves. "Now you." She turned to Julie and did the same.

In what seemed like seconds, the two were tied up and silent, staring at their captor with wide eyes. Blood from the pistol butt impact cut trickled down the side of Mark's face, but beyond that, except for some bruises and wrenched joints, they were unharmed. Mark's and Julie's faces strained with anger and defiance.

Max only took a moment to check for blood on her clothes, gloves, and face before rifling the equipment desk to find the boat keys.

With a quick check of the power panel, she flipped on the navigational lights and climbed up the stairs, closing the hatch behind her. Now came the next stress test, starting the engine.

Max had read the on-line manual for the boat. You couldn't simply start the engine without following a precise procedure. This was going to test her nerve.

The manual warned of stalling the engine. Step one, she engaged the neutral button and pushed the throttle forward to give the engine some revs for starting. Next, she inserted and turned the key full left to the "glow" position, to warm the diesel glow plug for a full ten seconds. Now, with sweat on her forehead, she turned the key back to the right in the "on" position. A continuous electronic alarm tone warned her to hold there for ten to fifteen seconds. She counted as it screamed. It seemed like forever, as the alarm echoed off the neighboring boats. She counted and watched for cabin lights to turn on, or for people to come out. Finally, one-thousand-twelve, she turned the key to start, and it fired up. She adjusted the throttle down a little.

Sweat dripped from her neck down her back as she stepped off the boat to release the lines. Two bow, two stern, and a single spring line held the yacht to the dock. Back on the boat, she pulled the throttle to neutral, switched to reverse, and pulled out of the dock. Within minutes she was away, and motoring at full speed south on the Washington Channel headed for the Potomac.

Chapter 51

On the Gozzard, Luca sailed into the Chesapeake Bay past a scenic tourist pier, and over the first of two underwater highway bridge tunnels. He had watched as the onlookers on the pier turned away to take selfies with the miniature pirate ship behind them as he sailed by. The first road was Highway 13, just north of the South Thimble Island tunnel entrance. He could just make out the Hampton Roads Bridge through the ocean mist, which, on a sunny day, could easily obscure the shoreline.

It was late and the sun would be setting soon, but he had made good time, leaving his mooring before dawn. He'd been lucky to find there was a stiff breeze off-shore. The boat handled well, running at its top speed in light chop. His careful planning the day before kept him from having to negotiate the harbor in the dark.

Although his seamanship had improved greatly, it was a great relief to sail over the two tunnels, instead of under bridges and between spans. Slight shifts in wind, rushing between columns of immovable concrete and steel, were unnerving.

He could have motored in, but he kept the sails up like the other boats. Fitting in was important to assure no side glances from the Coast Guard, or Navy. He gave large ships a wide birth while doing his best to adopt an easy going, day-sailor appearance. He even waved when people waved at him, but as he sailed past two aircraft carriers at their docks, the sheer enormity of the ships made him worry about being too close. The size of the two floating airports made it hard to judge distance. He tried to estimate whether he was outside the regulated distance. He didn't attract any notice, so he figured he'd guessed correctly.

Luca sailed down the far side of the harbor, heading into the Elizabeth river and toward his rented berth. If it wasn't for the tension in his stomach, it would have been a nice day on the yacht. As it was, he hoped that once this assignment was over he'd never have to sail another boat again.

The sun faded away just before he got to his berth. Lights from the nearby bridge and the pier helped him navigate. He almost slipped into the number fourteen slot by mistake. With a great sigh of relief, he tied off the bow and stern lines in number twelve. He had even learned from his reading how to put on a spring line. His boat looked as secure as any of those around him. With wobbly legs, he walked down the dock to check in with the office.

The Gozzard was now docked just a few miles due south of the US Navy Atlantic fleet aircraft carriers, and their docked support ships. He had no idea how much time he'd knocked off the trip by cutting the corner, but he knew he was now slightly ahead of schedule. He gave a long-awaited sigh of relief.

After checking in, he headed back to the boat to tidy up all the covers, lines, his gear, and then lock up. With everything shipshape, he hefted his duffle bag and headed for the office again. They had the number for a taxi service. Luca, with a huge weight off his shoulders, headed to the hotel. He ate, and then promptly fell asleep. His phone sat ignored in the duffle bag.

. . .

Max had been sailing all day. Through the night and dark morning hours, she had motored. Mark and Julie sat below. They had struggled a lot, testing the ligatures and tape to no avail. The mast was immovable, and the plastic tie wraps could not be broken or released, although they'd tried to finagle each other's bonds. Mark had tried to rise, but the tape around the mast and Julie's bonds prevented the action. He was left on the floor below her, while she stayed up on the bench.

Sitting topside in the cockpit, Max had eventually gotten the autopilot to take over the helm on a long stretch of the Potomac. The bay was getting wider—wide enough that the boat felt smaller and easy to maneuver. There was no oncoming traffic, so she could run a straight line for a while. She decided to check below.

Confirming that her two captives were not going anywhere, she went back up topside. The sun had come up, so it was time to raise the sails. It took a lot of muscle and some trial and error before she got the mainsail up. The first attempt failed. She was headed south, and the wind was blowing to the east. Raising the sail was impossible until she changed the heading to go straight upwind. This time raising the main was possible. Next, she pulled out the furled genoa and sheeted it in. Using the autopilot control, she fell off the apparent wind so the sail filled with air.

After a couple of sudden and unexpected jibes, she let out the sails a little to keep them on one side. She kept the motor running to force the boat up to eight knots according to the gauges, but that fought the sails. They flapped back and forth, making a lot of noise. The smell of diesel fumes came over the back transom, giving her a headache. Reluctantly, she put the engine in neutral. The navigation computer showed her speed-over-ground to be six miles an hour. She shut down the engine and became a sailor. The boat sailed smoothly and was wonderfully quiet.

Max's disguise was now complete. She was a sailor out for a cruise. It was oddly relaxing. She continued to sail for hours. The daylight was beginning to fade. Seeing another long stretch with no traffic, Max decided to go below while the light held to check on Mark and Julie. It smelled down in the cabin, reeking of urine. Both Mark and Julie had been tied up for hours and Mark had lost the battle for control of his bladder. The puddle of urine had pooled on the low side of the floor. Julie was looking painfully uncomfortable.

"I need to go." She said miserably.

Max realized she needed to use the bathroom, too, and without a word, stepped into the head. She relieved herself, then looked around at the washroom and how it was fitted. It was built with no solid loopholes, and she found nothing in it to which she could secure someone. There was no sure way to secure her prisoner in the space. They were more than halfway on a thirty-hour run, but Max determined the risk was too great to release either of them. When she came out of the head, she offered water to them. Mark accepted.

"Please, I genuinely need to use the head. I won't do anything." Julie pleaded.

"Water?" Max offered again, ignoring the request. She got only a glare from Julie.

Max went back topside.

It was an easy sail with the consistent east blowing wind. Max had sailed previously. She'd met a guy in Hawaii who took her out running up and down the beach on his Hobie Cat, just outside the surf. It had been fast and exciting. She'd learned enough of the basics to help out with the jib. A few years ago, she'd gone out on a Catalina 25 in Boston Harbor with a date and his friends who owned the boat. Again, she learned enough to not be completely stumped by a grinder or wench.

Looking at her watch, she noted that it was six. In fourteen hours the Hunter, still back in the harbor, would feel a jolt. It would then send a cloud of radiation into the air. There was something terrifying and ominous about that. It was also powerful, and that made her happy in a deep, visceral way she couldn't describe. It felt really good.

Chapter 52

Robert and Grady met, as planned, at nine a.m. the next day. They worked for hours on their progress report, which took them well through lunch. Then there were the extra reports needed for Homeland Security, the FBI, and the Pentagon. Grady needed the Pentagon report much more than Robert, but it was a joint effort. The fact that a dirty bomb had been exploded on US soil was a huge problem, well above both their pay grades.

It was only a matter of time before the radiation story would break. It was a miracle it hadn't, yet, but as soon as it did there would be a massive reaction. There would be hearings and investigations designed to give politicians airtime visibility. Soundbites would follow, along with an extended news cycle surrounding the explosion in Florida.

For now, it was all on a need to know basis. Robert and Grady had been reminded of that every hour, during every conversation. The official stand remained. Melbourne had a huge gas leak, forcing evacuations and medical treatment. There was the risk that the truth could leak out before they had all the answers, but that was Homeland Security's problem.

By three the brief was in Lorraine's hands for proofing and distribution. Robert and Grady were ready to hand the mess off, and it felt good.

Dinner time was fast approaching. Tracie and Katy had arranged a dinner for the two couples. Both men decided to use the next couple of hours to unwind before putting on their dinner clothes. Left on his own, dinner out was the last thing Robert would have chosen.

Grady was adjusting faster than Robert to the idea. He had been on the silent end of many top-secret events. After the last few days, he was ready for dinner with some lighter conversation. Plus, it was an opportunity to be with Katy on a strictly social basis. They were still having a hard time coordinating dates.

After showering, relaxing, and suiting up, Grady picked Katy up at her place. They rolled along Hwy 120 between I-95 and Arlington Boulevard. Katy looked great. She was dressed to kill.

"Just right for a casual get-together, I see," Grady teased her, grinning.

"Well, I wanted to look good for you, and you know Tracie will look stunning, as always," Katy told him.

Tracie and Katy were becoming fast friends, thanks to their weekly girls' investment club meetings. For Robert and Grady, the girls' preferred dinner topics were a welcome break from the office.

"You're looking forward to tonight, aren't you?" Katy asked.

"Sure. We haven't seen them together for a while," Grady affirmed. "It'll be a nice change."

"You were with Robert all day," Katy laughed. "Aren't you sick of each other?"

"Business-wise we might get that way, but we don't get any social time. It's not like hanging out with a buddy. And I haven't seen Robert and Tracie together for a while," Grady grinned.

"We had a call about stocks today," Katy informed him.

"You and Tracie?" Grady asked.

"And the other ladies in the club. Did you notice that the market took a small dip at the end of the day?" She asked.

"No." Grady never looked at the stock market. He didn't have time to spare.

"Most of the dip came from the sectors we were watching, and we got out just ahead of it, I think," Katy told him with some pride.

"The dip?" Grady queried. "Implying that it'll bounce back?"

"Right. We've been watching for this, so we were ready to sell. We'll buy back in on the rise." She said.

"That sounds good." Grady was not knowledgeable enough about what she was doing to add much to the conversation.

Katy moved to a new subject, deciding more of that story could wait. "Are you done with your most recent project with Robert?"

"I think we'll be working on this a bit longer," he told her. "There will be a lot of follow-up as usual. I'm still talking with police, fire, and the Secret Service from the last time Robert got me mixed up in something, so I've discovered that you never know how long these things will take. Any new projects or developments for you at the lab?"

"They finished analyzing the data MISTI collected at the Super Bowl. Everyone saw it hanging from the crane as trucks rolled underneath for inspection, but they didn't know we had another one watching sideways. We got some fantastic three-dimensional maps of the stadium, and everything around it. The techs got so bored at one point, they started mapping which concrete columns were the most radioactive."

"Concrete?" Grady asked, surprised.

"Concrete, granite, river rocks, beach sand—you'd be surprised how much small radioactivity is out there," Katy responded.

"I'll never look at sand or a granite countertop quite the same way again." Grady joked, making the turn onto Arlington Blvd. "So, your stock club is doing well?" Grady decided to have another try at showing interest in her club.

"Oh, you'll hear all about it over dinner." Katy was looking forward to telling the story with Tracie.

Robert and Tracie were already at the restaurant, but had not been seated when Grady and Katy arrived.

"Katy! Grady! How good to see you." Tracie gave them both a light hug and peck on the cheek.

Robert hugged Katy and had a hearty handshake for Grady. "Long time no see. How have you been?" He kidded.

"Great, you? Still working at the same ol' job?" Grady laughed. They grinned at each other.

Katy and Tracie jumped right in, talking about the trades they'd made after their lunch call. While they talked, the guys opted for the lounge and led them in while they waited for a dinner table to be ready.

Robert and Grady couldn't get away from office talk, going over their "Sandy Island" report one more time, using cleverly encoded wording to avoid eavesdropping. Katy and Tracie were absorbed in a discussion about oil prices, energy stocks, and mutual funds.

At the dinner table, after the inquiries of, "How are the kids," "How's work," and "How's your family," the conversations went right back where they started.

Eventually, the talk drifted to Grady's recent excursion to the islands, and Katy's small, but interesting role at the Super Bowl.

Tracie's tales of the past few weeks tended to include a bit too much name-dropping, which hindered the flow of conversation. Then she touched on a conversation she had with a Vice President from Lockheed, and the conversation turned to defense stocks.

An avid discussion of stealth, drones, ties to commercial aviation, autonomous robots, and surveillance ensued. Katy added tidbits of new technology trends, but when the subject matter slid back to energy stocks and oil prices, Robert glazed over. Grady kept up admirably, but lost the thread on covered calls and put option trades.

"That's twice tonight that 'covered calls' have come up. What exactly is that?" Grady finally asked. He wasn't afraid to show that he was in the dark on the subject.

"It's a stock strategy where you sell call options against stock you own." Tracie started explaining.

"Okay, and?" Grady needed more information.

"It's simple," Katy jumped in. "If you own one-hundred shares of a stock, you can sell one 'call' against it."

"Okay, what's so great about that?" Grady wanted to know.

"Well," Tracie took over again, "if the stock fails to reach the set price, your stock doesn't sell. You keep the stock *and* the money you were paid for the call option."

"And if the stock does get that high?" Grady asked.

"Then the stock is bought, you keep the call option money, and get the price you set. That should be higher than the original purchase price. The only downside is that if the stock goes really high, you don't get that extra upside."

"Or," Katy added, "the stock can go way down, and you're stuck with it. The trick is to only buy stock you are willing to hold through the down cycles."

"It's a win-win play," Tracie stated proudly.

"That sounds like something my Father would say," Robert commented with a frown.

"He's the one that showed us how to do all of this, and we have been making money on it every time." Katy was pleased with their accomplishments.

"Father has been showing you how?" Robert asked slowly.

"Yes, he has come to several of our meetings and helped out a lot. I told you that when we had dinner with your parents, remember?" Tracie tried to jog his memory.

"He got me into some really good trades," Katy happily added. "None of us are ready to try selling short, though; it's too risky. So, we're not getting into energy stocks until they bottom out."

"My father is helping you buy stock," Robert said it as a statement almost under his breath.

"Robert, we talked about this!" Tracie rolled her eyes at Robert's statement, annoying him further. "He's been very helpful to the whole club. In fact, he advised us to start selling on the rises a week ago, and we have been collecting some nice profits."

"Don't try to time the market." Katy and Tracie said together cheerfully, laughing. "Sell the rise, buy the dip." The two women shared a knowing grin.

Tracie continued. "We've done quite well. The whole club has." Tracie was not going to let Robert's competitive family issues cloud her achievements.

Both women went on to talk more about the ins and outs of stock trading with Grady, leaving Robert to sulk. He didn't make it too obvious that he was unhappy, but Tracie ignored him while he cooled off.

As Robert and Tracie were driving home, she chatted away. Robert half listened. Something was digging at the back of his mind. It wasn't that his father was helping the club that actually bothered him...there was something else that he couldn't put his finger on. It continued to dig at him all the way through saying goodnight to Alicia, as he watched her get safely to her car. It kept bugging him while he checked on the boys in bed, and while he took a shower. When he came out, Tracie was fast asleep. His mind was buzzing, but he didn't know why.

"What am I missing?" he wondered.

. . .

Vlad had waited patiently as the clock ticked closer to eleven-thirty p.m. Patience was not his talent. Most of the clients had sent confirmations. It was understood that they would confirm only after they had taken the actions they planned. Japan was thirteen hours ahead of Washington. The Tokyo Stock Exchange would be closed for lunch now. He held his tablet waiting for the email to update.

"Finally." He said aloud as the email popped up. The last client had confirmed.

Vlad quickly pulled up his blogs and websites in succession, posting the news, incriminations, and speculations. The Internet came alive with shock, fear, and recriminations against US government agencies and their inept management.

Vlad was pleased. He poured himself a celebratory drink and leaned back to watch the updates. They streamed across his social media channel consolidation app. He expected responses to be fast and reactions to be extreme. This was better than he had hoped.

Chapter 53

Lying in bed Robert couldn't shake the feeling there was a loose end, somewhere. It was an odd feeling; like a song stuck in his head with forgotten lyrics. Staring at the ceiling in the dark he made an effort to think about nothing. He finally managed to get into a half-awake stage, but his subconscious kept working on the problem. He dozed a little, rolling onto his left side which made him snore. Tracie pushed him to turn over. Rolling to his right, he stuck one leg out from under the covers because he felt too hot. Then he pulled the leg back in because it was cold. Robert was half awake for what seemed like hours. He finally gave up trying to sleep, and got out of bed to go to his study.

The house was cold. The setback thermostat brought the temperature down by fifteen degrees at night, and it wouldn't start back up until six-thirty. With no more than a bathrobe and slippers, Robert's ankles were freezing as he crossed them under the desk. He tried not to touch the chair legs with his bare skin. He was surprised to see the clock on his computer read five-fifteen. He had slept more than he realized.

When the news came up on his computer he absentmindedly thumbed through the headlines. One caught his eye. "Gas leak kills in Florida." Before he could click on it, the update spinner started. He had been seeing his last view of the site. Once the update finished, new headlines appeared. "Dirty bomb in Melbourne FL." "Terrorists attack Florida." There were at least six of these articles. Most looked like blogging junk, but two were legitimate sources. Above the official story in one was a short drone's eye video of Berg's Boats boatyard in Melbourne. On the ground was a police outline of a body. "Great, just great," Robert thought, as he watched.

For a moment, he actually felt good about the State Department and Homeland Security taking the lead on this. It was a hot potato and he was rid of it. They wanted control of everything—well, now they had it. He was glad it was their problem now.

As the video neared its end, the drone swung around the area for a wider shot. Robert was mulling over the legal issues surrounding the growing number of drones flown by citizens in unauthorized zones and through neighbor's backyards when he noticed something. He leaned into the computer screen to stare, but the video ended.

Clicking it again, he ran it forward to almost the end and paused the video. Now he could read the name on the boat: *Caroline.*

Robert stared for a long moment scratching his head. He jumped from his chair and ran upstairs to the bedroom. Flipping on the light, he crossed over to the bed.

"Tracie, wake up!" He shook her gently.

"What? What is it? Is it the boys?" She asked, squinting into the bright bedroom light.

"The yacht owners on St. Thomas—the couple that sold their boat. What were their names?" Robert asked.

"What are you talking about?" Tracie was still shaking off sleep.

"The yacht owners in St. Thomas who sold their boat," Robert said again. "What was the wife's name?"

"Their name was Barstow," Tracie told him sleepily. "Why?"

"No; *her* name, Tracie. What was *her* name, and the name of their boat?" Robert pressed.

"Caroline," Tracie remembered.

Robert turned toward the door.

"Turn the light off," Tracie called, rolling over as he flipped the switch and sprinted down the stairs to the telephone.

"Grady! Wake up!" Robert yelled into the phone.

"I'm awake. You just dialed my number and woke me, remember?"

"The dirty bomb is all over the Internet," Robert told him.

"Damn! That happened fast. So much for information blackout," Grady said irritably.

"There's more," Robert said. "The boat in Melbourne. It's named '*Caroline.*'"

"So?" Grady was still half asleep. He and Katy had come back to his place for a nightcap, and she'd stayed. She turned over next to him, grumbling a little.

"Jim and Caroline Barstow were two of the boat owners in St. Thomas, Grady," Robert was saying. "They sold their boat."

Grady sat up in the bed and switched on the bedside light. "You don't think it's the same one?" He asked slowly, considering the possibility.

"We've got to find out." Robert continued, "It could be the missing key to all of this. Mahaffey is working on the Melbourne boat problem, right?"

"Right," Grady affirmed.

"Get him on the phone. We have to find out if it is the Barstow boat." Robert was rifling through his valise. "Do we know where the other boats are?"

Grady was headed to the kitchen. "I don't know. You saw two of them last in Savannah."

"Okay. You get Mahaffey. Do you have a list of the boats and names?"

"No, try Mary. I'll get Steve on the phone." Grady hung up.

Robert went back up the stairs. This time he entered the bedroom quietly and felt around the bedside table in the dark for his smartphone. Once he had it in his hand, he headed back to the study and clicked Mary's number.

"Hello?" Mary sounded surprisingly awake for the hour.

"Mary, this is Robert Carlton."

"Good morning, Mr. Carlton. What can I do for you?"

"Mary, listen. Do you have a list of the five yachts from when we went to St. Thomas? I need a description of the boats, the name of each boat, and the names of the owners. Do you have it?" He asked.

"Yes, Sir. I have my notes on the computer. Well, I don't have the boat names—just the registration numbers, and the owner's contact information." She relayed.

"Do you have it with you?" Robert asked tersely.

"Yes, I take it home at night, because..." Mary began to explain.

"Great," Robert cut in. "Can you email that list to me right now?"

"I'll send it right away. Mr. Carlton, did you hear about the evacuation in Florida? There's talk of radiation and terrorists." Mary sounded excited.

"Where did you hear about it?" Robert questioned.

"It's all over my socials," Mary replied.

"Copy what you are seeing, paste everything in a document, and email that to me," Robert directed.

"Sure, I'll do that right now," Mary said.

"Good, thanks." Robert hung up.

While he waited for Grady to call or for his email to chime, Robert searched the news for more on the Melbourne boat. News headlines of ISIS and the terrorist attack in Florida were popping up everywhere he looked. Multiple sources were posting, tweeting, and reporting in a frenzy of social media feeding.

Finally, his phone rang. Grady's name came up on the screen.

"Grady, what did you find out? Have you seen the latest headlines? The Melbourne thing is going nuts."

Grady had flipped on his espresso machine to warm up and was headed into the bathroom. "Whoa, one thing at a time. Steve says they traced the registration number on the boat. The boat was recently purchased by a broker in Key West Florida for a Mr. Reese Krasinski. Steve got a hold of the broker late yesterday. It was paid for with an electronic transfer. They are tracking down the account holder, but it went through a non-US link to a Grand Cayman bank. Steve doesn't think we will find the buyer. The previous owners were Jim and Caroline Barstow of Palm Springs, Florida. There is nothing on the woman who paid for the boat work, yet, by the way. Maybe she is the buyer, or maybe she's a front. As for the headlines, Steve asked me who leaked about the boat."

Robert knew he was on to something. "I think we've got bigger problems than finding out who leaked that—we'll let State take that one. I think the boat in Melbourne is one of the five that were high-jacked. There were five missing irradiators. One shows up on Sandy Island. Now it looks like one was built into the Barstow boat..."

Grady knew where he was heading with this. He interrupted Robert, saying, "Leaving three more missing irradiators—and there were four more yachts high-jacked. Holy shit!" Grady said, as he pulled a towel off the rack and wrapped it around himself.

"We have to find those boats," Robert told him. His email chimed. "Hang on. I'm getting an email from Mary. It should be about the boats. Yes, that's what it is—I have the list. I'll forward this to you." Robert clicked and typed. "Okay, it's on its way. Do you have your computer?"

"Yes, but I'll pick up the email on my phone." Grady turned on the shower.

Robert was reading the boat list. "I'll track down Mark and Jeff in Savannah. You find Larry Bledsoe on his Gozzard, and Len Price and his Morgan."

"What do we do when we find them?" Grady wanted to know.

"Get them off the boats before they explode." Robert was thinking fast. "Get Steve to outline what the boat bombs might do, how we can get these people off safely, and how the boats should be secured. While you're at it, find out how he can help. With all the technician teams scattered around the islands, we don't have many people—and I don't know how much time we have."

"I'm on it," Grady replied, then hung up.

Grady came out of the bathroom with the bright white towel wrapped around his waist.

"Katy, are you awake? I need your help."

She turned his way with a sleepy grin. "A little early, don't you think, Colonel?"

"I like your thinking, but we'll have to table that idea for now." Grady came over to the bed and put one knee on the edge. Leaning over, he handed her his phone with the open email attachment. "Can you access registration information on civilian boats from the registration number?"

"What? What are you talking about?" She looked confused.

Grady started explaining, beginning with the boat in Melbourne.

"Okay, I'm awake now," Katy told him. "You can tell me the rest in the shower." She slid over to his side of the bed and grabbing his arm, pulled him into the steamy bathroom and hot shower.

. . .

Vlad's phone buzzed with a message.

"Carlton requested yacht list, names, and contacts." Mary was excited to have news.

Vlad smiled. His teapots were coming through. "Feed him the news leads."

"Already done."

"Good." Vlad was pleased, but this meant time was precious.

He quickly sent "Status!" to Max and Luca.

Max replied ten minutes later. "Boat one set. Boat two underway. ETA release for both 8am." Luca did not reply. Vlad dialed his number.

In Luca's room the phone lay dormant as he snoozed. The phone was on its "do not disturb" setting. It was a standard feature that came pre-set from ten p.m. to six a.m. Luca had updated his software and hadn't noticed the default setting. Promptly at six the phone illuminated and vibrated with the waiting messages. Luca groggily got up and went into the bathroom.

Chapter 54

Robert didn't have time to go to the office. He paced in his study with Grady and Steve on the phone simultaneously. The sun wasn't up yet, but the sky was turning a faint pink in the east.

"What are we looking at, Steve?" Robert was asking.

"First, let's talk explosives." Steve was ready. His team had analyzed the boat thoroughly. "Whoever did this knew precisely how the irradiator was designed, inside and out. The irradiator was mounted on the keel of the boat, along with two C-4 charges. One was a shaped charge, designed to crack open the irradiator protective shell. It also drove a wedge into the sealed source, exposing the Cesium-137 powder."

Steve took a breath, then continued. "The first charge should have sent the Cesium into the air through the mast. The second charge should have broken the boat in half, sending the Cesium, irradiator, and everything around or above into the air. The odds are that we would have had a much wider area of exposure if that had occurred. We believe that the explosions didn't take place as planned because of the victim's actions. While in the process of repairing damage to the boat, he cut a score line on one side. This dramatically changed the resistance on that side, unbalancing the explosive discharge."

"Right. I'm with you. So, let me just confirm what you are you saying. The way this was set up, it was created as a weapon, and the explosives weren't set up as defense mechanisms to protect a smuggling operation for the irradiator to be used elsewhere?" Robert asked.

"This absolutely was a weapon. They did a great job deliberately turning the yacht into a dirty bomb." Steve confirmed. "The yacht made it easy to transport, impossible to detect, and created effective disbursal."

"Impossible to detect?" Robert asked.

"Water is a great shield for radiation," Steve informed Robert. "It takes about fourteen feet of water to stop Gamma radiation from being detected. Much less water than that stops the Alpha and Beta particles from showing up. It only takes eight feet of water to make the radiation indistinguishable from background radiation. You'd have to be sitting on top of the boat with a Geiger counter to detect it."

"How about disbursal? Wouldn't it have been better if they just blew it up with one big blast?" Robert kept wondering why they needed two charges.

"Not the way they designed this. The shaped charge cracks the case exposing the Cesium. Then a fan turns on. They built in a fan that could draw air down a tube and blow a container of silica powder into the Cesium, and then out another tube. Both tubes were built into the keel's leading edge, then up to the hull, and finally into the mast. Holes were drilled in the top of the mast to allow for exhausting fifty feet or more in the air."

"That doesn't sound like an effective weapon to me," Grady argued. "I can't imagine the disbursal would be reliable, or widespread. From what I know, it seems unlikely they could deliver a lethal dose. There are more effective ways to kill people if that was their intention."

"You're right, the dosages wouldn't be lethal, but the Cesium would carry farther on the wind with this method than with most, and contaminate more ground. A single explosion, unless it was really large, might not effectively rupture the casing, and the Cesium powder wouldn't spread evenly—or maybe not much at all. Cesium salts bond well with silica, just like at the beach at Sandy Island. Silica powder has good resistance to moisture, so it can float a great distance on the wind. They seem to have thought this design would get more of the material up and out the mast if it was detonated as planned. That sounds like a good disbursal to me, and if being secretive is the goal, it's amazing. The second charge ensures the dispersal, in case the first doesn't do that job."

"So, they are pros," Robert assessed.

"I'd say that is probably the case." Steve agreed. "It takes a lot of know-how and money to get radioactive material smuggled anywhere, plus the plan included an expensive yacht and a sophisticated delivery method. They bought from the black market, and effectively smuggled over long distances dangerous, controlled materials. They created an unusual method of dispersal and obtained an unobtrusive, elegant way of shipping and delivering their weapon. Does that sound like something that would involve amateurs?"

"But why?" Grady asked. "If the plan wasn't to kill a lot of people immediately, what was the point?"

Robert was thinking about the other yachts from the kidnapped tourists. "We're going to have to figure out why later, Grady. Right now we have to find the other yachts. Steve, how can we tell if the other boats have these things onboard?"

"What other boats?" Steve asked.

Robert had forgotten that Steve didn't know about the kidnapped tourists and their yachts. He laid out the situation. "There were five sources of radiation smuggled to Venezuela. One showed up on Sandy Island. Another shows up attached to a sailboat that was one of five high-jacked all at the same time. The owners were kidnapped, and originally it was assumed this was part of a failed ransoming plan. The owners got away and were reunited with their yachts, which seemed to have been untouched. We now think the other three irradiator sources could be on three of those boats—and we don't know which three."

"Son of a bitch!" Steve shouted into the phone. He took a breath, then said, "If they are all mounted like this one was, you'll have to get on the boat with your meter to find out. Are all the boats about the same size?"

"They're pretty close to the same size, from what I understand," Robert said.

"Then the bottom of the keels will be six to seven feet below the water. If you are more than twelve feet away, that's fourteen feet of water on an angle. You'll have to get closer, like straight on top with a Geiger counter, or you won't find the stuff. And Robert, if any of them have been activated, nobody should get anywhere near the yachts. You definitely don't want to be downwind. Breath that stuff in and you're taking a big risk of cancer, or death."

"What about the Prussian Blue treatment?" Robert asked. "Doesn't that drastically reduce the risk?"

"Yes, if you ingest the Cesium. Ferric ferrocyanide reduces the biological half-life from one-hundred ten days to thirty—shorter exposure, so lessened risk; but I wouldn't bet my life on that idea."

"What about protective suits and masks? Don't we have something that will block any absorption?" Robert was trying to find an answer to dealing with the problem.

"We've got suits and masks that protect against inhaling or absorbing it through the skin, but they don't block the Gamma rays. Nothing you can wear protects completely from the radiation. You have to limit the time to keep the exposure within acceptable doses."

"Jeezus, Steve!" Robert's frustration was growing as the clock ticked the minutes away. "Grady, did you get connected with Bledsoe or Price on their yachts?"

"Price, yes," Grady responded. "I explained the situation and they immediately jumped off the boat into their dinghy and went to shore. The locals are blocking off the area. The good news is they're still in the Lesser Antilles, at Monserrat, which is a small island. The boat is at anchor in the middle of a bay. The bad news is that a lot of the almost 4,900 residents live around that bay, and there's an active volcano that doesn't make it safe to shelter on the other side of the island—even if there was a dock big enough to bring in large evacuation boats. Right now, everyone's hoping that yacht doesn't have the Cesium, or that it hasn't been active and won't be activated. One of our trainee teams is on their way there now to scan it. As for Bledsoe, all I get is voice mail. I gave all the boat information to Katy. She is coordinating the Coast Guard and Navy for us. I don't know what capability they have, but she'll get it done."

"So much for keeping this a quiet, non-event. The President will lose his mind." Robert was thinking out loud. He started going through his mental checklist. "Steve, were the explosives and fan hooked up to the boat for power, or on a separate battery?"

"The explosives and radio had their own battery, but the fan was hooked up to the boat," Steve told him.

"So, switching off the boat would minimize exposure," Robert theorized.

"I suppose," Steve admitted cautiously. "The Melbourne boat was wired directly to battery lines behind the power panel, so to be sure that it's switched off, the battery needs to be disconnected directly. But, yes, that would dramatically reduce exposure in the area."

Robert wrote that down. "Grady, advise your team of that when they get to the Price boat. Steve, can you get one of your experienced people down there to help with the Price boat?"

"Yes, but I'll have to have a bomb disposal guy go first," Steve advised him.

"Do that. I'll bring the State Department and local leadership up to speed." Robert was taking control. "The Florida Governor already knows, right?"

"Yes, he is in the loop," Steve confirmed.

"Good. I tried Jeff and Mark on their cell phones—they own the Beneteau and Hunter boats. I got voicemail on both. I contacted the Savannah Yacht Club, and the night harbormaster indicated both had left for DC several days ago. They must be on their way, or already in the Washington Harbor by now." Robert was trying to fit the pieces together with his limited resources. "Grady, can you get Katy and MISTI to scan the Washington DC harbor, and tell us if one or both of the boats are there?"

"From what Steve said, we won't detect anything unless they are spewing that stuff out," Grady reminded him.

"True, but if they are, we need to find out." Robert was grabbing his wallet and keys. "If the Cesium has been released, we'll have to have police lock down that area while staying inside their cars and using speakers. We'll need suits for boat to boat and door to door evacuations. If they haven't been activated yet, we can evacuate in advance, and keep the situation much quieter. MISTI is real-time, so we can use it as an alarm while that's happening."

"Hang on a minute, Robert, and I'll get Katy on the tug." Grady grabbed his coat and tapped Katy on the shoulder. She was on her phone talking to the Coast Guard. "We need MISTI to scan DC."

"Now?" She asked.

"A couple of hours ago," Grady replied, "but now will have to do." He grabbed Katy's officer's jacket and hat and handed them to her.

"We're headed out the door," Grady told Robert. "What are you going to do?"

Robert had been pulling up weather and maps from the Internet. "I'm going to Gangplank Marina in DC. The boats might be there. Jeff and Chrystal belong to the Port of Washington Yacht Club. If they're not there, they might be up the Anacostia River, or out on the Potomac. My weather map says the wind is blowing to the east. I'll come up from the Jefferson Memorial side. If you tell me it's safe, I'm going in to get them out quietly. Maybe the terrorists won't have time to set the bombs off before I can get them off the boats," Robert said, sounding more optimistic than he felt.

"We're on it." Grady and Katy were on the move. "We're getting in an elevator, but I'll be in the car in five. Call if you need me. Otherwise, I'll call when we start moving MISTI." Grady hung up.

"Have you got everything rolling on your end, Steve?" Robert asked.

"I already sent texts and I'll be making calls next," Steve replied. "When you find out where the other boats are, call me. I'll get my people there. I'll wake up everyone available on the East Coast."

"Do that, Steve." Robert hung up.

. . .

Robert was fighting morning traffic, stuck on sixty-six, trying to get over the bridge and to the Lincoln Memorial exit. He started hitting the steering wheel as he repeated over and over. "I should have taken the George Washington!" It was too late now. He had to exit on Ohio, go around the backside of Lincoln to the Jefferson Memorial, down to the golf course, then onto the three-ninety-five to the ninth street exit. "What a nightmare," he thought, as he watched the dashboard clock ticking.

A crescendo of bells went off in his pocket and he hit the microphone located on his earbud cord. "Barlow?"

"Carlton!" Grady called back. "We're at a dead stop on four-ninety-five, about two miles shy of the exit. Where are you?"

"Not quite to Lincoln. Get MISTI fired up. I'm calling the Metro PD to meet me at the Gangplank."

"Don't do it!" Grady cautioned him. "If the terrorists are watching, they'll set off the bombs the minute they see the police."

Robert realized that Grady was right, but they couldn't do this alone.

"Damn it, Grady!" Robert was getting boxed in. "We need support—probably on the water. How about the Coast Guard?"

"Katy already called the Coast Guard. They're positioning on the Potomac side of the golf course, opposite the yacht harbor. Another boat will be in position at the end of the runway at Reagan.

That puts them less than ten minutes from Gangplank or Buzzard Point on the Anacostia River, but out of sight."

"Good thinking. The Coast Guard doesn't need warrants to board or search any boat, so we won't have to find a judge if there's any lack of cooperation, but that doesn't help me find the boats." Robert was starting to feel the enormity of the task. "Wait a minute—that means if I find these boats, I have to get the owners off the boats myself! I was counting on police back up." He hadn't anticipated having to do this alone.

"Yeah, that could be difficult—and Robert, you'll have to get anyone near them off their boats, as well," Grady added. "You know those yacht owners, Robert. They'll listen to you." Grady intoned confidently. He looked at Katy, pressing the phone to his chest to cut off the sound. "Robert has to get them off the boats by himself. I don't know if he has any idea how to do that."

"That's if they're there, and he spots them," Katy pointed out. "Otherwise we have to find those yachts with MISTI, and he's stuck waiting. It could be awhile—we might not find them in time."

"Hey, Robert," Grady began.

"I heard all of that," Robert cut him off.

"What? You couldn't have. I had the face of the phone jammed into my jacket," Grady told him, bewildered.

"The microphone is on the end of your phone, not on the front," Robert sighed.

"Yeah; forgot about that." Grady skipped the backpedaling. "When you get to the docks, see if you can spot the boats. Katy's information says the name of the Hunter is 'Sail Away III.' The name of the Beneteau is 'E-Vent.'" Grady spelled that for Robert, then said, "The wind is blowing to the east right now, so start from the end nearest the Jefferson Memorial and work your way down. If they set off the bombs, at least you'll be upwind. Work your way downwind. By the time you spot one, we should be getting in position to take our first reading."

"Okay, then you can tell me if they've been activated," Robert said.

"Right, but we can't detect them if they are inactive, because of the water. We're pulling off on two-ninety-five, now. We'll have the boat moving in..."

"Twenty minutes, maybe less," Katy spoke loudly to Grady's phone. Grady handed the phone to her.

"Robert, this is Katy. The crew is on the boat, and MISTI is already hooked up. Bryston, one of my key techs, should be inside the gate by now. He'll have MISTI's electronics booted up by the time we get there. The Chief already has the boat engine running, and we'll have enough crew to do the job. I'll pull from the dock and steam west long enough for Bryston to read everything we can from there, then I'll turn north for a quarter mile, turn left, and read again. The zigzag should give us good readings, plus get us closer on each pass. Okay?"

"Good. Yes." Robert was halfway across the bridge in bumper to bumper traffic, headed toward the exit to the marina. "I'm about to exit. I'll be at the DC end of the dock in less than ten minutes. I'm on my headset, so stay connected if you have enough battery."

Katy looked at the phone display. "Grady is down to thirty percent. He'll call you from the boat." She hung up.

"Can he do this?" She asked Grady.

"Sure. He'll find a way." Grady hoped he was right.

Chapter 55

Coming out of the bathroom, Luca looked at his phone. He had three messages. The first one he read was the last text from Vlad.

"Melbourne confirmed compromised. Go Go Go."

It was hours old! Luca yanked on his clothes, grabbed his bag and broke into a sprint for the stairs. He ran for the front desk.

"I need a taxi, quickly!" The desk clerk picked up the phone and dialed.

"They'll be here in ten minutes," the clerk told him.

Luca acknowledged the statement and went out the front door to wait. As he listened to Vlad's voicemail, his heart skipped several beats. Luca had heard him that angry only once—that time he'd strangled a man in front of him. Luca wrestled with what to do. Call Vlad back, or get the boat moving and then call? If Vlad was nearby it wouldn't matter. Luca would be dead, and Vlad would be going to the boat. He decided texting "Yes" immediately was better than waiting and did so.

The taxi took less than ten minutes to arrive, but to Luca, it seemed like a lifetime. The trip to the harbor took just as long, even with a fifty dollar tip up front.

Luca ran down the dock to the boat. Ignoring the looks from other boaters, he frantically tried to start the engine. He didn't wait long enough to do it right and stalled it. It took three tries as he became more frantic, but finally, it caught and grumbled to life.

Throwing off the lines and dropping them haphazardly in the water, Luca accelerated out of the harbor toward the river. He overestimated the sailboat's ability to turn with the propeller spinning hard, and almost hit a pylon supporting the bridge. This drew attention from a few people on the dock.

Luca ran the engine at full throttle. He was finally heading north on the Elizabeth River. He had to get west of the Navy ships. His plan had been to wait for a wind blowing north, but that plan was shot. He wasn't sure how he could make this work. He stared at the map on his cell phone, zooming in and out, scanning up and down. If he went up the Elizabeth, he could head upwind toward the six-sixty-four Hampton Roads Beltway bridge. If he sailed up close to the manmade island where the bridge became a tunnel to go under the river, he could set the autopilot, then dive off the boat and swim to the island. It would take a lot of luck for no one to notice, but he had to take the chance. Just before diving off, with the boat motoring toward the aircraft carriers, he could activate the bomb. It was his only chance. Anything else would mean an impossibly long swim, or sailing into the hands of the Navy, assuming they didn't shoot him first.

Sirens erupted from three sides as Luca looked up from his cell phone. A big Coast Guard boat was in front of him, blocking his path. On his port side an inflatable Coast Guard boat was racing up, and another one was coming from behind.

"Sailing vessel 'Blustery.' Keep your hands where they are. Prepare to be boarded. Maintain course and heading." The message repeated over the loudspeakers as the inflatable, with its big orange stripe down the side, came close to the boat. The officers and men on board wore swat team gear and pointed military assault rifles directly at Luca. Luca stood frozen in place.

The first commando-type Coast Guard sailor landed aboard. The others pointed their rifles so close to Luca that he could almost reach out and touch the barrels. The sailor crashed onto the deck, hitting his helmet hard on the cabin. It didn't slow him down. Luca found himself face-to-face with a huge pistol held by an angry man.

"Hands on your head! Now! On your knees! Now!" The sailor yelled at him. Luca complied quickly. The sailor took over the controls and pushed the throttle down to zero, then spun the wheel to port. The sailboat pressed hard into the Coast Guard boat and slowed to a standstill almost immediately. More men climbed aboard. Luca was quickly surrounded by black uniforms. He was manacled hand and foot, and his pockets were pulled inside out as they frisked him. His belt, phone, and watch were put into bags and handed over to the nearby vessel. More bags were rapidly coming off the sailboat, as it was stripped of everything that wasn't nailed down. Luca was shackled to the sailboat as he watched a sailor carrying tools drop into the engine compartment. Luca now sat with his hands attached to the safety line behind his back, while he stared into the unyielding face of an officer.

"Describe the detonation trigger you were to use setting off the bomb," the officer commanded.

Luca looked at him, stunned into silence.

"You were going to set off a bomb. Tell me what the control looks like." The man insisted.

Luca fumbled his first words. Only a few disjointed syllables came out. His lips felt stiff and unable to move. The man's intense eyes watched closely, but with surprising patience.

"It is a white plastic box with two little dials, and a button a little smaller than a cigarette box," Luca finally got out.

"Chief!" The officer called to the other boat. "White box with a button and two small dials the size of a pack of cigarettes."

"Affirmative, Ensign! We have it. It was in his pocket." A sailor held up the device in a clear bag.

Turning back to Luca. "Is that it?" He wanted confirmation.

Luca nodded. "Yes."

"What else is there?" The man asked.

"Nothing," Luca said weakly. His shock was beginning to turn into a feeling of extreme fatigue.

"Is there a manual switch onboard?" He leaned closer to Luca's face.

"No, Sir. There is nothing," Luca just wanted to close his eyes.

The officer kept staring at Luca without blinking.

"Ensign!" The Chief called out.

"Yes, Chief?" The officer did not shift his gaze.

"Information from command," he yelled over the idling engines. "They say to disconnect the battery to disarm!"

"Did you confirm that?" The Ensign questioned.

"Aye, Ensign," the Chief answered.

The officer backed away and called to the man digging in the engine compartment. "Disconnect the battery!"

"Aye, Sir!" Came the response.

"Secure that remote trigger. Jones, you have the helm. Rig for towing."

The Ensign went back to his boat. The towing line became taught. They were headed just a few hundred yards to the Coast Guard docks. Luca had sailed just past their base to the harbor.

Back on board, the officer radioed the larger vessel.

"All secure, Commander. Remote trigger identified and secure, power disconnected."

"Good work, Ensign. Proceed to dock. Secure the vessel and prisoner." The larger boat powered up and turned down river to continue patrolling. A digital communication was sent to headquarters.

They had received Katy's warnings through channels. The boats' registration numbers, names, and descriptions had been broadcast to the Navy and Coast Guard. Visual recognition files had been digitally analyzed for matches at every Naval harbor with the new VR equipment. Luca's boat had been matched moments before he read Vlad's message. The Coast Guard and Navy had been looking for him before he left the dock. He'd sailed right into them.

Chapter 56

Robert sat in his car at the fish market, just northwest of the Gangplank Marina and a half mile east of the Jefferson Memorial. As he'd driven in, he'd left the heater off and put the system on recirculate, hoping that would bring in less outside air. He knew that cars had to bring in a minimum of outside air for safety, but the possibility of sucking in radioactive dust concerned him. Now that he was parked, he could turn everything off.

He was waiting for a phone call from Grady and Katy. They should have been on the tugboat with MISTI by now. He wanted a call saying there were no dirty bombs exploding in the yacht harbor.

Robert had a rush of thoughts running through his head. Assuming that the bombs hadn't released the Cesium, what was he going to do? He thought he could get the owners he knew to leave their boats, but how was he going to evacuate the whole yacht harbor without alerting the terrorists? If the bombs hadn't been detonated, his best option seemed to be to deactivate them by pulling the power.

From where he sat, he couldn't see any of the boats in the harbor well. He had a view of a portion of the first row. There was only one sailboat in that row, and it looked too big. It seemed to have two masts. He was going to have to get out and walk closer to the boats. Checking the weather app on his phone again, he saw that the wind was holding steady, blowing almost due east. He reflected on how important that was. The White House sat less than two miles north.

Legally, was he doing the right thing? He knew the Secret Service would throw him in jail for not alerting them. They would first protect the White House, then they'd swarm this area, and the terrorists would set off the bombs for sure, sending radioactive dust downwind over the businesses, apartments, the Washington Navy Yard, and the homes beyond. The President was in no danger at the moment—in fact, he might not even be at the White House.

Robert wasn't even sure the boats were in this harbor. Frustrated, he checked his phone again. When would Grady call?

...

Grady stood in the wheelhouse of the Navy tug in his usual spot. Katy went rapidly from one station to another, giving orders. Five crew members and Bryston were on board. Another crewman was running down the long dock as mooring lines were tossed off from the concrete pylons. Timing the release of the lines was critical to keep the tug away from the pier, and to keep the barge from colliding with the tug. As the last line was released the crewman jumped onto the tug. With a little more than half her normal crew, Katy commanded the tug forward, pulling the MISTI barge south smoothly away. They executed a tight turn to head north up the Potomac.

"Bryston, are you ready?" Katy called over the intercom to the technician in his instrument room.

"Aye, Captain." Bryston was getting into the Naval moment. His civilian laid-back day job craved the excitement. His youthfulness was enjoying the reality of the situation as he pulled up scans of northeast Alexandria. The turning motion of the boat swept the angle of MISTI's sensors around clockwise, across Daingerfield Island, then Ronald Reagan Washington National Airport. The screen popped up several known markers of low-level radiation. He found the one at the end of the runway, but as they continued their turn to the north, the sweep across Bolling Airfield did not catch the known target there. He hit the intercom button.

"What do you see?" Katy answered.

"We are out of range of the marker at Bolling." Bryston kept watching his screens. The sensors faced the eastern shore now as they pulled north.

"Very well. We'll steam north for two miles and turn again. Keep me informed," Katy told him.

"Aye, Captain," Bryston responded.

"Colonel, tell Mr. Carlton that we are twelve minutes from our first reading of the harbor. We may come up short, but we'll be able to see downwind of it." Katy used Grady's rank on board. It was proper protocol and maintained command structure for the crew.

"Will do, Captain." Grady made the call to Robert.

"Grady." Robert sounded understandably tense. "What do you have?"

"We are steaming up the Potomac. The system is working, but we are out of range. It will take five minutes to get two miles closer. From there we'll turn and sweep the area. It may not be far enough to read the harbor, but we'll be able to see if something is happening downwind."

"Five minutes. Got it." Robert said worriedly.

"I'll call back when we start our turn." Grady hung up.

Robert thumbed through his text and email messages. Nothing popped up that looked critical. The phone rang in his hand. It was Lorraine.

"Yes, Lorraine," Robert said.

"Mr. Carlton, I have an urgent message from Governor Collins of the British Virgin Islands. He wants you to call him right away."

"Can you patch the call?" Robert requested.

"Yes, Sir," she answered.

Robert waited. The clock read seven-twenty.

"Mr. Carlton, I have the Governor on the line," Lorraine said formally. A few digital clicks later the line became clear.

"Robert. Edward Collins here," the Governor said. "What is this I hear about a boat in Florida carrying a Sandy Island device?"

"Governor, this is confidential information and I'm on a cell phone in my car, so I'll have to be brief. Yes, we have found one like

Sandy, attached to the keel of a sailboat in Melbourne, Florida." Robert responded carefully.

"So, the rumor of five lost devices may be true?" The Governor asked.

"Governor, please, this is not a secure line. My team is tracking down several leads and will get an official communication to you through the State Department." Robert was uncomfortable with the breach of security protocols, but he knew it would be difficult to get the Governor off the phone.

"Robert, you know that there are official channels, and then there are those persons whom you can speak with. Am I to wait, or can you assuage my concerns about a BVI danger or a regional danger?"

"Governor..." Robert started, wondering how he could handle the Governor's concerns without breaching security.

"Edward," The Governor corrected, breaking into Robert's thoughts.

"Edward, I believe we have located four of the five, and the last one is here in Maryland. If we need them, can I call on you to lend us your newly trained teams, and have their equipment flown up here to help with cleanup?" Robert decided to be as direct as possible.

"Of course, Robert. You don't have to ask," Edward responded.

"Thank you. I will be in touch, but I must hang up." Robert replied.

"Cheers." The Governor hung up.

Four minutes. He had to wait four more minutes for Katy to make her turn, and then more minutes before he would get the call from Grady. Robert fretted in his seat.

Robert ignored the warning voice in his head and got out of the car. He was amongst fishermen selling their catch to the early buyers. Crates on two-wheel dollies moved back and forth, as Robert found his way around the buildings, construction barriers, and general confusion. Eventually, he stood facing the marina. Rusted, heavy barges blocked most of his view. They sat jumbled in disarray between him and the docked yachts. Robert assumed they must carry dredging and pylon equipment, but they looked like they had been dumped there, rather than thrown in an iron smelter to recycle.

He had to get closer. With increasingly hesitant steps he walked a hundred yards to get a better view, fighting the urge to run. He constantly checked flags and streamers for wind direction. It remained steady. A few small swirls made him hold his breath.

The first row of yachts was clearly visible, but most were motor yachts. Many had their bow facing him. He could only see the name of one sailboat, and it wasn't 'Sail Away III' or 'E-Vent.' This was going to prove harder than he'd thought. He walked as far as the first gangway and looked down the line. It was hard to read the names. Between the angle, the height of the dock, and the ropes crisscrossing the sterns, he could only make out the nearer half. Again, not the ones he was looking for. With a look at the boats themselves, he realized none were the Hunter or Beneteau shapes he had seen in Savannah. Neither boat was on this row. With effort, he could see half of the next dock. Again, there were mostly power boats, he looked closely and could tell that none of the sailboats were the right type.

Now he was faced with a dilemma. Go further and risk contamination, or stay where he was and wait. Then he realized he could move downwind to the next row.

Two minutes. It was coming up on seven-thirty. He headed quickly down the first pier so he could be sure about the last sailboat. None of them were the right yachts. He started jogging back down the dock when his phone rang.

"Grady, what do you see?" He asked quickly.

"Nothing. No readings. You're good to search. Be careful, they might be there watching. We're coming in close to read the harbor." Grady heard Katy answer her phone, then give the helmsman his new heading.

"I checked out the northern most row. Nothing." Robert was saying into the phone. "I'm on my way to the second." Grady wasn't listening.

"Katy is getting an update," Grady cut in. "They found the Gozzard. They picked it up on a visual recognition system that monitors the Naval Station, Norfolk, and the Norfolk Naval Shipyard. The Coast Guard has the boat and a man in custody."

"Was it on the boat?" Robert was asking, as Grady listened in to Katy over the thrum of the tugs' diesel engines.

"The guy admitted to a detonation device. He identified it to the Coast Guard. They won't know if the irradiator is on board until they get a Geiger counter to it." Grady sounded excited. "Katy, why don't they have a tester on it already?"

Katy waved him off with a scowl, as she stayed on her phone.

"I'll have to get back to you on that, Robert," Grady told him.

"We have to assume it is, and therefore the rest are armed, as well," Robert said. "I'm going to run down the dock and look for the others here. You scan as fast as you can. They could be setting them off at any moment."

"I'll call." Grady heard the line disconnect.

Robert had ended the call and pushed the phone deep in his pocket. He was in a full run now and headed for the second dock. He was halfway down when he spotted a Hunter. It was bow in. "Damn it!" Robert thought. "I left the list of registration numbers in the car." He had to risk being seen. He ran to the back of the boat. "Sail Away III Washington, DC" was painted on its hull.

Robert's heart jumped to the top of his throat, drowning out the panting of his chest. The boat looked empty and locked. He had not thought about that. The companionway hatch was a sliding top and front panel type. Both were teak frames with dark glass inserts. The hasp and lock seemed small enough to break. Robert looked around for anyone nearby, but the other boats seemed unoccupied.

Walking toward the bow and down the other side, he looked for an open hatch or some way to get in. It was buttoned up tight. He pulled out his phone and tried to call Jeff and Chrystal again, but only got voicemail.

"Jeff, this is Robert Carlton. I have to get in your boat and disconnect the battery. You may have a serious issue on the boat. If you get this message call me, and don't go near your boat without talking to me or to the police around the harbor first." He then called Grady. "I found the Hunter. It's on the second dock. No one is here, and it's locked."

"Disconnect the battery and get out of there!" Grady was emphatic. "Katy just got off the phone with the Coast Guard again. They confirmed the irradiator is on the Gozzard. You have to get out of there!"

Robert looked around. There were people downwind, but no one on the dock where he stood. "I have to break in to get the battery disconnected." Why hadn't he brought a toolkit? Robert shoved the phone in his pocket. He could faintly hear Grady yelling on the other end, but he ignored him and went searching for something to use to break into the boat.

The large power boat in the next slip had a heavy power tool lying in the open part of the cabin. Robert climbed in and grabbed it. The angle grinder was heavy, made of metal. Jumping into the Hunter he started hammering on the lock with the grinder. This brought the owner of the motor yacht up from below decks. "Hey, what are you doing?" He called out.

Robert looked up. "I'm the United States Deputy Attorney General and we have to disconnect the battery on this boat, NOW! Help me!" He yelled.

Whatever his voice sounded like, the urgency in it worked. The man jumped out of his boat and ran to the head of the dock. He flipped open a gray box and flipped the onshore power off.

"Keep at that lock. I'll get my tools!" He jumped back on his boat as Robert kept hammering. When the man came back up with a tool box, Robert stopped hammering for a second. That's when he heard it. A small click somewhere near on deck followed by a low heavy and distinct "Thump". Robert felt it, so did the man on the other boat. It shook the water.

"Quick, we have to get to the battery!" Robert swung with all his strength, breaking the hasp screws away from the teakwood. With a shove, he pushed open the hatch, lifting the front plate away and onto the deck. He was followed down the stairs immediately by the helpful neighbor and his tools. Robert did not know where to go next, but the other guy did. In seconds the engine battery compartment was open. With a big screwdriver, the helpful stranger loosened the ground cable and pried it off. Next went the positive cable. Both lay below and to the sides of the battery. The whirring sound they had been hearing stopped.

"Get off the boat fast! Hold your breath! Get everyone off the dock!" Robert's tone demanded action as the two men sprinted from boat to boat yelling. "Get off the dock!" then ran to the shore.

"What the hell is this about?" The helper exclaimed when they arrived on land, gasping for air.

"We have to get everyone off the downwind docks and upwind of the boats. There's no time to explain fully, but this is a life-threatening emergency. We'll split up, and get people to help. Don't run out on the piers. That's downwind of the boat. Just yell, and get everyone off the docks. We'll meet up at the fish market when we're done. If you see a Beneteau sailboat named 'E-Vent,' tell me immediately. Hurry!" Robert told him anxiously.

In moments people were running in every direction, banging on boats and yelling. Robert cleared two docks, then called 911. He ran to a spot upwind where he waved his arms, indicating that everyone should come his way. Sirens could be heard approaching. He then called Ron Crest's number at the West Wing to crash the White House.

As people came up to him, Robert informed them that there was a serious, airborne danger. The shocked look on their faces at the words, "You have to stay here together," was followed quickly by people moving to leave. Robert had a hell of a time getting his helpful boat owner and the other volunteers to keep everyone in one spot. Robert avoided any words like dirty bomb or radioactive, but he had to get these people the right kind of medical attention and they all had to be kept upwind from the Hunter.

When the police arrived, one four-striped officer seemed particularly authoritative. Robert pulled him aside to explain, but became frustrated after too many minutes of repeating instructions. "Stop," he told the officer, with all the authority he could muster in his voice. "This is the situation: we have an air born contaminant. I'm going to get you an expert who will explain what needs to be done. When his people arrive they will take control, but until then, you must keep everyone in this area." Robert dialed Steve on his phone.

"Steve. I found one of the boats. The Hunter. It went off, but I disconnected the power and the fan stopped. We evacuated the docks, and we are all standing upwind. I need you to talk to the policeman in charge here and get control of this area. Officer," Robert looked at his nametag, "Police Sergeant Trask, this is Steve Mahaffey of the Nuclear Regulatory Commission. He and his people are in charge of this situation. He will explain what you need to do." Robert handed over his phone. He could see that the word "nuclear" had changed the policeman's demeanor.

It only took a few seconds for the police to get everyone moved back after Sergeant Trask talked to Steve Mahaffey. As they organized the group, gathering names and ID, they corralled everyone behind yellow police tape. Minutes later, Steve was again talking to the police sergeant, who was using his own cell, now. Robert had his phone back. There was a voice message from Grady.

Robert listened to Grady's message. They had detected the release from the Hunter. The subsequent cloud was being tracked by MISTI as it floated over the area east of the dock.

Robert called Grady. "Grady, I know it was set off. I was on the boat when it happened."

"Did you get out of there?" Grady sounded understandably concerned.

"Yes, but not until we disconnected power to the fan," Robert admitted.

"We?" Grady asked.

"I don't know his name. I need to find him. What do you see now?" Robert questioned.

"A small cloud formed at the dock, but didn't build up very much. It is now floating east on the wind, settling along the way on the buildings and ground. Bryston thinks it will only just make it to the Anacostia River, but he is not sure. It depends on the wind strength. There is still a hot spot at the docks. I'll bet the dot is right on top of that boat. I hope you're away from that," Grady added.

Robert took in the information. "So, it looks like cutting the power worked. We checked the rest of the dock for the other boat but didn't find it. Have you seen any other radiation dots?"

"None," Grady told him.

"Okay. Dispatch the two Coast Guard boats to search up the Anacostia and Potomac for the Beneteau named 'E-Vent'. There is no point in being quiet about this anymore. The bomb went off on a timer of some kind. I heard it click just before it blew. You could feel it go off even on neighboring boats."

"I'll bet. You realize if we can still see a dot where the boat is, you probably have that stuff on you. Bryston tracked a number of smaller dots all around the area. You may be one of them."

"I know." Robert was hiding his anxiety, but there was nothing he could do about having been exposed. "I'm going to have to wait here for Steve's team and get decontaminated."

"You may need more than simple decontamination." Grady knew that Robert's situation was more serious. "Oh, and Katy's Coast Guard contacts say the trigger to be used on the Gozzard was a small white box. It has a button and two dials. It has a timer."

"There is probably one on the Hunter too, I didn't see it, but that's probably what I heard. I can't go back to look now."

"Do you think you ingested any of the stuff?" Grady asked.

"I tried not to, but without protective gear, who knows? We were running and yelling. Well, what's done is done, and according to Steve, it's cumulative, so I don't want to get anymore." Robert said firmly.

"Wait a minute. There was a second bomb on the boat in Melbourne. Didn't Steve say it had its own battery?" Grady remembered the conversation.

"Only the fan runs off the boat battery," Robert was saying slowly. He looked back at the dock as the sailboat suddenly exploded, sending fiberglass, wood, and aluminum straight up into the air.

Broken into two pieces, the boat fell back to the water as a geyser shot skyward, white spray arching over in the wind. It splashed down on several boats, as pieces of metal and Plexiglas crashed on the dock and rained down over the harbor. There was so much noise that Robert didn't hear the screams of civilians trapped by the barricades. He didn't notice the police with outstretched arms trying to contain them. People broke free and ran. Some were tackled by others or the police, but many escaped. Pandemonium reigned as the shattered boat and its pieces settled and sank. Robert couldn't see where the irradiator landed.

Robert didn't know if he should run. The wind was still eastward, but gamma rays weren't affected by wind. Robert's phone rang in his ear.

"Robert! What's happening?" Grady had hung up and called back.

"The boat blew." Robert was still trying to spot the irradiator.

"I know—we can see the water and smoke from here. The radiation cloud is bigger but still going east." Grady said.

"I'll call you back. We have to get everyone further upwind." Robert hung up.

. . .

It took forever to get everyone calmed down and all the way into the fish market, upwind of the boats. The explosion had wreaked havoc. Having the blast contained in part by the water helped focus its energy upward, doing much more damage than the one in Melbourne. The boat was fully underwater, except the mast, which leaned against the dock at a steep angle.

The police had control of the crowd again. Robert stood apart with Frank since they were assumed to be contaminated.

Robert's phone rang. "Grady?" He asked automatically.

"It's Lorraine, Mr. Carlton."

"Lorraine, I'm glad you called. I need to set up a call with Secretary Vance, or Lillian Morrison from State to bring them up to speed right away."

"I'll get right on it. Conference call, I assume?" Lorraine was perceptive.

"Yes, I will not be able to leave here, so I can't meet in person. Oh, why did you call?" He suddenly asked her.

"I have Mary Whiston holding for you," Lorraine told him.

"Good. Tie us together. You need to hear this, so stay on the line." Robert waited a second for the connection to be made.

"Mr. Carlton?" Mary queried.

"Mary, you and Lorraine need to know that I am stuck here at the yacht harbor on the other side of the Jefferson Memorial. I am with one of the boats we were trying to locate. The boat contained a bomb, which armed itself, and exploded. There will be decontamination going on here from radiation that it contained. This will undoubtedly hit the news hard. I can see some news van pulling up now, and I'm relatively sure that some individuals on the scene may have captured pictures or video with their smartphones. I need to brief Vance or Morrison on how this ties into the Caribbean situation, but first I have to get several agencies up to date. Lorraine, please coordinate the call with State. Use Mary if you need to get through. Set it up for a half hour from now."

"Yes, Sir," Mary replied.

"What were you calling for, Mary?" Robert asked.

"I just wondered if you needed anything else on the yachts," she parried. Mary had actually been looking for an update. The call had turned out better than she'd hoped.

"Okay. I'll call back once I get more people in the loop. Lorraine, track down Ron Crest and get him on the phone with me. I talked with him earlier. He's at the West Wing. They've crashed the building, so you might have trouble getting through."

"Yes, Sir," Lorraine said, sounding a little shocked.

It was only moments before she had Ron on the phone to Robert. Ron listened to Robert's situation, and told him that it would be a few minutes because of the Secret Service "crash," but the Situation Room was about to come alive.

Chapter 57

Vlad's phone chimed with an incoming call. It was Mary.

"They know about the boat here in DC," she informed him.

"They have found the boat?" Vlad questioned.

"Yes. It was in the DC yacht harbor, and it exploded," she said, wondering how he would react.

Vlad felt a surge of victory course through his body. "What about the others?"

"I don't know. They must be looking for them."

Vlad was thinking quickly. Luca had been headed toward the Navy aircraft carriers. He should have contacted Vlad by now. Vlad wondered if they'd found him before he could detonate the bombs. Where was Max? If they were looking for her, she might not have time to get to her destination.

"Is there more?" He asked Mary.

"No."

"You have done well. I want you to get more information about what they know, or what they find out. There is something I must do now. Contact me in one hour or less." Vlad waited to hear Mary hang up. He sent a message to Max.

He texted, "Want update 42."

Vlad paced, waiting for her reply. Had she'd already been found? He couldn't risk an incriminating message until she answered. The more he thought, the surer he was that Luca must have been compromised. He would have to resist texting him.

His phone beeped with a text. It was from another teapot girl. "State Department on global alert."

He answered, "Good work. Keep me updated."

Max replied to Vlad's message. "On boat eta target two hours=16."

Vlad smiled. She was on the boat and had used the safe code to reply. He was clear to communicate. His follow up text was, "DC activated. Norfolk may be compromised. Proceed to target and activate. Assume your area alerted."

Max looked up from Vlad's text, checking three-hundred and sixty degrees around her. No boats or aircraft were approaching, but Vlad's warning meant she could be found at any moment. Luca had either been captured, killed, or had failed to activate the charges on his boat.

She sent, "No problem here. Will proceed." Max put the phone back in her pocket and adjusted her course, continuing to sail near the islands and up the eastern shore of the Chesapeake Bay.

She was heading north-northeast, past Hoopersville Island. Her target was the new Liquefied Natural Gas ship loading facility, built a mile offshore from the LNG compressor station. Both were located on the opposite side of the Chesapeake Bay from Max. By sailing down the opposite shore, she kept five miles of water between her and the Patuxent River Naval Air Station. She didn't need one of their resident drones practicing visual capture on her, and the village islands gave her easy cover.

With a glance through the Plexiglas, she noted her captives were still securely in place. They were dehydrated and despondent, which always equaled cooperative. It wouldn't be much longer. They only had fifteen miles to go.

Inside the sailboat cabin, Mark and Julie were worn out. Mark had given up trying to get loose. The plastic straps had dug into his wrists, cutting enough to bleed. They'd grated his skin to the point any movement hurt. Julie had slumped forward away from the hard mast to lean against her bonds and the cushioned bench back. A series of waves from a larger passing motorboat jarred the sailboat several times. Mark, sitting on the floor, hit his head on the aluminum mast. Julie was thrown backward, then forward, yanking her arms and wrists. Mark heard a ripping sound.

When Max had put on Julie's zip tie handcuffs, she had been in the forward cabin. Mark was secured to the mast with the cuffs. Julie had been added to the mast later with duct tape. Now the top edge of that tape had been ripped.

"The tape. It's ripping." Mark said to Julie.

"What tape?" Julie was having trouble concentrating.

"She taped you to the mast. It's duct tape." Mark told her. "You can tear it completely if you yank on it hard."

Julie's adrenaline surged from the urgency in Mark's voice. She leaned her arms at an angle to feel the tape edge. She jerked and tugged at the tape. Nothing. Lining up again she pulled viciously at the bonds and heard a small rip.

"Harder," Mark pushed.

Julie's next tug was filled with desperation. Her shoulders snapped back as the tape tore further. Pain shot through her arms.

"Ahhh! Shit!" Julie lurched back in pain, then went quiet. They both looked up through the Plexiglas hatch. Max had not heard her. She was looking at something off the port side.

The tape still held. Julie inhaled deeply, and heaved forward, ripping the tape completely, and falling face first into the back of the bench. The cushions softened the blow to her face, but her head bent backward, twisting her neck as she fell to her side.

Her legs were still taped, and the handcuffs held her hands behind her back, but she was quickly up and hopping. She lost her footing and fell against the galley drawer where she had hoped to get a knife.

The hatch slammed open. Max stood glaring at the top of the steps, then came rushing down. She grabbed Julie by the hair.

"Don't touch her!" Mark yelled uselessly. Max snatched the duct tape from the galley counter, and dragged Julie, stumbling, up the stairs.

"I have something for you to do," Max told Julie.

"Julie!" Mark yelled, tugging vainly at his restraints.

Max pulled Julie across the top of the boat to the mast.

"Sit." She commanded. Julie didn't have much choice. Max pushed her down hard on the fiberglass. A cleat on the mast hit her shoulder as Max started to wrap tape around her wrists and the mast. It was difficult, so she made several wraps around Julie's waist at the belt. Julie's hands became trapped in the middle.

"That should hold you," Max said.

Max returned to the helm. Turning the boat she headed across the bay to a point of land. The land jutted out from shore about a mile from the LNG pier.

. . .

Robert stood with Frank Yoder apart from the police corralled crowd. Frank had helped Robert break into the Hunter, and both of them were dusted with radioactive Cesium. They didn't know how much, but they would be first in the decontamination tent being set up by the NRC team.

The crowd inside the makeshift corral of police tape and construction equipment were tense. The earlier panic had eased, but the violence of the explosion left nerves frayed and tempers short. Two policemen who had made physical contact with potentially contaminated bystanders were inside the corral.

Steve Mahaffey had directed the police sergeant through the setup and procedures. Now several of the NRC team had arrived and were in charge. The rules were being strictly enforced. The appearance of the protectively clothed technicians and the radiation warning signs they posted were intimidating.

Frank was amazingly calm, particularly for someone who may have just had serious radiation exposure. Robert was envisioning a federal lawsuit, naming him, for getting Frank involved. Robert might have an out with the good Samaritan law, but it could get ugly.

Robert spent his time on calls to Vance, Morrison, Mary, Lorraine, Grady, and the Caribbean Governors until his battery level was too low to risk more.

"So," Frank spoke when Robert put his phone in his pocket. "You're the Attorney General."

Robert's already tight stomach stiffened a notch more. "Deputy Attorney General."

"I didn't know you guys were so hands on. I thought it was more a bureaucratic job."

"So did I." Robert had to smile at that.

His phone rang. "Excuse me. I probably need to answer this. Robert Carlton," he said. The caller ID showed a number with no name.

"Robert? This is Jeff. Chrystal is here, too. What is happening on our boat?"

"It's a long story, Jeff, but first I need to know, are Mark and Julie visiting here in DC?"

"Yes, they are here," Jeff answered.

"You're sure they're here? They haven't left?" Robert asked quickly.

"I'm sure." Jeff wanted to know what was going on with his boat. "Why did you call about our boat? What's going on?"

Robert had his own priorities. "I'll get to that. I need to know where Mark and Julie are now."

"They're staying on their boat. They should be there now, unless... "

"Which dock?" Robert interrupted.

"Four docks down from ours; last slip on the left."

Robert stretched to see down the harbor, but the fish market buildings were in the way. "I can't see it from here, but I don't think they are there. Are you positive they haven't left?" Robert grilled Jeff.

"They were tied up next to a big motor yacht with a pink roof and a pink ribbon flag," Jeff told him patiently.

"Hang on." Robert got the attention of a suited NRC tech. After explaining the situation to him, Robert asked the tech to go look. He returned shortly, saying the boat was not there.

"Their boat's not there," Robert told Jeff.

Jeff was really starting to wonder about Robert. "What's this about?" He demanded.

"There was a bomb built into the keel of your boat. There could be one on Mark and Julie's boat," Robert apprised him.

"Jeezus!" Jeff replied. "There was a bomb on our boat?" Jeff started talking to Chrystal.

"Jeff," Robert called. "Jeff!"

"Yes? I can't believe this! Our boat had a bomb in it?" Jeff seemed single-mindedly obsessed by their own boat.

"Jeff! Stop for a second. I need to reach Mark and Julie. They are not answering their phone. We absolutely *must* find them, immediately. Do you know how we can reach them? If they left, what route would they take? Where might they stop? Can you think of anything to help us find them?"

"Sure," Jeff said, not surprisingly. "I have their cell number."

"Tried it. No answer." Robert repeated shortly.

"We have access to their route map progress chart."

"Their what?" Robert said, puzzled.

"We shared accounts on our route trackers. It's an Internet app that follows your cell phone and shows where you have been on a map. There are lots of these services now. It's a lot of..."

"Jeff. Look, I don't have much battery left. Can you tell me where they are now?" Robert looked at this phone. It was below ten percent. "Shit."

Frank was standing nearby and had been listening. He pulled his phone from his pocket and pulled up his number. "Tell him to call this number in case you go dead."

"Thanks—again," Robert told him. He got Jeff's attention, giving him the number, while Chrystal pulled up their route track on her laptop.

"They're near Barren Island on the Chesapeake Bay, headed north," Jeff told him.

Robert was repeating the words, trying to remember them.

"That's thirty-eight thirty-four north, and seventy-six twenty-seven west," Jeff was saying.

Robert repeated the numbers out loud. "Jeff, keep that map open and stay by the phone. We may need your help." He hung up. His phone was down to eight percent. He looked at Frank. "Can I borrow your phone?"

"Sure." Frank handed it to him.

"Thanks." Robert first dialed Grady on his own phone.

"Robert, I..." Grady began.

"No time. I'm going to call you from another phone." Robert hung up and dialed his number from Frank's cell.

"Robert?" Grady asked.

"Yes. I had to borrow a phone. Mine ran out of juice. Listen, Mark and Julie left this harbor, and we know where they are. I can't leave here. They're going to decontaminate me in a few minutes. I need you to get to them, and get them off the boat. Write this down. The boat is at..." Robert was suddenly drawing a blank.

Frank leaned over next to Robert and the phone, repeating, "Thirty-eight thirty-four north, seventy-six twenty-seven west. That's over by Hoopersville on the Chesapeake Bay. North of there a little."

"Did you get that, Grady?" Robert asked.

"Thirty-eight thirty-four north, and seventy-six twenty-seven west, Chesapeake Bay, north of Hoopersville," Grady echoed. "Got it."

"Right." Robert felt some relief. "I don't know how, but you have to get them off that boat before the bomb goes off. Disconnecting the battery is not enough. You have to get them off. Can you and Katy figure something out?"

"We've got it." Katy had been listening in. She'd already plotted the latitude and longitude on a map.

Grady added, "Katy already has it on a map. I'll call this number when we have a plan." Grady hung up.

Robert also hung up and offered the phone back to Frank. "Thanks."

"Hang on to it. I think you may need it, and I'm guessing we'll be here a while." Frank had a pleasant smile.

"I appreciate that." Robert really did. "How did you remember those coordinates so easily?"

"I've been sailing a long time. It has become kind of a second language."

. . .

On the tugboat, Grady and Katy were going through options.

"It's a hundred and forty nautical miles. At our top speed of fourteen knots, that's too far for us to get there as quickly as we need to." Katy had the map out on the chart table. "The speed of that sailboat, even with the engine running, must be less than ten knots. Probably more like eight." She pulled out a metal drawing compass and made four wax pen circles on the map, centered on the boat's location. Each circle represented one hour. She pointed to each circle, starting in the middle. "One, two, three, and four hour ranges. You said they were headed north. Norfolk and the Navy yard are about ten hours south, so it doesn't look as though they intend to go there."

"Where could they be going?" Grady asked her.

"Annapolis is here," Katy pointed far north, "and Baltimore over here." Katy pointed to the left top of the Chesapeake Bay. "Either could be a target."

"What's this pink rectangle?" Grady was pointing to a spot more or less in the center of the Bay, and at the edge of the two-hour circle.

"That marks a one-hundred and five-hundred-yard navigation boundary. The same as around the Navy docks in Norfolk." She pulled up an electronic version of the area and zoomed in. "Looks like that area houses the Cove Point LNG terminal for offshore natural gas shipping."

"So, pink is, 'don't go there,' and that sailboat is only two hours away from that spot." Grady looked up at Katy, but she was already moving.

She grabbed a phone on the side of the chart table. "Get me the Coast Guard dispatch. We need a boat near Patuxent River NAS."

"Aye, Captain," came the response. Putting back the phone, Katy picked up her binoculars and looked toward the shore of the Bolling Anacostia helicopter facility. There were three choppers there—two Marine and one Navy. The Navy helicopter had a flight crew milling around it. Picking up the phone again, she called her communications operator.

"Connect me with chopper operations at Anacostia. Grady, you and the Chief go down to the barge. Get hooked up with safety gear and transfer over to the barge. Climb up on the far MISTI container. I'm going to get you a ride out there. Wait—what's that new number for Robert?"

Grady gave her the number for the cell phone Robert was borrowing and left the bridge. The Chief met him on the fantail with a safety line and life jacket in his hands. When Grady was tied on and ready, the tug slowed down. The barge edged forward until it bumped. Grady hopped over. Once securely there, the Chief tossed him the safety line. He tied himself to the top of the container while he waited for the gray Seahawk SH-60 helicopter. He could see it lifting off from the nearby shore.

Katy was on a three-way call with Anacostia operations and Robert, who'd dropped the President and an Admiral's name to get the helicopter moving. The chopper had been on its way to Norfolk, but that trip was now over-ridden.

"Robert," Katy was saying, "Grady and I think the boat is headed for the Point Cove LNG facility. If that were to explode..."

"We'd have big problems," Robert finished. He knew what Liquified Natural Gas could do. New pipelines proposed in Maryland and Virginia had been hotly debated for years, partly due to the huge risks to public safety.

"Get Grady on that helicopter, Katy." Robert insisted. "I'll get the approvals. Stay on the line. I may need to tie you in." Robert called the situation room.

"The Admiral has just entered the room, Mr. Carlton," he was told. About time, Robert thought.

"Mr. Carlton. Admiral Strand here." Robert heard.

"Admiral, a bomb in a sailboat is headed for the Point Cove LNG facility. I need to get Col. Barlow on a Navy chopper out there fast to disarm the bomb."

"What is the situation?" The Admiral asked quickly.

Robert explained as fast as he could, with emphasis on the lack of other resources that could respond in time. The Admiral didn't hesitate.

"Do you have the air operations commander on the line?" The Admiral asked.

Robert clicked the join button, and Katy was tied in. "Captain Davies," he asked, "do you have Air Ops on the line?"

"I do. Captain Daniels, are you listening?" She questioned.

"I am," came the response.

"Captain, this is Admiral Strand." The Admiral took over. "Can you airlift Colonel Barlow immediately, and get him to the LNG location?"

"Affirmative, Sir." The Captain confirmed. "We are on final approach to pick him up now."

"Outstanding. Get it done on my orders, and we'll catch up on paperwork later," the Admiral told him. There were some rapid exchanges of information, and statements of military protocol. Robert could hear the discussion of further resource locations, and arrival times.

The Admiral had resources coming to life. They would soon be converging on the site from all directions, but Robert wondered if they'd get there in time to stop the bomb from exploding.

While Robert, Katy, and the Admiral fired up the entire mid-Atlantic emergency response network, the pilots were lining up for a mid-water pickup. A successful pickup would save at least a half hour, maybe more, compared to racing the tug to the dock.

Grady looked up as the Seahawk slowly dropped down toward the barge. Katy had the tug set at a consistent four knots, straight into the wind. The effect flattened out the ride to an almost motionless feeling, but it also headed them straight at the bridge crossing the Potomac. The tug and barge could fit under it, but Grady had to be off before they got there.

Grady had no time to think about the danger of the situation. He had to get on that chopper.

The wind from the helicopter blades blew Grady's hat off, as the chopper dropped in fifty feet above him. At the end of the line was a horse collar which Grady pulled toward himself, sticking his arms through it. He dropped his arms down to lock into the harness. The Chief on the tug signaled thumbs up, and the Seahawk lifted slowly up.

Grady suddenly remembered to release the safety line, dropping it down to the barge as he was lifted up into the air. The wench started pulling him up to the flight deck.

Robert had seen the helicopter flying from where he stood at the Gangplank Yacht Club. Along with everyone else, he watched Grady rise above the trees of the golf course to the chopper.

"Yes, Admiral," Robert relayed, "he is being lifted on board now. I can see him from my location." Robert was still on the three-way call, as the Flight Ops commander at Anacostia provided updates on flight time.

Chapter 58

"Thanks. I think you probably are aware of how much I appreciate your loan of this," Robert said, handing Frank's phone back to him.

Frank held his phone like an award statue. "I may have it bronzed." He was genuinely thrilled and having the time of his life—despite the radiation exposure.

Robert was pulled away to be priority-processed in the decontamination tent. Frank would go next.

Knowing that the radiation was Cesium-137 helped target the testing and treatment. The technicians checked to make sure there wasn't anything else, but the process was quicker once they'd verified the Cesium.

Robert's clothes were removed carefully to minimize spreading more radiation and bagged. He had, in fact, been exposed to the Cesium salt powder, so he was living proof that the bomb design worked. The technicians gave him something to make him throw up. Standing naked in the tent, he underwent every kind of washing imaginable. Every orifice was lavaged with cleaning and rinsing fluids. It was an unpleasant experience, but because Robert needed them to work fast, he said nothing throughout the process. He was glad to find scrubbing was no longer recommended—at least not for this exposure.

Robert had to get to the West Wing, so they allowed him one concession. He was to check himself into Walter Reed Army Medical Center for further treatment as soon as he was done at the White House—and in less than four hours. No one else would be given that leeway. Others, like Frank, were to be treated immediately at local hospitals that had the required training and treatments. They would be taken there, and not given an option.

His identification and car keys were given back to him in a clear bag. His phone and wallet had been confiscated. He would get them back if they could be cleaned of the radiation. Robert had tried to talk them into cleaning the phone on the spot, but they said that they couldn't get it clean enough, plus the solvent would ruin the speakers. He'd been given a government issued NRC blue jumpsuit to wear. The worst part of his new outfit were the slippers.

. . .

Robert sat in the Situation Room again. Coming through security his outfit raised eyebrows. He'd been cleared quickly since he had nothing to bring in except the baggy of ID cards, and a set of very clean keys. Both his house and car remotes had been cleaned in some spray can solvent and passed testing, but the plastic had been dulled.

This time he sat almost alone in the room. The Admiral was there, still driving resources toward the Patuxent Naval Air Station to support Grady, and ignoring Robert. The ever-present aide was focused solely on the Admiral.

Robert was distracted. The extreme stress was catching up to him as he looked down at his feet. He had never appreciated his shoes as much as he should have. After walking through the West Wing in slippers, he wished he had anything resembling a real shoe.

The Aide pulled up the situation map on the central monitor. The map of Maryland showed a red line that tracked from the yacht harbor to the Chesapeake Bay. It was the track for Grady's chopper, labeled Navy 1136. The helicopter was almost at the GPS location for the sailboat. Another red line came down from New Jersey. It had a USCG label. A blue, Navy labeled line was short, running along the Potomac. That was the tugboat and MISTI barge. A dozen more tracks and dots from around the area showed up in gray. There was a close-up map, centered on the Point Cove LNG platform and the Chesapeake Bay. Another monitor held a map of the DC harbor area, with a pink oval that indicated the radioactive contamination. It covered less than a square mile but was creeping slowly toward a residential area.

Robert was coming out of his distraction. "Can you get me connected to Lieutenant Davies, the Captain on the YTB-837 tugboat?" He requested.

"Yes, Sir." The aide responded. He tapped a touchscreen. Soon Robert heard ringing on the table speakerphone. The Admiral was talking on another line.

"USS Monacan, Captain Davies here," Katy answered.

"Captain, this is Robert Carlton in the Situation Room. Has the Coast Guard responded to the situation at Cove Point?"

"Yes, Sir. They have two vessels converging on the area. The ETA of the nearest one is two and a half hours. All of their units were out on calls. They have assigned our situation top priority. They also have a rescue helo on its way." Katy reported.

"Thank you, Captain. We are monitoring the situation and will keep you apprised." Robert knew that Katy would be worried about Grady, but the military leadership role left no room for it to show. He nodded to the aide who ended the call.

The Secretary of Defense Bill Trask and more generals suddenly flooded into the room. Conversation picked up, and Robert found himself the center of the discussion. It only lasted about five minutes before the President arrived.

"Ten-Hut!" The call from the sentry brought the room to their feet. The President strode in with Ron Crest right behind him.

"Let's get started," the President stated. He sat and everyone quickly followed. The President looked around the room and noticed Robert's attire. "Robert, you look ridiculous. I've heard of working in fuzzy slippers, but really! How many people got the decontamination treatment where you were?"

"The initial group counted about eighty, Sir," Robert answered. "There will be more as they sweep the affected area. The police estimate two-thousand are in the zone."

"How bad is it?" The President asked.

"The technicians believed that if I am the worst case, which should be the situation, then the radioactive contamination will prove to be medium or light. That means that no one exposed should have x-rays, MRIs, or CT scans for a year, except in case of emergency. No one is expected to die or have radiation poisoning symptoms, but more testing will be needed to estimate the rate of inhalation and cancer risks."

Those in the room were rapidly beginning to look at Robert with a higher level of respect. Robert had not realized there was a touch of heroism, even glamor, in getting hit by a dirty bomb.

"What kind of treatment?" President Baxter was actually interested, which surprised Robert.

"Prussian Blue," Robert replied.

"Not iodide pills?" The President seemed surprised.

"The source I was exposed to was Cesium-137. It had no measurable radioactive Iodine," Robert explained.

"I'll bet you can run down all the whys and wherefores that go with that, but let's save that for later, over a drink—when you're allowed to have one. Let's get to what is going on now, so you can go get the rest of your tests and treatment." President Baxter settled into his chair as everyone listened to Robert bring them up to speed on the day's events and some of what led up to it. All the while, the map showed Grady's chopper getting closer to the LNG, so Robert moved to the current situation rapidly.

"As you can see on the center monitor, we have Lieutenant Colonel Barlow in a Navy Seahawk headed toward the remaining target sailboat in the Chesapeake Bay. From the northeast, a Coast Guard HH-65 Dolphin helicopter is coming down from the Atlantic City Airport, where the USCG have their air base for the region. It will arrive in about forty minutes, according to the pilot. For reference, the flight for Colonel Barlow was about fifty miles. For the Coast Guard chopper, it's a hundred and twenty. This is why it was important to grab the Anacostia chopper, which was ready to lift off, and put Barlow on it—with the Admiral's permission." Robert nodded toward the Admiral and got a nod in response.

"Do we have a link with the Navy chopper?" Robert asked the aide.

"Yes, Sir." She connected the transmission to the table center speaker.

"Colonel Barlow, this is Robert Carlton in the Situation Room, can you hear me?" Robert asked.

"I read you." Grady's voice was clear despite the wind noise. "The copilot has tied you into our communication link. We are approaching the area now."

"Okay. We are listening." Robert and the rest of the Situation Room fell silent, waiting.

Robert stood up to approach the center monitor. "We were able to locate this last boat using the owners' cell phone tracking application. From that information, Colonel Barlow and Naval Lieutenant Katherine Davies determined the most likely terrorist target would be the Liquefied Natural Gas facility, or it's remote ship loading platform, located here." Robert pointed to the map on the monitor. There they could see the long north-south offshore platform, sitting about a mile offshore from a large facility of onshore white storage tanks.

"Do you have a live shot of the area, yet?" Robert asked the aide.

"No, Sir. We should when the helicopter gets within range."

Robert continued. "We also believe that one, or both of the boat owners are being held hostage on the yacht."

Robert went on to explain how they had come to their conclusions, and the actions they had taken. Robert was surprised and relieved that no one voiced any issues with the decisions made, or about what had been done. They just listened as he walked them through the information.

. . .

Riding in the Seahawk was a first for Grady. He had been on joy rides in Hueys before, which were wider inside. The Seahawk had much more comfortable seats. It held a crew of three, so with just him as a passenger, there was room to spread out—or fall out, as he soon realized, when the crewman slid back the side doors. Up until then, it had been warm inside.

Grady had been riding in the rear seat, facing forward. The opening of the door had given him a blast of cold air. Running at two-thousand feet, the air and wind chill were no joke. Grady was glad to have the warm coat and helmet the Sergeant had provided.

"Based on the coordinates you provided, Sir, the boat should be coming up on our eleven." The pilot told him over the comm system. Grady's microphone, headphones and face shield were all built into the helmet they'd loaned him. It didn't fit like his F-16 helmet and had no oxygen mask, so if felt a bit sloppy and awkward. If he hadn't been used to helmets, this would have felt claustrophobic, and heavy.

The Sergeant had been sitting on the floor with his feet out the door, watching for the sailboat.

"Got her! Ten-thirty, about three-ten degrees." The Sergeant called out.

Grady spotted the yacht a minute later. The boat was close to shore—about a hundred yards from a large point of land jutting out from the west side of the Bay, south of a gigantic pier. The pier held the LNG filling station and stood out in the middle of the open water. The boat had just turned and was pointed toward the pier.

On the Beneteau, Max had been approaching the shore when she spotted the helicopter in the distance. She had been looking for patrol boats, but the faint sound of a chopper drew her attention up. Time had run out.

Pulling the timer from her pocket, she judged the distance to the point of land, then the pier. She set the first dial to zero and the second to zero-point-two. She peeled off the tape backing and stuck it to the deck. With a quick look toward the chopper and a scan of the water around her, she made her decision.

Max moved up the deck to Julie, sitting by the mast. "You're the bait." Max tore Julie's blouse apart exposing her dark bra and contrasting light tan skin. With a pull, she had the blouse down behind both shoulders. "They'll see you for sure, now."

Running back to the helm, she turned the boat, setting the autopilot to the new compass heading. Then she adjusted the sails. She had been running the engine at full speed but pushed the throttle again to make sure it had as much momentum as possible. Picking up her shoes from the bench, she tied them together, running the laces through her pants belt loop.

Max made a last check of the autopilot and hit the button on the white remote box. The shaped charge down in the keel went off immediately, shaking the boat from the bottom up. She didn't look up at the top of the mast, but instead turned and jumped off the boat. As soon as she surfaced, she looked back. There was the slightest puff of white smoke coming from the mast. The smoke headed forward slightly faster than the boat. With less than a mile to the pier, the boat could reach it in ten minutes. Max turned away and began swimming toward the shore.

"Man overboard!" The Sergeant announced.

"Roger that, man overboard," came the response.

As the chopper descended, the crewman pulled a life vest from under the seat next to him. It was only moments before they were hovering above Max. She stopped for long enough to wave and then point emphatically to the sailboat. It was impossible to make out her face or even her gender in the spray created by the wind blast beneath the helicopter. It was clear however that she wanted them to go to the boat.

"Sergeant, deploy a life vest." The pilot ordered.

The crewman's accuracy was excellent. Even with all the wind, he landed the uninflated vest ten feet in front of Max. She waved, and swam toward it easily, grabbing it, and waving again.

"I can see someone on the sailboat!" Grady pointed forward.

They could all see Julie, sitting up against the mast.

"Head for the sailboat," Grady ordered. "She must be in some kind of trouble." Grady saw two problems, the bomb on the boat heading toward a natural gas pipeline, and an injured person on the boat. "Can you get me on that boat?"

"Sir, I can't lower you onto that boat. It does not fit our operating parameters," the pilot responded.

As soon as the chopper moved forward, Max let go of the life vest and resumed swimming to shore. It was a short distance; barely farther than the length of a swimming pool. She would be on land in minutes.

Back in the Situation Room, everyone had been listening to the communications with the mute button on.

Robert turned to the Admiral. "Admiral, we need to get Colonel Barlow on that yacht."

"I'm with you on this, Mr. Carlton. Commander, switch on your camera uplinks. Mr. Carlton, you should be aware that this is a dangerous maneuver even when everyone involved is fully trained, and lowered onto a smooth, still surface. A sailboat is surrounded with thin wire used for guy-wires and safety railings. It's easy to get tangled up. And there may be a strong static charge built up on the helo blades—strong enough to knock someone out, or worse. Drowning and injury are real possibilities." The Admiral switched his attention to the speaker box and tapped the talk button.

"Commander, this is Admiral Strand. Is your crewman surface-swimmer qualified?"

The pilot replied. "Negative, Sir. The flight crew is SAR certified, but we do not have a swimmer onboard."

"We should wait for the Coast Guard helo." The Admiral stated to Robert.

Robert looked him in the eye. The talk button was still on. "One of the civilians is in the water, and one is on the boat. The one on the boat must be in trouble. The boat is likely armed, like the other two have been. If it goes off with her on it, she'll be blown up. If Colonel Barlow can't get to that yacht in time, it'll hit the LNG."

No one spoke. Two monitors flickered on. One showed the straight forward view, and the other a wide-angle, forward and down. They could make out the boat and a woman sitting by the mast. In the distance, they could see a large ship tied up to the LNG pumping platform.

Robert turned to President Baxter. "Mr. President, the pilot says the crew is Search and Rescue certified. If the boat hits the pier and explodes, the natural gas explosion will be devastating, and the radiation will contaminate the entire area. That ship must be full or loading. There is no time to get the gas shut off, everyone out of the area, and pressure in the lines reduced. There's a chance Barlow can turn the yacht. The other Coast Guard chopper is too far away."

President Baxter didn't waste time. "Ron, get that LNG facility shut down and evacuated." Ron grabbed the phone as did two others.

Robert knew this was make or break time. "Barlow can handle this, Sir. If we don't try, people will die."

The President looked toward the Admiral. "Any options?"

The Admiral talked to the speaker phone. "Commander, this is Admiral Strand. How long before the sailboat reaches the pier?"

"Five or six minutes, Sir."

"Can your prop wash stop its progress?"

The co-pilot had observed engine propeller action behind the sailboat. "The engine on the boat is operating, Sir. We may be able to delay its progress, but how long is uncertain. Our chopper could knock the boat around, but the straight course indicates an autopilot."

"Admiral, tell the pilot to get Barlow down there." President Baxter ordered.

"Lower Colonel Barlow to the boat." The Admiral ordered.

"Aye, Sir. We are proceeding with the lowering," the pilot responded.

The crewman had already put Grady in the harness and attached him to the lowering cable. "Okay, I think I've got it. I need to make sure this tail hits some of the metal before I do," Grady repeated the directions.

"Affirmative, Sir. Not just a bump, but a real solid connection to dissipate the static." The Sergeant verified.

Grady was familiar with the static charge a plane or helicopter could accumulate while flying. It was a dry day, so that would help, but over the water it was always a little humid.

The pilot came in high, nearly the full length of the cable to minimize the prop wash effect on the sails. The boat still reacted harshly when the blast hit it from the side opposite the natural wind.

"We'll have to stay on the upwind side of the boat, then slide you over in the lowered position." The pilot said over the comm.

"How about doing it from the downwind side? Wouldn't the boat flop over when your chopper creates the stronger wind? In the meantime, it might slow down a little." Grady offered.

"Have it your way. If it looks bad, I'll switch sides and try a second approach." The pilot had no experience with a sailboat drop, much less one moving under sail.

With his feet out the door, Grady looked up at the winch, and then down to the hook on his harness. It looked small, and the cable looked thin. As he slid out, his feet fell into the open air.

The ride down was fast and smooth. The pilot could not see Grady and took his bearings from the Sergeant. A hundred feet below, the sailboat was struggling with the artificial wind. Off to the side, the helicopter blasted the sails, but inconsistently, making the boat flop back and forth. Once Grady was all the way down, the pilot began to sideslip toward the boat without changing altitude. It was a good thing waves were not a factor on the water surface. Normally, any operation like this would require that the sails be down. They didn't have any options today. The closer they got, the more the sails were pushed over. The boat struggled to stay on course. If the wind switched sides of the boat before Grady touched down, the mast could change sides wildly. That could be deadly for Grady.

The pilot had an idea. "Sergeant. Can you get him to five feet above the deck? I want to swing him into the mainsail."

"Aye, Sir. Can do." The Sergeant pulled up a couple feet, judging the distance visually. "Ready, Sir."

Grady, watching the boat fight the wind had become keenly aware of how many stainless-steel wires and aluminum poles covered the boat. It looked like a spider web, ready to tangle up his arms and legs. What had seemed like a stable boat from hundreds of feet above, now looked like a cork in a hurricane. He was regretting this decision. He thought maybe falling in the water in front of the yacht would be better. Then he could grab the boat as it sailed by. That idea was quickly tossed aside when he got closer and saw how high the rails were from the water surface. It would never work.

It looked impossible, but Grady could see Julie's face as she screamed for help. The yacht was too close to the LNG platform. He had to try.

On the shore, Max stood mesmerized, watching the show. The chopper seemed impossibly close to the top of the boat's mast, as it swung back and forth. The man hanging from the wire looked like a ball waiting to be hit by a bat. She wanted to stay and watch, but loitering on the beach was asking to get caught. She turned and headed deep into the woods. She was west of the Cove Point Light Station, and north of several houses. The woods were small and bound on the far side by marshes. It was time to escape, and that meant stealing a car, fast. She bolted away from the shore.

Hanging from the wire, Grady watched the boat. He understood what Navy guys meant when they said aircraft carriers looked like postage stamps during landings. He didn't know the pilot's new plan, but he had a feeling he was making his final approach. It was too fast. Grady prepared to hit hard.

Flump! Grady's body landed flat against the vertical mainsail and started sliding down. "Genius!" He thought. The sail cushioned the impact, held the boat more stable, and as he was lowered, he slid to the deck in almost a controlled manner.

The cable tail slid across the bare metal boom. When Grady's left foot landed on the cabin roof it felt great. Then his right foot kept falling. With frantic hands, Grady tried to hold onto something. That didn't work. Neither the smooth fabric or large round boom offered a handhold. With a series of thumps, crunches, and umpfs, Grady came to a hard-bouncing stop on the fiberglass. Both shoulders, his back, and one knee hit something hard. Grady lay in a heap on the cockpit floor. He gripped the hook and released it, tossing it far to the side of the boat. The helicopter pulled it rapidly away.

Without the wind blasting it, the boat stabilized. Grady got up on his knees. Through the dark Plexiglas door, he recognized Mark staring at him, bound to the mast. Standing up, he made eye contact with Julie. She looked like she was in shock.

Grady yanked his helmet off and rushed forward. He pulled an emergency knife from his life vest and hacked at the tape and plastic bonds. "We have to get you off this boat. There is a bomb onboard. I'll get Mark. Can you turn the boat away from the platform?"

Julie looked forward seeing the massive off-shore concrete and steel platform rising up in front of them. Behind it was a black wall of a towering ship. It was impossibly close. Feeling Grady snap the bonds around her ankles she rushed aft to the steering. "Get Mark!" She yelled.

Grady ran down the stairs. Seeing the bonds on Mark he lunged forward with the knife and got to work.

"Julie's turning the boat away from a natural gas loading platform," He told Mark while he worked. "There's a bomb onboard your boat. We need to get the yacht turned and you off it before it explodes."

Mark had his eyes on Julie up at the wheel. "Scissors in the drawer might work better." He told Grady.

The boat lurched and heeled far over to the port side, sending Grady crashing into the cabinets. Julie had shut off the autopilot, turning the wheel as far as she could.

Grady scrambled to get up. "I've almost got it." He told Mark as he sawed through the nylon tie.

"We felt something. It shook the boat." Mark said as he tried to stand up but failed. Grady attacked the ankle strap.

"There are two bombs. The second one is much bigger." Grady lifted Mark, who gained his feet. They both ran up on deck. The platform loomed overhead. Julie had turned the boat, but they were already beyond the turning point in the corner of pylons. The mast was almost touching the upper concrete walk and the wind was pushing the boat sideways.

With the motor already at maximum, Mark jumped past Grady and released the mainsail. The sudden loss of wind pressure made the boat flop to one side then back. Grady held on as the jib foresail, still full of wind from the side, pulled the boat by the bow back even closer to the platform. Mark grabbed for the sheet and released the jib. The boat came suddenly upright sending them all grabbing for a handhold. The mast moved away from the concrete several feet, but the wind continued to blow into the side of the boat. The upper guy wire of the mast snagged onto the iron safety railing of the platform, thirty feet above them.

The boat lurched to a halt. All three of them fell forward onto the boat deck. Grady, now flat on his back, scrambled back up.

"Jump! We have to get off the boat." He yelled. Julie didn't hesitate, diving head first off the boat. Mark looked up again at the snagged mast.

"Jump!" Grady yelled again.

Mark grabbed the life ring as he and Grady left the boat and landed in the water.

When Grady's head came up to the surface he yelled "Swim! Upwind!"

The three of them swam as hard as they could. Grady's continued prompting kept them moving. The life ring had a tether that Mark was able to hang onto and still swim. Grady's harness incorporated inflatable straps, but the extra gear was taking its toll.

"You okay?" Julie called to both men. She was easily outdistancing both of them.

They caught up with her as she tread water. Grady wanted to inflate his straps, but it would make swimming harder. Mark pulled the life ring up so they could hold on to it.

"I think we are far enough away." Grady was catching his breath again. "But the farther, the better."

They could hear a Coast Guard boat nearing. On the platform, workers were moving away from the tangled sailboat to the far end of the long filling dock.

The timer on the boat ticked one last time and the second charge exploded. The sound was deep and throaty, like a depth charge. Water shot upward higher than the fifty-foot mast. The center of the boat broke like a thunderclap. The center came out of the water first, the stern and bow pointing downward. The mast bent and folded up into the concrete above it.

The shockwave hit the swimmers, coming through the water as much as it did the air. They were pushed backward. Parts of the boat came flying at them. Grady was the last to duck under the water, getting nicked by a window from the cabin that hit the surface and sank into the back of his neck. The aluminum edge was jagged from the blast and cut into his neck and shoulder. It wasn't deep, but the sting of brackish water and shock of getting hit had him testing for blood with his hand.

"Are you hurt?" Julie asked.

"I don't know," Grady said, spinning in the water for her to look.

"It's not that bad," she told him.

"Keep swimming!" Mark called out, getting their attention. He pointed up at the platform. The boat was split in two and sinking. Above it, the concrete and steel were broken. Under its own weight, the platform was buckling, and the white twelve-inch natural gas pipes were bending down.

The increasing angle finally burst the pipes. Cold liquid, almost bright silver in the light rushed out, hitting the water. It instantly turned into an expanding frosty white cloud of ice, water vapor, and gas as it rose above the minimum minus two-hundred and sixty degrees liquefaction point.

They couldn't out swim the cloud, as it expanded in all directions. Back in the Situation Room, the helicopter video feed showed workers racing along the platform and the deck of the ship to escape. The cloud kept expanding and rising until a spark ignited it. A deep red to orange glow from inside the cloud turned gray, rushing toward the outer edges and changing to bright incandescent yellow before erupting. The blast knocked the helicopter away, the camera view careening upward and then around in a circle.

Robert involuntarily stood up at the sight.

On the water, Julie, Mark, and Grady dove as deep as they could and stayed down as long as their lungs could hold. They could see the yellow flames roaring above, endlessly supplied with fuel. The heat made the natural gas rise faster, and turned the flames upward into a mushroom cloud, glowing yellow on the water, and smoking black at the top. The supply of fuel continued pouring out of the pipes and the mushroom grew wider and taller, dwarfing the ship.

Coming to a clear spot on the surface gasping for air, the three swimmers found it hot; so hot they could not catch their breaths. They swam as fast upwind as they could, but the heat was sucking the air away.

In moments, an inflatable Coast Guard boat reached them. Blasting waves of flame pushed oven broiler temperatures at them. The men on the boat had trouble standing up against it.

"Grab the ropes!" One of them yelled.

The sides of the rubber boat were crisscrossed with rope. The three found hand holds there and hung on while the boat turned away from the flames and motored quickly away.

"Hang on!" There were sailors holding their wrists as Julie, Mark and Grady clung to the speeding boat. The flames from the burst pipe expanded as a second pipe failed and another mushroom cloud rose into the air with an earsplitting explosion.

The heat was enough to sear flesh without touching the flames. All of them felt the effect. Mark had one eyebrow half gone. The three benefited from being wet. The Coast Guard crew had helmets with protective jackets.

When they were far enough away, the crew helped them onto the boat. All on board stood in awe of the inferno. Concrete and steel bent from the heat as chunks of the platform fell into the water.

The President was now standing, watching the helicopter video turn back to the ship. The platform pipe was jetting flame at the side of the ship. It would not last much longer.

The blast ripped out the side of the ship, knocking it far over on its side. Multiple explosions ripped through the hull, as consecutive storage tanks onboard ruptured. The helicopter was pulling back, but the flames and cloud kept getting bigger than the screen until it was all yellow flames and black cloud.

The boat pilot pushed hard on the throttle as they all grabbed for a handhold.

Grady looked up at the rising fire and smoke. "Think it's done? I mean from exploding again?" He called out.

"I hope so," Mark answered.

The Coast Guard Chopper had arrived, hovering to the west. It moved to the end of the platform where some of the workers had made the thirty-foot leap to the water. Another Coast Guard boat was coming up fast from beyond the point. Their own inflatable was turning toward the people in the water to help.

By the time they stood onshore, the three were exhausted. Twelve survivors had been put on the dock before the Coast Guard boat raced out to continue rescue operations. Flames continued to jet out of the severed pipelines. They could tell the pressure was dropping, but even cut off, the liquid gas was six-hundred times more concentrated than the gas it became as it warmed and expanded. The flames would continue for some time.

"So, I guess you would like an explanation of just what happened to your boat," Grady said, turning toward Mark and Julie with a smile.

"I think we have time," Mark said.

"One thing I'm sure of is that we owe you a very big thank you," Julie added.

"If there is a bar over here, I'm buying," Mark said as he looked back at the burning ship, and where his yacht used to be. "I am bugged, though; I've never had to abandon ship before. I'm not sure I like it."

Robert and the men in the Situation Room had been watching and listening as the Navy pilot described the events. A representative of the Nuclear Regulatory team had been tied in and was giving instructions to the Coast Guard on what to do, and what to avoid. Military police from the naval air station had arrived at the LNG plant. Several boats were arriving to help evacuate the survivors from the platform and ship. The Sit Room became quiet as they all sat back down.

"So, is this it Robert? Are you done?" President Baxter asked.

"Yes, Sir. I believe that is it." Robert was showing the strain in his face.

"Good, then I will leave it to all of you to clean up." The President stood, and everyone rose. "Jason, Ron, full report, a.s.a.p., along with recommendations on how we handle the news cycle on this mess. You have ten minutes." He was almost out the door, then he turned back. "Good job everyone." He left the room.

"Well," Jason went to the stand to get a cup of coffee, "let's get this cleaned up. Robert, not you. You go to the hospital. Keep your phone handy."

"That's one thing I don't have. The decontamination techs have it."

"Airman," Ron called her attention. "Get Mr. Carlton a cell phone."

Chapter 59

Robert was sitting in the chair of his hospital room when Tracie arrived.

"Hi, Honey, how was *your* day?" Robert quipped, hoping to avoid what was inevitable.

The look he got from her could curdle milk, but she didn't say a word. She came over, kissed him on the cheek, and sat in the other chair. She was silent as she glared at the mechanical hospital bed. Robert fidgeted in his light blue bathrobe and paper slippers. The NRC jumpsuit hung in the closet. Under the bathrobe, he wore the typical paper gown with the obscenely ineffective ties in the back.

"Are you going to be all right?" Tracie finally asked.

"Tracie, I'm fine. I got a small dose. The Prussian Blue will flush out anything I might have swallowed or inhaled," Robert informed her.

She frowned, not looking directly at him. Her eyes were watery, but she wouldn't allow a tear to drop. "You scared me, Robert," she said, accusingly.

"I'm sorry. I..." Robert began apologizing.

"Why?" She cut in, still not looking at him. "There are people who do this—whose job it is to do this! They have training. Why did you have to put yourself at risk?"

"There were people in danger, Tracie. There was no time to get anyone else to do it—believe me when I say that if there had been, I would have. I was the only one there who understood the situation." They both knew Robert wasn't a natural hero.

"You have two sons," Tracie pressed.

Robert knew better than to answer too quickly.

Tracie sniffled and grabbed a tissue from her purse.

"Tracie, I..." Robert tried to start apologizing again, but she stood up and put her hand out, stopping him.

"Just give me a minute alone," She told him, walking out of the room.

Five minutes later the door flew open. Robert looked up, expecting Tracie, but instead a wheelchair containing Grady rolled into the room with a pretty nurse behind him.

"Seriously?" Grady was saying to her, "I'm not allowed to walk around, and you're expecting me to poop purple? What kind of place is this?" Grady had a big grin on his face as he turned toward Robert. "Robert! Do you believe this nonsense?"

"Blue." Robert corrected him, smiling.

"Blue?" Grady repeated.

"You poop blue while you're taking the Prussian Blue treatment," Robert said. "But the Cesium comes out with it, so that's good news."

"And they expect me to collect every bit of it, with a date and time, so they can track my progress. It's kind of disgusting, Robert." Grady shook his head at the nurse.

"Don't forget to wear gloves," Robert reminded him.

"That's what the blue gloves are for?" Grady looked up at the nurse. "If I don't wear the gloves, then will I get the whole body bath again?"

"Yep." She said with a devilish grin. "Every inch—but you'll probably get the male technicians again, Colonel."

Tracie came into the room through the open door. She looked recovered, but she was shaking her head at Grady. "Another bad macho influence. Proud of yourself, Colonel Barlow?" She asked sternly.

Grady looked over his shoulder at her. "No, Ma'am," he replied meekly.

"Good answer." Tracie held three bottles of water. She handed two to Grady and Robert. "I hope you both turn blue from head to toe."

Grady snorted so hard that all of them started laughing.

. . .

Max relaxed at a noisy tapas bar in Richmond, Virginia. It was time for a change of venue. She had quickly moved out of DC. Everything was in storage or the back of her leased SUV. The vehicle was not her style, but she'd had a hint that she would be needing it. She'd driven to Richmond, thinking she might be needed south. Vlad was prone to ask for her presence with very short notice.

In any case, it would be a long time before Max saw DC again. Right now it was important to stay away from any potential facial recognition. Tollways, airports, subways, and government buildings all snapped pictures that would be analyzed. Soon she would be back using her original personal phone, identification, and bank accounts, before assuming a new persona on a new job. For now, she was on hold. Until Vlad called the project closed, it was open.

She had concerns, as with all projects this complex. She had three loose ends—the two people on the boat and the guy at the boatyard bar. Each had gotten a good look at her. But there was good news. With three out of four boats activated, the mission would be considered a success.

Luca was Vlad's loose end. Max was waiting to hear what Vlad wanted to do about him.

She sat at a long dark wood bar and watched the TV mounted over the illuminated bottles. Her glass of deep red Rioja Reserva went down gradually with each appetizer-sized plate. Her Churrasco Con Chimichurri arrived as breaking news came up on the screen.

The news flash was labeled with a red and yellow bar across the bottom. Reporters introduced videos of evacuations in Washington DC, and shots of workers and rescue operations on the LNG pier in Point Cove. Then they switched to military personnel swarming over ships in Norfolk, with a long-shot video of the terrorist in custody. More emergency equipment was shown. Panicked mothers were pulling their screaming kids out of school, and freeways out of Virginia Beach and DC were clogged with people who were trying to leave the area. A few people were being interviewed, telling their stories of men in white suits scrubbing them clean of radiation.

What had started out as a gas leak story in Melbourne was now a national disaster and a terrorist act. People in the restaurant noticed. Norfolk and Virginia Beach were only one hundred miles away. Customers began waving for their checks. Cell phones started going off, and Max marveled at the over-reactions and panicked faces. No doubt, Max would have the restaurant to herself soon.

"What do you think?" A man next to her at the bar said, looking concerned.

"I don't know. Do you think it's even real?" She asked.

"Somebody must think so. Did you see the stock market? I just checked. It went down three percent in the last four hours." The effect on his portfolio got more reaction from him than the radiation issue.

"Vlad got that part right." Max thought to herself. She had pulled everything out of stock and put it in cash two days ago in anticipation. Vlad said to wait a week, then get back in.

Then it came, scrolling across the screen. "ISIS claims dirty bomb in Melbourne Florida! Airports on Orange Alert!"

Max had to fight back a smile. Vlad was a master. His last of three broadcasts had taken hold. Max pulled up her stock market app as her meal check suddenly appeared. The restaurant was closing. Market futures had already tumbled down another five percent.

. . .

Luca sat in his cell. He had initially been taken to the Coast Guard base but was swiftly transferred to the Navy base. Words like Homeland Security and National Security were tossed around, as competing factions pulled and tugged at each other to decide who owned him. The FBI showed up late to the party, churlishly demanding to know why they hadn't been called, and giving Luca some welcome humor in this nightmare.

The interrogations had been random and sloppy. He was threatened, then cajoled. The same questions came from a variety of different badges, suits, and uniforms. None of them talked to each other.

"Was it your plan to blow up an aircraft carrier?" They asked. "Where are you from? What religion are you?"

Every question he could imagine and more had been thrown at him. Everything except, "Do you want a lawyer or some water?" He had been told quite clearly that he did not have the right to anything. Being classified a terrorist was unpleasant.

At the last session, it was clear that Homeland Security and the Navy would be the last two standing in the battle for jurisdiction. The matter would not be decided speedily—at least not tonight.

. . .

Max stood outside the closed restaurant. It was barely eight. Her phone buzzed in her pocket. It was a message from Vlad. The message she expected, and dreaded.

Chapter 60

Robert took the long way to work, down the river and past Arlington Cemetery, so that he could take the 395 bridge past the Gangplank Marina. It had been a week since the bombs had gone off. The barricades were still up and would be throughout the cleanup.

He reflected that the situation could have ended with far worse results. There were a handful of fatalities, including Berg, the islanders, several workers at the natural gas dock explosion, and presumably Larry Bledsoe, who had yet to be found. The focus was on the one conspirator caught sailing an armed boat toward the Navy aircraft carriers in Norfolk. He was stubbornly refusing to say anything, which made for dull prime time commentary in the news. There were no follow-on threats by terrorists, no officially claimed responsibility, and denials from many suspected groups. Without more death to mourn, the country settled back into its accustomed, uneasy, post nine-eleven calm.

There were heroes to be congratulated. The Coast Guard sailors in Norfolk, Virginia and Point Cove, Maryland headed the celebrated short list. The NRC team, under Steve Mahaffey, were unsung as they cleaned up. It was their job. Robert and Grady got some hearty congratulations in their offices and in the West Wing—even a few pats on the back. Grady had a new ribbon on his chest, and stories worthy of a free beer at any airbase.

The days had been filled with doctors, paperwork, agency interviews, and appearances before the Senate investigation committee. There was no end in sight for any of these.

Robert thought about his calendar and upcoming testimony, as he walked up to the West Wing for his meeting with the President.

Grady stood talking with Steve as Robert entered the lobby.

Grady's crisp uniform and upright posture always disguised his disarmingly quick humor. "Hello, Robert. Finally cleared by the doc? No? Still feeling kind of blue? Guess who I just saw leaving as I came up?"

Robert only had a chance to answer the last question. "I have no idea, Grady. Who?"

"Our old buddy, Senator Gregg. He seemed in very high spirits. I guess retiring agrees with him after all." Grady smiled at the inside joke he and Robert shared. The last time Grady had seen Gregg, he and Robert had nailed him, ending his political career. It was gratifying for both to see a politician scumbag finally get his. Robert had beat him at his own blackmailing game.

Steve looked surprised. "Senator Daniel Gregg?"

"Yep," Grady said.

"He's not retiring. My sister is from his state. He's leading by a large margin to be re-elected, as usual."

"There must be some mistake." Robert was taken aback by Steve's revelation. "He wasn't going to run. He's retiring."

"I don't think so." Steve was shaking his head. "He came out gunning for re-election last week. From what she told me, the other two guys from his party dropped out the first day." He noticed Ron Crest motion them in. "They're ready for us." He pointed the way, and they started walking.

Robert and Grady exchanged looks, but the discussion would have to wait.

They spent the next thirty minutes debriefing with Ron. It had become routine. There were no particular surprises since the incidents had been gone over dozens of times. The Caribbean quieted down after the Price's boat had been found to be unarmed. The Governors were working hand in hand with the State Department and the CIA, who had no more missing weapons of mass destruction to report—or at least none they would talk about. The stock market was on the rise again, and the President's approval rating was back to normal.

The ability of the public to forget was astounding. Since no Americans got immediately sick, there were only a few angry victims, families, and activists remaining. Many with damaged property were happy with the zero interest loans for new roofs and landscaping. Helpful businesses and charity groups even provided much of the repairs for free. The yacht owners were enjoying celebrity status on talk shows and in the yacht clubs. It would be ten or twenty years before those exposed might begin showing signs of cancer from the radiation. Even then a direct correlation would be difficult to prove.

Their next meeting was with the President. Ron went with the three. Robert looked around as they entered the Oval and saw a cameraman by the fireplace. He realized that this was a photo op. They all stood with the President by his desk, smiling and shaking hands. Each, in turn, took center stage with the group, and then was individually photographed with President Baxter. Tracie would be happy with the addition to the wall in Robert's office.

"Robert, now that the pictures are done, let's start with you." President Baxter sounded very calm. Like the country, he had moved on to new problems, but a recap was in order. "Five yachts. Their owners taken captive down on a Caribbean island. The State department asks you to run cover for them, and two months later, you recognize a name on a boat. We end up with dirty bombs from Florida to within two miles of this office. Does that about sum it up?"

"Yes, Sir." Robert agreed.

"Well, you pulled this one out of the fire. I thought we were headed for nine-eleven again. But not so, thanks to the three of you. By the time we're done with this, you three will be national heroes who averted bigger disasters than what occurred—with the help of three armed services, and six agencies. This has to be the most spectacular performance of interdepartmental cooperation in history."

"Yes, thank you, Sir; it was a remarkable group effort," Robert replied.

"All right. So, that is our official story. That's the conversation that gets covered in every news cycle. Now let's talk about what really happened." The President said, looking annoyed.

"You had those boats in your hands, and you let them go. All the way to the fricking Jefferson Memorial! What the hell were you thinking? Did it ever occur to you that it was ridiculous for those tourists to be kidnapped, and their boats left untouched?" The President yelled at them.

Robert, Grady, and Steve were speechless. What appeared to be a congratulatory PR session had taken an ugly turn. They realized that they were going to take a beating.

Robert was unwilling to take the hit for what should have been the State Department's problem. "Actually, Sir, at that point my role was to merely help repatriate our citizens with as little political fallout as possible."

"But you were responsible for organizing the Caribbean anti-terrorism force, Robert. Didn't the two connect in your head?" The President was still angry.

"Yes, Sir, I was organizing that effort, but that was completely unrelated to the tourist kidnapping. It was a separate issue, made at the request of the State Department." Robert felt the ground giving way under his feet. He'd been set up from the start.

"But the connection should have been obvious—and because you were already working the region, the nuke on the island was handed off to you. How many hints did you have to have before you were going to put this all together, for God's sake?" The President persisted.

Steve felt he should step in at this point. "Sir, if I may, the CDC was called in when the victims on what we are calling 'Sandy Island' were discovered. The CDC called me and the NRC in when the head physician determined it was radiation sickness. Mr. Carlton was brought in because he had already organized the regional leaders to address terrorist imports of hazardous materials. There was no immediate connection to be made."

"Then you and Colonel Barlow went down to organize island searches?" The President inquired.

"And training. Yes, Sir." Steve answered.

"But it didn't occur to either of you that the tourist yachts might somehow be related?" The President wasn't letting go.

"There was no indication that the two were related," Robert interjected. "At that point, the boats were headed home. We had no evidence to suggest that they should be held—and they had been inspected by the Coast Guard. Nothing suspicious was found. Evidence pointed directly to a ransom plot. The CIA had lost track of 5 irradiators, but we knew nothing about that, then, so there was no connection to be made. We had three yachts sailing home, one sold, and one heading south to continue sailing in the islands, and a seemingly unconnected incident of a radiation poisoning on a small island. The island had no relationship to where the sailors were abducted or held captive. It was about a day's trip away by motorboat."

"Even after we determined that the irradiator on the island might be one of the CIA's missing five, there was no indication of where the other four might be." Robert continued, "When the incident in Melbourne occurred and was detected by Air Force personnel near the Kennedy Space Center, Steve's team was immediately called up from their work in the Caribbean."

"That was when some of my key people were pulled away, and we began to see a possible connection," Grady added.

"You were the organizer for Air Force technicians from the 2nd Bomb Wing?" The President queried.

"Yes, Sir," Grady confirmed.

"So, you just happen to recognize the boat, Robert?" President Baxter got up to walk around the far side of his desk as he talked. "From a news video, wasn't it?"

"Yes, Sir." Robert wondered if any of this was making a difference in the President's assumptions. "There was a shot of the boat, and I noticed the name on it was Caroline." It sounded less remarkable when said aloud in the Oval Office. "It drew my attention because of the double coincidence of sailboats and radiation."

"Not something you hear about every day." The President agreed, picking up a notebook and pen. "Go on."

"At that point, Sir, the three of us compared notes and pieced together that all five boats might be armed in the same way. Colonel Barlow and I split up to find them, with the help of Lieutenant Davies. The Coast Guard and Navy were brought in by Davies, and we set about shutting down the terrorist action as quickly as possible."

"You mean you were attempting to avoid disaster, to save lives, and to stop a war. You don't have to be humble." President Baxter returned to his chair. "As I understand it, you, Robert, jumped on one boat to manually disable the dirty bomb right behind the Jefferson Memorial, while you, Colonel, repelled from a helicopter to save the lives of two civilian kidnap victims. You planned to stop the bomb from blowing up a natural gas platform, saving everyone on it. The largest facility of its kind on the east coast, I believe?" No one spoke. "That would have been a hell of a mess—oh, wait. It was. None of the bombs were stopped. They exploded anyway, and the whole damn thing, plus a ship, went up in flames." The President finished sarcastically.

"I believe the Navy captured the one in Norfolk harbor," Jason Carlisle said as he walked in. "Sorry I'm late, Sir."

"The Coast Guard caught that one before its bomb could be activated," Grady clarified.

"Let me cut to the chase, then." They all waited for the President's next statement. "Two devices ended up on land, three in the water. They sailed right in because we have no detection capability and the terrorists successfully exploded all but one. Am I right?"

"Yes, Sir." Ron Crest answered.

"Ron, here's what I want you to do. Put together a comprehensive plan for early detection of these things coming in by land, sea, and air. Get the right agencies involved with the appropriate equipment and manpower. Jason, grease the skids so Congress can get rolling on appropriations, and get the cabinet in agreement. Control the message. Make sure everyone knows the message: we captured the bad guy and averted disaster, thanks to team effort and true patriots."

The President stood and left the office without a word to Robert, Grady, or Steve." Thank you, Mr. President." Jason and Ron said in unison, as he departed.

Once he was gone, Jason turned to the others. "I guess that about covers it. I'll have the staff come to you for the things we will need."

<u>Chapter 61</u>

As they left the West Wing, the three walked together. Robert and Grady were in shock.

"What just happened?" Grady asked.

"I'm used to it," Steve said. "No one likes us before or after incidents of this type. Radiation leaks are understandably unhappy events. I keep my resume up to date and handy, just in case somebody decides they need to place blame."

"I think I better start looking for a different position, too," Grady was not his upbeat self.

Robert was glum but attempted to get past it. "Don't worry, Guys. It started positive and ended positive. The Oval Office is always a rollercoaster ride."

"I don't think Six Flags needs to worry about the competition," Grady told them.

Robert and Grady shook hands with Steve, as he departed.

"I'm going to check into this Gregg thing. Can you see what the Intelligence Community knows about the irradiators, and if there are any more we haven't heard about floating around out there?" Robert asked.

"Sure. I'll get an update on the border protection plans, too. That might come in handy." Grady responded.

"Thanks. Are you seeing Katy tonight? You might want to warn her to expect an inquisition from the President's office," Robert warned him.

"She's out tonight, but I'll call her later," Grady said. "Stock night with the girls. She was bouncing off the wall happy since they sold before the crash. Then they bought at the dip, and made a bunch of money when it all came back up."

"I hope Tracie gets filthy rich. I'm not sure how much more of this I can take," Robert said. "It might be nice to kick back, and just sit on a corporate board or two."

"She still mad at you?" Grady asked.

"For getting involved, blown up, and irradiated? Yep. Still very angry." I have a feeling that's an, 'I told you so' for life." Robert was still getting daily lectures at home.

Grady reached out to shake Robert's hand. "I'll start pulling that info together. Let me know how it goes with Gregg. What would you say to a grilled burger on the deck this weekend?"

"I'd say, 'Count me in.'" Robert smiled.

Grady headed off while Robert got on his phone with Lorraine.

"Mr. Carlton, may I help you?" She answered.

"Yes. Can you get me in to see Senator Gregg as soon as possible? I'll head home from here unless Gregg has time now."

After Robert reached his car, his phone rang.

"Mr. Carlton, I have Senator Gregg on the phone for you. He says he does not have a meeting time available, but he's got a few minutes if you can take the call." Lorraine explained.

"Yes, connect us." Robert agreed.

"Robby. How good to hear from you." Gregg sounded loud and gregarious.

Robert wondered why Gregg felt the need to call him "Robby." Did he know how much he hated that?

"Dan," Robert said. "I was surprised to hear that the party forgot and put your name in for re-election?" It was a direct inquiry—maybe too direct, but Robert had lost much of his diplomacy in the last few weeks.

The Senator bristled at being called by the casual diminutive of his first name. "Actually, I am enjoying a nice lead in the race,

Robby, but I never take a lead for granted. I plan on running a strong campaign."

"I think, Senator, that we agreed you would retire and spend more time with your family, or don't you recall that conversation?" Robert was not letting this slide. He had pictures Gregg wouldn't like being made public. He got into the car and started the engine.

"Things have changed, Robby, and I think I owe it to my constituency to uphold my state's rights in congress."

"Nothing has changed," Robert stated flatly, lowering his voice. His fingers dug into the steering wheel.

"I know you don't realize it just yet. You should check with your lovely wife. It seems that your portfolio has seen a pronounced growing spell with the recent events. You might reconsider what it means to throw stones, now that you have so much new and valuable glass of your own to protect." Gregg sounded almost gleeful.

"What are you blathering about?" Robert stopped any pretense of polite conversation.

"Ask your wife about her sudden success, and even greater rewards to come. I think you will find that you need to be very supportive of my campaign, Robby. I look forward to having lunch to discuss it. Well, I have to run. Have your girl set up a luncheon with my girl." With that, Gregg hung up.

"What the hell was that?" Robert knew he needed to talk with Tracie. He put the car in drive and pulled out of the lot to get home as fast as possible.

Putting on his earbud headset, he voice-dialed his house and got the answering machine. He left a message, trying to get Tracie to pick up. When that failed, he dialed Tracie's cell phone.

"Robert, I'm in a rush right now," she said.

"Have you been making inappropriate stock investments?" Robert suddenly realized how ridiculous that sounded. "I mean, have you been doing insider trading or something?" That didn't sound much better.

"What are you talking about? We're just buying stocks based on what looks good, and what makes sense. We don't have any insider information. How could we?" Tracie was surprised.

"Yes, of course, I know that. I mean—what stocks are you buying?" Robert was fumbling with this. He didn't have any idea what to look for in her portfolio. Only Gregg's implication that he had something on Robert kept him asking questions.

"You're acting funny," Tracie complained. When you get home, sit in with us, and you can see for yourself what we're doing."

"I guess I do need to look at what you've been buying," Robert decided.

"Fine, I'll see you at home." Tracie hung up.

Robert fretted about the problem as he drove, but he still had no idea what could be so damaging that Gregg would suddenly think he had the upper hand.

When he arrived home, Tracie was busy getting the house ready for guests.

"Here, you can look all you like." She handed him her laptop open to a listing of transactions on her online trading account.

"Thanks." Robert took the laptop and headed for his study.

It was a complex listing filled with buys, sells, calls, and puts. It was admittedly beyond Robert's full understanding. He knew the basics, but not enough to really grasp the strategies. Tracie and the girls had become very advanced in their stock trading in an incredibly short time. Robert's interest was more on the what than the how. What was she buying, and how could that possibly look bad for Robert?

He focused on the stock symbols, looking up the companies one at a time. Her account had an easy lookup system and information on each of the companies.

Tracie and the girls had been buying a wide variety of stocks until two months ago when they seemed to divest those and focus on using their money to buy energy. They focused particularly on natural gas producers, and the companies that transported the gas. Then ten days ago, she was selling some stocks. She sold covered calls on the ones she didn't sell, and she'd been buying puts on others.

Robert spent a lot of time trying to understand what was in the listing. He heard the girls arrive and the noises of the kitchen, food being plated, and drinks being made. Then they settled into talking in the living room. He couldn't hear them well, nor was he really paying attention. A pattern in the data before him had emerged. He needed to be sure that what he saw was real.

For months, Tracie had been buying energy stocks, then suddenly a week ago, she started selling. Not all at once, but at every rise, she sold twenty percent until everything was gone. The next day the news about the boat in Melbourne came out, and the market crashed. For the next three days, it went down dramatically. Yesterday Tracie had bought back in, but she'd changed to energy stocks with different names. At first, he thought she must be trying to time the market bottom, assuming the terrorist scare was over and people would buy back in, but her buys were timed differently. The puts and calls were baffling.

The more he looked, the more it appeared she had timed the market perfectly with the bad news. How had she known when to sell? Then there were the companies she'd bought yesterday. His Father's company topped the list, then came a string of defense and tech stocks that looked strangely familiar. It took a while, looking up each company.

When Robert started seeing the pattern, he opened his email and pulled up the listing of products Steve had recommended they buy. Tracie had purchased the same list of equipment manufacturer stocks needed for radiation detection and cleanup. The list of companies was nearly identical. There was also a group of companies that made underwater detectors, both remote controlled and stationary—new concept detectors that Steve's team did not have yet, but would be needed. There were several companies that made radiation detectors and software that attached to phones for commercial use, and chemical companies that specialized in cleanup for hazardous waste.

All of these companies would soon be getting a windfall in sales if Congress approved funding for the list Robert and Steve just provided to them.

Tracie had started with twenty-thousand dollars and had successfully grown it to almost sixty-thousand. A spectacular performance, but not a lot of money. "Would that matter under scrutiny?" Robert wasn't sure. It was a murky area in the law when a wife's account was in question, but if a tabloid got the information, they would blow it way out of proportion.

He was thinking this over when the door to his study opened and in walked Tracie and his Father.

"Hello, Robby." He said confidently as he walked in and sat down.

"I need that." Tracie grabbed her laptop and left the room closing the door behind her.

"Hello, Father." Robert had been surprised, but quickly realized why his father was there. "Have you come by to help the ladies with their stock club?"

"Yes, you, as well, it would seem." His father said.

"Me? How do you mean?" Robert wondered what his father was getting at.

Instead of answering, his father said, "I see you are working with Tracie's list. Do you have any questions?"

"No. It seems pretty straight forward to me," Robert wasn't sure he was ready to discuss this with his father. He'd prefer to talk with Tracie first and understand why and how she'd done this.

"I'm sure you have seen the pattern, companies, and technologies by now. They have done quite well for themselves, don't you think?" His father seemed determined to make a point.

"Yes. Do you mean they all have similar portfolios?" Robert inquired.

"The ladies? Yes, almost Identical." His Father got up to pour himself a scotch. "Would you like one?"

"No, thanks. Go on." Robert was feeling the stress mounting. His Father had that effect, even on a good day.

"She could have made more, except that small stake made it hard to do many covered calls. You understand, I'm sure."

"Of course." Robert didn't really, but he wasn't going to admit it.

"I'm glad. We thought you would agree. You see, she tripled her money with the small account, but with just thirty percent of yours, she has grown it over two-hundred-thousand dollars." His father said casually.

"What are you talking about?" Robert turned to his computer and pulled up his 401K portfolio. It was filled with the same list of stocks. Clicking on the history, he saw the same long list of trades, made with a much larger sum of money. She was buying and selling with his retirement account. He had given her access ages ago. It was a joint account, but if an outsider looked at these stocks, then combined that knowledge with what he was working on—it was a political noose around his neck. Insider trading. plus a violation of national security.

"What have you done?" He looked at his Father in abject horror. "How could you do this?"

"Me? I've done nothing." His father lifted an eyebrow condescendingly. "Oh, I gave some advice here and there, but they did the buying. They did the research, and they acted on it as a team. They've done quite well, don't you think?"

"But why?" Robert was in shock. How could his father have knowingly put him in this position?

"See that one?" His Father pointed to the stock in his own company. "And that one?" The stock of his competitor. "Buy one, sell the other. If something were to go badly for them, she wins twice."

Robert didn't need to look it up. The offshore LNG pier belonged to the competitor. Now the press was calling it the most unsafe platform in the world and naming it a national tragedy. His Father's company had run their pipeline to the gulf. Right now, it was safer and more secure.

When the news had broken about the LNG platform, Tracie had already bought and sold with timing that was too coincidental to look anything but "informed." Robert's face flushed with the realization.

"These, I'm sure, will go up very quickly now." Robert's father was pointing to the stocks that would soon be getting billions in appropriations, and which would be selling radiation detection gear to the government on Robert's recommendation.

"You set me up." Robert glared in anger, not knowing what he could do about it.

"I protected you." His father said smoothly.

"Protected me?" Robert's disbelief echoed in the room.

"Shhh," his father warned. "You don't want to disturb the ladies. Yes, Robby, I protected you. From Gregg, and from more than a few others like him."

"What are you talking about?" Robert demanded. "You've put me in a terrible position! I could be prosecuted for this."

"You pulled the tiger's tail when you went after Gregg, Robby. Do you think he and his compatriots would let you ride happily away into the sunset? Now, thanks to me, they have leverage that is worth more to them than your demise. You are no longer a threat; you're one of them. They don't have to ruin you. You have something on Gregg, and he has something on you. Mutually assured destruction. Classic politics. Who do you think the military learned it from?"

Robert was appalled. The full meaning of the situation had hit him. "You did this? You brought nuclear weapons—dirty bombs, into the United States? You endangered people's lives, people died, just to arrange this situation and put me in my place? Are you out of your mind?"

"Of course I didn't do that. How ridiculous of you to think so, Robby. I would never do such a thing. We are talking about investing. You've never understood that there are investments beyond real estate and stock. Sometimes a truly unique opportunity is presented to a very select group of people. Those people don't control the opportunity, but they can profit from it. You are now one of those people." Robert's father explained.

"Investment? You bought shares in a terrorist attack? How is that even possible?" Robert couldn't shake the feeling that he was in the midst of a nightmare.

"Don't be naïve. This happens all the time. It's about information. Events happen, and there is profit to be made. It's about knowing where to invest and when." His father said casually.

"This is impossible. Don't you realize how wrong it all is?" Robert was frustrated and wrung out.

His Father smiled again. "It's right, Robby. It's the way it has always been. You are in the inner circle, now. You'll learn where real power and money come from. To begin with, you get to keep your position, and Gregg gets to keep his. You get to keep your money, as do all those nice ladies out there. Keep it straight in your mind that this is not just about you, and you'll be fine. I think you will find you have more helpful friends than ever before." He stood up, composed and arrogant. He set his glass lightly down on the desk. "I've been away from the ladies too long. I need to get back to congratulate them, and answer any questions they may have." He walked to the door.

Robert wanted the last word. "Let me just get this straight. You paid for information. You and the rest of your 'investors' bankrolled terrorists?"

"No. We did not." His father sighed. "Things happen, Robert. We are simply better informed than others. That's the way it is. Those in the circle of knowledge benefit—if they know how to do so, and are prepared." He placed his hand on the doorknob. "You have become one of us, Robert. You can't change that." He opened the door. "Don't think you can outsmart me. You have a lot still to learn. You should realize that now." The door closed behind him.

Robert fumed. How could his father have done this? He went over the list of stock trades again, waiting for the stock club to adjourn. When the last one finally left, Robert left his office to talk with Tracie.

"Hi! You should have come out to say hello." Tracie was in good humor. Her success was making her feel important. Tracie had no trouble taking the credit and accolades from her friends, even though Robert's father had orchestrated the accomplishment.

"I need to talk to you about what you're doing," Robert told her, trying to suppress his anger.

"Oh?" Tracie said lightly, putting some glasses into the dishwasher.

"You need to stop," Robert said bluntly.

"What are you talking about?" Tracie had begun wrapping trays to go into the fridge.

"Listen to me, Tracie. This is important. The stocks you bought, particularly the ones in my name, have put me in a bad position politically, and maybe legally." He was getting angrier the more he thought about it.

"Don't be ridiculous," Tracie laughed. "How in the world could our little stock trades put you in a bad spot? If anything, I'm ensuring our future."

"Look, I'll be frank," Robert stopped, realizing that beginning a sentence like that would annoy Tracie. Her arms folded and her face went sour immediately, but he persevered. "I won't go into who, but a politician I was forcing to resign now has incriminating evidence against me—because of your stock trades. He's not going to resign now, and I can't do anything about it. You've created blackmail that he can use against me anytime he likes. The stocks you've purchased are affected by the purchase of products by the government—products and companies I recommended because of this investigation. It's fraud, collusion, and insider trading all wrapped up in government funded contracts."

Tracie was starting to look a little pale. "I only followed the market and made good picks," she defended.

"Under father's guidance," Robert pointed out.

"So?" Tracie didn't understand what he was trying to get across.

"He did it on purpose, Tracie. Father set you up, and me along with you." He wondered how he was going to get her to understand the enormity of this problem.

Tracie was looking skeptical and a little angry. "He and this politician are in cahoots? Don't be ridiculous, Robert."

"What's ridiculous is how much of this goes on. Father just declared I was now part of a 'club' that does this regularly. They've got this to hold over my head. I have to find a way to openly declare this so that they can't keep using it against me, but in the meantime, you must stop all of your stock trading activity."

"Are you saying that I have to sell the stock, and not make any trades whatsoever? I can't even trade completely different stocks?" Tracie was seething.

"Let me talk to a lawyer first. I'll do that tomorrow morning." Robert said.

"*You're* a lawyer," Tracie reminded him.

"I need an expert on SEC violations, Tracie. I don't know much about this. I should have thought of that the minute you started getting involved with stocks. I knew there had to be something wrong when Father started helping you." Robert was berating himself for not having figure the situation out. Why hadn't he checked into Tracie's activities after that dinner at his parents' house?

Tracie was silent. It was becoming obvious to Robert that the silence would outlast his ability to stand still and not say something more. He felt a chill in the room, more from the strain on their relationship than from any temperature drop.

"We can't talk about this with anyone," he warned.

"What do I tell the girls?" Tracie asked icily.

"Nothing," Robert advised. "You may have to make an excuse for staying out of the club for a few weeks, but they shouldn't have a problem. As for me, the lawyer may not see a good ending to this and may advise that we keep our own counsel—meaning that we keep our mouths shut. I don't know. I *am* sure that you will need to move out of those stocks. I don't know how, or how quickly you'll need to do that. I know you need to stop trading in my name, and most of all stop asking questions of or listening to my father."

They went to bed angry at each other. The house stayed silent.

Chapter 62

Robert sat on Grady's deck. They had beers in hand and burgers on the grill smoking. Tracie and Katy were inside.

"It's none of my business," Grady ventured, "but Tracie seems a bit frosty."

"We had a fight," Robert said shortly.

Grady didn't say anything.

"It's about the kids," Robert lied. "It'll blow over." Robert sipped his beer. "I need to catch you up on Senator Gregg's situation."

"I have a feeling I won't like it," Grady grimaced.

"Probably not. He's running again. He'll probably win. He got a get out of jail card." Robert hoped he'd be able to gloss this over.

"How?" Grady asked grimly.

"It's complicated." Robert felt like a jerk for not being able to explain everything to Grady.

"Another crooked politician wins. Are there any that aren't crooks?" Grady questioned bitterly.

"I don't know. Maybe, but it's hard to believe that anymore." Robert set his beer down. "We still have some leverage with Gregg, but not enough to get him out of Congress. He can't do just anything he wants, as long as we are watching. That's the best we're going to get."

"You mean while you watch. I think I'm done with this bullshit." Grady told him. "Give me a stand-up fight any day over this."

"You think terrorists are any better? That's who we have to fight, Grady. This other stuff stinks, but it's nothing compared to the people who are determined to take down our country and culture." Robert was concerned. He didn't want to lose Grady from his team.

"I don't know. I liked it when good guys wore white hats, and bad guys wore black." Grady sounded tired all of a sudden. "Bad analogy, but you know what I mean."

"Yeah, in the movies, Grady. In real life, they all dress alike and always have," replied Robert.

"So, he wins and we lose," Grady stated.

"To some extent." Robert wished he had a better answer.

"Whatever." Grady dismissed the subject and pushed back into his chair. "What about border defense?"

"The House will pass the appropriations bill to up our game for waterway protection, but the customs law isn't going to change," Robert informed him.

"Boats can still come in without going through some kind of scanner?" Grady asked.

"Correct. They deemed it impractical, restrictive, and bad for the states' economies. It probably also seemed too immense a problem," Robert speculated.

"And, as a result, this whole scenario could happen again." Grady was dejected.

"The thinking is the Coast Guard can already board and search without a warrant, so they want to enforce the existing law, rather than write a new one."

"So, it's the Coast Guard's problem. They're supposed to enforce a law with an understaffed, under-budgeted program." Grady was shaking his head.

"Right. They did fund a DARPA project to find alternatives, though."

"Katy ends up with a new kind of MISTI at the Navy Labs?" Grady wondered.

"Maybe." Robert wasn't sure what they were going to appropriate when all was said and done.

"How many people have to die before politicians—hell, I just answered my own question, didn't I? Until a lot of people die, and the public riots, they're not going to change anything, right?" Grady was becoming resigned to the situation, but he didn't like it.

"Afraid so." Robert nodded.

"You know; I can live with that."

Robert looked skeptically at Grady.

"No, really. Hasn't it been that way all along? You can't protect against everything, or you stop living. You buy locks to stop amateurs, and insurance to stop pros. Drive defensively, wear helmets, don't drink from water hoses—you do what you can, but in the end, you fight the big ones and watch out for the rest." Grady's positive nature was rebounding. This was the way life was, and he lived it as well as he could.

"I guess that's true," Robert said, picking his beer back up and taking a drink.

"Okay, I can handle this." Grady sounded more like himself every minute. "I understand that a few must fight and risk their lives so that others can complain, or veg on the couch playing video games. What matters is what I do, not what everyone else doesn't do."

"You're a philosopher now?" Robert felt a little better.

"It's just military philosophy," Grady grinned.

"Never has so much, been owed by so many, to so few." Robert smiled for the first time in days. "Churchill."

"That about sums it up." Grady held out his beer bottle. He and Robert tapped the necks together.

<u>Chapter 63</u>

Max had been waiting deep in the woods surrounding the Naval Consolidated Brig Chesapeake facility. Known as NAVCONBRIG, the complex served as the joint mid-Atlantic correctional facility for all the armed services. It was the one place all the jurisdictions could agree on using. Located south of the Navy Yards, the facility was right next to the North Carolina border. There was nothing near it except some support housing.

The woods gave good cover. There was no electronic security, except inside the perimeter, but getting a clear shot would be problematic. The undergrowth made a prone shot impossible without getting too near the boundary. The flat ground gave an unacceptably low chance of success shooting over the brush and through the tall chain link fence.

Max had one option, to climb a tree. Moving slowly, she stayed tight to the trees and undergrowth, looking for her best vantage point. There was no rush, she had all night. As the light came up, she would have to be still. Even in camo, a sharp-eyed sentry might spot her in daylight. Darkness let her get into position, hanging from her climbing rope and harness.

She had practiced shooting at hundred yard increments from eight-hundred to fourteen-hundred yards. Now she rested her .50 Barrett M82 in a limb sling fifteen feet off the ground, four trees back from the fence. The rifle bipod legs were braced on a limb with a bungee for three-point stability.

The M82, or Light Fifty as most called it, could handle the distance extremely well. Originally designated an anti-material rifle, the recoil operated semi-automatic rifle had become a favorite sniper weapon. At less than ten-thousand dollars retail, it was a bargain. Weighing just thirty pounds and forty-eight inches long, the Light Fifty's range and hitting power were amazing. Max was thinking that next time she would get the .416 M82A1 which was said to be even more accurate.

Suspended in the tree, Max was confident. She had a long firing line down the length of one building, which gave her the best angle over the fence and down the yard to the door.

She had been getting constant messages from Vlad. One of his teapots was "whistling," as he called it, supplying updates. Max was not going to be waiting for long.

Three vans pulled up to the doorway. Max watched through the scope. She had ten rounds in the clip, but wanted to only use one. The slight sway of the tree made visibility through the scope tougher. She would have liked to see someone in her target zone to use as a reference point, but no one was there, yet.

When the door opened, three guards emerged with Luca. He walked proudly, his head held high, looking at the blue sky. He wore a helmet and bulletproof vest with a high collar. Shackles on this feet and hands made progress down the two steps slow, but he moved with comparative grace. Halfway to the van he stopped. Standing tall, he looked up at the sky again as if to take one last free breath. He turned his head to look straight down the length of the yard and held still for a moment.

The bullet pierced his head just below his right eyebrow, racing through his skull, and exploding outward through the back. It tore away his helmet, spraying one of the guards with blood, bone, and brains. The shot rang out an instant later or seemed to with the distant report of the heavy fifty caliber round.

The recoil nearly knocked Max out of the tree. She steadied herself to see if Luca was down. He was, and his guards weren't trying to help him. They were ducking and searching for the shooter.

Max repelled quickly down the backside of the tree. The rifle and all her gear were left behind as she made her way out of the forest. Hidden in the thick brush at the road's edge was a small on/off-road motorbike. It was a short time before she was rolling down Ballahack Rd., looking like a local farm girl in a t-shirt, jeans, and a baseball cap.

After miles of empty country road, she reached the southern edge of Chesapeake and the credit union where she had parked the SUV. Not wasting time to put the bike back into the SUV, she abandoned it. With the numbers ground off, they were unlikely to trace the stolen bike back to its owner, much less her.

With the adrenaline wearing off, Max pulled over at a gas stop where she could get something to eat and drink. It was starting to hit her. Luca had been a lover and a friend. It was business, but it still hurt.

The strain, exertion, and emotion reddened her nose, blushed her cheeks, and filled her eyes with tears that did not flow.

"Are you all right honey?" The woman behind the counter asked.

"Yeah, thanks." Max placed a drink on the counter next to a protein bar she'd chosen. "I just broke up with my boyfriend."

"I'm sorry to hear that, but a pretty girl like you—well, there'll be others." The woman smiled understandingly, taking the ten-dollar bill Max offered.

"Yeah, I know." Max accepted the change and headed out.

<u>Did you like the Two Dirty For D.C. ? Tell your friends.</u>

Reviews are the easiest way to say thank you to an author. Books with more reviews get more views on sites like Amazon and reach more readers. Post a review! Readers want to see what you thought about my book, and I do, too. It can be short. Just type this link into your browser and it'll take you directly to Amazon reviews.

Amazon Review: http://amzn.to/2zqos4K

The Washington D.C. Series Book #3 is coming!

THREE STRIKES
YOU'RE DEAD

Want to be the first to know when it is released?
Go to www.jrussbriley.com and register.

To know more about me and my books:

On Amazon   http://bit.ly/BrileyonAmazon
On Goodreads   http://bit.ly/BrileyonGoodreads

Thank you,
J Russ